Margaret Wade Campbell Deland

Philip And His Wife

Margaret Wade Campbell Deland

Philip And His Wife

ISBN/EAN: 9783743302921

Manufactured in Europe, USA, Canada, Australia, Japa

Cover: Foto ©Andreas Hilbeck / pixelio.de

Manufactured and distributed by brebook publishing software (www.brebook.com)

Margaret Wade Campbell Deland

Philip And His Wife

PHILIP AND HIS WIFE

BY

MARGARET DELAND

AUTHOR OF "JOHN WARD, PREACHER," "SIDNEY"
"THE STORY OF A CHILD," ETC., ETC.

"Marriage is not a result, but a process"

BOSTON AND NEW YORK
HOUGHTON, MIFFLIN AND COMPANY
The Riverside Press, Cambridge
1894

PHILIP AND HIS WIFE.

I.

The postman and the people of the place knew where each family lived. As for the rest of the world, what has one to do with the rest of the world, when he is safe at home? — JACKANAPES.

"Now, mother dear, you are all comfortable, are n't you? Here is your Prayer-Book. And see, I 've put the roses over on the chest of drawers; I don't believe you 'll notice the fragrance here."

Mrs. Drayton moved her head languidly and glanced about. "Yes, as comfortable as I can be. But I 'm used to being uncomfortable. I think perhaps you might move my chair just a little further from the windows, Lyssie. Might n't I feel a draft here?"

This was too important a question for a mere "yes" or "no." Alicia Drayton knelt down beside her mother, and leaned her fresh young cheek towards the closed window. "I don't feel the slightest air, dear," she said anxiously.

"Ah, well, *you!* I suppose you don't. What color you have, Lyssie! I don't see why I have n't some of your health. I 'm sure, when you were born, I gave you all of mine."

"If you would just go out a little bit more?" Alicia suggested hopefully.

"Oh, my dear, don't be foolish," said Mrs. Drayton. "Go out! How can I go out? It tires me to walk across the room. Yes, you had better move my chair. I 'm sure there is a little air."

"Well," Alicia said cheerfully, "there! Can you look out of the window if I put you as far away from it as this?"

"I don't care about looking out of the window," sighed Mrs. Drayton; "there is nothing to see; and I 'm going to read my chapter as soon as you have gone. I 'll tell you what you may do, Lyssie. You may go over and ask Susy Carr to come in some time this morning. If she is out anywhere on the farm, see if you can't find her, and tell her I hope she 'll come. It 's very foolish in me, but I don't like to be alone. I think I feel my loneliness more as I grow older."

"I wish papa were going to be at home this summer," Lyssie said. "Of course it 's lonely for you with only me."

"I was n't finding fault with your father," Mrs. Drayton answered quickly, "and I have no complaint to make when I have you; but now Cecil and Philip are coming, I suppose I shan't see anything of you."

"Of course you will! and Cecil and Philip and Molly, too."

"Oh, don't call the child by that ridiculous name!" said Molly's grandmother, or rather, her step-grandmother; "though her real name is ugly enough, poor child. Why Cecil should have named the baby after Philip's mother, when she never knew her, and could n't have had any affection for her, I never could understand."

Mrs. Drayton's unspoken inference that it would have been more fitting to have given her name to the child did not escape Alicia; but inferences are generally best left without comment, so she only said, "Well, dear, everything is in order now, so I 'll run up to Cecil's. Eliza Todd is to bring a woman to help her with the windows, but I 'm going to take the covers off the pictures, and just see to the finishing touches. I think everything will be fixed by the time they get here; and I 'll stop and ask Miss Susan to come in and cheer you up."

"Very well," said Mrs. Drayton, with that weary closing of the eyes which every one who has had the care of an invalid knows too well. "I want everything to be nice for Cecil, I 'm sure. But it 's a little bitter to be so much alone."

"Oh, I 'll be back by dinner time," Alicia reminded her brightly. "Do you want me to take Cecil a bunch of poppies from you?"

"Certainly, I do," said Mrs. Drayton, opening her eyes. "Cecil does n't really care for me — no, don't interrupt me, Lyssie! *I know;* — but no one can say I don't do everything in the world for your dear papa's daughter. No one can say she is n't exactly like my own child."

"Why, of course," said Alicia soothingly.

"I don't know why you say 'of course'!" cried Mrs. Drayton. "I'm sure there are a great many step-mothers who might have made a difference."

"I only meant of course you loved Ceci," Lyssie explained.

"I remember," Mrs. Drayton proceeded, with a hint of tears in her voice, — "I remember perfectly well, once, when you were both little things, somebody asked Susy Carr 'which was Mr. Drayton's child by his first wife.' I think that shows how I treated Cecil."

Cecil's step-mother almost sobbed, and her daughter had to stop to kiss and comfort her, though it was getting warmer every moment, and the walk to her sister's house was long and sunny.

"Oh, go, go!" said Mrs. Drayton. "I felt you look over my head at the clock. I'm sure I don't want to interfere with your plans about Cecil. I suppose you've told Esther about my eggnog? Give my love to Philip. I must say he's never let Cecil teach him to be disrespectful to me; he is always properly attentive."

Alicia Drayton was only twenty-one, but she excelled in the art, which is taught to perfection in a sick-room, of knowing when to ignore complaints. A certain angelic common sense gave her at once discrimination and tenderness, — those two qualities which must be together for the full development of either.

"Yes, Esther will bring the eggnog at eleven," she said cheerfully. "Good-by, mother darling."

She gave an anxious thought, as she went downstairs, to that possible draft; and her face sobered
as she stood for a moment in the open doorway of
the dark, cool hall, and saw the blaze of June sunshine over the garden. The thought of her mother
sitting all alone, in the half-light of lowered curtains
and bowed shutters, struck on the girl's tender heart
with a sort of shame at her own young vigor. She
knew how Mrs. Drayton's pallid face and weak eyes
would have shrunk away from what she always
spoke of as the " glare," and how the hot fragrance
of the roses would have made her poor, heavy head
ache. " But it does seem as though she might look
out of the window," Lyssie thought, sighing. Yet
she had been content to let her mother be comfortable in her own way. From which it will be seen
that Miss Alicia Drayton was an unusual young
woman. Indeed, very early in life this girl had
displayed the pathetic common sense of the child
whose mother's foolishness forces her into a discre-
tion beyond her years. The village had acknowledged her merit long ago, — acknowledged it with
the slight condescension with which Old Chester
commented upon Youth.

" A very good girl," said the village, " but " —
Old Chester was apt to balance its praise with a
" but " — " it 's a pity the child has n't more accomplishments. She 's been so busy taking care of her
poor mother all these years that she has n't a single
accomplishment."

Mrs. Drayton, however, would have explained that

an invalid could not be expected to think of such trivial things as accomplishments. "I've brought her up to be a good child," said Mrs. Drayton; and certainly nobody could deny that. In fact, Alicia's mother did very little beside read her Bible, and meditate over certain small good books of the nature of Gathered Pearls and Daily Foods. She kept a stand at her elbow for her half dozen devout and well-worn volumes. Thomas à Kempis was there; and her Prayer-Book, with flowers pressed between the pages of especially significant saints' days, and small marginal ejaculations scattered through the Psalter, — ejaculations which Mrs. Drayton not infrequently read aloud to her callers. There was also upon the stand a little calendar, with a text, a hymn, and a prayer for each day. This was a distinct interest in the poor sick lady's life, for there was the element of surprise in tearing off each slip; she was apt to inclose an especially beautiful page to any correspondent to whom she chanced to be writing, and she would add "True!" or underline a word or phrase, to show how personal were these printed outbursts of religious feeling.

Her husband, compelled by ill health to live abroad, was greatly favored in this way. Yet he had been known to say that "Frances's goodness was the worst part of her." Indeed, irreverent lips whispered that Mrs. Drayton's goodness was the peculiar disease which needed European treatment.

"But then, why did he marry her, if he didn't

want to live with her?" the village reflected. "Everybody knew what Fanny Dacie was. And why did he marry again, anyhow? His child by his first wife had a good home with the Ashurst Draytons. He had no need to marry again."

Mr. William Drayton, however, had thought differently.

After the calamity of his first wife's death, he had left the baby Cecil with his sister-in-law in Ashurst, and, dazed and bewildered by his grief, had gone away to forget. For several years he wandered aimlessly about the world. And when he drifted home again, and found Cecil, with her mother's eyes and her mother's name, — which made him wince whenever he had to address her, — when he found her irritable and discontented among her cousins in Colonel Drayton's household, why, then he married again. He did not love the child, but it was *hers,* so it must have a home. He took Cecil and went back to Old Chester, and opened up the house he had closed when his wife died. What the associations were, what strange certainties came to him of that dead wife's sympathy in his search for a new wife, he did not confide to any one, least of all to Miss Frances Dacie, while he sought to impress upon her that his happiness and her welfare — a more truthful man might have reversed these terms — depended upon their marriage. Miss Dacie was thirty-one; she yielded to his entreaty without that foolish hesitation which younger ladies sometimes deem necessary. Having thus provided a home and a mother for little Cecil, William Drayton found, in a year or two, that his health demanded foreign travel.

"And the unfortunate part of it is," said Mr. Drayton, forty years old, gray, *blasé*, standing with his back to the fireplace in the Rev. Dr. Lavendar's study, — "the unfortunate part of it is, my wife is such a wretched invalid (she has never been well, you know, since little Lyssie was born) she is n't able to go with me. She could n't stand traveling; and traveling, King says, is what I need. My only consolation is that I can live so much more cheaply in Europe, which of course is a good thing for Frances and the girls."

And thus it was that Mr. William Drayton became a fugitive from matrimony.

He did give a thought sometimes to the task which Miss Dacie had assumed because of her desire to promote his happiness. But he consoled himself by reflecting upon her welfare. "She likes living in the Poindexter house," he thought, his cold, heavy eyes closing in a smile, "and it 's a great satisfaction to her to be married, even if she does have to wrestle with Cecilla; but I 've no doubt that little monkey, Lyssie, will improve Cecilla."

That Cecilla needed to be improved no one could deny. Her aunt, Mrs. Henry Drayton of Ashurst, used to testify to that emphatically.

"I had that child seven years," she would say, "and nobody can tell me anything about her. She is the strangest creature! — though I 'm sure I tried to make her a good child. Poor Frances ! I must say I pity her."

Indeed, Mrs. Henry Drayton had continued to try to make Cecil a good child even after she had handed her over, " with a sigh of relief," to Mrs. William.

" Cecil, my dear, you ought not to call your mamma ' Mrs. Drayton,' " she instructed her niece.

" My mamma is dead, and I don't love Mrs. Drayton," Cecil answered, with a little pause between her slow sentences.

" That has nothing to do with it," said Mrs. Henry. " She is your father's wife, and you should treat her with respect even if you don't love her ; and it is n't respectful to say ' Mrs. Drayton.' "

" I 'd just as lief say ' Miss Dacie,' " the child said.

Her aunt gasped and cried, " You are a naughty little girl ! Of course you are not to say ' Miss Dacie ' ; she is your papa's wife, and — "

" How many wives can papa have ? " Cecil interposed calmly ; " my mother is his wife."

" Your mother is a saint in heaven ! — at least, I hope she is," said Mrs. Henry, horrified. " If I were your mamma, I 'd send you to bed without any supper."

" I 'm glad papa did n't marry you ; that would have been worse than Mrs. Drayton," her niece announced.

And then Mrs. Henry wept with Mrs. William, and said she pitied her with all her heart ; and mobody was more rejoiced than she, when, at eighteen, Cecil, just home from boarding-school, became engaged to Philip Shore.

"I rejoice on your account, dear Frances," she wrote to Cecil's step-mother. "What a relief it must be, after your noble devotion of these eleven years, at last to hand her over to a husband, — though I must say I pity the young man! The colonel and I are delighted to hear what an estimable person he is, though I'm sorry he hasn't expectations from his uncle. However, Cecil has money enough for both. I hope, for your sake, they will be married at once."

But they were not married at once. Philip spent three years in one of the Paris studios, so Mrs. Drayton was still obliged to endure her step-daughter's indolence, and willful ways, and occasional black tempers; and also her cold indifference, not only to herself, but, it must be admitted, to Old Chester!

When at last she married Philip Shore, the village drew a breath of satisfaction. "Dear Philip," it said, — "such a really superior young man! Now poor Cecil will improve."

But except that Philip took her away for a year, no improvement was visible. She came back when Molly was born, and then everybody said they hoped the baby would make a difference in Cecil. It did; it added to the strange, passionate, untrained nature the passion of maternity.

"Though I don't care now what they say about me," Cecil said languidly to her husband, looking down at the small head upon her arm; "I have *this!* And really, Philip, you must admit I am of some value to Old Chester? I give it something to gossip about. If I were suddenly to grow good, people would be disappointed!"

There was truth in this. All her life Cecil had afforded to her friends that interest of shuddering disapproval which is so delightful. Even her father had felt it when he came home to see her married. "There are possibilities in this affair," he thought, watching her with amiable, impersonal interest. "If this Philip would get drunk once in a while, or swear at her, I think it might turn out pretty well. But he won't, he won't," said Mr. Drayton, with real regret; "he'll be too damned polite to her." He was surprised at his fatherly solicitude; for the paternal tie is weakened after twelve years of absence, broken only by occasional visits. "The young man," he meditated, standing on the threshold, bidding adieu to the departing bride and groom, — "the young man is in love; there's no doubt about that. And as for her, I suppose he is the first man she has seen, and so she's in love, too. But very likely she'd have married the Devil to get away from Frances." He was really interested; perhaps, could his visit have been prolonged, he might have felt some anxiety in spite of himself. He was absent-minded as he listened to Old Chester's praise of Philip, and ominous omission of Cecil's name. "The boy is an ascetic," he was saying to himself, "and she — " He closed his lips; at least she was Cecilla's child. He had not seen her since, for, the winter that the young husband and wife were in Paris, there were reasons why Mr. Drayton could not ask his daughter to visit what he called his "humble roof" in Cannes; and so, to avoid embarrassing inhospitality, he had found it necessary to be in Egypt for his health. The next time he came to Old Chester, Philip and his wife were living in town, and, as Mrs. Drayton explained, "dear William was unwilling to take a moment from me, though he would have been interested to see Molly, of course."

When her step-daughter married, the consolation of living in the finest house in Old Chester was taken away from Mrs. Drayton. The Poindexter house had belonged to the first Mrs. Drayton, and had been settled on her child, as was also her not inconsiderable fortune. But when the plans for Cecil's wedding were made, Mr. Drayton arranged that his wife and younger daughter should take a house in the village, "where," he wrote, "as soon as my miserable health permits, I shall hope to join my dear ones permanently." But thus far his health had not permitted.

That moving from her sister's house had been a great trial to Alicia, who had been born there, and had spent a happy childhood in its gardens and orchards; but she had not been able to think very much of her own feelings. All her childish courage was needed to sustain her mother, who wept and moaned, and said that Cecil had turned her out of doors. "Papa has made this arrangement, Mrs.

Drayton," her step-daughter reminded her briefly; and Mrs. Drayton's pride refused her the luxury of finding fault with her husband. It was nine years ago that this change was made, but Alicia's deepest home feeling was still for the great brick house on the hill, where she had spent those twelve happy years. She could see it from her window in the village, lifting, above the foliage on the hillside, its square, flat roof with the white balustrade. The house had white corner trimmings, and white lintels and copings, and the worn brick floor of the veranda was darkened by a roof lifted above the second-story windows by four white columns. It was cool on this porch, even on a June day like this on which Cecil and her husband were coming back to Old Chester to spend the summer, — a day brimming with hot sunshine, and with not a breath of wind to carry the scents of the garden up to the open windows of the house.

Alicia Drayton had sheltered herself under a big umbrella when she climbed the hill; but she was glad to sit down on the porch steps and rest, and fan herself with her hat, before going indoors to her pleasant task of giving the final touches of order and comfort to her sister's house. Eliza Todd, who was scrubbing somewhere within, came clattering through the hall to tell Miss Drayton that all the mopboards were cleaned, "and cleaned *good*," said Eliza; and that consciousness made her feel enough at leisure to stand leaning on her broom listening to Miss Lyssie, who was incapable of seeing any reason why she should not tell her scrubbing-woman how happy she was to have her sister at home again.

"And Molly; Molly is my little niece, Eliza; she's just eight. Oh, she is the dearest little thing! Though she can't be very little now; she was five the last time I saw her, and of course she's grown since then."

"And have they just the one?" said Eliza.

"Yes; I'm sure I don't know what my sister would do if there were any others, she loves Molly so much!"

"Well," Eliza commented, "a mother, she's always got love enough to go round, somehow. I wish you could say the same of shoes."

"How is Job, Eliza?" the girl asked kindly.

"He's been sober for three days," said Job's wife. "If your sister had to count days between sprees, she might say she was glad there was only one. And me with six, an' another coming! Well, Miss Lyssie, the Good Man's judgment ain't just like ours, is it? Me with six, an' only one in a nice house like this. — Well, I guess I'll go back to that hall; it wants to be swep' once more."

Alicia followed her in pitying silence, and a grave look lingered in her face even when she was busy with her pleasant work. Her scrubwoman's domestic infelicities were very puzzling to Lyssie. Once, hesitatingly, after discouraging efforts to reconcile the husband and wife, whose violent quarrels were commonplace village gossip, she had suggested to Miss Carr that Eliza be advised to leave Job.

"They don't like each other, Miss Susan," the girl said, "and he treats her badly, and we have to support the children."

"Why, he is her husband, Lyssie Drayton!" cried Miss Susan. "You don't know what you are talking about, child!" And her horrified disapproval closed Alicia's lips.

"But I'm going to ask Ceci what she thinks," Lyssie said to herself, when, late in the afternoon, a half hour before it was time to expect the stage, she went out on the porch again to rest. And then, in her own happiness, she could not help forgetting poor Eliza and her troubles. A red rose leaned its chin upon the balustrade and looked at her. Alicia pulled it down against her cheek in a pretty caress ; it made her think of her sister. It was brimmed with sunshine, and hot and sweet with passionate color. She remembered how Cecil liked to sit in the sun, with lovely, lazy, half-shut eyes, and strong white fingers clasped behind her head. Alicia twisted the thorny stem, but dropped it quickly, and put her finger to her lips and said, "Ouch!" and then tried again to pluck it. "I'll put it on her dressing table," she reflected, "and tell her it looks like her."

II.

CECIL SHORE'S house was all ready for her, when, at five, the yellow coach, swinging, pitching on its big springs, came rumbling up the lane with much clattering of harness and cracking of the whip. Philip was on the top seat with the driver, his hand on the collar of a big dog, whose trepidation at his swaying elevation was manifest; his master's face broke into a smile at the sight of Alicia, standing in happy excitement on the steps, and before the horses could come to a standstill he had swung himself down and kissed her, with one hand on her shoulder, and the other dragging Eric back, for the dog had followed him with a flying leap. Then he turned and opened the stage door, which was glowing with an Italian landscape of mountains and lakes, and Lombardy poplars.

Cecil, in the dark cavern of the coach, was smiling at some one beside her. "Yes, that is Lyssie; that is my sister," she was explaining. "Lys dear, here we are! Have you worked your little hands off for us?" The soft, dark feathers of her wide hat brushed the top of the stage doorway, as, slowly, touching her husband's arm to steady herself, she came down the two hinged steps; then she smiled up at Alicia, and put two fingers under the girl's chin and kissed her. "Bless your dear little heart!" she said. "I hope you are not worn out by house-cleaning?" And then she looked over her shoulder at the gentleman who had followed her from the coach, and upon whom Eric was bestowing a warm, wet welcome.

"This is Mr. Carey, Lyssie; my sister, Mr. Carey. Oh, don't let Eric jump all over you! Well, Lys dear, how are you? Oh, Lyssie, I left my book in the stage; get it, dear, will you?"

Alicia had no eyes for any one but Cecil. She ran back for the book, and stopped to hug Molly once again, and said no more than "Excuse me" when she brushed past Mr. Carey and followed her sister into the drawing-room. There she put Cecil into a big chair, and then stood and looked at her, her breath shaken by a happiness which brought the tears to her eyes.

"Oh, my *dear!*" she said; strangely enough, the older woman stirred all the mother in the girl. "Oh, Ceci, to think you are here!" She slipped down to the floor, and put her arms about her sister's waist and kissed her shoulder. "Are you well? Is Philip well? Molly looks as blooming as a rose. Oh, Ceci, there never was anybody so dear as you!"

"Molly is an angel," Molly's mother declared. "Lyssie, here is Mr. Carey. Mr. Carey, a declaration is being made me." She bent Alicia's face back and kissed her, smiling, and then she glanced about the long, pleasant room.

"Oh, how familiar it all looks! Mr. Carey, my sister has put this whole house in order for me."

Mr. Carey, standing in the doorway, was civilly surprised at Miss Drayton's goodness and cleverness, but he was plainly more interested in Eric, who ought to have some water, he said.

"Here, you brute," he protested, "don't jump on me! Mrs. Shore, may Eric come into the parlor?"

"You must ask Lyssie," she said, leaning back in her chair. "May he come in, Lys? How cool it is in here with this white matting on the floor! Lyssie, the house looks as though it had been lived in always; and let me see — it's three years since we 've been here, is n't it? Those poppies are superb. Oh, what color, what color! Mrs. Drayton sent them? She's very good, I 'm sure. I hope she is quite well? Molly, come pull off mamma's gloves. And how is Old Chester, Lyssie? Is everybody asleep? Do you think they will waken up to talk about me? Oh, do put those poppies here beside me; that scarlet is — I think it is an expression of religion. Poor Lys, how I shock you! Mr. Carey, did you know that Mr. Shore was the Example of Old Chester, and I the Warning? We come like two traveling evangelists."

"Well, I will go and assist the Example," said the young man, and went out into the hall, where the master of the house was giving directions about trunks and boxes.

Alicia was so far used to the excited happiness of the arrival that she glanced at Mr. Carey, and thought that his short, rough, blond hair made him rather good-looking. He also glanced at her with a pair of candid, obstinate blue eyes, and said to himself, " To think of those two women being sisters ! " Indeed, his impression of her was deep enough to make him say, while he was looking after Eric's comfort, " She seems like a mighty nice girl."

Cecil, meantime, in her big, cool bedroom, was explaining her guest to her sister. " I hardly know him ; I 've only seen him twice. He 's a friend of Philip's ; he 's a lawyer, but quite an authority on pig iron, too. He looks it, somehow, don't you think he does ? The word suggests him, — pig iron. Well, you know Philip is writing a book on the chemical changes in pig iron, — Heaven knows why ! One would think he had enough on his hands with his scholarship fund and his political people ; but he persuaded Mr. Carey to come down for a fortnight and help him about something. Philip thinks him charming," she ended, and smiled, with the corner of her red lip drooping ; " but really, he is n't bad."

She had taken a gold pin from her hair, and two braids fell heavily upon her shoulders. Lyssie, her elbows on the toilet table, and her chin in her hands, sat absorbed in looking at her. " Oh, Ceci, I wish you would never go away again," she said.

" My dear ! I should die here," Cecil assured her seriously. " A summer is all I can think of. I wanted Molly to be in the country, in some quiet place, and I wanted to see you, so I thought I could stand Old Chester for three months. But this room is certainly very nice," she broke off, with such a kind look that Alicia forgot the fatigue of her day's work. She glanced at the white curtains in the four deep windows, and reflected how she had hammered her thumb in putting them up; but what did that matter? Cecil liked her room ! There was matting on the floor, and white covers on the furniture, and a deep white valance about the bed, whose four tall posts were crowned with a tester. It, too, was hung with white dimity. There were two silver candle-sticks on the table, and an India china bowl full of pale pink roses. There was also a deep red rose in a glass on the toilet table.

" I thought it looked like you, Ceci," the younger sister said timidly.

" No, not a rose, Lys," she corrected her slowly, with a melodious break of silence between her sen-tences. " I 'm a peony. I 've no soul. Put it in Philip's room. He is all soul ! Philip has almost converted Mr. Carey (his name is Roger, — Roger Carey) to his political opinions. Not quite, though, as he has an interest in a rolling-mill at Mercer, and iron rust doth corrupt, so he 's still a Republican. But I almost wish he would get converted, I 'm so tired of hearing the excellent Philip plead with him. They talked about it in the train, all the way to Mer-cer. I composed a new soup in my mind to keep the refrain of ' reform ' from putting me to sleep. Well, what do you think of him, Lys ? "

"He looks rather nice," Alicia commented, "and he was good to Eric."

"Oh, he is given up to dogs and horses and all that sort of thing; he's that sort of a man. But I like to talk to him; though he is rude. I think, if he had been born in a different class, he would have knocked his wife down sometimes, or sworn at her, anyhow."

"Is he married?" Lyssie said.

"Oh dear, no; he has n't money enough to marry. What do you think of his looks?"

"I'd rather think of yours," Lyssie declared. "His eyes seemed nice, and I thought he was rather a rosy person; oh, quite good-looking, I think. But, Ceci, I think *you* — oh, when you bring those two braids around behind your ears and cross them on top of your head, with those little tendrils of curls sticking out of them, they look like a chaplet of laurel!"

"You are rather nice-looking yourself," said the other, thrusting the gold pin through these same splendid braids, and glancing with kind eyes at her young sister, who, indeed, had no more claim to beauty than is given by mere youth, with perhaps a fresh color, and frank eyes, and a well-shaped head set on a slender, girlish neck. "Yes, though not a raving beauty, you are nice to look at. How is our dear papa, Lys? I have n't heard from him for six months. He never included me among his 'dear ones.'"

"About the same, I think," Alicia answered soberly. "Mother had a letter last week. I wish she were able to join him, Ceci. I think, if she just got through the voyage, Cannes would be good for her."

"Good gracious!" cried Cecil. "Well, Lyssie, don't let Mrs. Drayton come down upon him unexpectedly; don't surprise him, dear."

"Oh, there really is n't any chance of her doing it," Lyssie said; "but why not? I always thought that it would be so pleasant, to be surprised?"

"I — I don't think it would be pleasant," Mrs. Shore answered briefly; and added, "for our dear papa." And then she laughed, and pushed her chair back from the dressing table, resting her fingers on its linen cover, and glancing into the long mirror which stood behind it, between the windows.

"Well, is there anything interesting going on in Old Chester? Oh, I forgot to tell you. Mr. Carey is a sort of relation of some Mrs. Pendleton (or rather of her husband) who has come to Old Chester to live. He had forgotten it, but Philip discovered it in some way. Who is she?"

"Well, she 's a widow; she 's — oh, I 'll tell you who she is, Ceci: she was the Miss Amanda Townsend whom we used to hear about when we were children, — don't you remember? She was engaged to Mr. Joseph Lavendar, and they quarreled; and she married some rich man right off, — oh, in a month, I think, or something like that. Well, he was Mr. Pendleton; he died nearly two years ago. Such crape! She must have been very much attached to him; she's all covered up in crape yet. And he left her a house here, and quite a lot of money," said Lyssie, with some awe; "they say five thousand a year!"

Cecil laughed, and rose. "What a fortune! I should think Mr. Joseph would try to make up."

"I think he'd like to," Lyssie said; "but they say that if she marries again she has to give up the money; and then I don't think Dr. Lavendar likes her, so Mr. Joseph could n't."

"Is Dr. Lavendar just as dusty and tangled looking as ever?" Cecil inquired. "People really ought not to be allowed to offend the world by their looks! I had such a time this spring with my coachman. He appeared, if you please, in blue spectacles. It did n't interfere with his driving, of course, but he was a perfect object! I told him I could n't have it. He could take off the spectacles or leave. He left: so annoying in him."

"But the poor man's eyes," protested Lyssie; "perhaps he needed blue glasses?"

"Well, that was n't my affair," Cecil said, much amused.

"But he must have felt rather discouraged," Lyssie persisted, "to lose a place just because—"

"Oh, those people don't mind," Cecil interrupted her carelessly. "Come! let's go to the nursery. Molly is delicious. Have you seen her?"

The visit to the nursery delayed supper, but that did not trouble Mrs. Shore. She brought Molly downstairs with her, and kept her at her side at the table, feeding her with lumps of sugar dipped in coffee, to the child's delight, and her father's great but reticent annoyance.

Mr. Carey's keen eyes noticed the annoyance in spite of the reticence. " Funny match," he thought, glancing at his hostess across his wineglass; and he reflected that the other sister was " more like Shore."

" The other," sitting opposite him, was defending herself from a charge of neglect.

" It's very ungracious in you," Mrs. Shore had said, " to leave me the moment you've had your supper ! "

" You know I'd like to stay, Ceci," the girl pleaded, " but I don't want to leave mother alone all the evening. I was here in the morning, you know."

" You rushed home to give her her dinner," interrupted Cecil gayly; " I am certain of that ! Molly, will you be as good to mamma, when she is old and fussy, as aunt Lyssie is to grandmamma ? "

Alicia's color rose a little. " *Of course* I went home; I wanted some dinner myself. But I was here all the afternoon, and I couldn't be away in the evening, too ? " she ended anxiously.

. And Roger Carey, listening, said to himself again, " She's a mighty nice girl." But he laughed, notwithstanding his appreciation of her character, when Mrs. Shore declared drolly, " Oh, Lyssie, your especial form of selfishness is unselfishness."

" At least it is an unusual form," Philip said, smiling; " but anything unusual is very bad, Lys ! "

Then the group about the table broke up, and Alicia said she must go home. Cecil reproached her, and her brother enticed her, and Mr. Carey said that, as an unprejudiced outsider, he must say he thought she was neglecting her family. But she was charmingly firm; so, through a mist of June moonlight, full of the scent of dewy leaves and blossoming grass, Philip and his guest escorted her to her door.

Cecil, left alone upon the porch, cuddled Molly in her arms, and thought how tired she was, and how delightful it would be to have nothing whatever to do for the next three months.

The summer night fell like a perfumed curtain across the valley; the dusk had a certain richness of texture, as though one might lay one's face against it and feel its softness. From the pool below the terraces came the bell-like clang of frogs. Katydids answered each other in the tulip-trees, and the shrill, monotonous note of the cicada rose and fell, and rose again. Molly had fallen asleep, and Cecil felt the little limbs relax, and the head grow heavy upon her arm; she looked down at her, and leaned her face towards the child's soft, parted lips to feel her breath upon her cheek; then she lifted the little limp, warm hand, and kissed it gently; but Molly stirred and fretted, and her mother was plainly relieved when the nurse came to take her to bed.

" How heavy she is getting, Rosa! " Mrs. Shore said, with that frowning pride common to mothers when any pain comes to them from the child's strength; and her eyes followed the little figure in Rosa's arms with a sort of passionate tenderness, before she allowed herself to sink back into her chair, and yawn, and think that her arm was really stiff from the child's weight.

"Yes, it will be good for her to be here," she reflected; "the duller it is, the better on her account. But, good heavens! I don't know how I am going to stand it. Perhaps I was a fool not to have sent her to Alicia, and taken Philip abroad for the summer?"

. No nicety of thought prevented Mrs. Shore from regarding her husband's entire financial dependence upon her with anything but a crude truthfulness; but she was apt to confound such dependence with a certain silent acquiescence in her plans, and to feel that she really might have "taken" him abroad, or that she had "brought" him to Old Chester.

In the half-light there upon the old porch, where the climbing roses and the wistaria grew so thick about the pillars that they made an almost impenetrable lattice against the faint yellow light still lingering in the west, the singular and distinguished beauty of Cecil Shore's face was less noticeable than was that peculiar brutality one sees sometimes in refined and cultivated faces which have known nothing but ease: faces which have never shown eagerness, because all their desires are at hand; nor pity, because they have never suffered; nor humility, because their tributary world has made their sins those of omission rather than of commission.

"But this Mr. Carey is entertaining," Cecil was thinking, — "if a friend of Philip's can be entertaining!" She sighed, and looked wearily about her. "Yes, it *must* be good for Molly," she repeated, as though for self-encouragement. Sometimes the sense of a lack of interest comes over one with a horrible physical sinking. "And nothing ever has been interesting except that first year I was married!" she said to herself.

She was just thirty: nearly half her life, perhaps, was lived; why in the world should another thirty years seem so horrible? She had so many of the conditions which are supposed to mean happiness. She had Molly. "But, after all, Molly is not myself," she thought. In a mother this keen sense of personal identity is significant; it was even conceivable, with this sense, that Cecil Shore's little daughter might some time bore her. As she lay back in her chair, her face grew dull, as though for very weariness of her well being; and then a faint amusement came into her eyes at the remembrance of her husband's excellence, and with it a contemptuous impatience of her own good humor. For she was very good humored with Philip. Even Old Chester, snubbed and shocked and honestly grieved at a thousand faults, — even Old Chester had to admit that she was very agreeable to Philip. "She makes him very comfortable," Old Chester said. "She is a good housekeeper, and that is most praiseworthy. She gives a great deal of thought to her food. She is lazy, but she trains her cook herself!"

Her faults were all obvious enough : — impertinence
to her elders and betters ; extravagance ; indolence ;
the failure to bring Molly up according to Old Chester traditions, — but, nevertheless, she made Philip
" very comfortable."

" How he hates it ! " she thought to herself, a
keen humor lighting her eyes. " He does n't want
to be made comfortable. I think he would really
like it better if I were not so agreeable to him. Oh,
he ought to have been a monk, — he ought to have
been a monk ! "

III.

A small neighborhood where we know every one, are known of every one, interested in every one, and authorized to hope that every one is interested in us. — MISS MITFORD.

MRS. DRAYTON had been quite right in saying that Philip was always properly attentive. His first call in Old Chester was upon her; and though he was careful to say that his wife had sent him, with her love and apologies that the fatigue of the journey kept her from coming herself, no credit was given to Cecil.

"Sent him!" Mrs. Drayton said afterwards to Alicia, aggrieved, but shrewd. "As if I did n't know what that amounted to! She does n't even know he has been to see me. Oh, when I think how I took her mother's place to Cecil, it is a little bitter to feel that she does n't care for me." Her eyes filled, and Lyssie knelt down and put her arms about her and comforted her, with that sincere and troubled tenderness — love knows it well — that dares not stop to think of truth.

"Ceci was so tired with her journey. Of course she wants to see you, dearest, but — "

"Oh," cried Mrs. Drayton, "you don't understand. Only a mother can understand the pang that a child's ingratitude causes. And Cecil was always like my own child to me. Did I ever tell you that somebody once asked Susy Carr which of you was your father's child by his first wife? Well, that shows how I loved her. And I'm sure, only the other day I made you carry her some poppies. I'm always showing her my affection, and she despises, despi—" And Mrs. Drayton broke down and wept.

Alicia, very pitiful of what her clear eyes told her was not wounded love, but wounded vanity, stayed in the darkened room for an hour, though she had not given Esther her orders for the day, nor picked the roses, nor fed her pigeons, nor had a moment to run up the hill to see Cecil.

On this particular occasion, however, in spite of Mrs. Drayton's insight into Cecil's feelings, her stepdaughter did know that Philip was being "properly attentive." That morning, as he and Molly and Mr. Carey had started down to the village together, Cecil, standing on the porch to see them off, said gayly, "Spare Mr. Carey Mrs. Drayton, Philip. He has done nothing to deserve Mrs. Drayton, I'm sure. And make me as fatigued as possible, do! I shall not be equal to a call for a week."

Molly, hanging on her father's hand, said gravely, "Why does n't mamma like grandmamma?" At which Roger Carey, under his breath, said something about little pitchers, and Philip laughed in spite of himself, but looked annoyed, and called Molly's attention to the fact that she had better pick some daisies for her aunt Lyssie.

They left Mr. Carey at his kinswoman's door before Philip went to make his call upon Mrs. Drayton. "Turn up at the tavern about twelve, Carey," he said, "and we 'll walk back together."

"Twelve!" thought Mr. Carey, with dismay. "Must I stay with the old lady until twelve?"

Mrs. Pendleton was plainly of the opinion that he must, for she had many things to talk about. She was a pretty little woman, in spite of the heavy crape in which she was swathed; her face was round and rosy, and her light brown hair waved down over a forehead as smooth as though she were fourteen instead of forty-five. There was hardly a wrinkle on her placid face. Dr. Lavendar had been heard to say, in this connection, that "thought made wrinkles." And the inference was obvious. Yet the fact that Mrs. Pendleton was known in the world of letters might seem to contradict such an inference. To be sure, it was only as "Amanda P.," but almost every one who had seen the thin volume of verses had heard Mrs. Pendleton's modest acknowledgment of its authorship.

"I suppose," she used to confess whenever she gave away a copy of the book, "I suppose it was unfeminine to publish, but 'Amanda P.' is not like appearing under my own name. That I never could have done; it would have been so unfeminine." Indeed, in Old Chester Mrs. Pendleton was as distinguished by her femininity as by literature. Her delicate manners were of the kind that used to be called "genteel," and she always displayed the timidity and modesty that are expected of a "very feminine " female.   She had fainted once when a little mouse ran across the chancel in church, and she had been known to say that she thought certain words in the service " most indelicate."

As she talked, Mr. Carey felt again his old impatience with her, which he had forgotten, as he had forgotten her, and he wished he could intercept Philip somewhere before the hour for meeting him at the tavern was up.   Mrs. Pendleton did, however, give him a good deal of Old Chester gossip, for which he was not ungrateful.   She told him that Frances Drayton, Cecil Shore's step-mother, was a most lovable character, and Alicia a devoted and dutiful daughter, " though not what you would call a clever girl."   That Susan Carr was quite philanthropic ; " but, I must say, she seems rather stern, sometimes," Mrs. Pendleton said, with a little qualifying laugh, and then she told him how Jane Temple had married very much beneath her.   Mrs. Pendleton had lived in Old Chester only a short time, but it was another of her characteristics, this of speaking of persons whom she knew slightly by their first names.

The hour was nearly up when Roger went away, saying that he wanted to have a look at Old Chester before going home.   He walked down by the church, and wondered what philosophy Dr. Lavendar exploited ; for plain religion would scarcely have warranted Mrs. Pendleton's appreciative remark that old Dr. Lavendar was *very* learned, though — though a little shabby.

It was a pretty little church, the walls all rustling

and tremulous with ivy, and with a flutter of spar-
rows' wings about the eaves. Philip had told him
that Miss Drayton sung in the choir on Sundays.
" I 've a great mind to go to church while I 'm here,"
the young man reflected. And with this thought in
his mind, it was natural enough to turn and walk up
on the other side of the street, past a low, whitewashed wall crowned by a dusty hawthorn hedge. It
was remarkable how often Mr. Roger Carey glanced
over that hedge at the white house behind it. " Perhaps she 'll happen to come out," he said to himself.
Possibly to keep such a chance open he stopped, and
seemed to examine, with frowning interest, the fringe
of grass which straggled out from the lawn and hung
over the wall; but no door opened in the silent,
sunny house, and no light step came down the path,
and he was obliged to walk on. He wondered
whether, when Mrs. Shore had presented him to
Miss Drayton, and he had bowed, and said nothing
but that Eric ought to have a drink, he had seemed
like a cub? He really felt a little anxious. " The
next time I see her I 'll make myself agreeable ; I 'll
make a pretty speech," he promised himself, his
pleasant eyes crinkling into a laugh ; and then his
whole face suddenly beamed, and he pulled off his
hat, for there was the lady of his thoughts before
him. The barn, connected with the house by a line
of outbuildings, faced the street; its double doors
were open, and on the threshold, with the cavernous
dusk behind her, stood Alicia Drayton in a blue
print gown, her soft hair blowing about her forehead,

and a crowd of fantail pigeons strutting and cooing and tumbling over one another at her feet. Lyssie had a basket in her hand, and now and then she threw a handful of oats among them; they walked over one another's pink feet, and pressed their snowy breasts so closely together that the grain fell on their glistening backs and wings before it reached the floor. Lyssie, as she let the oats drop through her fingers, made a low coo in her throat, or stopped to admonish her jostling friends. "Don't push so, Snowball. Puff, you're rude. There! there's some all for yourself." Then she looked out across the sunshine in front of the barn and saw Mr. Carey. She remembered quickly that her hair was rough, and she brushed the stray locks back with her wrist, but she smiled and said, "Good-morning. Yes, do!" when he called out to know if he might come in and admire her flock.

"Why, are n't they tame!" he said, as he took her hand, and then watched the pigeons flutter back after their moment's consternation at his footsteps. He had really meant to look at Alicia, she made so pretty a picture standing on the barn floor, with the shadowy haymow behind her, and a dusty line of sunshine from the window in the roof lying like a bar between them, — he had intended to look at her, and perhaps even make his pretty speech; but the pigeons interested him too much; he had a dozen questions to ask about them.

"Have you any swifts? Do you call the young ones squabs or squalers? The sheen on that one's neck is like a bit of Roman glass!"

"Is it? That's Puff. Indeed they are tame;
look here!" She knelt down and stretched out her
hand. "Come, come, come," she said, with the cooing sound in her throat; and one of the pigeons
hopped upon her finger, clasping it with his red,
hard little feet, and balancing back and forth with
agitated entreaty to be careful, the fleeting irides-
cence of his rimpling breast striking out into sudden
color. And as she knelt there, Roger, looking down
at her, and seeing the pretty way her hair grew
about the nape of her white neck, found the pigeons
less absorbing. Then she said she would·show him
something else that was pretty, and stepped back
into the dusky gloom of the barn and called "Fanny,
Fanny! Come, Fan!" There was a scurry of uncertain little hoofs back in the recesses of the stable,
and a bay colt, long-legged and shaggy, with small,
suspicious ears pointed at the intruder, came with
hesitating skips to her side.

"Isn't she a beauty?" Lyssie said. She had
forgotten all her embarrassment at her rumpled hair,
and looked at him with the frankest, kindest eyes.
Roger, examining the colt's mouth and stroking its
absurd legs, said "yes," and called her attention to
several good points, as certain of her appreciation as
if she had not been a girl. Fanny's mother thrust
her serious head over her manger, and watched the
young people, and the pigeons, and the long shaft of
sunshine falling in a pool on the rough floor at
Fanny's forefeet.

"She's named for my mother," Alicia explained;

and after that they talked as easily as if they had known each other for years. Philip was making a lot of visits, Mr. Carey told her. "Yes, he's been here with Molly," said Alicia. "It's so sweet in Cecil to send them to see mother the first thing; Cecil was too tired to come herself."

"Yes," said Mr. Carey; "so — ah — she said. I went down to see the church, Miss Drayton. Philip says we can come and hear you sing on Sunday."

"Oh, it is Miss Susan Carr who sings," Lyssie explained; "she has a beautiful voice."

She looked at him with such placid candor that it would have been absurd to make a "pretty speech." As he thought it over afterwards, Roger Carey was surprised to find that he had not made a single pretty speech in their whole talk as they stood there in the barn with Fanny and the pigeons; perhaps it would have come had the talk been longer, but Alicia chanced to speak of Philip, and Mr. Carey, conscience-stricken, remembered that it was after twelve.

"Philip!" he said. "What will Philip say to me? I was to have met him half an hour ago." Then he said good-by, and rushed away. But his haste was unnecessary; Philip had not yet reached the tavern; so he had to walk home by himself, thinking all the while, with regret, that he might have stayed a little longer in the barn.

The fact was, his host had forgotten him. After he had done his duty in calling upon his mother-in-law, there were many old friends whom he wanted to see. Then, too, he had to stop to point out familiar landmarks to his little daughter, which took time.

"Look, that's where father went to school."

"Is that where you used to draw pictures on your slate instead of doing sums?"

Philip's confession would not have been approved by an educator: "Yes; it was a great deal better than doing sums."

After that they stopped to buy some candy at Tommy Dove's. "I used to waste lots of my allowance here when Mr. Tommy's father kept the apothecary shop," Philip said; and the purchase of a red-and-white-striped candy whistle, very stale and very strongly flavored with wintergreen, detained them for some time; and it took at least a quarter of an hour longer for her father to show Molly how to make a strange, husky noise through the whistle, while between her lips it was melting into sticky sweetness.

It was nearly noon before they reached the rectory, — a small, rambling house, with vines growing thick about its doors and windows. When they crossed the threshold, the visitors took one step down into a narrow hall, and then turned sharp to the right to enter Dr. Lavendar's study, a small room, smelling of tobacco smoke and leather bindings. There was a work table, with a lathe beside it, standing in a flood of sunshine by a south window, but vines darkened the other windows, and the book-covered walls filled the room with a pleasant dusk. The old clergyman looked up from his sermon when Philip and Molly broke in upon his solitude. His eyes shone with pleasure; he took his pipe from his lips, and stretched out his hand to them without rising.

"Can't get up," he said, frowning, with great show of annoyance; "this abominable dog has gone to sleep with his head on my foot! Dogs are perfect nuisances!" But as a shaggy old Scotch terrier rose, yawning and stretching, from the floor beside him, he did rise, and clapped Philip on the shoulder, twinkling at him from under bushy white eyebrows.

"Good boy! Good boy!" he said. "And the child? Nice child. Go and play in the garden, my dear. I can't remember her name, Philip?"

Molly, obedient, and glad to get out again into the sunshine, would have stepped from the open French window into the deep, tangled sweetness of an old-fashioned garden, but Dr. Lavendar called her back. He put his pipe down on the mantel-shelf, and searched slowly in all the pockets of his ancient dressing-gown. "There," he said, "there's a nickel! Now go." And Molly, with a wondering glance at her father, went.

Dr. Lavendar sat down in front of his work table. "Back again, boy? How long do you intend to stay? How's your wife?"

"Well," Philip told him briefly; and added that they should spend the summer in Old Chester.

"You did n't see Joseph in Mercer, as you came through? Well, never mind; he 'll be here on Saturday, — never fails to come on Saturday. Hi, there, Danny! Do you see that dog getting into my armchair? I won't have it; I 'll give him away. Daniel, you 're a scoundrel." Then he got up and poked a cushion under Danny's little old gray head.

"I have seen only two or three people beside Mrs. Drayton," said Philip, — "but I 've seen the new inhabitant! I stopped at her house to present my friend, Roger Carey, who is staying with me. He is a connection of her husband's."

"Yes, yes; Ben Pendleton's widow has come here to live," said Dr. Lavendar, the eager sweetness of his old face changing suddenly. "You know who she is? She 's the girl who broke off with Joey. She lived in Mercer then. That was twenty years ago; but she 's the same woman, — the same woman ! "

"Perhaps she 's had a change of heart," Philip suggested.

"Can the Ethiopian change his skin?" cried Dr. Lavendar tremulously. "No, no, Philip. She threw Joey over for a rich man. And she has a small mouth. I will never trust a woman with a small mouth. Why? When you 've had more experience in life, you 'll know why. Women with small mouths think of nothing but themselves."

"But if your brother has forgiven her — " Philip began; but Dr. Lavendar would not discuss Mrs. Pendleton.

"I'm afraid I seem irritated," he said apologetically; "sometimes I almost lose my patience in speaking of her. Yes, Joe forgave her, and I ought not to be resentful, I'm sure. I'm the gainer. I'd have lost him if she'd appreciated him. She's the kind of woman who comes out three or four words behind the rest of the congregation in the responses, Philip. If you were a clergyman, you'd know what that means!" He pulled his black silk skullcap down hard over his white hair that stood up very stiff and straight above his anxious, wrinkled forehead and his keen dark eyes. Then he sighed, and said, with a little effort, "Look here, I've something to show you."

He turned his swivel chair round a little, and began to fumble at the lock of a drawer in his table. "I always keep the key in the lock," he said, chuckling. "If I didn't, I should lose it twenty times a day!" He pulled the drawer open, and took out some small packages of soft white tissue paper; he unfolded them with eager haste, his lips opening and closing with interest.

"Look at that!" he said, and spread on his thin palm a dozen small, glittering stones. "They are hyacinths. Joey got 'em for me. Look at this one." He took a single stone up in his pinchers, and held it between Philip and the light. "Some time, Philip, when you are a rich man, you shall give me a diamond to cut?"

"You shall have it, sir," Philip assured him; "but I'm afraid I'll never be a rich man. How

The old clergyman shook his head. " Fairly, Philip, fairly ; I think it will be done in about three years. You see, The History of Precious Stones cannot be written in a day. (That's the title, — The History of Precious Stones. Don't you think that is a good title ?) No, it can't be written in a day. It is the history of the human race, when you come to think of it. And that's a large subject, sir, a large subject. You see, there are so many discursions from the main subject necessary, — subsubjects, as it were. Take, for instance, the story of the emerald of Artabanus ; of course that brings up his wife, and she at once recalls to the thoughtful reader the incident of her father and his general. Or say rubies : one is reminded of the dancer who lost his bride because Clisthenes objected that he ' gesticulated with his legs.' You remember the story of the ruby there, of course, Philip ? "

Philip was prudently silent.

" Yes, I think it will certainly be three years before the book is finished. Then I 'll rewrite it and polish it. I 've no patience with those crude writers who don't polish. Books are like sapphires ; they must be polished — polished ! or else you insult your readers."

" It will be a very valuable book, I 've no doubt, sir."

" Why, certainly," Dr. Lavendar agreed, rather curtly (the young man's observation seemed trite) ; " of course it will be valuable. It gives me pleasure to feel that I am going to be able to leave Joey a

snug little sum; he 'll have a regular income from
The History of Precious Stones, when I 'm dead and
gone, sir."

Philip, suppressing any astonishment he might
have felt at the profits of literature, examined an
amethyst of very beautiful color, while Dr. Lavendar
explained that all his stones were cheap. "Joey
can't afford valuable stones," he said; "but for
beauty, what is more beautiful than those drops of
immortal, unchangeable light? Look here!" He
rummaged in another drawer, and found a cracked
china cup, half full of small, roughly cut stones.
"Topazes, garnets, green garnets, — look!" He
took up a handful of them, and, standing in the
stream of sunshine from the deep window, let them
slip by twos and threes between his fingers, a flash-
ing drip of color.

Philip went away, smiling and sighing.

"What do you breathe such long breaths for,
father?" said Molly; and he turned his sigh into a
laugh, and said he was thinking it was pretty nice to
live in Old Chester.

"Everybody 's so happy, Polly," he explained.

"But why do they all fuss so?" Molly inquired
gravely; and when he bade her remember that little
girls did not know enough to talk about grown persons, she looked up at him and made her small excuse with puzzled face. "But mamma said so.
Mamma said that everybody here was awfully fussy,
and they bored her to death."

Her father was too busy pointing out a martin-

house in the fork of an oak to make any comment on
" mamma's " views, and she did not look up to see
the irritation in his face.   She went springing along
by his side over the short pasture turf, in search of
Miss Susan Carr, who was, they were told, looking
after some late planting on her farm.   They crossed
a brook, that went bubbling between green banks,
making whirling loops of foam about the larger
stones in its path ; a cow, standing ankle-deep in its
shallow rush, sighed, as they passed her, in calm and
fragrant meditation.   Old Chester was behind them,
and high up on a hillside on the left the balconied
roof of Cecil Shore's house gleamed whitely above
the treetops.

" Oh, father," said Molly, " can't I take off my
shoes and stockings, and wade ? "

Philip, nothing loath to light a cigar and sit in
the sun, said, " Yes, by all means !   Miss Susan has
to cross this field to get home, so we 'll wait for her
here."

He stretched himself out lazily under a beech, and
with half-shut eyes watched, through the cigar smoke,
the child holding her skirts well up out of the water,
gripping the slippery stones with little bare white
feet, and balancing herself in all the delightful excitement of a possible tumble.   The beech leaves
moved and whispered in a fresh breeze, and the
brook kept up a low argument broken into chattering
bursts ; the sun shone warm on the green slope of
the field, and far off, behind the hills, great shining
clouds were piled against the placid blue, like the

white domes of some celestial city. A man could forget the harshness of living, in such warm peace. Philip was almost sorry when Miss Susan Carr's cordial, strident voice hailed him with affection and surprise. She came towards him, all unconscious of her heavy, muddy boots and her hot, red face.

" My dear Philip !   My dear boy ! " she said, her kind, near-sighted brown eyes dimmed with pleasure. And then she kissed him heartily, and asked a dozen questions about his health and his concerns, and hugged Molly, and said she hoped Cecil was well. She stood there in her short linsey-woolsey skirt and loose, baggy jacket, one hand on her hip, looking at him with those quick, anxious glances which, to be sure, do not see very deeply into a man's soul, but are full of that mother comfort that often speaks in the faces of childless women. Philip's affection answered her in his words and eyes. He and Molly went home with her; and Molly had a cake, and went to visit the kittens in company with Miss Susan's old Ellen ; and Philip drank a glass of wine, and Miss Susan talked and beamed. She gossiped, like all the rest of Old Chester ; but by some mysterious method, Susan Carr's gossip gave the listener a gentler feeling towards his kind. When she spoke of her neighbors' faults, one knew that somehow they were simply virtues gone to seed ; and what was more remarkable, her praise had no sting of insinuation in it, no suggestion that she could speak differently if she chose. Susan Carr's heart was sound and sweet ; she seemed to have brought from her fields and pastures the courage of the winds and sunshine, and the spirit of the steadfast earth.　Her face was as fresh as an autumn morning; her nut-brown hair, with a large, soft wave on either side of the parting, had not a thread of gray, though she was quite forty-five; on her cheek there was the glow that a russet apple has on the side nearest the sun, and her dark eyes crinkled into laughter as easily as they had done at twenty.　She had a great deal to say to Philip, and all in a loud, breezy, vibrating voice, full of eager and friendly confidence in his interest.　She told him that Lyssie was the dearest child in the world, " and devoted to Frances," she declared.　" Of course she has n't Cecil's looks; but she 's such a pleasant girl, and such a good child, too."　She had a good word for Mrs. Pendleton, though there was a little effort in her voice.　She laughed good naturedly about the Lavendars.　" Yes, the dear old doctor still preaches on the Walls of the New Jerusalem.　He is wonderfully learned, Philip, about precious stones; and I don't mind hearing about jacinth and chrysoprase and all those; it 's really interesting.　And it is about heaven, too," she added reverently.

" I suppose you and Lyssie do a good deal of his parish work for him?"　Philip said, lounging up and down the room, his hands in his pockets.　" How familiar everything looks, Miss Susan!　How well I remember the first time I came into this room with uncle Donald!"

" Do you?" she said, her face softening.　" How proud he was of you, Philip!　Well, yes, Lyssie

and I help the doctor sometimes. He's getting old,
dear old man. But he won't spare himself. Careless as he is in his dress and about small things, in
his work he's as exact and as punctual! Dear me,
I wish the rest of us were half so methodical. You
can't make him remember to order Jones to clip the
hedge by the church, or to tell his Mary to mend his
surplice ; but if he has promised to see a poor soul
at the upper village, he's there on the minute ; or if
he thinks Job Todd has been drinking, he's sure to
call just at the time he gets home from the shop, so
as to keep him from abusing Eliza."

Philip, listening and smiling, said " yes " or " no "
as Miss Susan seemed to expect ; but he paid sudden
attention when, in speaking again of Alicia, she
referred incidentally to Eliza Todd's unhappiness.
Miss Susan did not speak of Eliza as a " case," and
the absence of that objectionable word was sweet to
Philip's ears.

" Yes," Miss Susan said, " Lyssie is really very
useful in parish work. The way she has induced
Eliza to stay with Job, when I was ready to give it
up and let her go, is quite remarkable. Of course,
there are matters that Lyssie can't help us in ; for
instance, that poor Ettie Brown and her baby. You
remember you sent me some money for her, Philip ?"

" Cecil sent it," he corrected her ; " I am only her
almoner."

" It's the same thing," said Miss Susan, with that
positiveness which confesses an unwillingness to
acknowledge what is painful ; " it's *just* the same.

Well, it would n't have been proper to have had
Lyssie have anything to do with that; but she 's in-
valuable in most things, and it 's wonderful how she
has kept Eliza to her duty."

" Her duty ? " cried Philip sharply. " Do you
call it duty ? " The worn lines in his face deepened
suddenly as he spoke. " Why, Miss Susan, a thousand times better let Lyssie help the poor girl than
meddle in the unspeakable viciousness of — " he
seemed to try to shake off his sudden earnestness —
" I mean have any hand in keeping two people together who don't love each other."

" Why, but, my dear Philip ! " said Miss Susan,
aghast.

But Philip offered no explanation ; he looked annoyed at himself, and said he must call Molly and
go home.

" I 've forgotten all about Carey ; I was to meet
him at the Tavern. He 's one of the Mercer Careys,
you know; he 's staying with me. I 'm going to
bring him to call."

Miss Susan was so bewildered by Philip's extraordinary view of what was proper for Lyssie that she
made no protest at his departure ; but her confused
look changed abruptly when, with his hand upon the
door, he made some careless, friendly comment upon
Joseph Lavendar.

" He still plays at the morning service, I suppose ?
What a grave, splendid touch he has ! " And then
he went away.

" Oh my ! " said Susan Carr. " I 'd almost forgotten it. Oh dear!" She sighed, and sat down as though suddenly tired. She sat as a man might, leaning forward, her clasped hands between her knees, and staring with an absent frown at her heavy boots; then she seemed to realize her masculine attitude, and drew herself together with an effort to achieve some feminine grace. There was something pathetic in the·constant endeavor of this gentle, robust woman, whose occupation had made her clumsy, to express in her body the very genuine and delicate femininity of her soul. "Though I never can be silly," she had long ago admitted sadly to herself.

The worried look which Philip's allusion to Mr. Joseph Lavendar had brought into her face deepened, as she sat there frowning and tapping her foot upon the floor. After a while she rose, and tramped up and down the room, with her hands behind her, absorbed in thought. Then she stopped before a big, old-fashioned writing-desk, littered with farming papers, and with packages of vegetable seeds overflowing from crowded pigeon-holes; accounts and memoranda and ledgers lent it a most businesslike and unfeminine look. Miss Susan took a letter from a little drawer, and read it, standing up, twisting her lip absently between her thumb and forefinger.

MY DEAR MISS SUSAN, — I have found a very good Te Deum in C. I send it with this. Will you be so good as to look it over, so that we can try it on Saturday?

Very truly yours,   JOSEPH LAVENDAR.

P. S. May I add, although the somewhat business-like tenor of my letter might seem to preclude the mention of tenderer sentiments, that I have long desired to address you upon the subject of my affections? Delicacy only has restrained my pen or lips, and also the doubt (proper to a gentleman) of my own worthiness. But I cannot longer remain silent. I feel that the time has come when I must beg your amiable and ever ready sympathy and kindness,—for I believe that my future lies in your hands; with your help, I venture to hope that I may become the happiest of men. I am sure that my brother has a warmer regard for you than for any one else whom I might mention, and your sympathy with my suit will mean very much to him. May I beg that you will think this over, and let me have an opportunity for free discourse upon the subject?

Yrs. tr.   J. L.

"I never encouraged him," said Susan Carr. "Oh, I am so sorry, for I like him so much!"

She put her hands behind her, and began again to pace up and down the room. Philip's coming and this letter made her think of his uncle, Donald Shore. She and Donald were to have been married, but Philip came into his uncle's life, an orphan nephew, whose support was so much of a consideration that the quiet, prudent Donald felt it necessary to put the wedding off a year, and then two years, and after that another year. Then the postponement of eternity came between them, and Donald died. Susan

Carr had felt no bitterness towards Philip. She loved him, at first because he was Donald's nephew, and then for his own sake. Indeed, even while he postponed her marriage, he made another tie between herself and her slow and sober lover, whose affection for his nephew seemed to reconcile him to the delay in winning the hand of his " admirable Susan," as he called her. When he died, she felt as though Philip belonged to her: it was she who made it possible for him to go abroad and study when he had finished college; she who rejoiced with practical good sense when he married Cecil Drayton, who had plenty of money; and she who watched the unsatisfied, disappointed look deepening in his eyes, with the pang that his mother would have felt, had she lived. And through all these years the old love for Philip's uncle lay fragrant in her heart. But now came this letter from Joseph Lavendar.

" It 's out of the question," said Miss Carr, reading it over again, the color deepening in her cheeks. " And it 's too bad, for I do like him so. Well, I won't give him ' an opportunity ' ! That is the only kind thing I can do."

IV.

No deeply rooted tendency was ever extirpated by adverse argument. — G. H. LEWES.

DR. LAVENDAR always said that his brother Joseph lived with him; but the fact was, Mr. Joseph Lavendar could spend only his Sundays at the rectory. He used to come down from Mercer on the Saturday morning stage, but he traveled back again on Monday morning to his music-teaching. "My profession takes me away from home during the week," he used to explain. That one day with his brother really made a home for this simple, honest gentleman, whose occupation was to drill short-petticoated misses in their scales.

But although Mr. Lavendar came to Old Chester only to spend Sundays, the village, quite as much as his brother or himself, would have resented the suggestion that his home was not at the rectory; for everybody loved Joseph Lavendar. To be sure, he was something of an exquisite, which is not usually endearing: his suit of brown broadcloth was immaculate, his linen spotless, his shoes knew the polish of his brother's precious stones; indeed, he had more than once been seen to brush a speck of dust from them with his pocket handkerchief. But, though finical about himself, he was tolerant of other people's dusty shoes, to speak generically, and such

tolerance is always endearing. Besides, the eager
kindliness of his face was irresistible ; his mild,
somewhat prominent blue eyes were without a
shadow of suspicion of any of the human race; his
bald, high forehead, with little tufts of reddish hair
above each ear, was forever wrinkling with sympathy for somebody else. It was nothing more than
sympathy, for he never dared to offer advice ; it
being his instinct to believe that other people
knew more than he did. He accepted, joyously and
gratefully, the opinions of his friends, especially his
brother's opinion, for Dr. Lavendar's judgment was
quite ultimate with Mr. Joseph, — except, indeed,
when he disapproved of people. Then, almost always Mr. Lavendar acquired an opinion of his own,
and ventured to differ. He did it in an apologetic,
deprecating, timid way, but he differed. It seemed
as though he were constitutionally obliged to take
the side of the under dog.

It was this amiable and unreasoning tendency
which brought the first note of discord into the
friendship of the two brothers.

Mrs. Pendleton came to live in Old Chester ; and
Dr. Lavendar, who had quite forgotten her in these
twenty tranquil years since she " threw Joey over,"
suddenly found that he had not forgiven her. And
certainly, the poor lady, with the best intentions in
the world, did not endear herself. The fervency of
her responses in church distracted the old clergyman from his own devotions ; her foolish bene-
volences amazed him ; her efforts — those pitiful

efforts of the outsider to seem on terms of intimacy with recently acquired acquaintances, efforts which are betrayed by speaking of comparative strangers by their first names — seemed to him only the unpardonable vulgarity which indeed they are. When she said " Susy " Carr behind Miss Susan's back, Dr. Lavendar winced ; and when she spoke of " Jane " and " Tommy," he took immediate occasion to refer to Mrs. and Mr. Dove. Poor Mrs. Pendleton meant well, and in truth there was nothing upon which Dr. Lavendar could put his finger as his special reason for disliking her. Perhaps that was rather an aggravation in itself ; our sentiments toward " Dr. Fell " are probably heightened just because we " cannot tell."

But it was in connection with Mrs. Pendleton that Mr. Lavendar's constitutional tendency began to threaten the life of mutual admiration in the rectory. Mr. Joseph did no more than speak well of the little widow. He, too, had almost forgotten her, and he had quite forgiven her ; but, spurred on by Dr. Lavendar's dislike for her, he hunted in his memory for her good qualities, that he might defend her to his brother. No doubt the reviving remembrance of the pain she had made him suffer so long ago added to the warmth of his defense ; which, to be sure, was eloquent in intention rather than in words, for he only protested, timidly, that he thought Mrs. Pendleton an exceedingly pleasing person. But that his discernment, his judgment, his taste, should be so at fault confounded and irritated Dr. Lavendar.

It would be as incredible as it is amusing, if

only all the world did not know it to be true, that a difference in taste can be absolutely disastrous to friendship, and even to love. The absurd unhappiness begins at the moment when it becomes plain to each friend that the other ought to be convinced. What starts as a matter of opinion deepens into a question of principle.

This point had been reached by the two brothers. It was a long time since the amiable routine of Joseph Lavendar's thought had been so broken in upon as by his brother's injustice to Mrs. Pendleton. Never before had Dr. Lavendar's indulgent admiration for Joseph's unreasonable good nature been shocked into a suspicious doubt of Mr. Lavendar's intelligence. Each brother had been amused at first, and then amazed; and now each had become almost indignant.

"But, brother James," Joseph would say, his mild, prominent eyes full of reproachful anxiety, "you don't seem to be fair to the lady. It is n't like you not to be fair."

Even Dr. Lavendar saw the humor of that. "Ho!" he said, and grinned a little. "Well, perhaps I 'm not always fair, Joey; but I 'm never prejudiced; and I have a memory, sir!"

"Oh yes, I know what you mean; but that was twenty years ago, my dear Jim, and it was entirely my fault. She is a lady of great kindness, and—"

But Dr. Lavendar would fling out impatiently that Joey did not know what he was talking about!

"Kind? Well, yes, she has a good word for

everybody. I think she'd speak well of the devil.
I don't call that 'kindness,' Joey. I call it silliness ; silliness, sir, for the devil does n't deserve a
good word. You speak up for her as if you were
going to — to marry her!" Dr. Lavendar had cried
once, sawing the air with his pipe, and searching
for the most preposterous illustration he could find.

"Marry — her? I never — why, I never thought
of such a thing," stammered the younger brother,
his high forehead growing faintly red. "I never
dreamed of such a thing."

"Well, well; there! I beg your pardon," said
Dr. Lavendar. "I may have seemed irritated, but
not at all, not at all. I was merely emphatic. I
can't help being amazed at your lack of intelligence. An unintelligent person distresses me ; and
you ought surely to be able to see, Joey, that she — "

And so they argued on ; each convinced that he
was right, and each sincerely troubled at the attitude
of the other. Again and again, Mr. Joseph, with
timid and anxious persistence, suggested that Dr.
Lavendar should show more marked kindness to
Mrs. Pendleton, because she was a stranger and —
and his friend. Again and again, Dr. Lavendar
asserted that he would do his duty as her clergyman,
but nothing more, because he did not like her, and
he saw no reason why his private opinions should be
at the mercy of his official duties. "I 'll call twice
a year, or I 'll bury her, cheerfully, — that 's my
duty ; but I won't pretend that she 's a personal
friend when she is n't!" he would insist.

It was in the winter that he had used the extraordinary illustration of marriage as a means of showing his brother how unreasonably far his defense of the little widow had gone. Until he said it himself, Dr. Lavendar had really never thought of anything so bad as that; yet, even as he used it, the illustration became a possibility to him, and he realized in a flash that defense, if persisted in, will create a certain tenderness in the defender for the defended. All through the spring his own suggestion rankled in his mind. "But no," he would assure himself, "Joey has too much sense. It's only his ridiculous amiability." It never occurred to him that Joey, too, might brood upon that sarcastic suggestion, until the acceptance of it would seem natural and even chivalrous, and not sarcastic at all. By midsummer, Mrs. Pendleton, or rather their disagreement about her, was actually marring the brothers' Sundays to such a degree that each secretly found Monday, and Joseph's departure, a relief.

Dr. Lavendar was the first to recognize this, and it sobered him into momentary indifference to the object of their dispute. "Joey and I fall out!" he said to himself, dismayed and almost frightened. "Joey and I quarrel about that foolish woman! What nonsense! We'll just drop the subject." Was there ever a disagreement in a matter of opinion which was not broken into chapters, as it were, by this determination to "drop the subject"?

The next Saturday, when Mr. Joseph climbed carefully down from the stage, and carried his carpet bag into the little hall in the rectory, Dr. Lavendar was saying to himself that he and Joey must not get into any more discussions about that person! Oddly enough, Mr. Lavendar, too, had determined to drop the subject, and, with this end in view, substituted another.

"My dear Jim," he said, "I have found a very admirable garnet. I saw it at Soomby's, and got it for a song, a mere song. But it needs a good deal of polishing." Mr. Lavendar pulled open a little leather pouch, the mouth of which was gathered on a string; he carried his notes in this, each carefully rolled up like a lamplighter and folded four times; he shook out of it, carefully, a wad of tissue paper. Dr. Lavendar, pleased and eager, bent his thin old hand into a cup to hold the stone.

"Yes, yes; wants a bit of cutting, a bit of polishing. Joey, you are an extravagant dog! How much did this cost you, sir? I saw young Shore yesterday. (Yes, they 're here. Came Thursday.) I told him he had got to give me a diamond when he gets rich. He says he 'll never be rich. Very likely not. A man with a rich wife is a pretty poverty-stricken fellow, sometimes. I heard that she once sent her check for his club dues; think of that!"

"Poor boy!" said Mr. Lavendar, his face wrinkling with pity. Mr. Lavendar's face showed his emotions as a little sheet of placid water shows the wind. "But I 'm told she 's a good housekeeper?" he defended her.

"Yes," Dr. Lavendar agreed; "as far as the bread which perisheth goes, the boy's well fed. But that's not enough, Joe?"

"No, that's not enough, Jim," said the other; and then they went out, as they always did on summer Saturday afternoons, to make, arm in arm, with Danny at their heels, the tour of the garden behind the rectory.

"The hollyhocks are not looking as thrifty as they did last year," Joseph observed, with concern.

"They've never done so well as they did eight years ago, — no, nine; it was the summer Philip and Cecilla were married. Joey, how many pears do you suppose there are on that little jargonelle? I counted 'em last night."

The two brothers went across the deep soft tangle of the grass, and stood under the pear-tree. "It has twenty-seven pears, Joe!"

"I thought I saw twenty-nine," Mr. Joseph said mildly, after a moment's pause to count the still green fruit; "but no doubt I was mistaken."

After that, as they went down a little brick path, past the honey-locust hedge and the big laburnum bush, over to the south wall where the two beehives stood, Mr. Lavendar told, as usual, the little details of his week's work. Dr. Lavendar knew the names of the pupils, though he had never seen them, and he had his questions to ask and his comments to make; then he told Joseph all the Old Chester news. But both were conscious of an effort; each was aware that the other disapproved of him, and that made a strange, intangible barrier between them.

The afternoon sunshine, piercing through the trees and bushes, stretched in level lines across the grass; it lay warm upon the red bricks of the rectory, and slipped, glistening, over the mat of ivy on the south wall, and it struck a sudden shine from all the little panes of glass set in their deep window frames. The brothers sat down under a trellis where the wistaria hung its bee-haunted blossoms above their heads; syringas pressed close about this little arbor, filling the air with heavy fragrance; and a thicket of lilacs, their dark, heart-shaped leaves spotted with white mould, made a dense shade behind it. There was a small wooden table in the arbor, and on it were a decanter and two glasses.

Dr. Lavendar, with a careful hand and an intent, puckered face, mixed the proper proportions of water and sugar and lemon with the contents of the decanter; then, his legs stretched out before him, the front of his waistcoat sprinkled with ashes from his pipe, his black skull-cap pulled down over his stiff white hair, he gave himself up to comfort. Danny had stretched himself luxuriously upon the grass checkered with moving leaf shadows, and was opening one eye occasionally to snap at an impertinent fly. Dr. Lavendar sipped, and sipped, and talked. Joseph listened, and agreed, and held his glass up before his eyes, narrowed to a beaming line to catch the light through the liquor. It was not unnatural, everything being so harmonious, that Dr. Lavendar, with a view to dropping the subject, should do so with some well-chosen words.

"Joey, in connection with what we were speaking of last week, — I don't mean to discuss it, of course every man has a right to his opinions, and you have a right to yours ; I 'm the last person to dispute that, for, whatever else I may be, I 'm tolerant! — but, in that connection, I just wished to say to you that, in formulating your opinion of your friend Mrs. Pendleton, it seemed to me you overlooked one fact which I think bespeaks character: she enjoys giving away money to the poor so much that she gives it where it does harm. Now, that 's pure selfishness, not generosity ; she — "

"Brother Jim, do you not overlook the fact that she has a kind disposition ? "

"I was not talking about her disposition !" declared Dr. Lavendar, frowning. "I 'm not in the habit of discussing a lady's disposition, sir. I don't know anything about her disposition. But I hope I am not trespassing upon any propriety when I say that her intelligence is at fault? She is not intelligent. She has gone and given some money to Job Todd. He does n't have to work, and so he gets drunk."

"A kind deed," Mr. Joseph began to explain, "may be an error of judgment, brother Jim, but — "

"It is n't kind if it 's an error of judgment, brother Joe," cried the other; "you have n't any business to make errors in judgment in dealing with people like Todd."

"Well, but," protested Mr. Lavendar, his face quite agitated, and his kind, prominent blue eyes distressed and entreating, "everybody makes mistakes sometimes."

"No, they don't. Look at Susan Carr. Never made a mistake in her life! At least — you make me emphatic — I mean her judgment is good. Now, there's a woman I admire!"

Mr. Lavendar's face softened; he even blushed a little. "An admirable lady, yes; I agree with you," he said. "I am sure she has a kindly feeling for — for the lady of whom we were speaking. And you respect her judgment, brother Jim?"

"Of course I do. I don't know her views on this subject, but Utile Dulce is intelligent; and she —"

But Joseph did not follow his brother's dissertation upon the estimable Miss Carr. "Miss Susan and I are going to look over a new Te Deum," he said; "I wrote her about it, and I shall take the liberty of stepping over to her house after tea."

"Good idea," assented the old clergyman, with a pleased look, — Joey was not apt to give up these discussions upon Mrs. Pendleton so readily; "excellent plan. I have a great regard for Susan Carr. Ah, Joey boy, *there* was a woman! When you were both younger, I used to hope — But you'd had your deathblow, poor boy; yes, your deathblow. It's queer that an unintelligent person can have such an effect. Well, I did n't mean to discuss it. Let's drop the subject. Yes, of course, go over to Susan's. I think I 'll step in with you myself."

"Oh, will you?" said Mr. Joseph, a little blankly; "that will be very agreeable."

V.

What do you think of marriage ?
I take 't (as those that deny purgatory)
It locally contains or Heaven or Hell ;
There 's no third place in it.

Duchess of Malfy.

MRS. DRAYTON had just declared that it was a little bitter to take a mother's place to a child, and then be forgotten. "For Cecil has been here three days, and has n't called," she was saying, when she discerned her step-daughter walking indolently up the village street.

"Oh, *at last!*" she said, and glanced at the mirror at her side, to see if she were tidy. Mrs. Drayton was always careful to have the cheval glass near her, so that she might be sure of the delicate precision of her invalid costume. "The light hurts my eyes," she used to say patiently, with the air of one who suffers for a principle, "but I must be tidy!" And so she patted her faded hair, and pulled the ruffles down about her lean wrists, and looked again swiftly into the glass.

There was a nervous quiver in her small, blond countenance; she was afraid of Cecil. A certain smile at the corner of her step-daughter's lip confused and terrified her. At heart, she much preferred the diversion of being neglected, the interest of Cecil's unkindness, to the shivering apprehension which her dutifulness aroused.

" How well you look ! " Cecil said cordially ; and Mrs. Drayton kissed her in an agitated way, and responded, " I don't look as I feel, then. I am far from well, — far from well ! "

Lyssie glanced at her sister imploringly ; had Cecil forgotten that her mother did not like to be told that she looked well ?

Cecil answered only by a surprised " Really? Well, one can't tell anything by looks. It seems to me you look younger and better than when I saw you last."

The frightened attention in Mrs. Drayton's face relaxed. " Well, I suppose I *am* a little older, but confinement indoors does spare the complexion, — I must admit that." As she spoke, she glanced at the mirror again, which made Cecil say that the re-flection from the glass must try her eyes ; and she even took the trouble to rise and throw her wrap across the tall carved frame and over the gleaming oblong of the mirror. She looked sidewise at her step-mother as she did it, and smiled. Mrs. Dray-ton gave a gasp, and had the air of one searching for a repartee. She found nothing more impressive to say, however, than that she thought Molly was looking well when Philip brought the child to see her. " Philip came three days ago," she declared significantly.

Lyssie, hovering on the outskirts of the conversa-tion, ready to rush in as peacemaker, or to be silent when either of the two whom she loved best in the world seemed to be doing herself justice, said, hurriedly, something about Mr. Carey. Was he going to stay long? Did he like Old Chester?

"He is quite agreeable," Mrs. Drayton announced, before Cecil made any effort to reply. "He called yesterday. Your company came to see me, Cecil, though you did not."

Cecil opened her eyes in frank astonishment. "Why, he does admire you, Lys!"

The invalid frowned, and drew her little pale lips together. "Really, Cecil, such talk is quite indelicate. Young girls in Old Chester are not in the habit of hearing that they are admired."

"No, I should n't think they were," Cecil said dryly. "Lys is an exception. But perhaps you don't mean her ever to have an admirer?"

"Ceci, you 're a goose!" Alicia broke in. "How can anybody have an admirer in Old Chester? I am going to succeed Miss Susan as a model spinster."

"When the proper time comes," Mrs. Drayton said severely, "I hope Alicia will be suitably settled. But I don't approve of talking flippantly about a serious matter."

"It is serious," Cecil agreed, with an amused look. "But it does turn out well sometimes. Look at me! And your marriage, too; though you can hardly expect Lys to find a widower. I 've heard you say that widowers make the best husbands."

Mrs. Drayton sat up very straight, and seemed to consider where she could strike a blow. "Yes, you are quite right; they do. And as for your father's being a widower, as you are unkind enough to remind me, Cecilla, I can't help saying that I don't mind being a second wife, but I never would have consented to be a second love!"

She almost sobbed, but Cecil said soothingly, " I am sure you were not a second love, Mrs. Drayton."

There seemed to be nothing objectionable in such an acknowledgment. "But she means something," the poor little woman thought, and repeated, with a catch in her voice, that there were people who said there was no husband so good as one who had learned a lesson of patience with a first wife, "even if it was a very youthful experience."

"Ah, well," Cecil objected seriously, "somebody's got to marry first, to make the widowers, I suppose?"

"Unfortunately," Alicia broke in, "we have no widowers, only a widow; and she can't get married unless she gives up the money her husband left her. Wasn't it unkind in him to make a will like that?"

This well-timed remark diverted the threatening storm, and Mrs. Drayton began to gossip about her neighbors, and to deplore their failings, which made her exceedingly good natured. For a virtuous discontent with other people imparts a sense of rectitude and a peace of mind hardly equaled by virtue itself. Cecil, looking out of the window, and watching the blowing silver of some willows at the foot of the lawn, and beyond them, now and then, the faint, rocking flash of the river, listened lazily. Alicia breathed freely, and doubtless all would have gone well had Mrs. Drayton only refrained from going back to her first grievance. " Yes, everybody in Old Chester is very kind to me; all my friends come to see me; they don't forget how lonely I am."   She sighed, and glanced at her husband's miniature, which she wore on a long, slender gold chain about her neck.

Cecil was unable to resist this.   " You must miss papa very much ? "

" Oh, you little know! his absence is a great cross; my one prayer is that — "

" That he will return ? "

" That his health will permit him to return.   I could never be so selfish as to wish him to run any risk for my sake; that is not my idea of love, Cecil."

" I should be so interested to know· your idea of love," Cecil answered slowly; " but I was sure you would not wish him to return."

" Mother is so nervous about people's health," rushed in the tender, young, troubled voice; and then poor Lyssie said, breathlessly, she " wondered when Cecil and Philip would come to tea."

" Why, you don't seem to want to talk about our dear papa ? " her sister said, laughing and rising; then she bade her cowering step-mother good-by, and regretted that she must remove her wrap from the mirror.

" Ceci, how can you tease mother so ! " Lyssie said hotly, as they went downstairs.   " You know how nervous she is, and you know, in spite of — of the things you make her say, she really loves you, and — "

"Which of us is Mr. Drayton's child by his first wife?" Cecil broke in drolly.

"Cecil!"

"Ah, well, I ought not to tease Mrs. Drayton, —you are quite right," Cecil confessed frankly. "I won't. I'll stay at home. Lyssie, come to supper to-night and entertain your mother's admirer. Why did n't he tell me he had called?" And then she went away, smiling to herself at Mrs. Drayton's fright.

But Lyssie could not be spared that evening. Her mother had been so much agitated by Cecil's visit that she was too unwell to be left alone.

"Oh, I am a poor useless creature," said Mrs. Drayton, her voice quivering. "I interfere with your pleasures. I'm a burden to you. Yes, you need n't deny it, Lyssie; you would rather be with Cecil than stand here and comb my hair. I am a miserable burden; and if it were not wrong, I should wish that my heavenly Father would take me to himself!"

While Lyssie, with great good sense tempered by tenderness, was combating these opinions, Cecil, in the fragrant twilight on the terrace, talked about her step-mother to her husband and her guest; or it would be more exact to say, she talked to her guest, for Philip, sitting smoking on the steps of the terrace, took no part in the conversation. Molly, nestling down in his arms, listened to her mother's talk, and frankly resisted her father's efforts to gain her attention.

"I'd rather hear mamma talk. Mamma is so funny!" she said; and Philip had no choice, at last, but to lure the child down into the garden, to spare her some little childish delusions about her grandmother.

Roger Carey, listening, laughed and looked annoyed, and then laughed again. "The old lady is preposterous," he thought, "but she's Miss Drayton's mother. Mrs. Shore does n't seem to consider that." Nevertheless, he laughed until the tears stood in his eyes, when his hostess told him, with unsparing and clever truthfulness, this or that incident in which poor foolish Mrs. Drayton had taken herself seriously.

"And the funny part of it is, Lyssie does n't see how amusing her mother is," Mrs. Shore ended; "she takes her seriously, too, — dear little thing!"

"Well, that's fortunate," Mr. Carey commented.

"Fortunate? Why, not at all; it simply encourages Mrs. Drayton, and —"

"Yes; but don't you see," interrupted Roger Carey, "it would be fatal if she were ridiculous in her daughter's eyes. Absurdity is the one thing love can't stand; it can overlook anything else, — coldness, or weakness, or viciousness, — but just be ridiculous and that's the end of it!"

"Ah, but not that kind of love," Cecil said. "My sister's feeling for her mother is not the lover's love, nor even the filial love; it is the maternal passion. One is never ridiculous to one's mother."

Love is a most interesting topic between men and

women. Mr. Carey's cigar went out while he laid down the law with all the emphasis of the theorist; until, by some chance, — perhaps it was in the way of an illustration of married love, — they came back to Mrs. Drayton again, and Cecil began to tell another absurd story about her. Then Roger Carey lighted his cigar, and frowned a little.

"It's awfully funny," he said, " but I feel as though I ought to apologize to your sister for listening to it."

His blunt rudeness made Cecil Shore look at him with attention. But he never thought of apologizing; instead, he began to talk of other things, with that good-humored determination to change the subject which is so irritating to the listener. Mrs. Shore felt it, and was almost relieved to see her husband appear. Philip had mounted Molly on his shoulder; she was pulling his head over sidewise upon her little breast, and rumpling his hair about his eyes. When they reached the steps of the terrace, he slipped her gently down from her high perch, and made great pretense of horror at his disheveled condition, which enchanted Molly, who shrieked her desire for another ride.

"No, a merciful little girl is merciful to her beast. And it's your bedtime, too. Oh, what dissipation! It's a quarter past eight. Run along, now, to bed."

"Oh no, I want her," Cecil said gayly. " Don't you want to sit up with mamma a little while ? "

And Molly, nothing loath to escape her nurse and her father's rule of bed at eight o'clock, climbed up

into her mother's lap. Cecil clasped her in her
arms and kissed her, rocking the child backwards,
and catching her with a storm of caresses. Philip
looked away, and then back again, and opened and
shut his hands nervously. His glance had in it none
of that deep and beautiful meaning with which a
man may look at the woman and the child who are
his, who stand to him forever as that other Mother
and Child who belong to our humanity and divinity.
Roger Carey felt the peculiar unhappiness which is
experienced by a guest conscious that a domestic in-
felicity is occurring in his presence. He said impetuously, and with no regard for relevance, something
about some stock quotation, and bewailed his luck.

"Hang it, the day after I bought, down it went!"

Philip, turning his back on those two on the terrace above him, said calmly, why had he not done
thus and so? why had he not taken advantage of
this and that? and then gave him a bit of information which made Roger slap his thigh and cry out in
grateful enthusiasm, "By Jove, that's neat! I did n't
know you were up to this sort of thing? You
ought to be on the street; what a business man you
would make!"

"Philip is a good business man," said Cecil kindly.
"Since he has managed my property, my income has
increased fifty per cent.,—no, forty. How much
did you tell me, Philip? Fifty per cent.?"

Roger drew in his breath in a noiseless whistle;
he did not look at his host.

"Your income has increased forty per cent.,"
Philip answered.

"Well," said Roger, "if you have any more of these ideas lying around loose, do hand them over to me. I 'm amazed to find that you have a genius for speculating."

"I have n't. It is Mrs. Shore's wish to invest her money in this way; I merely act for her. That 's how I happen to know about it."

"Philip's one fear is that I shall grow what he calls disgustingly rich," Cecil murmured, over Molly's head. ("Now, Molly, go to bed. Mamma is tired. Come, don't be so slow! I hate people who dawdle. You absurd little monkey! you don't want to go to bed? Well, then, climb up in mamma's lap again.) Mr. Carey, you don't know all Mr. Shore's remarkable qualities: he is a single-tax man, a woman's-rights man, a philanthropist, a — a — an artist, — all in one. Oh, and a financier; though that is not genuine; he prefers poverty, don't you, Philip?"

"I think I prefer a walk, at this moment," her husband said lightly, "if you will excuse me? Carey, shall I leave you with Mrs. Shore?" And then he lounged down into the summer dusk and disappeared.

Roger Carey debated with himself a moment, and looked after him. He did not like Mrs. Shore, but he liked to hear her talk; so his half-uttered excuse died upon his lips. "Shore 's too polite to her," he thought, and gave himself up to the pleasure of looking at her and listening to her. But Cecil saw the moment's hesitation with an astonishment that had in it both amusement and annoyance.

VI.

> I took you — how could I otherwise ? —
> For a world to me, and more ;
> For all, love greatens and glorifies
> 'Till God 's aglow, to the loving eyes,
> In what was mere earth before.
>
> BROWNING.

ALONE, Philip Shore drew a breath of relief; he
let himself out into the grassy lane by the great iron
gates at the foot of the garden, and as they clanged
sharply behind him his face lost its look of restraint,
and settled into the worn lines of habitual and troubled thought. It was an interesting face, gentle,
intelligent, sad; the face, as Mr. William Drayton
had recognized, of an ascetic, of a man who might
even be a fanatic, but one in which the harassed bitterness could melt into sweetness when his eye caught
a flower nodding against a blue sky, or when he
heard the murmur of water under a vague moon, or
when a child's hand touched his own. Even now,
with eyes oppressed and heavy with thought, he
stopped to notice some distant cypresses standing
like black spires against the fading yellow in the
west. He seemed to have no objective point in his
walk; he went at first towards Miss Susan Carr's
house, then hesitated, and turned down the road,
walking slowly and aimlessly until he reached the
bridge which crossed the river, like a gray ribbon

stretched between green banks. Though the sky was still faintly light, it was quite dark down there, for the river ran close to the hills; it was very silent, too.

Philip folded his arms upon the stone coping, and watched the slight heaving of the lily pads; there was a faint lap and slip of the water against the pier in mid-stream. As he leaned there, looking down at the black current, a sudden tremulous sparkle wavered up from its depths, and he lifted his eyes to see a star hanging low in the melting, translucent dusk above the hill; the star in the river shook and trembled, plunging down like a golden plummet, or blotted out when a lily leaf swung across its upward track; but it grew brighter, for the darkness deepened, and still he leaned and watched it. He was saying over to himself words which clamored in his ears in all his silent moments: "How far is a man's own conception of his duty to weigh against accepted standards?"

It is a serious question. Most conscientious men and women must answer it one way or another in their lives. Philip Shore had been trying to answer it for three years. For it was just three years since he had acknowledged the hopelessness of his marriage, and had said to himself a hard saying: "*Marriage without love is as spiritually illegal as love without marriage is civilly illegal.*" This once admitted, that unanswered question inevitably presents itself: May a man be base in his own eyes, because the law approves? May he live a lie, because expediency

and custom condone the offense? Or shall his own
conception of duty weigh against accepted standards?

Philip Shore was thirty-three that summer; but
he looked older, for he had hardly known youth in
the sense of joyous unconcern and divine, full-blooded
humanness. The years before he went to college had
not been young years; his uncle had made the lad
his companion, and kept him reading and studying
with him when he should have been at boarding-
school, among boys of his own age. Philip's passionate feeling for color Donald Shore admired, with
reverence, because he was himself quite without it.
The boy should be an artist, he said; and Susan
Carr agreed with him, and so they put their wedding
off a little longer, that Donald might take Philip
away for a year's study before he went to college.
"When you are through college, boy," the uncle
said, "we 'll go abroad!" But before that time
came Donald died, and Philip had to arrange for
that study abroad without the encouragement and
stimulus of Mr. Shore's deep and quite unwarrant-
able belief in him.

Philip had been so happy with his uncle that he
had not cared very much for the society of those of
his own age, except indeed for Cecil Drayton's society, and hers not at all because she was the Everlasting Feminine. "Cecil has brains," he told his
uncle; "she is n't girly." So it was not until he
had finished college, and had come home to Old
Chester for a month's visit before starting for Paris,

that he fell in love with this tall, silent, mysterious Cecil. At least she seemed mysterious to him. Perhaps love, like art, needs mystery, for it does not always thrive in the unreserve of realism. Certainly, Philip's absence for the next three years kept him very ignorant and very devoted. He was very much in love in those few weeks before he went away. He said to her the old, beautiful words which every lover has whispered, and every mistress has believed: " No woman was ever loved as I love you, because there never was a woman like you! " Cecil, just home from boarding-school, wondering what life meant, still altogether potential, — Cecil smiled, and sighed, and consented; gazing with calm, innocent eyes at the extraordinary agitation in his face. She thought he would kiss her, but he knelt down and kissed the hem of her dress, and went away silently, leaving her amused, but not displeased. Then had come the three years of engagement and absence and letter-writing, — three things which most perfectly conceal character. When they ended, these two young persons knew each other less than at their beginning.

Cecil had been impatient for the engagement to end. She wanted to go abroad; she wanted to live the strange, fascinating Bohemian life of which her lover wrote her; she wanted — oh, how much she wanted! — to get away from Old Chester. " I'm rich, you know," she wrote him once, shyly; and though he adored the noble frankness of her love, he must, he told her, feel that he was able to support her, and then — *then!*

And so he worked, his soul kindling with the thought of the woman he loved. His love was a form of art to him; it was religion; it was life; it was his inmost self. It created in him the purity, the truth, the reverence, which it revealed in her. That she should love him filled him with that fine humility which exalts instead of depresses. It was the mystery of the Divine coming down to earth for us men and for our salvation; it was not to be understood; it was to be accepted. Her potentiality did not trouble him; her sweet ignorance of human passion exhilarated him.

Love such as this dwells less upon the beauty of the beloved, the touch of her hand, the ivory curve of her soft throat, — the things on which a young lover writes lame verses, and of which he is as proud as though he were responsible for their perfection, — such love thinks less, or not at all, of those things, and much of the God who is revealed in them. Of course, with the pathetic belief of youth that absolute confidence is possible between human souls, Philip used to write to her of all this spiritual significance of love; and she, with gentle and non-committal sympathy, would answer that what he said was true, or wonderful, or beautiful; and her lover's heart would glow at the "reserve," the "insight," which those words indicated.

Philip Shore was a man capable of sustained ecstasy; a man who lived, not upon those occasional sunlit peaks of emotion which most of us touch now and then, but upon a high plateau of noble idealism,

and the three years of waiting became almost the noviti-
ate of a holy life, so complete was his idealization of
marriage, of love, and of the woman he loved. Very
likely there was a touch of the mystic in this young
man; mysticism is latent in most artistic tempera-
ments, though it does not always show in artists,
perhaps because the mercantile instinct which they
so readily acquire chokes anything so unprofitable
as mysticism. And Philip, unhappily, was never to
be more than artistic; his ability fell just short of
making him an artist.

They were married rather unexpectedly. The
three years' study had not found Philip very far on
the road to fame, and the engagement might have
been prolonged, had not Mr. William Drayton met
him one day in Paris, and, in a burst of sudden
fatherly interest, told him the engagement had lasted
long enough. "She's got plenty of money, so
what's the use of waiting? Take her or leave her;
don't shilly-shally!" said the unromantic father.

And Philip took her.

And so at last came the wonderful day. Now,
nine years after, Philip, leaning over the parapet of
the old bridge, staring down at the rocking lilies,
remembered it, the color burning suddenly in his face.

The night before he arrived in Old Chester was
as much a holy vigil to him as were those sacred
hours which young knights spent on their knees before their armor. He was too solemn to know that
he was happy; his thoughts were prayers. The
next day, as a priest might go to the altar, — nay,

as a soul to its God, — Philip Shore went to the woman he loved.

Thinking of that supreme moment, here in the summer darkness on the bridge, he drew a breath that was like a groan. He remembered what he had meant to tell her; he knew the very words in which he had intended to say that in these three years of absence the white thought of her had shown in every dark place of his nature; she should see that the man's soul in him knelt before her womanhood. He meant, too, to share with her, with the generosity of only the highest love, a deep distress of his own, at which, in his letters, he had only been able to hint, — the knowledge that had come to him of his own mediocrity in art, and the alternative of going on with a work which he loved, in which he could never excel, and the giving it up to put his shoulder to the wheel of life, and be of some use in the world. That she would counsel him as his own soul had counseled him he had never doubted. It was in this spirit that he met her.

Still in her eyes he found the same deep smile, the smile into which he had read every solemn meaning of life and death and love; still, still, that wonderful, sympathetic silence, which had again and again by all its unuttered intelligence, revealed him to himself. There was all this, but there was something more. They sat together alone in the June dusk. There was the scent of jessamine about them ; a star shook in the tender sky ; far down in the orchard, a bird cry, as clear as a drop of honey, fell into the beating silence. Cecil, leaning back in her chair, bent her arm behind her head, and the full sleeve slipped up above her elbow; the warm shadow of her white chin fell across the curve of her bare throat; the dusky rose in her cheek deepened; she drew in her red lower lip, and lifted her eyes, full of the glints and lights of dark wine, and brimmed with meaning, and for a silent instant looked full at him. Then she laughed.

It seemed to Philip that she said something, — he did not know what, — some commonplace about the wedding, perhaps; he did not hear it. A mad, un-recognized, latent Self leaped up. All his love burst into flame; the spiritual passion vanished. His hands tightened upon each other; his eyes glowed. He crushed her hand in his savagely, kissing the warm palm, until she gave a little cry and laugh, and said he hurt her. "*Mine!*" he said to himself.

Those three years, in which his thoughts of her had been prayer, were forgotten; all he meant to say to her, face to face, heart to heart, man to God, was forgotten; all the solemn glory and whiteness of love went out, as a star in heaven might be blotted from a man's sight by the roar of some hot fire here on his little earth. Oh, love! love! love! This, then, was love, — this supremest expression of self?

Philip, remembering, his elbow on the crumbling parapet of the bridge, his chin on his clenched hand, ground his teeth. Well, so it had gone. Looking back upon it, he saw earnestness and ambition

and responsibility flung aside; he saw art forgotten,
or followed for the personal ends of amusement or
occupation; he saw himself the prisoner of an ignoble passion, hiding his chains behind the cloak of
marriage. He knew every step of the shameful,
splendid, glowing way. He knew the ghastly moment when he looked back at the heights from
which he had come, and recognized the dishonor he
had done to love and the woman he loved. The remembrance of that moment, of that time of anguish
and of struggle, turned him sick now, eight years afterwards; for it was a year before he awoke, a lurid,
drunken year, in which he had no thought of anything but self. His awakening dated from their
first quarrel which had in it anything deeper than
some selfish irritation; there had been plenty of
such contentions, followed by equally selfish recon-
ciliations. This quarrel had sprung from his reviving determination to give up his painting. Cecil
had refused to listen to anything so foolish. She
adored the life in Paris, a life which had in it all the
freedom of the Latin Quarter and all the luxury of
the Champs-Elysées. Her resistance woke the old
arguments for truth, the old reverence for art.
There had been a violent altercation: Philip, in a
half-dazed way, standing out for what, blindly, as
though through some mist of memory, he knew to be
right; Cecil saying insolently that the money was
hers, and she "would not allow it."

"Then you can stay by yourself!" he had flung
back at her. "I've done with this pretense." And

with a high hand he had carried out his wish, and they had come back to America.

That was the beginning. The old ideals crowded upon him, and he knew that he did not desire them. It was a time of dreadful remorse that seemed like some sickness in the very substance of the soul. Then it was that he turned to his wife for forgiveness, only to discover, with confusion and incredulity and dismay, that Cecil was not aware that she had anything to forgive.

After that came the long struggle to waken her dormant soul, — a struggle which amused, and then bored, and at last irritated her beyond words. At first she endured it with rallying tenderness and temptation, and he would fall for weeks or months into loathful ease and satisfaction in the comfort of his life; for, except when he teased her with visions and ecstasies, Cecil made his life full of lazy and beautiful comfort. With Molly's birth, which came just after their return to America, the revelation of fatherhood summoned him with solemn and irresistible voice to his spiritual manhood. That summons seemed to him so conclusive that he found Cecil's deafness to it incredible. She loved the child with a fierce unhumanness; she caressed it in a way that made him sometimes turn away his eyes. Yet, through Molly, with kindling hope, again and again and again he appealed to her. He called out with anguish to something which was dead, or had never lived.

But they came no closer together because of the

child; their constant and bitter disagreement concerning her training made her little life like a wedge driven into the very heart of their marriage.

To Philip first had come the recognition of the hopelessness of the situation : he had thought to marry a beautiful soul, but had married instead a beautiful body. The woman whom he had loved had never existed. The woman who had for a time chained him to his senses, stifled his soul, insulted his heavenly vision, — that woman he had never loved, as he counted love. And that woman was his wife.

Cecil, by and by, had come to feel, with a dull sense of disappointment, that love, by its very nature, was a temporary and passing experience, but she was much too philosophical to be unhappy. She used to look at young lovers with some amusement, but no bitterness ; her life was too comfortable for that. Besides, she did not dislike Philip. In those first days, when she had been fond of him, and they had quarreled, she had almost hated him ; but that was all past, and now she was both tolerant and good natured.

" How far is a man's own conception of duty to weigh against accepted standards?" said Philip Shore to himself again, looking down at the swaying glimmer of the star. It was very dark now on the bridge ; it was very silent. But the silence was clamorous with incisive questions : Is not a man's own conception of duty a dangerous and an egotistic guide ? Is not obedience to an unwritten law merely fantastic and absurd when it interferes with all material well being; when it robs a man of a home; when it bids him turn his eyes away from the beautiful, unloved woman who is his wife; when it even means the possible renunciation of his child? Again and again Philip Shore had said to himself that such obedience was impossible.

And yet, coming back to the associations and ideals of his youth, here in his old home, he recognized, almost with terror, that it was possible. Those high demands spoke in all the silences of his luxurious living: "*Is not marriage without love as spiritually illegal as love without marriage is civilly illegal?* And if it is, what is your duty?"

It needs a brave man to answer that question.

VII.

MISS Susan Carr's distress at Joseph Lavendar's folly was so genuine that she did not strain the truth when she said she was not well, and could not go to church, the first Sunday after she had received his letter. "No self-respecting woman will let a man have the chance to be refused," said Miss Susan, and she was glad that a headache came to her assistance in saving Mr. Lavendar from mortification.

Then it occurred to her, as a respite, to accept a long-standing invitation from some old friends in Ashurst, and so escape the next Saturday and Sunday. "But after all," she sighed to herself when, on Friday, she said good-by to the Misses Woodhouse, and turned her face again towards Old Chester, "after all, I can't be away from home every time Joseph Lavendar is in town. I suppose I 've got to meet him some time. But my manner shall show him that I 'm not thinking of — such things !" She was saying this to herself as she climbed into the empty stagecoach at Mercer, and then sat waiting for it to start, and looking at the rain streaming on the window. "I will be severe," said this amiable woman, frowning at the vacant seats opposite her ; "it 's better that Mr. Joseph should think me dis-

agreeable than misunderstand any mere friendliness.
I could not respect myself if I allowed —" Just
here the stiff handle of the door turned with a jerk,
and Mr. Joseph Lavendar stepped into the coach.

"Oh *dear!*" said poor Miss Susan, shrinking
back into her corner.

Mr. Lavendar sat down on the middle seat of the
stage ; it had a swinging strap for a back, and was
quite narrow and far from comfortable. Mr. Lavendar took it for that reason; for though the stage
was almost empty at present, it would doubtless fill
up, and as a matter of course Joseph Lavendar took
the least desirable seat. When he looked up and
saw Miss Susan sitting opposite him, he felt the
compensation which unselfish people are forever discovering in their sacrifices.

" Why, my dear Miss Susan !" he cried. " Why,
this is very delightful, quite an unexpected pleasure.
I feared that your visit was to be prolonged over
another Sunday."

" I did think of it," said Miss Susan faintly.
(" If nobody else gets in, I will get out," she decided
desperately; " I 'll say I forgot something, I 'll say
I 'm ill — I 'll — oh, how can he be going to Old
Chester on Friday ? ")

Perhaps the distress in her face asked the question ; at all events, he began, cheerfully, to explain
his presence. One of his little pupils was ill, —
poor dear child ! a most pleasing child ; a son of
poor Thomas Townsend. Miss Susan recalled
Thomas Townsend ? He died some fifteen years

ago; he was a relative of — of our friend Mrs. Pendleton. "But as his illness is not serious, I can be grateful for the opportunity, which I very much appreciate (as you know, my dear Miss Susan), to spend an extra day in Old Chester."

Miss Carr began, nervously, to gather up her umbrella and bags. "I think I must — " she said hurriedly, but paused, and fell back into her corner again, for a large lady, in a tight black alpaca, was climbing, laboriously and with panting breath, into the coach. "He can't speak now," thought Miss Susan, relieved but unhappy.

The stage sagged forward, and started with a swaying jog; the rain clattered on its ribbed top, and on the rubber aprons that covered the trunks piled at the back; and its three occupants resigned themselves to that peculiar jolting discomfort which only the inside rider knows.

"Let me see," said Mr. Lavendar pleasantly; "you have no later Old Chester news than I have myself? In fact, I have the most recent, as I only left town on Monday. But you can tell me something about our friends in Ashurst. I trust they are all well?"

"Yes," Miss Susan assured him, and made haste to repeat all the Ashurst gossip she could think of.

The large lady, whose chins were in terraces, was swaying about in her corner, as the coach swung and lurched, but she was so comfortably protected by her personality that she was able to doze a little, though sometimes, at a decided jolt, her eyes would spring sharply open, and then drop shut again. Miss Susan looked at her imploringly; if Mr. Joseph should see that she had fallen asleep, what might not happen?

"I was sorry not to see you last week," Mr. Lavendar said, when Miss Susan came to a pause in her Ashurst reminiscences; "and the week before you were indisposed, Lyssie told me. I was much disappointed."

Miss Susan murmured her apologies for having missed the choir practicing. She searched her memory desperately for further Ashurst news, but nothing presented itself.

Mr. Lavendar lifted his left leg across his right knee, and looked at it critically, brushing a little dust from the neat brown broadcloth.

"I was very much in hopes to have had a short — ah — conversation with you, my dear Miss Susan," he said; and then, the color mounting in his face, he added, "You received my letter, of course?"

Susan Carr dared not look at him. Was he going to — here? in a stagecoach? "Letter?" she said. "Oh yes, I believe I did. Don't you think we had better open a window? It's quite warm. At least, if it will not inconvenience this other lady," said Miss Susan, raising her voice, so that Mr. Lavendar was quite startled, and their fellow-passenger opened her eyes in a sleepy gleam.

"It is warm," Mr. Joseph agreed, and he tugged at the window strap with an energy which made his face red, and wakened the stout lady so thoroughly that she sat up for a moment and looked about with frowning surprise. Then a gust of cold, wet air blew in upon the swaying, pitching occupants of the coach, and Susan Carr wondered if it would not keep her protector awake. "How fresh and delightful the air is, ma'am!" she said to the lady pleadingly.

"It's damp," returned the other, and closed her eyes.

"My letter did not call for a reply," Mr. Lavendar proceeded, in a low and confidential voice, "but I thought I should have seen you before this. There is so much I want to say," he ended simply.

"A man who talks on such subjects in a stage-coach must be — very much so," thought Miss Susan despairingly. "But I won't let him!" And, with this determination, she burst into eager and emphatic views about the weather. The rain beating against the closed windows made the landscape waver and glimmer; the woods were gray with mist, and the streams under the creaking wooden bridges were swollen and laced with tangles of foam.

"I think this is the equinoctial," announced Miss Susan breathlessly. "Just see how it pours! And the wind is very high! And did you notice, as we crossed the river, that the water was up to the middle of the pier, and — " Here, to Miss Susan's joy, the other traveler awoke, and found the subject so interesting that she too expressed her opinion, while Mr. Lavendar said protectingly, "It's only a passing shower, ladies, — a passing shower," and watched patiently for a chance to go back to the subject which was plainly uppermost in his mind.

As for Miss Susan, remembering her one experience in love-making, recalling Donald's quiet, matter of fact affection, his tranquil yielding to circumstances, she felt this intensity on the part of Joseph with a certain quickening of the heart. "Oh, I wish he would n't," she said to herself, "for this will spoil everything, though we 've been friends all these years." She was almost ready to cry with the trouble and worry of it; and when at last, damp and tired, she reached home, and sat down in the diningroom to her solitary cup of tea, the tears really did stand in her kind eyes. In her thoughts she went over Mr. Lavendar's looks and words in the coach, and the result of her meditations was that another Saturday afternoon's practice passed, and "Miss Susan was a little under the weather, and could n't come." That the robust Susan Carr should be indisposed began to be food for comment in Old Chester. Alicia Drayton, as she walked down to the church to go over the hymns for the next day with Mr. Lavendar, wondered a little about it. "Why, this is the third time she 's missed the practicing!" said Lyssie to herself; and then an absent look came into her eyes, and she thought no more about Miss Susan.

The rain of the day before had washed the July dust from the roadside weeds and grasses; the trees, all in a shining rustle with the fresh wind, made pretty shadows on the path, and the lines of moss between the flagstones were like strips of green velvet. The very air seemed washed and shining and full of the Saturday afternoon feeling, — the feeling of order and cleanliness and readiness for the morrow.

Alicia, with her green singing-book under her arm, glanced along the river road. "Will he come before we begin to practice?" she said to herself. Ah, what chance for sympathy have elderly ladies with headaches when such questions come into a girl's mind? She stood a moment on the threshold of the church, looking out at the sunshine, and hearing Mr. Lavendar up in the organ loft pulling out the stops and running his fingers along the keys.

"Miss Susan is n't coming this afternoon, Mr. Joseph," she said, as she pushed open the little baize door of the loft; "she is n't very well; so you and Mr. Tommy and I will have to practice by ourselves;" and then she nodded pleasantly at the other member of the choir, who, with his spectacles on, was poring over a manuscript of music.

"Dear, dear, I am sorry to hear that she is indisposed," said Mr. Joseph; "exceedingly sorry. Will you be so kind as to say so to her, Lyssie, if you see her this evening; say I had meant to call, but, as she is indisposed, I will not intrude?" But he sighed as he spoke, and then he pivoted round on the long wooden bench to his organ; his feet, searching for the keyboard, made a muffled sound in the listening silence of the church. Down below, the cheerful red cushions on the seats were all turned over to preserve their color, and the chancel was ghostly with white covers on the altar and the reading-desk; there was the scent of Prayer Books and dust, with strange, wandering hints of flowers which had lain here with the dead all these years, or denied death on Easter mornings.

From a little round window high in the wall behind the organ a bar of yellow sunlight shot down into the dusk: it threaded its noiseless way among the singing-books upon the benches; it struck a sudden sparkle from the ring on Mr. Tommy's thin, veined hand as he held his music-book close to his eyes; and it shone through the soft hair about Alicia Drayton's forehead, turning it into a delicate aureole of light around the shadowed seriousness of her face. She had been listening for a hand on the outer door of the church, a step on the graveled path, and she had even suggested timidly to Mr. Lavendar that — that perhaps the church door was locked, and perhaps — some one was trying to get in? Mr. Lavendar said mildly, "You came in last, Lyssie; did you lock it? Then of course it is n't fastened. Miss Susan can get in, if she changes her mind and wishes to come."

"Oh yes, so she can!" Lyssie answered. But still she listened.

Yet when Roger Carey did slip in, closing the door gently behind him, and starting the muffled echo of the empty church, Alicia, singing, the sun making that powdery halo around her head, did not hear him, and he looked up and saw her, and the young fellow's clear, positive, honest eyes filled suddenly with a reverence which the church itself had not brought into them.

When Lyssie saw him there was a tremor in her pretty voice; which is natural enough in any nice girl's voice when she finds that somebody is listening to her. This, not being a conceited man, was the explanation Roger Carey made to himself while he waited for the practicing to end. He sat in one of the square pews, which had a straight, uncomfortable back covered with prickly red cloth, and a door whose lifting brass catch had doubtless invited many of those idle fingers for which Satan, even in Old Chester, finds some mischief still. Roger Carey's fingers began to lift it now, and then to let it fall with a clatter, while he wished Mr. Lavendar would not try " *We praise thee, O God!* " for a fifth time, and while he thought, smiling to himself, of this or that which Miss Alicia Drayton had said to him. Her quaint truthfulness, her enchanting modesty in matters of opinion, her wisdom unto that which was good, her simplicity concerning evil, had delighted him as he had come to know her better. When he watched her or listened to her, it was with the pleasure of the man who has found something new.* But he said to himself that he was not in love with her. Certainly, his appreciation of her sweet young womanhood was of the nature of his appreciation of a limpid morning in spring, or of a star, or of the pathos of innocence and happiness in a child's face, rather than that more selfish appreciation which

comes when a man is falling in love. Roger Carey
was profoundly stirred and happy; he felt lifted up
to good things. But he was not, he said to himself,
" in love with her."

He was impatient for the practicing to cease; he
liked to hear her pretty voice, but he liked better
to see her and to hear her talk. As he sat waiting
for her, smiling now and then at some thought of her,
and playing with the little brass catch on the pew
door, he read the inscriptions on the two or three
tablets on the walls, and that upon the brass plate
in the chancel, in memory of the first minister of the
church, — his name, his virtues, and the exhortation
to " mark the perfect man," and after that those two
dates which bound with solemn meaning the weakest
or the meanest of lives, the dates of birth and death.
The empty church, the silent tread of the light from
the window in the organ loft up the aisle and across
the chancel, the moving shadows of the leaves outside, and, through all, Alicia's voice, " *O Lord, in
thee have I trusted; let me never be confounded,*"
— all these things, the scene, the waiting, the old
and beautiful words, fell into the young man's heart
with a strange touch of melancholy, and his face was
serious when he met Lyssie at the door and they
went out into the sunset.

It was pretty to see these two young people together, and to mark the change that each produced
in the other. Lyssie's shy anxiety, the anxiety that
a girl just beginning to fall in love feels, and does
not understand, — a desire to seem her best, to

please, to win, all the little humility that, when she is alone, makes her sigh and say to herself that she means to try to improve, — all that was gone in a flash, and instead there was a soft arrogance, a charming girlish imperiousness, and such joyousness!

Roger Carey seemed to have acquired all that Lyssie put aside; his impulsive dogmatism and careless good nature and frank criticism were lost, and in their place was a humbleness which was new to him, and an enchanting sense of delight in the sweetness of this young creature; he wanted to hear her talk, to see her smile, to protect her, to care for her. It was rather the feeling of the discoverer than the more serious joy of being himself discovered.

They did not go home at once, but wandered about in the churchyard and talked to each other. Once they grew so earnest that they stopped, and Lyssie sat down on an old tomb that stood like a low granite table under the shadow of a tulip-tree. She wore a little gray-and-white-striped gingham, and she had a bunch of laburnum in her belt. She took off her hat, and sat leaning her open palm on the lichen-covered name, looking up at Roger Carey with candid eyes of that color which lies on distant hills, and is neither blue nor violet. The sunshine touched her face and dress; a leaf shadow swung back and forth across her hand and over the assertion of endless love and grief on the old stone; and there they talked and listened, and looked and lived.

It was the usual talk: the girl's tentative expressions of opinion on great subjects; the man's instant acquiescence in them; the mutual astonishment at their unity of thought.

"You think so, too? Why, how strange! I've always felt that."

"You would rather see Egypt than any other country in the world? How odd that is! Do you know, I've always said I'd rather go to Egypt than any place else."

"You really feel that a lie is the only thing you couldn't forgive, Mr. Carey? Well, if I couldn't forgive everything, — forgiveness isn't hard to me, — why, I think I should draw the line at a lie!"

Ah, well, well, it is the old, beautiful story. We laugh at the two souls and the single thought; the conviction of the glorious and harmonious future, built up in a moment, because views of Shakespeare and the musical glasses coincide; but all the same, it is a divine time and a true time, *and it does survive!*

VIII.

We are such friends, my little girl and I,
That, tho' her summers scarcely number nine,
I need none other as I go my ways,
With her small fingers closely clasping mine.

A little world we two make of our own,
And people it with all things fair and sweet;
The stars that twinkle overhead at night
Drop down at dawn in daisies at our feet.

BROWN.

EVERYBODY watched little Lyssie's romance with approval and interest, for Old Chester loved her. It had been recognized as a romance the moment it was known that Mr. Carey's two weeks' visit was to be prolonged to three, and then to four.

"Oh, thank you very much," he said eagerly, when Mrs. Shore first proposed that he should stay another week; "I 'll be delighted to." And then he added, rather ruefully, "I might just as well, since you are good enough to ask me; for the fact is, I have n't anything on hand just now." That a client might knock at his door in his absence did not seem to trouble him, and Cecil, smiling to herself at the confession of his prompt acceptance, did not remind him of it. Indeed, his visit had done so much to relieve the intolerable dullness of Old Chester that she was glad he was going to stay. "Even his impudence is refreshing," she thought; for she had winced once or twice under some blunt expression of his opinion.

Still, such rudeness showed itself only at the beginning of any conversation they might have; towards the end, admiration would, for the time, thrust out the dislike which was, oddly enough, his real, sober feeling for Miss Drayton's sister. He felt this dislike more keenly when he saw them together; indeed, he did not like to see them together. Alicia seemed just a little childish, in the presence of this strong, clever woman. Nevertheless, Roger Carey was too glad to talk to little Miss Drayton to slight any chance of seeing her, whether it was in Mrs. Shore's presence or not; and he certainly would not have taken Eric out for a run on the hills, one charming morning, had he known that Lyssie was coming up to her sister's at that very hour. He had left Mrs. Shore struggling to make up her mind to pay the inevitable calls which were the price of a visit to Old Chester, and he had advised her, gayly, to find out when people were to be away from home; then, whistling to Eric, he had tramped off into the sunshine, thinking with satisfaction how incapable Miss Lyssie Drayton would be of any such forethought.

Mrs. Shore, however, had scarcely required his instruction.

"Tell me, Lys," she said, as, with Molly clinging to her hand, she walked down the path to meet her sister, "when does the next sewing society meet?" Then she put her finger under the girl's chin and lifted her fresh young face, and kissed her. "Mr. Carey has gone off to exercise Eric," she added significantly.

"I 'm sure I hope he will do it properly," Alicia returned, her head high; but she laughed and blushed. "What do you want to know about the sewing society for? Do you mean to go?" She slipped her arm about her sister's waist, and brushed her cheek against her shoulder. Lyssie smiled readily in those summer days; it seemed such happiness to be alive; she had recognized no other cause for happiness, either in herself or in Roger Carey. It is generally so with a girl; the spoken word has to fall like some subtle chemical into the luminous nebula of bliss, to crystallize it into a jewel that she can recognize, and claim, and wear as the crown of life. Alicia's bubble of laughter at her sister's interest in the sewing society was only this vague happiness seeking expression.

"*I* go? Lyssie! I must make my manners to all the old ladies, and I wanted to know when I could call with safety."

"Oh, Ceci!" Alicia remonstrated. "Indeed, I won't tell you; you shall find them all at home."

"But mamma does n't want to see them, aunt Lyssie; that 's why she goes when they are out," Molly explained, astonished at her aunt's dullness.

Cecil laughed. "Intelligent Molly!" she said.

The two sisters and the child had come along the flagged walk below the terrace to the pool, which was almost hidden now by water-plants. The flags ended in three mossy steps leading down to the water's edge. Two ancient Lombardy poplars stood here, with gnarled trunks, and mournful breaks of dead branches through their dark foliage. They made a spot of shade on the sunny, faintly undulating expanse of shimmering lily leaves. A frog splashed from the bank at the sound of footsteps, and made for a moment a widening, rocking circle on the still surface. Molly was instantly desirous of catching him, but her mother said peremptorily, "No. Now don't bother me, precious, or you'll have to go into the nursery. Sit down here beside mamma. Lyssie, is there anything so important in one's domestics as health? The honest, temperate, capable young woman amounts to nothing compared to the robust one! Molly's Rosa is ill, and I, in one of those moments of rash good nature that we all have at times, and on which we look back with such astonishment, — I said I'd take Molly to walk this morning. Didn't I, you nuisance?" And she drew the child's head down upon her lap and mumbled her little neck with kisses.

They were sitting on an old stone seat between the two poplars; the sunshine, sifting down, touched Cecil's head, and flecked Lyssie's cotton gown, and shone into Molly's eyes until she said she did not like it, and wished mamma would go to walk. "Anywhere," Molly urged. "You *said* you would!"

"It's too hot, Polly. Yes, Rosa has been creeping about with a white face for two days. So annoying to see her."

Lyssie was full of sympathy for Rosa. Had Dr. King seen her? What was the matter?

"Oh, nothing," Cecil answered impatiently; "a little feverish, perhaps. Of course I have n't sent for the doctor. One might as well start a hospital at once as keep five or six women. They always have something the matter with them, — or they think they have." And then she began to tease and cuddle Molly, until the clang of the iron gate at the end of the garden broke in upon the child's laughing cries; and Cecil, leaning backwards, glanced through the shrubbery. "'Good Lord, deliver us!'" she said, under her breath, "it's Mrs. Dale. She has come to tell me her opinion of young women who don't call upon their elders and betters! But I was going; you'll bear witness to that, Lys?"

"Yes, when she was at the sewing society," Alicia returned, with malice.

Cecil slipped Molly down on her feet. "Molly, my angel, run! Say to that lady that mamma is not at home; say I've gone down to the village. Run! She has n't seen us, and you can meet her at the front door."

Molly went, with the matter of fact obedience that found such a command no surprise.

"Why, Cecil!" cried Alicia Drayton.

"What? 'Not at home'? Oh, Lyssie, what a funny little thing you are!"

"But Molly?" Alicia protested, her eyes widening with dismay.

"Oh, you really are delightful," Cecil said, much

amused, looking at her with kind eyes. “ How very far from the maddling crowd you have lived ! ”

“ But, Ceci, I ’m — horrified. To tell Molly — ”

Cecil put her hand suddenly, softly, over her sister’s lips. “ Fault-finding is the wind that blows to the Place-we-don’t-believe-in, and it sends more people there than anything else. Do be quiet. Look ! there is Mr. Carey.”

Philip and Roger, with Eric at their heels, were crossing the meadow on the further side of the pool. When the two men reached the stone seat under the poplars, Lyssie’s face was still so serious that Roger Carey looked blank.

“ I wonder if she ’s offended ? ” he thought, frowning. “ I wonder if Mrs. Shore has been saying nasty things about me? Why, she ’s hardly smiled ! ” And he himself hardly smiled, while Cecil told him how Molly had come to the rescue and dismissed Mrs. Dale.

“ But I wish you could have seen my sister’s horror,” she ended gayly.

Roger sat down on the grass, and Eric squatted behind him, leaning his chin on the young man’s shoulder, and blinking his honest yellow eyes at Philip, who was talking to Alicia. Philip did not look at his wife until she said, breaking into something she was telling Mr. Carey, “ There, Polly, don’t lean on mamma. Come ! run and tell Rosa she really must take you out to walk.”

“ No, you take me ; you promised,” Molly teased. “ Rosa ’s sick ; she says she feels — ”

But Mrs. Shore was not interested in Rosa's feelings. "My little Polly, I adore you, — you are an angel; but don't bore me. Run along, like a good child."

"I will take you to walk, Molly," said Philip over his shoulder.

Cecil leaned her head back and laughed. "Philip never surprises one. Of course he'll take Molly to walk!"

"Is Rosa really ill?" her husband asked. "Shall I send King up to see her?"

"Oh, if you want to. I suppose we ought to make sure it is nothing contagious," Mrs. Shore said indolently.

Roger Carey looked as though about to whistle, but checked himself, and eased his mind by pulling Eric's ears until the amiable dog squealed, and then licked his hand, as if apologizing for having allowed his emotions to overcome him.

Philip was indifferent, apparently, to the nature of his wife's consent. "Very well, I'll tell him to come up. Come along, Molly." And he whistled to Eric, and started toward the village.

"Philip's goodness leaves nothing to the imagination," murmured Cecil.

"I have known people who left it all to the imagination," Mr. Carey observed.

"If you are going to be epigrammatic, I shall leave you," his hostess assured him.

"Oh, are you going in?" Roger said cheerfully, rising as she rose, but instantly sitting down again to talk to Miss Drayton.

Cecil laughed, but the color came into her face as she went back alone to the house.

As for Philip, he walked along with Molly, his face grim with the restraint he had put upon himself in the talk by the pool.

"To deliberately tell the child to lie!" he was thinking; and then he told Molly that he was going to take her into the woods. "You'll like that, won't you, old lady?" he asked absently.

"Oh, yes," cried Molly, "let's go to the woods! Mamma promised she would take me last week, but she did n't. And can I pick some flowers for her? And shall we watch the ants carry their babies into the sun to keep them warm? Oh, and, father, will you tell me the story you told me when I had the measles, about the man who rode to the moon on a wooden horse? And, father — " Her little, bubbling flood of questions caressed his ear.

"Yes; yes; yes," Philip answered blindly, as she seemed to expect. His indignation at Cecil's carelessness about Molly's truth-telling deepened into a bitter sense of his own helplessness to protect the child. This sort of thing was always going on. So far as Cecil was concerned, Molly knew nothing of the sacredness of a promise; the duty and grace of kindliness to inferiors she had never seen; truthfulness, according to her mother, was always secondary to good manners, and, in consequence, a matter of expediency. Cecil caressed or punished the child with the most absolute selfishness, and lived her own life without a thought of the responsibility of example.

Any protest from the unloving husband to the unloving wife only made matters worse, by adding to carelessness the deliberateness of antagonism. The effect of all this upon Molly was, of course, deplorable.

The child of unloving parents, illegitimate in a deep and terrible sense, — for love is the fulfilling of the law, — suffers, as whatever is in opposition to law, human or divine, must always suffer.

Philip said to himself that this little human soul, this little child of his, had wandered into a home polluted by the presence of the dreadful dead body of Love ; and if a man fears corruption and its train of disease for his child physically, what must he feel for a corruption which may taint her spiritually ? He held Molly's hand in his in a rigid grasp.

" Oh, father, you hurt my hand ! " she cried, pulling it away from him, and dancing on in front of him, across the upland meadow toward the woods ; then she ran back to adorn the lapel of his coat with a stalk of early goldenrod. " Tell me the wooden-horse story now ! "

" Oh, not now," Philip objected. " I 'll tell you what will be nice ; let 's sit down here, and father 'll smoke, and you shall tell him a story."

" That would be nice for father," Molly said, pushing out her lips, " but it would n't be *very* interesting for me."

" Oh, but to entertain me ? You did n't think of that," he reminded her.

Such confidence in her amiability could have only

the desired effect, though she qualified her consent, by the condition that they should tell the story together; for collaboration was a frequent amusement of these two friends.

Philip scratched a match on a stone, shielding the spurt of flame with a curving hand; then he lighted a cigar, and stretched himself out on his back, his hands under his head and his hat pulled over his eyes. "All right," he said. "Go ahead."

"No! You begin," Molly insisted anxiously. And with a little sigh Philip resigned himself to fiction.

It was a still July morning; the leaves overhead moved slightly back and forth across a sky that was deeply blue and cloudless; there was a flickering play of shadows on the grass and moss. Down in the valley lay Old Chester; here and there a gable showed through the thick foliage, or a chimney-stack rose well above it; beyond, on the opposite hillside, was the house from which they had just come, — "Cecil's house." Philip, staring out from under his hat brim at that house, and telling the story of a green-haired banshee, was reflecting upon that extraordinary folly of sentiment which, when love, which constitutes the home, has died, holds a husband and wife together, lest the "home be broken up." "As though the family idea meant the mere living together of the father and mother!" he said to himself.

Molly, cuddled against his side, with one arm thrown across his breast, watched him as he began his tale, her round, serious eyes full of profound interest; the more so as her father's stories were not apt to end with a moral, or to contain those indirect insinuations of virtue which children find in as bad taste as do their elders.

"Well, this green-haired banshee," Philip declared, after having described a banshee suitable for the infant mind, "went down to the seashore, and she saw a sea serpent. He had a mane all about his head, and it was covered with barnacles and little pink shells, and they rattled and clashed; and his sides were all wet and shining, and they were blue and green and gold; and he had diamond eyes —"

"Oh, draw him, father, draw him!"

So Philip hunted in his pocket for a pencil and an old envelope, and proceeded to sketch a strange beast unknown to natural history; on its back, clinging with bony fingers to its mane, he put a banshee, with wild hair and eyes, and a dreadful mouth full of sharp and jagged teeth.

"The banshee waded out and got on the back of the sea serpent, and he began to career around. At first she thought it was pretty nice; but sometimes the sea serpent would go under the water for an hour or so, and that made her wet, you know —"

"Why, she'd get drowned, father!" Molly broke in, with some sternness.

"Oh, she was a land-and-water lady," Philip explained.

But Molly frowned. "She was n't a lady; she was a creature."

Her father looked at her admiringly. “Your distinction is fine, Molly. I ’ve known ‘creatures.’ Well, anyhow, once when the sea serpent came up to the surface of the water, the banshee looked up into the air, and away up in the air, about nine hundred miles, she saw two rocs fighting.”

“ Rocks ? ” said Molly, following him breathlessly.

“ I mean birds; don’t you remember the rocs in Sindbad? They were fighting up there eight hundred miles, and — ”

“ You said nine hundred,” Molly interrupted threateningly.

“ Why, yes, it *was* nine hundred; what am I thinking of ? Their great wings were like four gray clouds, and they covered the sun. And just then a feather from one of their wings floated down into the sea, and lay rocking up and down on the waves like a boat. So the banshee climbed on to it.”

“ You did n’t draw her with any legs, father,” Molly objected.

“ Oh, we must give her some legs,” Philip said gravely, and, putting his cigar down on a flat stone, he indicated, among the voluminous folds of flying drapery, the very thin legs proper to a banshee.

“ Well, she climbed up on this great gray feather, and pulled up the big end for a sort of sail, you know, and then she went sailing and sailing and sailing; and after a while she came to a desert island.”

Molly sighed deeply, and nestled close to her father, her chin on his breast, and her eyes watching his lips.

"She came bump up against this island, and the great gray feather grated against the pebbles on the beach; and she got off and ran up on the shore. It was a very rocky island; there was n't a single green thing anywhere on it, — not a tree, nor a bush, nor a blade of grass."

"Nor any goats?" Molly asked anxiously. "Robinson had goats."

"No, no goats. But right in the middle of the island was a great white roc's egg that looked like the Mormons' Temple. No, you never saw the Mormons' Temple, but never mind. That's what it looked like. And what do you suppose the banshee did? She knocked a hole at either end of the roc's egg, — just as if she were going to suck it, you know; and then the wind blew right straight through it, and there it was, empty! a beautiful, white, shining house for the banshee, who immediately turned into a beautiful princess; for it seems a wicked magician had enchanted her and turned her into a — a creature. Oh, and the inside of the egg, the part we eat, I mean —"

"Do we eat roc's eggs?"

"I never have, Molly," Philip admitted, "but I should like to. Well, anyhow, it all ran out on a rock where the sun had been beating for a thousand years, so it was very hot, and of course it cooked the egg into omelets; so you see the beautiful princess had plenty to eat. Now finish it; it's your turn."

Molly gasped. "Oh, father, not yet?"

"Yes, it's your turn. What are you going to do with the princess?"

But he did not follow her adventures. His thoughts went back to the old question: "What is my duty?" He said to himself again, as he had said so many times in these last few years, "Molly!" He knew, of course, that if he ended what he believed to be an ignoble and a lying relation, if he and his wife separated, the court would take no cognizance of his subtleties, and Molly would unquestionably be given to her mother; that is, if the matter were pushed to any legal decision. And if it were not made a legal question, he knew equally well that Cecil would never consent to give the child to him; the only possible arrangement would be a division of Molly's time, — that arrangement fatal to the father and mother idea in a child's mind. All the embarrassment and pain of such a plan to the growing girl came before his mind: she would have no fixed home; she would have to make explanations; she would be surrounded by the horrible atmosphere of antagonism in which each parent must live in regard to the other, who, in so many months or so many weeks, would steal the child away again. On the other hand, suppose that he were to give up his desire for integrity, his passionate belief in the honor of marriage, and continue this miserable life, so that Molly's little existence be kept unruffled: what would be the result to her? What would be the effect upon her of the incessant contradiction and bickering between her father and mother, the teach-

ing of each denying the teaching of the other; and,
more subtle and deadly possibility, what would be
the effect upon her of the lie which the father and
mother lived?   Was not the truth safer?   Was it
not to be trusted?   There was surely less danger to
her from the sad, outspoken acknowledgment that
because love was the supreme thing, because they
honored marriage, her father and mother had parted!
Again and again he had argued this with himself;
again and again he had answered, " Yes, the truth is
best!"   And yet, how could he give her up, how
could he trust her to Cecil even for half the time?
— *Molly!*   It was as though upon the fine and delicate and admirable machinery of his theories this
little unconscious hand was laid, and everything
jarred and snapped and broke.   Ah, we take a great
deal upon us, we men and women, when, all uncertain
of ourselves and of each other, we dare to bring a
child's soul into the strife and confusion and cruelty
which any lack of love between us will create out of
marriage !

Philip was not listening to Molly's story, — it was
something about Indians and sponges, — when suddenly she broke it off with a question : —

" Father, why does n't God kill the devil? "

" Well," said Philip, knocking off the ashes of
his cigar with a careful finger, " candidly, I don't
know."

" Why, father ! " cried Molly.   " You ought to
know," she said severely.

" I don't," Philip confessed meekly.

Molly sighed. "I don't know why He does n't, either. He's the biggest."

"What do you know about God and the devil?" her father inquired.

"Oh, everything."

"Well! do impart your information, Polly."

"What?"

"Tell father; he does n't know 'everything.'"

"Well, God lives in a garden. I think the stars are the bushes growing in it. And He hides somewhere in the bushes, 'cause we never see Him, you know."

"Yes," Philip said, "it does seem sometimes as if He hid Himself, Molly."

"There is a river in the garden, and a gold house for Him to live in. And He keeps crowns in a box under the bed, and gives 'em to the angels, an' the angels keep throwing them down in front of Him. I don't see why."

"It does seem singular," her father agreed.

"Well, and the — Other. He has ears like a cow, and hoofs. He makes people bad. He makes 'em say — 'damn'!"

"Oh, *dear!*"

"Yes, he does; he's awfully wicked. And God does n't like him. So why does n't He kill him? I would." She dropped her head on her father's breast, so that her soft, straight hair touched his lips. "I really don't understand it, father?"

"I've known others who are confused by it,

Polly. But if I were you, I would n't bother about it. If God knows, why, that 's enough."

"Well," returned Molly reluctantly. Then she looked up and said, "Mamma laughs and laughs, but I think it is a good deal better to say a prayer to both of 'em. If God is n't quite big enough to kill him, why, it 's safer to say a prayer to him, too. Then he won't be mad."

Philip's hand, holding his cigar, hid his face for a moment, but when he spoke his voice was very serious. It was better to think of what was good than of what was bad, he told her. "And so," he ended, "I would n't pray to the devil, darling."

" Well," said Molly doubtfully ; " but it seems to me — *just as well.* Mamma said my devil prayer was naughty, — oh, she thought it was real wicked, father," she said proudly, — " but it made her laugh and laugh ; she made me say it to Mr. Carey. Want me to say it to you ? It will make you laugh like everything. 'Dear Dev — '"

" No ! "

At the change in his voice, Molly's little face puckered into excuses and defense. " Why, mamma laughed ; she — "

" No," Philip said again, but gently. " You must not make an exhibition of your prayers, Mary."

" A what, father ? "

" An exhibition. Let 's see if you can understand. Your prayer is only for the One to whom you speak. If it is only one word, 'God,' it is a prayer ; and if you say it to make father laugh — "

He stopped and set his lips; how was he to spare
the mother to the child? "Your prayers must be
reverent, dear," he ended lamely; "will you remember? Whether it is a devil prayer or a God
prayer, you must not think of any one else. Do you
understand, Molly?"

"Yes," Molly answered. "Oh, quick! Look at
the ant walking around your hat!"

Philip let her chatter on, with a word now and
then to keep her happy. Once the look in his face
called out her rebuke: "Don't wrinkle your forehead so, father. It is n't pretty. Father, you look
cross."

He laughed, kissed her; but he was angry. "I
will see her to-night," he was thinking. "I must
speak to her. This sort of thing has got to stop.
Oh, the child!"

IX.

Good nature is often mistaken for Virtue. — INGERSOLL.

BUT Philip had no opportunity to speak to Cecil that evening.

Alicia came to dinner, and, watching the pretty drama enacting under his eyes, his harsh and silent thought of his wife seemed to him a sort of sacrilege. No shy inflection of the girl's voice, no humid look from the undeclared lover's eyes, no meaningless badinage that hid all meanings, escaped his reverent appreciation. He was like a man struggling and drowning in the mire, yet seeing, far off, firm sunlit uplands. He had not attained them, but he was still able to believe in them. There are the lowest deeps, where a man ceases to believe in what he has missed; but Philip Shore believed in love with all his soul.

Cecil watched the lovers, too; and when Lyssie went home, with Philip and Mr. Carey as escorts, she thought tenderly of her little sister, but with half-bitter amusement of the situation. "She takes it seriously!" she thought. She was distinctly interested, however, and checked Molly's persistent chatter that she might follow her own thoughts undisturbed; but the child's teasing questions annoyed her, and she sent her into the house for some candy.

"You can have all you want, if you'll only keep quiet; but if you bother mamma, you must go to bed."

Molly, delighted to find herself possessed of a whole box of candy, was very obedient, until Rosa, looking pallid, came to say that it was her bedtime; then she cried, and Cecil kissed her, and promised her a present if she would be good.

"Give her that little Japanese box on my dressing table, Rosa," she said; and added a kindly word to the woman about her own health; "you had better take a glass of milk before you go to bed," she suggested; and Rosa went away, beaming. Cecil Shore was adored by her servants; perhaps, sometime, we shall know why it is that the u. scrupulous, generous, selfish person arouses in his inferiors a devotion which virtue itself, with all its justice and sense of responsibility, rarely commands.

Cecil's bribe to Molly left her to the peace and quiet she desired, and her thoughts went back to the lovers.

She had a small silver flask in her hand, full of some thick golden perfume, and she opened it slowly: "To think it should be Lys! What a pity Philip is married; he would be so much more appropriate for her." The natural sequence of this statement occurred to her and she meditated upon it with some interest.

Cecil Shore was a singularly clear-sighted woman, and she was in the habit of observing herself as truthfully and intelligently as she did other people.

But truthfulness of this sort is in no sense spiritual; it is only a calm, material dealing with facts. Hence she felt no shock or shrinking at the tendency of her thoughts, or her serious admission that it was a pity things could not be more appropriately arranged; she only sighed a little, and began to plan how she might make this sweet, unreal, fleeting time sweeter for Lyssie. "I must have her here oftener," she thought, but remembered Mrs. Drayton, and half laughed and groaned. "I 'll have to step into the breach and be agreeable to her, so that she 'll let Lys off. I 'll have to go and sit with her sometimes, and talk about her soul, — Heaven help me!" Then she started, and said sharply, "Who 's that?" for a figure moved down among the shadows at the foot of the steps, and then stood still.

"Me, ma'am," a frightened voice answered.

Cecil, still feeling her heart beating, sat up, and said, "Well! who are you? Eliza Todd? What do you want, Eliza? You should n't come creeping about this way; you frightened me to death!"

The little gray figure came out into the faint light from the house. "I — I thought Miss Lyssie was here, ma'am. I 'm sure I did n't mean to frighten you, Mrs. Shore. I thought Miss Lyssie was here."

"She has gone home."

"Oh, has she, ma'am?"

"Yes."

"Well, it don't matter. 'Tain't no great odds. I 'm sorry I disturbed you, I 'm sure."

Eliza was creeping back into the shadows, but

Cecil stopped her: " Why did you want to see Miss Lyssie, Eliza?   Anything wrong ? "

" No, 'm; oh no, 'm.   I just thought I 'd — I 'd get her," said Eliza, her voice breaking; and then she lifted the skirt of her calico dress and wiped her eyes. " I 'm all shook up, Mrs. Shore.   I 'm sure I beg your pardon for giving way before a lady like you.   But I thought Miss Lyssie was here."

" Oh, don't cry, whatever you do ! " Mrs. Shore said cheerfully.   " Tell me what troubles you.   I think I 'll do as well as Miss Lyssie.   Is it the rent ? "

Mrs. Todd laid her worn, thin hand across her mouth, as though to steady the nervous tremor of her lips.   " I 've been doin' your windows to-day, Mrs. Shore, and the girls said Miss Lyssie was here to dinner, and was out setting on the porch with you; and so I come round from the back of the house to see if I could get her.   That 's all."

" But what do you want Miss Lyssie for, at this hour of the night ?   Oh, come, Eliza, you must n't cry !   I never can do anything for people that cry." Then, after a moment's pause, seeing the little, crouching, crying figure at the foot of the steps, Cecil added kindly, " Come up here, and let 's have a little talk ; tell me what 's the matter."

Eliza came, slowly, catching her breath as she tried to stop crying.   She sat down on the steps, and Cecil, stretched out in her long chair, could see all the details of work and poverty in her face.

" 'T ain't anything, ma'am, only I was afraid to

go home.   I thought maybe Miss Lyssie would go
with me.   She can do anything with *him*."

"Miss Lyssie!" cried Lyssie's sister, resentment
and amusement in her face. "Why, my sister
could n't go home with you at this time of night,
Eliza.   I suppose you mean that you and Todd have
quarreled; but Miss Lyssie can't do anything."

"Oh no, ma'am, we 'ain't quarreled," Eliza explained eagerly. "Only your Rosa said that Mr.
Shore's John told her he seen Todd going home,
full.   Well, I expect my baby in six weeks, ma'am,
and I ain't real smart; an' when he 's full, he 's just
as like as not to jaw at me.   And I thought I 'd
just get Miss Lyssie to speak to him.   She 'd get
him pleasant, if he was n't real drunk.   If he 's
real drunk, he sleeps, and then I don't mind.   But
Rosa said John said that he were n't more 'an half
full.   So I thought I 'd get Miss Lyssie."

"Is Miss Lyssie in the habit of going around at
night to pacify Todd?" said Cecil curiously.

"Ma'am?"

"Does she often come and talk to your husband?
She ought not to go at night, Eliza."

"Well, yes 'm, she comes sometimes.   There 's
nobody can do anything with him but Miss Lyssie,
— the nasty brute!"

"Oh," said Cecil, surprised, "is that the way you
feel about him?   Well, I 'm sure I should think you
would.   It would be very disagreeable to live with
a man who ' jawed ' at one."

"Well, that 's just what he does," Eliza said resentfully. " My! nobody knows what I 've put up with in that man. An' he 's just a worthless brute; I 've told him so a hundred times. I 've told him the Lord only knew why I demeaned myself to marry him."

" That must have been encouraging to him," Cecil observed.

But Mrs. Todd went on passionately : " Me, that was well brought up! I had my music lessons, Mrs. Shore, when I was a girl, and I had an instrument; I could play 'See the dewdrop.' I suppose you know that piece, ma'am ? "

" I don't recall it," Mrs. Shore confessed.

" And then to think I married that — that — that *carpenter!* " ended Eliza, at a loss for an adjective.

" Well, you were very foolish to marry a man who drank," Cecil said, yawning.

" Oh, but he signed the pledge," Eliza excused herself, — " he signed it as many as six times before we was finally married. And now look at him ! And look at me, slavin' ! I never thought I 'd come down to washing people's windows, Mrs. Shore. My father was a respectable man. He was never took up for anything, and he never kept company with them that was took up. So I had advantages ; course, now, I feel it. We 'ain't got any instrument. My goodness! we 'ain't got anything. Oh. it 's no good talking ; it makes me real put out. But to-night I thought I just could n't stand him if he got to jawing ; so I came round to get Miss Lyssie to speak to him."

" Well, Eliza," Mrs. Shore assured her, " I think, considering your powers of invective, there may be something to be said for Job. However, never mind that. I wish you 'd tell me one thing : why in the world do you go on living with him? I should think the simplest way out of it all would be to leave him ? "

" My! I 've threatened to do that a hundred times. But then, when he ain't drinking he gets good wages. I suppose I 'm more comfortable, ma'am, takin' it all together, than if I had n't his wages coming in sometimes? And then, Mrs. Shore, *I* 've got a tongue."

" I 've noticed that," Cecil murmured.

" An' I can give it back to him! It 's only when he licks me — well, he 's only done that three times. I could have had him took up, but then there would n't 'a' been any wages, you see ; so I just content my-self by telling him that he 's a brute. An' he is! — my baby coming, and me afraid to go home for fear he 'll get me in a tremble! I thought Miss Lyssie would make him pleasant," she ended, and whim-pered, and wiped her eyes on her skirt again, and rose. " Oh, I 'm that scared of him! " She stood there, her poor gaunt little face full of the fright-ened resentment of selfishness, but with no gleam of pity for the sinfulness of the poor sinner who was her husband.

" You are a very foolish woman to live with him," Cecil said impatiently. " As for to-night, I can send John home with you — But no, that would n't do any good. Oh, well, you poor silly little creature, come, I 'll go home with you myself." She got up lazily. " Run into the hall and bring me that white wrap that is on the sofa. Yes, yes ; I 'll walk home with you," she insisted good naturedly in answer to Eliza's tremulous protest.

They were outside the gates before Cecil remembered that she should have had John follow her, that she might not have to come back alone. Still, in Old Chester one does not mind being out after dark by one's self. So she said one or two kind things to Eliza, promised her some baby clothes, told her she might come up to the barn every night and get milk for the children, and then, silently, walked along in the starlight down to the village, to the miserable little house where the Todds lived. There, Eliza slipped behind her while she knocked gayly, and then instantly pushed the door open and entered.

There was a moment's pause on the threshold of the squalid room. Job, who was sitting with his head on his arms, at a table on which were some unwashed plates with scraps of meat upon them, and a pitcher of tea, and a sugar bowl black with flies, lifted his head, and looked at her with dull eyes ; a child, wailing fretfully on a bed still unmade, stopped, open-mouthed. Cecil, with a quick glance, took in the scene. Job Todd's jaw dropped in blank and sheepish astonishment as she came toward him.

"Oh, Mr. Todd," she said graciously, " I 'm so glad you 're at home. You 're just the man I want to see. Can you do a piece of work for me to-morrow, in my stable? Ah, Eliza, that little woman on the bed wants her supper! Mr. Todd, I'm afraid I kept your wife very late, but she is such a capital cleaner I really could n't let her go sooner."

Job had gotten on his feet, and was grinning in a silly way, but at Eliza's name his heavy red face darkened. "I had to get my own supper," he began threateningly.

Cecil, with a charming smile, broke in: "I have heard people say that men are better cooks than women! But you've had your supper, Mr. Todd? I'm not interrupting you?"

"Oh no, 'm; not at all, I'm sure," Job said, jerking his head up and down in a bow.

"I just wanted to ask you about this piece of work," Cecil went on, aware that Eliza was slipping the children away to an inner room, and clearing the table, and turning down the lamp which was smoking on the mantelpiece above the untidy stove. "I know what a good carpenter you are; I remember hearing some one say what good work you did."

Job shook his head, with a pleased look, and thrust out his weak lips. "Well, I don't know. Used to be." Then the drunken anger came back into his face. "*She* wastes all my money, an' I have to get my own supper; no good in being first-rate in your trade, if —" He glared at Eliza, and Cecil was in despair. Well, there was nothing for it but to take him away. She shivered a little, but she said, courteously, that she wondered if he would be so good as to walk up the hill with her?

"I forgot to tell my man to come for me; but if you will walk home with me, Mr. Todd, that will be better, because I can tell you about the work."

That Job was flattered was so evident that Cecil could hardly keep the gravity of countenance which was essential; he came stumbling out into the street with her, murmuring, "Yes, 'm, yes, 'm," to everything she said. And she said much, and always with "Mr. Todd?" at the end of her sentences, spoken in that enchanting voice which made the poor fellow straighten himself, and feel more like a man than he had in many a year, — far more than Dr. Lavendar's invectives, and Miss Susan's sensible reproaches, and Miss Lyssie's entreaties had ever made him feel. Cecil did not refer to the work again, and she devoutly hoped that he would not. "What *shall* I say, if he asks what it is?" she thought nervously. She spoke of the weather, and was "so glad" Mr. Todd thought it was going to be fine; she asked him about his politics with all the gravity in the world, and took him to task for not voting. "American men ought to vote, and not leave the ballot to aliens, don't you think so, Mr. Todd?" And Job, who had not paid his poll tax ıce he was twenty-one, said, "Yes, 'm, yes, 'm. er right, 'm. We had ought to vote; yer right, 'm." It seemed to Job that she had forgotten that he was a drunkard, as Dr. Lavendar and the others had assured him he was, over and over. A glow came about his heart. He was so elated that he did not notice the relief in her tone, when, halfway up the hill, she interrupted herself suddenly by saying, "Oh, there's Mr. Carey, — there's Mr. Shore and Mr. Carey, Mr. Todd. I shall not have to trouble you to go on up the hill with me. Philip!" she called out sharply, and the two men turned, astonished to see her and her companion. When they were beside her, she laughed a little at her own relief, but she said, still with that gracious politeness that stirred Job as nothing but flattery can stir a fool, "I had to go down to the village, and Mr. Todd was so kind as to walk up the hill with me. Good-night, Mr. Todd. Thank you so much."

And Job Todd made a jerky bow, promised to attend to the stable job, and went off with a brisk step that surprised himself.

As for Cecil, she drew her wrap about her, with a shiver and a laugh. It seemed as though she still felt his heavy presence, and the smell of liquor near her. "*Oh*, what a beast he is!" she said. "How glad I am I met you! Mr. Carey, that is one of my sister's protégés. Philip, find something for him to do to-morrow, will you? I've told him I had some work for him. Can't you break down a stall, or something? I told him the work was in the stable." And then she shook her head and laughed. "No, no! please don't talk about him, — horrible creature!"

She was plainly nervous, and yet full of the drollery of the situation.

It was useless, Philip saw, to think of having any talk with her about Molly that night.

X.

I am often filled with wonder that so many marriages are passably successful, and so few come to open failure. — STEVENSON.

THE next morning, in accordance with her plan of being agreeable to Mrs. Drayton so that Lyssie might have a little more freedom, Cecil went to see her step-mother; and she was agreeable, though the repression she had to put upon herself in her conversation with this foolish little woman made her tired and cross, — so cross that when, at noon, Rosa came to ask what work Mrs. Shore wished Job Todd to do in the stable, Cecil replied impatiently, "I don't know, I 'm sure! Don't bother me about it, Rosa. Just tell John to find something for him to do. Anything; I don't care what. Let him build a kennel for Eric."

"Eric has a very good kennel, Mrs. Shore," Rosa said hesitatingly.

"Well, let him tear it down and make a bigger one," Cecil commanded, relieved to have the matter decided; and then she called the woman back. "Oh, I suppose I must go myself," she said, crossly, with that impatience which we all feel when we would do evil, but find good present with us. So she went out across the hot sunshine of the courtyard, said a dozen pretty words to Job, and came back again, touched and amused by the poor stupid fellow's slavish admiration.

She had a delicious nap that afternoon, Rosa fanning her softly until she fell asleep, and when she awakened, warm and flushed, bringing her a sangaree so cold that the goblet was frosted with beads of mist.   Cecil was very comfortable by that time, and very good natured: she had planned an unusual salad for dinner (tomatoes set in aspic, with a delicious accompaniment of stuffed eggs) ; also, she had arranged with Mrs. Drayton that Lyssie should have a whole day off ; and two such successes could not fail to make her good natured.   She intended that Lyssie's day should be charmingly spent with Philip and Mr. Carey on the river.   For her part, she would go and sit with her step-mother, and then have her nap as usual in the afternoon.   Cecil very frankly hated excursions, — they involved too much exertion, and the sun was generally hot ; but, provided she could stay at home, she was willing to arrange them for other people.   In fact, she liked the pleasure, which in some natures is almost sensuous, of giving pleasure to others.

When she announced her plan to Mr. Carey that evening, his quick look of delight annoyed her.   She did not know why.   " One would think he would be a little bored by a whole day of it," she thought ; and when Philip, who had been walking restlessly up and down the porch, turned to go into his library, she stopped him rather curtly, and told him what she had arranged.

“That will be very nice,” he said absently. “To-morrow, you say? I’m glad of that; I must be away the next day, unfortunately.” Then he explained to Mr. Carey that he had been called up to town. “I’ve just had a letter from Woodhouse, saying that he can go over Miller’s work with me on Thursday.”

“Miller is Philip’s little artist,” Cecil said. “You know Philip keeps an artist as some people support missionaries. He thinks he can create genius by encouraging ability. Now, Philip, I hope you are not going to be hard on him?”

“I hope not,” Philip returned briefly. “I’m sorry, Carey, to clear out in this way, but I have to take Woodhouse when I can get him. Miller is his missionary as well as mine. Poor Miller sent the pictures over six weeks ago, and I suppose he is beside himself with anxiety to know what his chances are. We withdraw the money, you know, if the excellence of the work does n’t warrant it.”

“What are his chances? Has he the real stuff in him?” Roger asked. He knew all about this plan of Philip Shore’s for lending a young artist money for three years’ study abroad. One man had already profited by this arrangement, and now Philip was watching with some anxiety the progress of the second.

“Well,” he said doubtfully, “I don’t know. This examination will settle it. He does not seem to me to stick as he should.”

“Sure you ’re not holding too tight a rein?” Roger suggested. “He ’s young, you know.”

" Indeed he is holding too tight a rein ! " Cecil broke in. " Philip's idea of the artistic passion is to die in an attic. Now, I think one can be an artist, and yet not die in an attic. Here 's Philip himself," she ended, with a droll glance.

Her reference to the life which he had put aside because he had recognized his limitations — put aside with agony and truth — stung like a lash across his face ; but he said, carelessly enough, " Oh, very likely I was n't capable of dying at such an altitude," and would have gone away, but Cecil detained him by a gesture and a laugh.

" You did n't sell your pictures ; that was the real reason. Come, now, Philip, was n't it ? "

" Of course it was. If they had been good, they would have sold ; and fortunately for me, no misguided friends purchased what was n't good, to encourage me in devoting myself to mediocrity."

" It 's a pity your view is n't more general," Roger Carey observed. " Misguided friendship and weak-kneed benefaction are harder on art than hunger and cold ever were. I 'm glad you won't support your man unless he has the real stuff in him. But, poor devil, I 'm sorry for him, if his work does n't come up to the scratch."

" So am I," said Philip Shore ; and there was something in his voice which told that he was acquainted with that grief.

" Ah, well," Cecil said lightly, " somebody may die and leave him some money, or he may marry a rich wife ; that will destroy any passion for dying in attics. But really, it would be very hard on him to have .to give up, now, without such compensation. If you decide against him, I 'll send him the money to go on with his work myself."

Naturally the conversation ended with this remark. Roger Carey looked at his hostess with a wonder at her possibilities which was almost admiration. As for Philip, he excused himself to his guest because he had some letters to write, and went into his library, setting his teeth hard, and closing the door behind him with a vicious bang. As he did so, he heard Cecil's voice saying, " Has she talked religion to you yet? She has it in its most malignant form " — and he knew that poor Mrs. Drayton was serving as a stalking-horse for his wife's wit.

He did not hear Roger Carey's blunt rejoinder: " Oh, now, look here, Mrs. Shore, I like Mrs. Drayton! You must n't abuse her to me."

Cecil laughed. " My dear Mr. Carey, what has liking to do with it? You don't suppose that I am not deeply attached to my step-mother? But I can't help seeing that she is amusing."

" You would see something amusing at a funeral ! "

" Ah, well, you have n't experienced her religion," Cecil defended herself. " She has n't told you how intimate she is with her Creator, and you 've never heard her purring on about infinity by the hour ! I assure you, Mr. Carey, she empties her soul of its emotions just as a boy pulls his pocket wrong side out to show you that there 's nothing in it. And to think that I am going to sit with her to-morrow morning, so that my sister can have a little spree, poor child!"

Roger felt the reproach for his somewhat aggressive goodness, as she meant he should.

"You're very good, awfully good, to sit with her instead of coming out on the river. But is she too sick to be left alone?"

Cecil laughed. "Sick? She is the most robustly delicate person I know."

"Well, then, why does she object to being alone?"

"But don't you know?" said Cecil, surprised;— "there is never any '*why*' in Mrs. Drayton's objections!"

Again Roger Carey frowned, and said that at any rate Mrs. Drayton spared Miss Lyssie to do lots of charitable work; and for his part, he thought there was nothing more attractive in a woman than just that sort of thing.

"Oh, nothing!" Cecil agreed, smiling.

But Mr. Carey had nothing more to say of little Lyssie. Indeed, he did not like to talk about her to this strangely different woman; to discuss her with his hostess was like analyzing a violet upon a gaming table. Instead, he took Cecil to task for having told Molly to fib, the day before. "I should think it was awfully important to teach children to tell the truth," he said. "'I speak as a fool,' for I don't know much about 'em; but judging from the experiences of my own youth, I should say they took to lying pretty easily. You instructed Molly so gracefully, the young one will think fibbing is a fine art."

This led to a discussion upon truth, in which Mr. Carey aired very noble sentiments, and Cecil insisted that truth was governed by the law of benefit. " And I consider that I was a benefactor to you all by saving you from the old lady," she said, with some earnestness. Mr. Carey's carelessly frank astonishment at what she had done annoyed her to the point of self-defense. " Besides, the child discriminates, you know."

" Yes, against Mrs. Dale, no doubt," Roger said ; but was so little interested in her explanations that he hardly waited for her to finish another excuse before he began to talk about Job Todd ; his admiration of what he called in his own mind her " sand " in walking at night with an intoxicated man spoke plainly in his voice.

" Do tell me how you happened to do it," he said, scratching a match upon the sole of his boot, and lighting his cigar.

And she told him ; commenting, when she ended, upon the absurdity of the situation. " Here they are, living a cat-and-dog life ; and we have to support their miserable little children ! I told her she was a great goose not to leave him."

" She was a goose to marry him, but she ought to stick to her bargain. I hope your dangerous views did n't strike in ? "

" Marriages are queer things, are n't they ? "

Cecil returned thoughtfully. "Did you ever notice how we say of all our friends, 'Why in the world did *he* marry *her?*' or, 'What possessed *her* to marry *him?*'"

"Yes, I—I 've noticed it," said Roger Carey, looking at the tip of his cigar.

"Ah, well, there 's a mistake somewhere in this idea of marriage," Cecil informed him gayly. "Talk about matches being made in heaven! If they are, they light the fires of — the other place very successfully."

"Well, you help to light the fires with bad advice," Roger insisted dogmatically, and with that good-humored contempt of a woman's opinion which does not condescend to argument; but he moved his chair so that he might see her face as she talked. His first repulsion always faded after he had been with her a little while. Perhaps it was her repose which charmed him, — a repose so absolute that to see her eyes when she lifted her white lids he had thus to move his chair, for she would not turn her head when she spoke. Her voice, between her melodious silences, was deep, for a woman, and soft, and it had in it the delicious clearness and color of dark wine; she spoke slowly, too, so that he could feel the caress of sound without the tension to catch the sense. He heard her excuse Job Todd because of the fatality of his environment; he heard her advocate the irresponsibility of temperament. She talked well and cleverly, touching, with the conventional unconventionality of our day, on subjects which a generation ago were tabooed between men and women, but which now we see fit to discuss, declaring that there can be no consciousness in the commonplace — though every man and woman of us knows better! Once he contradicted her sharply, and once he laughed; but he was not listening closely. "Oh, now, look here!" he said vaguely, with the intonation with which, to a man, he would have said, "Bosh!" He was following — for her sleeve was of some sheer muslin — the line of her arm from the shoulder to the finger tip: he saw the exquisite curves, unmarred by any ornament, he saw the faint color of her relaxed palm, and it came into his mind, with that primitive ferocity which lurks below the product of civilization which is named a gentleman, that a man might grasp the satin smoothness of the round flesh, above and below the elbow, and kiss the blue vein on that warm curve of the inner arm, — kiss it, and kiss it, until —

Roger Carey rose hastily. "I must go in; I have some letters to write. Beg pardon for interrupting you, but I must go in. I just remembered." He dropped her hand carelessly when he said "Good-night," and then went hastily to his own room, where for a long time he stood before the open window frowning out into the darkness. But after a while his face cleared, and he smiled and drew a deep breath. "She *is* a dear little thing!" he said.

Roger, capable of forgetting himself, was also capable of forgetting Cecil; but she did not readily forget him. When she went upstairs there was some annoyance in her face. " How unpleasant he is ! " she thought, and sat down in front of her mirror, looking absently into its shadowy depths. " Very unpleasant, but — " Then she half laughed and sighed, and, leaning her elbow on the table, looked long and deeply into the glass. .

The room was lighted only by the candles on the dressing table, for the night was warm and still. Cecil, moving about, stopped to trim the wicks, and then stood, the snuffers in her hand, absorbed in thought. Some one knocked, and she answered absently, without turning her head, " Come in ; " then, with a start, she saw her husband's face in the mirror.

" What, you ? "

" Yes ; can you spare me a few moments ? " said Philip; but, involuntarily, he stood still on the threshold, in the quick delight of the artist at that sumptuous figure, standing there in the faint dusk of the candlelight. Somehow, the beauty of it, and the sense of his absolute ownership, took him by the throat for one bad moment that sent the blood into his face. All this beauty which enchanted and invited him, this length of shining hair, the white column of the stately throat, was his; for was she not his wife ?

But the soul of the man knew better.

" Of course I can spare you a few moments." Cecil answered, smiling, and sitting down, one white bare arm along the back of her chair, and the other on the dressing table.

" I am afraid it is late," he said, " but I saw your light, and I was anxious to speak to you. I won't detain you very long."

" I don't see why you should be apologetic," she interposed good naturedly. "Sit down, won't you?"

There was a certain intent look in Philip's face that did not escape Cecil. " I have attacks of nerves," she had once said, " but Philip has attacks of soul! " Such attacks were not agreeable to her, though she bore them with remarkable patience. She thought now, watching him with amused, critical eyes, that such an attack was imminent. "I suppose," she reflected, " that this sort of thing attracted me at first, because it was odd. Yes, and there is an intellectual value, too; Philip is no fool."

" I hope nothing has bothered you?" she said, aloud.

" I want to speak to you about Molly."

" Molly! Why, what is the matter? Is she ill? What about Molly?" Her face changed sharply, and she half rose.

" No; nothing, nothing; she is quite well."

Cecil sank back in her chair, with a quick breath of relief. " Oh, you startled me so! " she said, her color coming again. Her hair, falling over her shoulders, was pulled sideways by her change of position; she caught it and twisted it in a rope, and wrapped it about one bare arm; a faint gleam touched a gilt thread here and there in the soft coil, as the flames of the candles behind her bent and flared in a sudden light draught. " I wish you would n't come

in and frighten me this way," she told him irritably.
" Well, what is it? What do you want?"

" I want to ask you " — he spoke slowly, and his
manner was guardedly polite — "I want to call
your attention to the danger of giving Molly an idea
that truth is not important. I noticed yesterday
morning — "

" Yesterday morning?" she broke in. " Oh, you
mean ' not at home '? Oh, now, really, Philip, do
you think it worth while to discuss a social form?
I 'm pretty patient with your ideas generally, but
really ! "

" I 'm not talking about a social form; I 'm talking about the spirit of truth. We debauch a child's
soul when we allow it to sink its directness in what
we call a social form. Molly can't discriminate.
She tells what she thinks is a lie, and finds it in-
dorsed, in fact suggested, by us."

" ' Us ' ! " Cecil repeated, and laughed. " Philip,
your politeness leads you dangerously near this same
debauchery yourself. Pray don't consider my feelings. Tell the truth, and shame — me. Oh, I 'll
not send any more such messages by her, if it distresses you so much. But don't, don't, at midnight,
begin about the ' spirit of truth'! Must you,
Philip?"

All her good nature had come back again, for she
was sleepy.

Philip Shore made no appeal for any deeper motive in her acquiescence than this mere contemptuous
consideration of his wishes; the time for such appeals

seemed to him long gone by. "Thank you," he said. "And there's one other thing. Molly happened to speak about that prayer of hers — to the devil, you know?"

"Yes, well? What of it? It was very funny. Did she repeat it to you?"

"Repeat it? Of course not. Do you suppose I'd let the child think her prayer could be amusing? That is what I wanted to speak to you about; it was outrageous to make a jest of the child's prayer!"

Cecil dropped her arm on her dressing table with a soft crash. "*Oh*, dear me!" she said, and then swallowed a yawn which brought the water into her eyes and made her smile. "(I beg your pardon.) Philip, if you had the slightest sense of humor, you would be spared much. The idea of being harrowed because I laughed at Molly's prayer! And really, I must protest; I can't have my child praying to the devil, — if that is what you want. I mean that Molly shall have some religious teaching, and know that one does n't pray to the devil."

"Certainly. Check it, by all means. But the point I make is this: when you treated her prayer, which according to your theology was bad, as a joke, you robbed the child of reverence."

"Your ideas of reverence are interesting: Reverence, and a prayer to the devil."

"It is the prayer which I revere. The name 'God' or 'devil' is nothing, the instinct of prayer is everything; and you laughed at it, and made the child repeat it; you turned it into a show. It was shocking!"　His anger with her grew as he put it into words.　"I know you have no reverence yourself, but, for Heaven's sake, don't rob the child of it."

Cecil sighed.　It was nearly a year since Philip's last attack of "soul;" she felt that she owed him a hearing for so long a holiday, but she wished he would hurry.　"Go on," she said resignedly; but could not help adding, "It is interesting to hear you advocating religious teaching, — you, a skeptic.　Oh, Philip, there!　I didn't mean to call down a statement of your faith!"

"Don't be alarmed," he said dryly.　"I shouldn't make such a statement to *you*."

"There's one thing that always interests me about you good people," returned Cecil, yawning: "not your certainty that the rest of us are swine, — no doubt we are, — but your certainty that your opinions are pearls."

"My only certainty is that there is no skepticism so dreadful as that which finds no seriousness in life," he answered significantly.

"If you mean that for me," she protested, "my dear friend, no one finds life more serious than I; especially on such occasions."

"You don't know what it means, even," he said angrily.　"If you did, you would be incapable of treating lightly the instinct of worship in a child's soul!"

It seemed that his words had some effect, for she sat without speaking, tapping one foot upon the floor, and pulling with a restless finger at her red lip. But her flippancy was so intolerable to him that he turned to leave the room. "I don't often interfere," he said, pausing on the threshold, for her continued silence restrained him like some spoken word, — "I don't often interfere about Molly, but in a thing of such vital importance as —"

"Look here, Philip," she interrupted. "You and I will never agree about Molly, so what is the use of talking about it? I will never allow her to be taught your dreadful agnostic ideas; I'd rather have her pray to the devil upon the housetops, to the amusement of everybody. No, we'll never agree about her; but oh, life would be so much more comfortable if you would just make up your mind to that fact. You go your way, and I'll go mine."

"*What?*"

"I mean, you teach her your ideas, and I'll teach her mine."

"Oh, I — I misunderstood you!" he exclaimed, his voice suddenly harsh; and then he was silent a moment until he said, "That's perfectly absurd; it would be as though you said a thing was white, and I said it was black. She would end by not believing either of us. No, I shan't contradict your religious teaching; but you must not ignore moral teaching, — that I shall insist upon. I shan't say that this or that doctrine seems to me ridiculous; but I do insist that while your teaching is, as I think, intellectually crooked, it is not, also, morally crooked."

Cecil's face had grown slowly white. "This is insufferable!" she said, in a low voice. She turned her back upon him, and, shaking her hair loose, began to braid it with trembling fingers. "Philip, I shall do exactly as I please. You can make up your mind to that. Good-night. Please go. You are perfectly impossible. Please go." Anger vibrated in her scantily civil words. She saw him, in the mirror, hesitate, and then turn away.

As the door closed behind him, she said, violently, under her breath, "You fool!"

XI.

Women never reason, or, if they do, they either draw correct inferences from wrong premises or wrong inferences from correct premises; — and they always poke the fire from the top.

WHATELY.

"I 'LL go and see Utile Dulci," said Dr. Lavendar to himself, with a sigh.

It was Friday afternoon, and Joseph was to be at home the next day; but in spite of that his brother had received a letter from him.

Dr. Lavendar had been working at his lathe, for it was five o'clock, and this was his free hour. As he worked he thought very much about his book, and he perceived, suddenly, a chance for a new subdivision, — The Relation of Precious Stones to the Science and Practice of Medicine. The very title was rich with suggestions! He saw at a glance the possibilities of psychical investigations; delusions and illusions, and their uses; and of course a dozen instances and minor histories. He sighed with happiness, and made a little mental calculation, as he had done many times before, as to the probable amount of money the book would earn for Joey.

The window was open beside him, for it was hot, and the hum of the bees outside mingled with the buzz of his diamond-wheel; his thin, veined fingers were grimy with oil, and his face was full of that satisfaction in accomplishment which has no relation to the value of the thing accomplished. One sees it on the face of a child who surveys with ecstasy his mud pie, or in the eye of a woman measuring the day's toil on a piece of embroidery for which the world has no need. It must be a comfortable frame of mind, this satisfaction with achievement without relation to value; perhaps still higher beings than we who observe the mud pies and embroidery may envy us our anxious and happy preoccupation in our little reforms, or philanthropies, or arts, — who knows?

Dr. Lavendar, his stiff white hair standing up very straight, his spectacles pushed up on his forehead, his head sunk between his shoulders, was saying to himself that he had never got so fine a polish on a carnelian. He sat on the edge of his chair, his knees together to make a lap for a dropping tool or stone, his gaitered feet wide apart to afford room for Danny to lie between them. His sermon was written; he had made three parochial calls, — one of them upon Mrs. Pendleton; he had seen a little blind horse — bought because it was blind and ill treated — installed in his stable; and he had put an unequaled polish upon the carnelian. No wonder his face beamed with satisfaction.

And then arrived Mr. Joseph's letter.

It startled him so that he must have stepped upon Danny, for the little grizzled dog yelped sharply, and Dr. Lavendar, frowning with anxiety lest Joey should be writing to say that he was ill and could not come home on Saturday, paused, the unopened letter in his hand, to feel the little gray legs remorsefully and pull the ragged ears as an assurance that his awkwardness was unintentional.

Then he read the letter.

The experience of the human race should have decided by this time whether it is best to communicate unpleasant news by word of mouth or in writing; but Mr. Joseph Lavendar, like all the rest of us, had had twenty minds about it. He had something to say which his brother would not like to hear. Should he tell it or should he write it? One or the other must be done, for Mr. Lavendar was meditating an important step, and he was incapable of such disloyalty as acting, and then telling. The week before, he had decided to talk it out over their pipes in the arbor; but it had rained, and they had smoked indoors. Now, it is a fact that, if one sets one's mind on doing a thing in one way, it is quite difficult to do it in any other way. So Mr. Lavendar, owing to the rain, had carried his secret back with him to Mercer. But the consciousness of secrecy was misery. So he wrote his letter; carried it about in his pocket for one uncertain, hesitating day; mailed it on a sudden impulse, and had regretted it ever since; because perhaps he ought to have spoken its news?

He followed the letter in his thoughts on its journey in the battered leather mail-bag down to Old Chester. His heart burned and ached as he fancied his brother opening it and reading it; he knew the old clergyman's pipe would go out, that he would turn his back upon the lathe, — perhaps even upon an unfinished sermon. Oh, when we receive, as we all do now and then, a letter that strikes us to the heart, at least let us feel that the writer, too, calculating to the moment its arrival, may be turning hot and cold, as do we while we read it.

"I am sure, my dear James," Mr. Lavendar had written, — "I am sure you will be glad to know that I have placed my affections upon a lady for whom I have the highest respect. Indeed, I am confident that you will feel as warmly as I do toward her when you truly know her, — which, my dear brother, judging from your opinions expressed about the estimable Mrs. Pendleton, you do not at present. It is my intention to beg her to accept my hand ; and my deepest desire, apart from the hope that she may accept it, is that I may have your sympathy in my suit."

It was after supper that Dr. Lavendar, still quite shaken from this distressing letter, said to himself, "I 'll go and see Utile Dulci."

He sighed deeply as he took his hat and stick, and called Danny, and went plodding up the road to Miss Carr's house. Of course he did not mean to speak to her of his dismay at Joey's plan, but he might perhaps skirt the subject, if only in his thoughts ; and she, being a strong, good woman, an "intelligent person," would, quite unconsciously, give him some sort of comfort.

There was no light in Susan Carr's parlor as Dr. Lavendar went groping through the hall, — for, in

friendly Old Chester fashion, the front door was
open, — and the house seemed quite empty and deserted. He could hear Miss Susan's Ellen moving
heavily about in the kitchen, singing in a thin voice
and with unmistakable camp-meeting emphasis one
of those fierce evangelical hymns which display such
a singular and interesting conception of the Deity.
Dr. Lavendar sat down in the twilight of the silent
room, and drew a long breath ; his head sunk upon
his breast, and his eyes fixed absently upon the floor.
He was thinking, as most people do at some time or
other in their lives, that this matter of falling in love
knew no rule of reason, or common sense, or obvious
propriety.

"There ought to be a law to prevent foolishness,"
he said to himself despairingly. It seemed to him
that there was a great deal of foolishness in the
world; why, even in little Old Chester, just see what
folly there had been: Could anything have been
more absurd than for William Drayton to marry
that ridiculous Fanny Dacie ? Could anything be
sadder than for a man like Philip Shore to have
bound himself to a selfish, sensuous, soulless creature
like poor Cecil? And there was Eliza Todd, running into the trap of marriage with a drunkard
whom she hoped to reform. "Foolishness! foolishness!" said Dr. Lavendar, nodding, and pressing
his lips together, his forehead wrinkling up to his
short white hair. "And now to think that Joey
should be foolish!" Then he heard Susan Carr's
step, and looked up with a vague apprehension of

comfort to be found in her mere presence. She struck his hand, man fashion, in a hearty welcome, and said in her clear, strong voice that he had scared her when she saw him sitting there alone in the dark.

"I've just been in to say good-evening to Mrs. Pendleton," she explained. "Why did n't you tell Ellen to run over for me?"

The dogmatic, gentle old man felt his heart suddenly come up in his throat; if he could only tell her all about it! She looked so wise and simple as she sat there in the dusk beside him; her face was full of that clear, fresh color that tells of rain and sunshine; her whole strong, vigorous body seemed to bring the scent of the friendly earth and the breath of growing trees into the still room. And to think that Joey should be foolish, when here was Susan Carr, whom he might have had! For of course she could not — no woman could — resist Joey. His voice actually trembled when he said he had just dropped in for a moment. "No, no; nothing special. So you 've been to call on your neighbor?"

Now, Susan Carr had that reverence for her clergyman as the vehicle of grace which all good women feel, — a reverence often so devoid of reason that it may be accompanied, where the clergyman is their junior, with a recollection of having dandled the vehicle of grace upon their knees, or even spanked him in his tender youth. But in spite of Susan Carr's reverence she could not help feeling that sometimes Dr. Lavendar was hard upon her

little sleek neighbor. She felt it now in his harmless
question; and though she would not for the world
have seemed to reprove her pastor, she made haste to
say a good word for Mrs. Pendleton: " She's a
pleasant person, I think."

" Ho ! " said Dr. Lavendar.

At which Miss Susan cheerfully changed the subject. She asked him about his book; and he told
her, listlessly, of the chapter upon The Relation of
Precious Stones to the Science and Practice of Medicine. He said he had not talked it over with Joey,
but he felt sure Joey would think it an admirable, in
fact a necessary discursion. " Though it will delay
the book a little; but, fortunately, Joey is in no
hurry for it, financially."

Then he fell into a moody silence, and Miss Carr
talked; she spoke of Lyssie and Mr. Carey, and, a
little sadly, of Cecil. " She has never belonged to
us as Lyssie does," said Miss Susan; and in a
troubled, hesitating way she added something about
Philip and his wife: " They don't seem as affectionate as I could wish. I can't help feeling anxious
about them ? "

" I have n't seen them together since they 've been
here. But I was always doubtful about that marriage," Dr. Lavendar answered, nodding his head.
" Look at 'em, — fire and ice. He's a good fellow,
fine fellow ; but she never had a chance, poor child.
Just think of being brought up by Fanny Dacie ! "

" Well, it was n't always easy for poor Fanny,"
Miss Carr reminded him, good naturedly.

"Oh well, nothing ever was easy for her, was it?" said Dr. Lavendar. "Dear me, how she does enjoy misery! That was a queer marriage, too, — Willi.. Drayton and Fanny Dacie. Well, well, marriage is a very strange thing, Miss Susan?"

"I should think it was," Miss Susan agreed, with the modesty of one who has really no right to an opinion. Then, to her dismay, she felt herself blushing. What would Dr. Lavendar think if he knew that Joseph was meditating this "strange thing"? As for Dr. Lavendar, he sighed deeply.

"Miss Susan," he said abruptly, "do you think your neighbor has any — ah — wish to marry again?"

"Dear me! why, I never thought of such a thing. Oh no, Dr. Lavendar; I 've heard her say that she could not endure second marriages. And just see what deep mourning she wears."

"Have you really heard her say that?" he asked eagerly. "Well, now, well! I 'm pleased to hear it. I 'm glad she has so proper a feeling about marriage."

"She has to give up her money if she marries again: at least, so they say. I think that shows how attractive her husband thought her," Miss Susan observed, with mild reproof.

"It shows him to have been a dog in the manger!" Dr. Lavendar cried joyously. "But no, I had not heard that. Well, she 'll never marry, — unless she finds a man with money enough to cover her loss. Joey and I — ah — differ a little in our judgment of your neighbor. I wonder if he knows this about the disposition of the money?"

"I'm sure I don't know," Miss Susan answered constrainedly: even such careless reference to Mr. Joseph made her conscious.

Dr. Lavendar felt suddenly cheered. Of course Mrs. Pendleton would not marry Joey. Give up her money for a poor music teacher? Not she! Dr. Lavendar was almost gay.

"Come, Danny," he said, "we must be going home. Well, Utile Dulci, I'm always the better for a talk with you. The fact is, I had something on my mind when I came up, but I believe it will all come out right."

"Has Job been troubling you again?" Miss Susan asked sympathetically. "Is there anything I can do?"

"No, it wasn't Job. I was a little anxious about — about some matter in which I feared Joey was going to be disappointed. Nothing of importance — at least — yes, it's very important; but I didn't mean to speak of his affairs, I'm sure. Well, you've done me good, as you always do, and I'm sure everything will come out all right."

Susan Carr's face flamed; she stepped back from his outstretched hand, the quick tears stinging in her eyes. "Oh — Dr. Lavendar," she stammered.

"Why," he said, peering at her in the dusk, and blinking with astonishment, "why, do you — has he spoken to you?"

"He wrote," faltered Miss Susan, "but that was

a month ago.　I hoped — by this time, he had forgotten it."　Her agitation was apparent.

("Why, how she feels it!"　Dr. Lavendar thought. "*She* knows what a fool the Pendleton woman is.")

"You are a good friend," he said warmly. "Joseph couldn't have done better than write to you, — though he did not mention to me that he had done so.　No, he hasn't forgotten it; and, my dear Miss Susan, this is the time to prove your friendship for Joey; he never needed it more than he does now. Of course I couldn't have spoken to you before he did, but I can't tell you what a relief it is to know that he has done it himself.　I depend on you, Susan.　I might as well tell you I have been very anxious and distressed about it."　He sighed deeply; "However, what you have said makes me feel better."

Poor Susan Carr nearly wept.　"Oh, Dr. Lavendar, *please* don't!　I can't bear to have you speak of it.　It's no use — and — and I'm so unhappy, so disappointed."

Unhappy? disappointed?　Dr. Lavendar stood, with his mouth open, looking at her.　Why was Susan Carr so overcome at this prospect of Joey's foolishness?　He saw how tightly her hands were clasped on the back of a chair in front of her; he heard her voice break and tremble.　Could it be that — Dr. Lavendar was appalled.　A terrible possibility flashed into his mind.　"My dear Miss Susan — my dear Miss Susan!" he said.　He forgot the danger that threatened Joey, in his grief at this other grief which he had never suspected. "I can't tell you what this is to me! I had no idea — I never supposed that you — "

"I can't help it," she said faintly; "I'm very sorry. I'm sure I'd do anything I could; but one can't make — affection."

Dr. Lavendar's jaw actually dropped with dismay; he saw in a flash Susan Carr's mortification when, alone, she should reflect upon this extraordinary loss of self-control; he felt his very ears burn for her; he was glad the room was dark, so that he could not see her face; he wanted to get away; and yet her trembling voice went to his heart. He took her hand very tenderly in his. "Good-night, my dear friend," he said. "This — this is very dreadful. But I hope it will not be what we fear. I'll do my part, you may be sure of that; there's nothing I want more, — I'll do my part. Good-night, my dear Susan. God bless you." He took his hat, and went stumbling into the hall, where he paused for a moment, and swallowed once or twice, and winked hard; then she heard him come back. "Susan," he said tremulously, "never mind having spoken to me. I feel your confidence just as though you were my sister, and — and I wish you were!"

XII.

June takes up the sceptre of May
And the land, beneath his sway
Blooms, a dream of blossoming closes,
And the very wind's at play
With Sir Love among the roses.

HENLEY.

"LYSSIE — I beg your pardon — Miss Lyssie" — Roger Carey paused to be told that he was forgiven, and perhaps to hear that he might drop the title; but Miss Drayton did not even smile at the slip or the apology. "Do you know that I've got to go away from Old Chester next week? In fact, by rights I ought to have been at work a week ago."

Alicia, with great presence of mind, asked no explanation of this neglect of duty; she only said that she wondered that anybody liked to be in town in such weather.

"Why, I don't like it!" cried Roger. "You wouldn't think I could like it, Miss Lyssie, if you knew how much I cared for Old Chester."

"Have you really liked Old Chester?" Lyssie said, and blushed; she wished she had said anything but that.

"It is like heaven!" Roger Carey declared, in a low voice.

"Is it?" Alicia asked, with entire seriousness.

" I have n't traveled about very much, but it always seemed to me pleasant."

Lovers, so far as they themselves are concerned, have no sense of humor; Roger never noticed Lyssie's literalness.

" Yes," he said, " like heaven ! "

It was dusk, and he, instead of Philip, was walking home with Miss Drayton. Eric was jogging along behind them, leaving them for moments to themselves when a rustle in the hedge or the whir of a wing was too enticing for the responsibility of chaperonage, but coming back again, with a side-wise, deprecating glance which said, " My young friends, this shall never happen again."

Roger was enchanted to be alone with her, but not because he had any special purpose in view. In fact, he had quite made up his mind that a young man with no special income has no right to have any special purpose in regard to a nice girl. Indeed, a lack of income, together with periods of uncertainty as to whether she is, after all, completely and exactly the woman who can satisfy every need of a man's soul, is surely an excuse for being without such purpose when walking home with her.

Yet, as Roger Carey was going away from Old Chester, he was, not unnaturally, glad of this last chance to see Miss Alicia Drayton. He had not had the forethought — he would have seen fit to name it conceit — to consider that, as he had no special purpose, it might be well to shield her from himself. He was too absorbed in watching her ; in answering her little questions, drawing out her little opinions, smothering his laughter at her sweet, unworldly views; too absorbed in feeling that he should like to kneel down and kiss her little feet, and tell her she made him want to be a good man, to give any thought to such responsibilities.

"I 'm not in love," he had assured himself several times during the last week. The sort of woman with whom Mr. Carey had long ago decided that he should probably fall in love was far enough removed from this good child. Still, it must be admitted that he had insisted upon his loveless condition far less during the last day or two, and he did not think of it at all as they walked along now in the dusk, talking of nothing in a voice that meant all things.

He told her that he hoped he should not forget to go and say good-by to Mrs. Pendleton ; and she assured him, simply enough, that he could not forget it.

"Why, it would be unkind to forget it!" she reminded him, with a surprised look.

"Well, the fact is, she 's not overfond of me, I fancy," Roger defended himself. "I 'm one of the relations to whom her money would go if she married again, you know. That was an outrageous will of my cousin's. Ben was a cub."

"I should n't have thought he would have wanted to *buy* her faithfulness," Lyssie announced, with a little toss of her head.

"No, would you? Love like that is not love. Love does n't need any chains." Here he sighed deeply, for joy of the moonlight, and the scent of the new hay in a field on their right, and the glorious word sweet upon his lips. " Love is immortal, don't you think so? Second marriages, anyhow, seem to me sacrilege."

This he really felt, being at the moment very young. But Alicia said, nervously, with a suspicion of age in her manner, " Well, not always."

And Roger, much confused, remembered Mr. William Drayton, and turned the subject.

" Let's go out on the river; that little boat down by the bridge belongs to you, Philip said. Won't you? "

" Oh, I'm afraid I ought n't to," faltered Alicia, — " mother might need me; but I'd like to so much! Oh well, just for a few minutes."

So they turned, and walked down the street and out toward the bridge, where, under a leaning birch, Alicia's rowboat was tied to a small float, which rocked and swayed as Roger jumped down on it. He hauled in on the painter slippery with dripping water grasses; some yellowing birch leaves had drifted under a thwart, and he brushed them out, and said, ruefully, that the boat seemed a little damp, but —

" Oh, dampness does n't matter," said Alicia, (the idea of thinking about dampness!) and she laughed, and took the hand that Roger, kneeling to hold the skiff against the float, reached up to her. But there was a look in his upturned face that made her heart give a sudden beat. " Oh, really, I'm afraid I ought n't to go," she said, breathless. " It's late, and — "

"Get in, please," said Mr. Carey; and she got in, meekly, for there was that in his voice that took the matter out of her hands. She felt that she must talk, rapidly, without a single pause, of — anything! Eric would do: was n't he the dearest old fellow? Sometimes she thought he had some spaniel blood in him, he was so fond of the water. He often went in after sticks. Did Mr. Carey think he would swim after them now?

"I hope you don't think I 'm a stick," Roger retorted, his breath catching in a nervous laugh at his own feeble joke.

Eric, however, sat down upon the float, and made no effort to follow them. He thumped his tail a little, as though to say, "I trust you; but I shall stay right here and watch you, my children;" and as the boat pushed rustling through the lily pads and out into the middle of the stream, he looked at them benignly, until his big black nose dropped between his paws, and it was an effort to lift one eyelid for an occasional glance into the twilight.

The river, full of shadowy quiet, was so deep that there was not even the silken, slipping sound of a ripple. Roger Carey had fallen silent. How sweet she was, in her white dress, sitting there in the little old boat, her eyes looking so shyly into his, her voice speaking what was always his own best thought. "Dear little soul!" he said under his breath; he wanted to take her in his arms and kiss her. He did not stop to inquire whether he was in love with her; the moment and the moonlight were too much for such cynical speculations; he felt his heart beating fast as he looked at her; the tears stood in his eyes. "Dear little soul! how sweet she is, how *good* she is." Roger Carey was experiencing religion.

"How black the trees look, don't they?" said Alicia.

"Yes."

The skiff rocked and swayed, and the water gurgled softly at the prow; the branches of a sycamore on the left and a beech on the right nearly met in midstream; the green dusk began to wink with fireflies, and from far above, through the domes of the treetops, the faint moonlight filtered down, and broke here and there upon the water in a slipping film of icy shine, that sparkled and was lost, and sparkled again.

"It's growing pretty dark?" Lyssie observed.

"Yes, rather."

Another silence, melodious with the rhythmic dip of the oars and the low brush and rustle of lily pads. "I never supposed I could be so much in love," Roger thought, profoundly moved. The water ran black and silent between the straight staves of the arrowheads and past the sides of the boat; he could see her finger tips dragging lightly upon it; once she leaned over and caught a lily, and there was a soft tug of restraint upon the skiff's smooth progress, until the long stem yielded and she pulled it in, and then seemed absorbed in studying its fragrant, tremulous heart.

“The lilies are lovely, are n’t they?” she said. Her voice had a nervous thrill in it.

“Yes; oh, very.”

“I think perhaps we ’d better go back now?”

“Yes!” he assented, with sudden alacrity. “I — I can’t seem to talk, somehow; you seem so far off, down at that end. Let ’s go ashore.”

“Oh, I don’t mind staying out a little longer,” Alicia said quickly. She held tightly to the sides of the boat, as though she would detain it, and postpone that beautiful moment whose gracious steps she heard coming nearer and nearer.

But Roger cut deep into the flowing blackness of the slow current, and the skiff swung in a rocking circle and pointed down stream. “It ’ll take me ten minutes to get back to that float!” he said savagely, and sighed and bent to his oars. His thought, if he had spoken it, would have been, “Why did I get into this confounded thing? Why did n’t I speak on the road?” The boat shot with steady pulls down the river.

“I don’t like to talk at arm’s length,” Roger announced.

Lyssie seemed to have nothing to say.

“If we were in the house it would be better. I could — I could — we could talk, I mean.”

Lyssie, apparently, had no opinions. He looked over at her, and his lips trembled.

“Just see the fireflies!” Alicia said faintly; and Roger Carey, struggling to hold both oars in one hand, flung out the other toward her.

"Oh, Lyssie, Lyssie, I love you! I — did you know I loved you? Do you love me a little? Lyssie!"

Oh, that wonderful shining moment of silence while a girl gets her breath after hearing those words; when the tears rush to her eyes, and her soft throat trembles, and her heart swells suddenly with the passion and the pain of joy! "*I love you! Did you know I loved you? Do you love me a little?*" She says the words over and over, and thinks she has answered him; but she is silent.

"I 'm not good enough to tie your little shoes; of course I know that. (Oh, this boat!) I can't talk about it, somehow, here. But if I can ever get back to that float I can — I can say, you know, that you are as far above me as a star in heaven."

"I?" said little Lyssie under her breath. "Oh!"

The skiff came pushing through lily leaves, and bumped softly against the crumbling wooden pier; the low voice of the river sang between them.

"*Lyssie?*"

He let the oars catch and swing backwards, and rose with an impetuous step. The boat rocked and dipped. Lyssie caught desperately at the sides.

"Oh, don't — yes!" she said, the happy tears breaking in her voice.

Roger sat down. "Did you say Yes?"

Alicia nodded; she could not speak.

Without a word, Roger pulled the boat in against the pier; he got out very carefully, and with a silent but not ungentle movement of his heel instructed the affectionate and joyous Eric to keep out of the way; then he knelt down to tie the skiff, and felt sharp between his fingers the cold smoothness of the river grasses tangled along the rope; he saw the white feather of water under the boat's prow as the current struck it; he heard the wash of the float swaying under his weight; he heard the soft break in the breath of the girl who loved him. How alert, how conscious, how wonderful, the supreme moment!

"Lyssie! say it — just once more?"

He had no difficulty in talking now; he could hardly wait to hear again that enchanting word before he burst into the telling of his love. And how she listened! Her listening was almost as beautiful as any words she spoke. But she did not speak many.

"Yes;" "yes;" "yes." She loved — she knew — she felt — Oh, symphony of assent!

Roger said he was poor; Alicia loved poverty. He said he had no "prospects" outside of his profession; she thought "prospects" ruinous to real achievement. He confessed that his practice was small; Lyssie felt that if it were large it would be a sign that he was eager to make money.

"There's so much more than that in living," the young girl said, looking at him with believing eyes. "I know how you feel about mere money-making; I heard you talk to Philip and Cecil about responsibility, and — and I liked what you said."

"I didn't know you ever listened when I talked. You always looked so remote — so — so above all

the rest of us. Oh, Lyssie, when did you first begin
to care the least bit?"

"I think — I think it was the day you looked at
the pigeons; no, it was the day before that. Oh, I
don't mean that I" — she looked the word she
could not speak — "but I liked to hear you talk."

Perhaps it is only when a man looks back upon it
that he realizes the charm of a little coquetry on such
occasions; at the moment, Roger felt only the noble
simplicity of her confession, the benediction of her
tender, overflowing eyes.

"Why, that was the day I came!" he said rap-
turously.

"When did you first know that you cared?" she
said, divinely shy and bold at once.

"I? Why — well— Oh, I think it must have
been the minute I saw you; only, of course I did n't
recognize it myself, you know, until later."

They walked slowly along the road. It was dark,
and they were leaving Old Chester behind them;
but Lyssie was not aware of either fact; she did not
remember her mother and her duty for nearly an
hour, and then it was with a start of dismay and
remorse.

So they came back to actual life, and Roger
Carey realized that he had fallen in love, and was
an engaged man. He was very much astonished,
but he found it very delightful.

They turned toward Old Chester, and Roger began to be silent. Lyssie's stillness fell into his like
chords of music melting into some larger harmony.

She would have been content never to speak again, she thought. It seemed as though all were said, forever. But Roger had something to say, though he did not say it until they stood at Alicia's door. Then, very low, very anxiously, "Lyssie, do you know? I'm going to kiss you before you go in."

"Oh!" said Lyssie, "are — are you?"

"Yes," Roger answered, very gently. And then he took her hands, and, with delicate precision, he kissed her on her left cheek, just below her ear.

"Oh — oh!" said Alicia. At which he took her instantly in his arms, and kissed her heartily right on her lips. After that, it took nearly twenty minutes of adieus to fortify themselves for absence overnight.

"You will come to-morrow morning?"

"Yes! Yes! May I come as early as half past eight?"

"Oh, I'm afraid that is a little early — "

"Well, eight forty-five?"

"And I will tell mother to-night; and will you tell Cecil?"

At which Mr. Carey said abruptly, "No; you tell her, Lyssie."

Tell Cecil Shore? Speak to such a woman of such an experience? He thought, tenderly, that Lyssie could never understand why, at such a noble moment, a man could be repelled by her sister. He rejoiced in her ignorance; perhaps because at that time he did not need the tolerance or the sympathy which such ignorance of life forever precludes.

Lyssie, after yet one more impassioned "Good-night!" went into the house and closed the door upon her lover. She stood still in the hall, listening to his retreating footsteps, with her hands over her face and the sound of her own pulses in her ears.

Then she went into her mother's room, where, in the lamplight, her eyes vague with happiness and the summer darkness, everything seemed blurred and dazzled; perhaps that was why she did not see the fretful look on Mrs. Drayton's face. She went, like a child, to her mother's knee, and, slipping down on the floor, hid her face in her bosom. "Oh, mother, mother!" she murmured.

"What is it? Is anything the matter?" cried Mrs. Drayton, with nervous sharpness.

"Mother — *Roger!*"

Mrs. Drayton fell back in her chair. "Oh, Alicia, can you never remember how weak I am? You come bouncing into the room, and at such an hour, too! It's nine o'clock. I've been terrified about you. I thought something had happened. You have no consideration at all; you know how anxiety makes my head ache — " She fretted on, half in tears, and then suddenly seemed to remember Lyssie's whispered word. "Roger? What do you mean by 'Roger'? Why, do you mean — has he — Why, Lyssie!"

"Oh, mother darling, yes! Just think of it. *Me!*"

The tears sprang to Mrs. Drayton's eyes. She put her arms about the kneeling child, and they trembled with unconscious tenderness. "Oh, my dear, my dear!" Mrs. Drayton forgot herself; she kissed and cried over the girl with honest mother love. She asked a hundred sympathetic questions, which Lyssie answered dreamily, with little tender reserves, which would break suddenly because of the bliss of putting such wonderful facts into words.

After the first reality of it, Mrs. Drayton could not help glancing over Lyssie's head into the mirror. It was a pretty picture : the frail mother, with her delicate, pallid face ; the girl kneeling at her feet ; the flood of soft lamplight shining on the open pages of the Bible on the table.

"My *child!*" murmured Mrs. Drayton, resting her cheek on Lyssie's hair. It was a charming scene.

"Oh, mother," said Alicia, with a long sigh, "putting aside any personal feeling, — I mean, speaking impartially, as a matter of judgment, — I am certainly a very fortunate girl. He is not at all like anybody else ; he is — well, mother, just wait till you know him!"

Mrs. Drayton was not disturbed by Lyssie's halting language ; she had plenty of words of her own. She began to speak of the glory of duty, the joy of self-sacrifice, — in a word, of love, — in a way which satisfied even this young lover at her feet. Indeed, so perfect was the situation that it would have been still prolonged but for Lyssie's sudden realization that it was long after Mrs. Drayton's bedtime. With a happy sigh she rose, and made

haste to begin her loving task of maid. Mrs.
Drayton's hair had to be brushed steadily for a
quarter of an hour before it could be put up in curl
papers; then a psalm must be read, and the selec-
tion for the day in Gathered Pearls.

" Oh, mother dear, how selfish in me to have kept
you up!" Lyssie said. " It will be nearly eleven
before you are in bed."

" Oh well, a girl can't be engaged every day,"
said Mrs. Drayton magnanimously. " I'm willing
to sacrifice something; we won't read to-night. I
can think of my blessed Bible, and repeat a hymn
while I lie awake. Of course I shall lie awake after
this excitement. But never mind that."

Lyssie winced; but she thought that now, since
Roger loved her, she would be, for the rest of time,
unselfish and considerate. She would be *good!*
She was very tender to her mother, with a tender-
ness which was half remorse because of her own joy.
" I have n't done all I might to make her happy,"
Lyssie was thinking; " and her life is so empty with-
out papa."

The emptiness of life may have struck Mrs.
Drayton, for she took occasion, when Lyssie kissed
her good-night, to say that she had been lonely.

" You were very late in coming home," she said.
" It was rather sad to sit here all by myself. But
you were happy, so I don't complain."

Alicia opened her lips to speak, but stopped; a
strange apprehension gathered in her heart. It was
too vague for words, but a little mist crept across

her joy. Her mother lonely without her? Well, but how would it be when she was — She did not say the word, but she adored it in her heart. How would Mrs. Drayton feel when —

Lyssie kissed her again silently, and crept softly o her own room.

XIII.

BLAKE.

OLD CHESTER grew quite wide awake over Alicia Drayton's engagement. There had been no such sensation since Miss Jane Temple married beneath her, and found happiness and content in the home of the village apothecary. Of course Lyssie's romance could not compare in interest to Miss Temple's; it did not have in it anything of which Old Chester could disapprove, — and to be truly interesting to the world about us, we must not be too good. Lyssie's engagement only gave opportunity for conversation and speculation. "What will Frances Drayton do when the child gets married?" everybody said to everybody else, although, so far, no one had said it to Mrs. Drayton, who was enjoying very much the importance of being the mother of her daughter. It was almost as good as making a sensation herself; indeed, she entered into the situation with so much histrionic earnestness that she was obliged to take to her bed, and receive Mrs. Dale and all the other ladies, reclining upon her pillows, attended by Alicia. It was thus that Cecil found her listening to Mrs. Pendleton's congratulations, allowing Lyssie to fan her, and saying many noble things about a mother's joy in a child's happiness.

" I enter so into Lyssie's romance," said Mrs. Drayton, " that I live my own over again."

" Except," Cecil returned, after that meditative pause which gave such weight to her slow words, — " except that no youthful indiscretion made Mr. Carey a widower, he must indeed remind you of papa. But I almost think, Mrs. Drayton, that in entering into Lys's romance yourself you keep her out of it a little. She can't listen to lover's vows and fan you at the same time."

There was an eager disclaimer from Lyssie, and Mrs. Drayton said tearfully that it was a little bitter to have Cecil, who was exactly like her own child, (some one had once asked Susan Carr which was Mr. Drayton's child by his first wife; she did not know whether she had ever mentioned that to Mrs. Pendleton?) — it certainly was a little bitter to have Cecil speak so to her.

As for Mrs. Pendleton, she thought to herself that there was some truth in Mrs. Shore's remarks; but she only said, soothingly, that she had no doubt dear Roger would rather have Miss Alicia dutiful than have her society.

" I am inclined to think," Mrs. Shore observed, " that Mr. Carey would feel that one included the other." And then she wrung from Mrs. Drayton an angry consent that Lyssie should dine with her that night, and went away, saying to herself that she hoped she had done some good.

"He leaves Old Chester in three days," she thought, "and Lys, poor little thing, ought to see more of him." But she was not very hopeful; she knew how probable it was that Lyssie, from a sense of duty, would yield to her mother's demands upon her time; indeed, Mrs. Shore had long since recognized that Alicia's especial form of selfishness was unselfishness.

This immoral unselfishness is characteristic of many excellent women. They practice an abnegation of their comforts, their rights, their necessities, even, which they feel endears them to their Maker, and at the same time gives them real happiness. Apparently they are unable to perceive that this unselfishness of theirs brutalizes and enslaves to self the man (for men are generally the victims of this unscrupulous virtue),—the man who accepts the sacrifices made for him, indeed often thrust upon him in spite of his gradually weakening protests; and young Alicia, painfully conscientious as she was, never once realized that, if it were selfish for her mother to accept a sacrifice, it was a sin for her to make it.

As for Cecil, she did not put it quite that way to herself, but little Lyssie's foolishness struck her with a sense of being pathetic. "Little goose," she thought, smiling. But she was very gentle with Alicia, looking at her with a half-wondering amusement.

"You are very happy, kitty, are n't you?" she said that evening, when, before dinner, the two sisters were alone in the library. "You are very happy?"

Alicia's face, so radiant and young, sobered suddenly, almost to tears. "Oh, *Ceci!*" she said, and put her face down on Cecil's shoulder and was silent for a moment. Something came into the eyes of the elder woman, that mist that sometimes dims the eyes of a dog, which cannot weep, but yet can suffer; it is unutterably sad, but it is not a spiritual pain.

"You poor little thing," she said, almost passionately.

Lyssie looked up, wondering. But Cecil only laughed, though the tears stood in her eyes.

> "'Always to woo, and never to wed,
> Is the happiest life that ever was led!'"

she cried gayly. "Go on being engaged, pussy; it is really very good fun."

"I never *thought* of anything else!" protested Alicia, even her slender neck crimsoning; and Mrs. Shore laughed until she cried at the innocence of the child. But the situation seemed to her a cruel one; Lyssie was so happy!

Cecil did not think very much about Mr. Carey; if she had, she would have discovered in herself an astonishment at his conduct which was almost contempt. Her mind was dwelling upon certain miserable facts which are thrust upon all of us men and women when we soberly observe the marriage relation as we see it about us, especially when we observe it in contrast to this first beautiful dawn of love in the faces of two young lovers; two who believe — as they all do, or else they are not lovers — that they, out of all the world of failures about them, shall make permanent that which is by its nature evanescent and fleeting, the mystery and passion of young love. They need — ah, what deep experiences, before they can know, two such sweet optimists, that it is as foolish to hope that they will keep love forever young and mad and wonderful as it would be to seek to hold back the dim beauty of the dawn, which must change, perhaps into a leaden and dreary day, perhaps into the calm glory of the sunlight; into a noon serene and perfect and secure as the light upon the face of God, — the noon of married love!

Cecil Shore believed only in the dawn. "Poor little thing!" she thought again, pityingly, as she watched Alicia's frank happiness. How cruel it was that it could not last! These two sometime would be among that great army of husbands and wives who are not unhappy, not incompatible, who "get along very well with each other," as they would say, — the very husbands and wives who give little smiles and shrugs at the ecstasies of young love as they observe it; the men and women who, simply, have missed the best. Cecil was not thinking of the miserable marriages, — there were such things, no doubt; there were infidelities, cruelties, baseness; but when they happened in her class they were concealed. No, it was only the grotesque disillusionment of it all that struck her with grim amusement. "Poor little Lys!" she thought.

But no one could have seemed to need pity less than Alicia Drayton. It might better have been bestowed on her lover, who felt conscious and half irritated all the time they were at table. He wished Philip were at home; he was grateful to Molly for talking to him; he wished Lyssie (bless her dear little heart!) would not be quite so — so young; he wished Mrs. Shore, with her slightly cynical smile, were drowned in the depths of the sea. Without the slightest reason, he began to be angry with her; he answered one of her assertions apropos of some discussion about the working classes so curtly that Alicia looked apprehensively at her sister; but Cecil, strangely enough, seemed more hurt than offended. She colored, and said that Mr. Carey had certainly misunderstood — she had not meant quite what he supposed; and she tried by a hasty explanation to bring a certain seriousness into her flippant statement that the submerged tenth was as necessary to the higher civilization, to the culture of the few, as a fertilizer was to a flower garden.

Roger Carey said carelessly, " Do you think your culture and mine quite worth such manure ? Think of the misery of the sweating system, for instance ! Perhaps you are worth it, Mrs. Shore, but I 'm sure I 'm not."   But when he saw the pain and truth in Alicia Drayton's face, as she said, " When I see ready-made clothing, I always wonder, ' Who suffered for that ? ' " he felt ashamed of having paraded his irritation in the dress of a fine sentiment; so he became rather more frankly rude to Mrs. Shore to console himself.

Lyssie was quite discouraged, and gave him that little appealing look which we see so often on the faces of those dear souls who long to have us do ourselves justice. It said, "Oh, be nice, Roger; don't be so — not-as-pleasant-as-usual." But Roger continued to be "not-as-pleasant-as-usual" until he got away from Mrs. Shore; and then — ah, well, a girl knows of no adjective to describe her lover in those adorable first moments when she has him to herself, and he is even more pleasant than usual.

Roger was to go away on Tuesday, and he wanted to be with Lyssie every moment that he could. He was still vaguely astonished to find himself in love; but he liked it. And he was distinctly cross when Mrs. Shore mentioned, casually enough, on Monday, that he would not be able to see Lyssie that afternoon.

"Really you must be a little firmer," she said. "She was to have gone to the upper village this morning on some stupid errand for her mother; but Mrs. Drayton wished to be fanned, so she had to put it off until this afternoon; she could just as well have gone this morning. You must teach her some of your firmness, Mr. Carey."

"This afternoon!" said Roger blankly. "Why, I thought I could see her this afternoon."

"Oh well, later you *can* see her, — when she comes back; about five, I think. Meantime, I'll entertain you by taking you out to drive. No, you can't go with Lyssie," she silenced him, smiling. "She has started by this time. The people dine here, you know, at half past twelve, so she started nearly an hour ago."

Roger resigned himself to a drive with his hostess with an ill grace. "She'll be back by five, surely?" he asked, and intimated to Mrs. Shore that he cared to drive with her only until that hour.

And no one was more surprised than Roger Carey to find himself at half past six, driving into Old Chester on the way back to his hostess's door.

"Why," he said, "why, what time is it? Are we back again?" He looked at his watch, and turned red, and said something under his breath. How *could* he have forgotten? He asked himself the question a dozen times, finding no satisfactory answer. But it was not so very remarkable; human nature is human nature. For one thing, his companion was a beautiful woman; but beside that she could talk. To Roger Carey discussion was like the breath in his nostrils, and when Mrs. Shore took him to task for a statement of his, that, without the great human experience of friendship, a soul was still potential, he grew keen and interested, and intent upon making his point. Cecil had declared that friendship was very beautiful, — if there were such a thing, and he had burst out in condemnation of the insinuation. But her remark had been genuine enough: she had never experienced friendship; she had known no schoolgirl frenzies of letters and copied poems and exchanged locks of hair, — all that rehearsal of love with which young women so seriously amuse themselves, but which so often cools into sincere and lifelong regard. Roger told her, frankly, that he was sorry for her, and added his conviction of her potentiality. Curious that this topic of friendship is so especially alluring to a man and woman between whom friendship is impossible !

After that their discussion turned upon the abstractions of truth and duty and conduct, and Roger Carey, in his perfectly straightforward earnestness, fell into that courteous trap of " you and I ; " " you and I think," or " feel," or " know better."

There is no more subtle flattery from an intelligent man to an intelligent woman than this " you and I ; " it is an intellectual caress, and the mind responds to it with an abandon which betrays its ethical effect. Roger was too interested to be aware of anything more than an added brilliancy in his companion's look, an added force in her words. But his interest made him forget that Lyssie would be back from her errand to the upper village at five. Now, realizing his forgetfulness, he was angry at himself, with that painful anger which was only a form of astonishment at his own possibilities. He was plainly sulky with Mrs. Shore, which was most unjust, for Cecil, though she laughed at him a little, was really sorry. " I never thought of Lys," she said ; " it 's too bad ! You were too entertaining, Mr. Carey. She will never forgive — "

An exclamation from Roger made her turn, and she saw, in the meadow on her right, Lyssie and Molly, and, further off, her husband struggling with a drunken man.

XIV.

ALICIA, it appeared, had come hurrying back from her errand to the upper village, and, finding no Roger awaiting her, looked half puzzled and half disturbed, until Esther told her that she had seen Mr. Carey drive by with "Miss Cecil." It was all right, if Roger were being entertained; but before she had time to speculate as to his return Philip came striding up the path and into the hall.

"Lys! where are you?" he called out, so heartily that she knew, as she ran downstairs, that he knew — the one thing in the world worth knowing! "Carey wrote me about it," he said, "and I got off the stage at the gate to come in and tell you that he's a good fellow, but he'll have to do his best to be good enough for you!"

"Were n't you very much surprised, though, Philip?" she said, with a blush all over her happy face.

"Well, no, I can't say that I was *very* much surprised," Philip confessed, greatly amused.

"Oh, were n't you? I was," Alicia answered him, shy but serious. "Oh, Philip, you're laughing!"

But his face was so tender that Lyssie forgave the laugh. Then he asked where Roger was, and, learn-

ing, had a suggestion to make. "Let's go over to
East Hill and look at the mowers; you can watch
the street from there, and see the carriage the moment it appears."

There was something in the simple way in which
Philip took for granted the impatient and pretty
folly of a lover that made Alicia full of happy ease.
He had not that laugh in the eye which says, "Oh,
it is sweet, it is pretty ; but you'd better make the
most of it while it lasts."

"I'll go and get Molly, and join you there,"
Philip said, when she had agreed to come as soon as
she had seen whether her mother was quite comfortable.

But it takes a good while to make some people
comfortable. Philip had been in the field ten minutes before Alicia, her face sobered, arrived. Mrs.
Drayton had seized the opportunity to implant an
arrow in the child's tender conscience, by speaking
of Alicia's indecorous haste to see her lover, and her
selfish indifference to her mother's loneliness.

"Here I sit all day long, and you never think
what it is to me to be shut out from society," she
sighed. "If it were not for the companionship of
my blessed Bible, and my own thoughts of how I
shall be recompensed some day for all I've borne
here, I don't see how I could endure it !"

"Mother, dear, of course I won't go, if you want
me to stay," Alicia protested.

But Mrs. Drayton shook her head. "I want you
to *want* to stay, Lyssie. I don't care for unwilling

service. Go, go! you'll be late." Then she drew
in her breath in a meek sob. "Perhaps, though,
you will be willing to wait one moment, if it's something for yourself? I want to pin this rose in your
hair. Kneel down."

Alicia, with a little sigh, knelt, and her mother
put the rose against the soft coil of hair behind her
ear. Mrs. Drayton did not declare that she was returning good for evil; but Lyssie felt the scorch of
coals of fire, as her mother intended she should. Indeed, as an expression of pure malice, the heaping
of coals of fire may be as telling as a blow; poor
Lyssie, feeling, as she walked over to the meadow,
the soft touch of the rose upon her neck, heard those
words about loneliness ringing in her ears, and asked
herself again, with dismay, "What will she do
when —"

The grass on the long slope of East Hill had been
cut and stacked into cocks some days before, but in
the level light the stubbly floor of the field, barred
by long shadows from the buttonwood-trees that
edged its western side, looked smooth and soft.
There was the scent of new hay in the air; and the
whole stretch of the valley, clasped by the far-off
curve of the river, lay like a green cup, brimmed
with warm and silent peace. Going from one small
haymow to another was a cart drawn by two white
steers; three men were loading it, and a woman,
who had climbed into it, was forking and trampling
the hay into place, her strong young figure standing
out clear against the ochre glow of the sunset.

Alicia perceived with amusement that one of the men was her brother-in-law; and then she caught sight of Molly, curled up against a little haystack, plaiting three stalks of grass to make a ring. Molly welcomed her eagerly.

"Aunt Lyssie, shall I have to say 'uncle Roger' to Mr. Carey?" she inquired.

"Oh, Molly, hush, you little goose!" said Lyssie, her face full of charming color. "Look at your father making hay; and is n't that Eliza Todd, raking, on the other side of the cart?"

"I saw father long ago," Molly announced. "Is n't it funny for father to work when he does n't have to? He did it once before, all day. Mamma said he was singular. What's 'singular,' aunt Lyssie?"

"What you are when you are remarkably good," Alicia said significantly.

Molly did not pursue the subject. She returned to braiding her bits of grass, and sang a strange rune to herself, something after this fashion: —

> "Minnows, minnows, minnows,
> Live in water,
> Wriggling,
> Wriggling.
> The sun shines on 'em in the water.
> They wriggle,
> Up the stream.
> Where the sun shines in the water,
> The spotted minnows wriggle."

Alicia laughed under her breath, and motioned to Philip, who had joined her, to listen. They looked at each other, smiling. Philip, fanning himself with his hat, waited until Molly's song sank into a whisper, and then said : —

"The epic is in us all, is n't it? Have you been here long, Lys? Oh, Lyssie, this is the way to live! It is splendidly material, and a man takes to it so that I begin to think the other side of us is abnormal, the soul is an excrescence. Yes, I 'd like to make hay or dig potatoes."

"I should n't like to work!" Molly announced, coming to clamber over her father, and then settling comfortably down in his arms. "I 'd rather play. Mamma said you were ' singular ' to work, father. Mamma said —"

"Philip," Alicia broke in, with all the haste of embarrassment, "did Mr. Miller's work satisfy the judges?"

"No; I 'm sorry, but it does n't warrant any further encouragement."

"Cecil said, if it did n't, she was going to send him some money," Lyssie said. "She 's awfully generous, is n't she?"

"She enjoys giving, I think," Philip answered briefly, and added, irrelevantly, that he thought the haymakers had a pretty good time. "Oh, see that attitude!" he interrupted himself, sitting up straight, and putting on his glasses to look at the woman in the cart. She was standing, her weight on her left hip, her face crimsoning with exertion, the muscles of her arms, as she raised a forkful of hay and leaned backwards to balance it, lifting into swelling curves. The hay in its place and trodden down, she stopped

to draw a full breath, and with her bare oent arm
brush back the hair that had fallen across her hot
face. Even at this distance Alicia could see her
splendid vigor. There was a certain superb well-
being about her, as absolutely material as the warm
scent of the grass, or the stretch of shadows over
the clean field, or the faded colors in the stubble.
Standing there knee-deep in the hay, flecking the
sweat from her forehead with an impatient finger,
she seemed as organic and unconscious as the rocks
and trees. Philip, watching her, said again whim-
sically, " Yes, yes, it 's better so ; she is n't going to
tear her soul for any mere ideals ! "

A sense of spiritual weariness came upon him; a
longing for that life which is as far from sin as it is
from virtue, — the life of some men and women, and
of the beasts that perish.

Molly, who had trotted off to pick a flower, came
running back out of the sunset with two red lilies,
which she presented, in solemn childish fashion, to
her father and aunt. " There 's a man over there,"
she said, — " I guess his legs are sick ; they wabble.
Look, father."

"Oh, I fear his legs are sick," Philip agreed.
" Poor Job ! Lyssie, suppose you go along with
Molly. I 'm afraid he may be conversational."

" Oh, Philip, is n't he a little — "

" A *little !* " said Philip, as he caught Job's
raised and stammering voice. " I should say so.
Go, dear, go ! " Then he picked himself up lazily,
and brushed the hay from his coat, and lounged

down to the other side of the field, where he stood, his hands in his pockets, observing the situation. Cecil's carriage had just come in sight, but his back was toward the road, and he did not see it.

Job Todd was not an attractive object; he was drunk, but, unfortunately, not quite drunk enough to have passed the ugly stage. His poor brute face was dully purple, his small, cunning eyes swam in stagnant film, and his loose lips moved in thick, stumbling words.

"Where is that damned woman o' mine?" he demanded, putting his legs wide apart, to stand more steadily.

"Oh, Job!" quavered Eliza.

The girl who was forking the hay into place stopped and peered over at the scene, and the two men drew together, and said pacifically, "There, now, Job."

"Job, don't! Oh!" Eliza cried out, writhing away from the heavy hand he laid on her shoulder.

"You come home. You get my supper. I 'll break your damned head if you don't tend up to your business."

"Oh, I 'll come, I 'll come," she said tremulously, dropping her wooden rake, and walking along a little in front of him.

Philip walked in the same direction. "Hullo, Job," he said good naturedly. "Don't you think you 'd better let Mrs. Todd go on with her work?"

But Job, with vast contempt, refused to notice Mr. Shore's remark; he stooped to pick up Eliza's discarded rake, and brandished it in the air, catching himself with a jerk as he lurched forward.

"The old woman," he called out to the group about the cart, "is —" Job's drunken fluency in regard to his wife made some one laugh, and the man, instantly infuriated, turned upon her and struck her, and then staggered and fell, tripped up neatly by Philip Shore's outstretched foot.

"Don't, sir!" the two mowers called out. "He ain't safe, Mr. Shore; don't meddle with him, sir!"

The shock made Job sober for an instant; he got on his legs with surprising quickness. "You want to fight, do you," he said, "you" — and added a string of epithets which made Philip laugh in spite of himself.

"What command of language you have, Todd! No, I'm not anxious to fight. Come, now, behave yourself. Don't be a fool."

"Whose wife is she?" roared Job. "I'm boss in my house. It's more 'an you are in yours, and for a good reason: your wife's worth two of you! But I keep *my* woman in order. Do you see that?" and he made a lunge at Eliza, who ducked and whimpered.

"I'll knock you down if you do that again," said Philip pleasantly, walking between Job and his wife.

"Ye will? Look a' there, then!"

A flame leaped to Philip's eyes. The men, calling wildly to him to "come off," to "stop it," saw him strip off his coat, and, holding up his left arm to guard his head from Job's rake, plant a blow under the drunken man's ear; and then there was an instant of really sharp struggle, until Philip's arm hooked about Job's neck and his right hand caught him under the chin. Todd roared and kicked for a moment, until Philip flung him on the ground.

"Do you want some more? The next time you strike a woman I'll give you some more!" he said, breathless, touching him contemptuously with his foot.

Roger Carey, who had come running down the field, had just reached him, disappointment in every feature.

"You've had it all to yourself!" he cried regretfully, and then gave Job a hand and pulled him to his feet. "Have you been bullyragging Mrs. Todd, you brute?" he said. "I wish I'd been here in time to get a hand in."

As for Cecil Shore, after her first instant of quick admiration for her husband standing there in his shirt sleeves, his clenched hand drawn back as though his very fingers were tingling with desire to leap at Job's throat, she thought of the man's mortification should he realize that she had witnessed his humiliation, and gave the order to drive on. "But Philip really did that well!" she said to herself, smiling. Then her face darkened, and she sighed; her vague dissatisfaction with Lyssie's engagement, or rather with Roger Carey's engagement, came back. She was half sullen and quite absorbed that evening, as poor little Molly learned to her cost.

She came dancing into her mother's room while Cecil was dressing for dinner, and was kissed and cuddled to her heart's content, until Cecil pushed her away gently, and said, " Don't bother me, precious ; mamma must dress. There! you can play with mamma's rings, if you want to."

Molly, enchanted, seized the small satin-lined box, and shook the rings into her lap in a shower of light. How beautiful they were, piled stiff upon her little fingers until she could not shut her hands! Then the charming thought occurred to her that she would string them all on a stalk of grass, and hang them around her mamma's lovely neck. The very joyousness of the plan kept her silent, and, gathering up the front of her dress to hold all this glitter and gleam, she crept out of the room.

Cecil did not notice her absence. She forgot the child and the rings too, until she heard a wail from the garden, down below the terrace. Of course the inevitable accident had happened. A moment later Rosa brought Molly to her mother, and the little girl, catching her breath with fright, tried to explain that the stalk of grass had broken, " and — and the rings — spilt!" In fact, three of them had leaped as though from a sling out into the pool. It seemed as if the smouldering irritation of Cecil's thoughts sprang into flame.

" You naughty little thing!" she cried. " How dare you take my rings out of doors?" And while her lips were still set with anger she punished the child, who screamed with pain and terror, and then pushed her toward Rosa. "Just put her right straight to bed, Rosa. Don't speak another word, Molly, or I'll spank you, you wicked little girl! Rosa, send John down to the pool at once. Tell him he must find the rings to-night. Which are they? Oh, Molly, you horrid child! Rosa, my sapphire has gone! The other two are not so important. But John must find them to-night, somehow."

XV.

And yet she was a happy woman, and a woman whom no one named without good will. It was her own universal good will and contented temper that worked such wonders. She loved everybody, was interested in everybody's happiness, and quicksighted to everybody's merits. — JANE AUSTEN.

OF course the tussle in the hayfield was discussed in Old Chester, and it brought up the question of Eliza's possible danger in remaining with Job. Her possible degradation had been long ago dismissed, or never thought of. The economic propriety of placing upon the community the burden of supporting Job's neglected but increasing family had been pointed out only by innocent, straightforward, sensible Lyssie. The indignity done to marriage by urging the continuance of a relation from which love and respect and tenderness had fled, leaving in their place brutality and lust, had never been considered. But when it came to the chance of physical injury to Eliza, then indeed Old Chester was aroused and perplexed.

"Perhaps we ought to tell her to leave him?" said Miss Susan, worried and anxious. "Maybe, if she left him, he would really turn over a new leaf for the mere discomfort of it; but to separate husband and wife!"

Miss Susan Carr sat in front of her writing-desk, thinking what had best be done. It would be no use to ask Dr. Lavendar; he would say that Eliza must stick to her duty, even if Job cut her throat some fine day while he was drunk. Mrs. Dale took this view too; and these two people certainly ought to know. Dr. Lavendar had had so much experience, and as for Mrs. Dale — well, everybody knew poor Eben Dale's failings. But Susan Carr's first, simple, unecclesiastical, common-sense impulse was to say that Job and Eliza had no business to live together.

Miss Susan, in her swivel chair, staring absently at the cluttered pigeon-holes of her desk, her heels stretched straight out in front of her, her hands thrust down into the pockets of her short sack, pushed out her lips in puzzled and troubled reflection. But suddenly, catching sight of the corner of a letter, she winced, and drew herself together, and thrust back into the half-open little drawer the envelope which held Mr. Joseph Lavendar's proposal.

So far, Miss Carr had succeeded in " staving him off," as she expressed it. No doubt her firm words to Dr. Lavendar had helped her good work, for of course the disappointed older brother must have told Joseph that there was no hope for him; but her own efforts had been unceasing. As this crumpled corner of his letter brought him swiftly to her mind, she congratulated herself upon her success in preventing the declaration which would have resulted in his mortification; but, glad as she was for his sake, she could not help a little pang on her own account. It is hard to lose a friend just because one has acted from a sense of duty. Susan Carr had in all honesty done the kindest thing she knew; but in consequence Joseph Lavendar treated her with unmistakable coldness and offense. In fact, it appeared that he had taken the hint she had tried to give him; and now, with an unreasonableness most admirably feminine, Miss Susan was conscious of feeling, as Mrs. Drayton would have said, "a little bitter."

"He would have had no cause to be unfriendly even if I had refused him, instead of just keeping him from speaking," she reflected, with some spirit; "and I *will* be his friend, I don't care how angry he is!" She did not add, as she had often done before, that he had been Donald's friend, and so of course must be hers; for once she forgot the sweet, faded romance, which lay between her youth and her middle age like a rose pressed between the pages of a book. She sat there in her revolving chair, looking at the confusion of her desk, and wishing that at least Joseph Lavendar knew how heartily she respected and liked him, notwithstanding what she had done. Well, unjust as he might be, it was a comfort to see with what friendliness his brother treated her. Dr. Lavendar showed no resentment; only a troubled gentleness, "as though," said Miss Susan to herself, "he realized just how hopeless it was." She reproached herself for not making more of this comfort. "I *ought* not to be unhappy," she thought. "I 've done my duty, and I 'm sure that ought to be enough of a consolation." But she sighed deeply.

Miss Susan was quite right about Dr. Lavendar's

friendliness. He made a point of seeing her oftener than before; and although he never spoke to her of Joseph, the whole melancholy situation was continually in his thoughts. At first he had been quite overwhelmed by it and altogether hopeless, and, with an injustice as natural as it was deplorable, more bitter than ever toward "the Pendleton woman," as he called her in his own mind.

Indeed, when Mr. Joseph, conscious and uncomfortable, had followed his letter down to Old Chester, his brother had been so unmistakably cold to him that poor Joey felt all his courage ooze away; consequently, that week Mrs. Pendleton's affections did not become engaged. But Dr. Lavendar had not breathed freely until he saw the coach roll off on Monday morning. "Well, he's safe for five days!" he said. Then his mind went back to the estimable Miss Susan; and by and by, in spite of himself, he began to hope. "If Joey can just be made to appreciate Utile Dulci!" he thought; and he decided to try to make Joey appreciative. Now Dr. Lavendar was a wise man, and therefore he was aware that the effort to induce one person to care for another person is generally as successful as the effort to make water run uphill. If he had wanted any proof of this axiom, there was Mr. Joseph's own endeavor in behalf of himself and Mrs. Pendleton. Mere insistence, Dr. Lavendar knew, was not only useless; it was almost prohibitive of the result desired. "So," said Dr. Lavendar in his own mind, "I must be subtle!"

The next Saturday, when Joseph came home, he found his brother in quite a different mood from that which had made his previous visit so melancholy. Dr. Lavendar was eager to tell him about Lyssie's engagement; he had much to say of the way in which Philip had thrashed Job Todd; he was full of the new chapter in The History of Precious Stones; in fact, he spoke of anything and everything but the old bitter subject. And through all his conversation singularly irrelevant remarks about Utile Dulci came in, like the chorus of a Greek play. As for Mr. Joseph, while he was interested to learn of Lyssie's happiness, and was sorry about Job, and listened to Miss Susan's praises respectfully, he had his own business to attend to.

"Brother Jim," he said, as they sat at the tea table that night, and there came a moment's pause in Dr. Lavendar's excited flow of conversation, "brother Jim, it seems only proper to say to you that I mean to — to — to do it to-night."

"Do what?"

"Request the honor of — "

"Oh, Joey, Joey, what a fool you are!" groaned the old clergyman. He pushed his chair back a little, and beat a tremulous tattoo on the table with his shaking fingers. In a moment all his assumed interest in other things disappeared; it was not a time for subtlety, but for action. "Joey, of course I'd never think of betraying the affairs of any of my parishioners to any one else, even to you, but — I

—the fact is—*why don't you go and see Miss Susan?*"

" Miss Susan?" said Joseph Lavendar. " Why should I?   She is no more in sympathy with my views than — than you are, brother Jim," he ended sadly.

Dr. Lavendar, pouring out another cup of tea for himself, his fingers gripping the teapot handle till his knuckles were white, swallowed twice, and said, " Joey, you make me seem impatient; but not at all, not at all.   I am merely — ah — infuriated by your folly !"   Here he noticed his overflowing cup, and put the teapot down.   He was trembling.

Joseph rose silently, and wiped up the tea from the table.

" If you speak to this — lady, that implies, I suppose, marriage?" said Dr. Lavendar, his voice husky with fear.   " But it occurs to me to ask you whether you know that if she marries she must relinquish her fortune?"

Joseph was silent, but his face changed.

" It is asking a good deal of a lady to request her to relinquish her fortune," Dr. Lavendar proceeded breathlessly.

" I did not know that," Mr. Joseph said, in a low voice.   " At least, I may have heard it, but I had forgotten it."

The two brothers looked at each other, and neither spoke.   Dr. Lavendar had played his highest card; he hardly dared to speak, lest he should undo any good which that appeal to Joseph's chivalry might have accomplished. The little dining-room was not very light, and the bare dark top of the table between the brothers made it seem still more sombre. Dr. Lavendar poured out another cup of tea, and drank it defiantly. Mr. Joseph got up, and stood at the window. "It looks a little like rain," he observed.

"That — that will be good for Susan Carr's farm!" Dr. Lavendar exclaimed, breathing hard.

Joseph made no reply.

"Susan is a very superior woman, Joey, don't you think so?"

"Very superior," Mr. Joseph agreed listlessly. There was a look of pained bewilderment in his large, mild eyes. Dr. Lavendar could almost have wept for his brother's lack of intelligence, and for his good Susan's disappointment.

So Joseph did not "do it" that night. He lit the lamp in the library, and pretended to read. He must not give in to James! It would be dishonorable, and a slight to the lady, if his kindliness of word and manner were not followed by a declaration; unless, indeed, this hint about the money and the will should be true? In which case Mr. Joseph would rather suffer the imputation of dishonorable conduct than request a lady to make a sacrifice for his sake. Dr. Lavendar had judged his brother well when he used that argument. Poor Mr. Joseph was very miserable; he said to himself that he hoped Jim was mistaken. Who would know? He thought immediately of Susan Carr. He could ask her help again.

" She *is* kind," he said to himself, — " though she has seemed a little unfriendly of late about this. But Miss Susan has certainly a kind heart."   And so, on Sunday evening, after supper, — which was dull enough, with the constraint and pain between the brothers, — Mr. Joseph said he was going to consult Miss Susan about a voluntary.

" Well, he 's safe for to-night," Dr. Lavendar thought.   " But poor Susan! poor Susan!"   He walked to the gate with Joseph, struggling to find some word to say about her and for her; but nothing came except his rather purposeless insistence upon the fact that Utile Dulci was an intelligent person; " most intelligent, Joey.   Of course I can't talk about other people's affairs, but — but — give her my love, Joey; give Utile Dulci my love, boy, do you hear ? "

Miss Susan was sitting by her round centre table, her feet on a high footstool, her elbows propped on the arms of her chair; she was holding a large book close to her eyes.   She had, for the moment, forgotten her anxieties about Joseph Lavendar in following Smith's directions for ploughing under a potato field to supply the soil with humic acid.   Miss Susan, presenting the soles of stout boots to the caller, and frowning with interest, did not invite any tender confidences; still less so when, hearing Mr. Lavendar's voice, she dropped her book, and, with an awkward clatter, pushed away her footstool, and stood up, red and embarrassed, and almost angry.

Mr. Joseph steadied the tottering footstool, and picked up a newspaper that had slipped rustling to the floor, and made his apologies for having startled his hostess.

"We men are apt to forget the timidity of the gentler sex."

"I 'm not timid," Susan Carr said decidedly.

But Mr. Joseph would not listen to such self-depreciation. "Oh, come, come, Miss Susan, there is nothing more engaging in a lady."

"Well," Miss Carr retorted, her self-possession returning, and struggling to defend herself and him from the inevitable moment which she felt was approaching, "well, you ought to admire my neighbor, then; she, poor little soul, is afraid of a caterpillar!"

"Is she, indeed? Is she, indeed? Yes, I have noticed it in her, — very pleasing; yes." He sat down, his hands on his neat brown broadcloth knees, his face a little wistful and anxious. "I suppose you see a good deal of your neighbor? Your life must be quite lonely, and she doubtless enlivens it, and — "

"Not lonely at all," interposed Miss Susan, the color mounting to her face; "and anyhow, the poor little lady is really so — I don't want to be unkind," cried Susan Carr, scarcely knowing what she said, but willing to hide behind Mrs. Pendleton for protection — "she is so silly, you know. I 'm sure I should rather be alone than talk to Mrs. Pendleton!" There was no malice in this attack, only she must keep Mr. Lavendar silent. She wondered if she might not introduce the subject of soil dressing? "Yes," she said desperately, "I am not lonely. Since Donald's death I have grown used to spending my evenings with my books. I was just reading to-night — "

Mr. Lavendar let her talk on; when she had finished her excited résumé of Smith's admirable work, he said, resignedly, that he did not know much about farming; he remembered that Donald had been very wise in matters of that kind. He spoke absently and rather sadly; and Miss Susan felt that her desperate reference to her dead lover had saved her. And so, although it hurt her curiously, she spoke again of Donald. It seemed to Susan Carr, as she tried to shelter herself under his name, that he had never been so far removed, so truly dead. Far off, with dismay and pain, she saw a strange moment approaching, — a moment when she must acknowledge that her grief for Donald was dead.

Joseph Lavendar did not return to her loneliness; he only asked her, in a constrained way, did she see much of Mrs. Pendleton? And by the bye, did Miss Susan know whether it was true, this gossip that one heard about the will of the late Mr. Pendleton? Mr. Lavendar thought it a most unjust will for any man to make; for his part, he believed that a lady's affections could be engaged a second time — did not Miss Susan think so? — without disloyalty to their first object.

"Indeed I *don't*," she said emphatically, "indeed

I don't! The will? Well, I'm sure I don't know. I've heard so, but of course one can't tell certainly. Perhaps not. But I'm sure it does n't need a will to keep one faithful!"

She was so flurried that Joseph Lavendar looked at her in bewilderment. "You appear to find this subject displeasing," he said mildly. "I did not mean — "

"Oh," stammered Susan Carr, "I don't want to seem unkind, but *don't* — don't! Mr. Joseph, I can't let you. Please *never* speak of it, never!"

Mr. Lavendar rose; the color came into his face, — even his high bald forehead was faintly mottled with red; he opened his lips twice before he said, "Certainly not; certainly not! I beg your pardon, ma'am."

A moment later he bade her good-night, and, with pursed-up lips, bowed himself stiffly out of the room.

As he went home, he hardly remembered to congratulate himself upon the fact that there was at least some uncertainty about the testament of the late Mr. Pendleton, so dumfounded and nearly angry was he at Miss Susan.

"And she used to be so intelligent!" he thought, almost as Dr. Lavendar might have done.

As for Susan Carr, when he had left her, she put her head down on the open pages of the book upon subsoils and cried heartily. "And I like him so much," she said, again and again, "and now he is dreadfully offended!"

She was more worn out by the excitement of this

fencing with her old friend than she would have been by a day's tramp over her farm. After a while she dried her eyes, and looked about the silent room. Yes, it was lonely; Joseph was right. She got up, and, with her hands clasped behind her, walked up and down; once she stopped before Donald's picture. "It has been lonely," she said, staring hard at the faded photograph; "yes, it *has*, Donald!"

She did not sleep well that night; the sense of the solitude of her life was heavy upon her. Even the next morning she stopped once in her busy work about the garden, to sit down on the upper step of the porch and think about her loneliness; her cheery face grew dull, and showed a hint of age about the lips.

"And now, I suppose, I shall even lose the interest of the choir," she thought; "for if Joseph Lavendar will go on being foolish, I've got to give that up; I can't be meeting him without a third person by. And Lyssie won't be very regular, now that she has this new interest. Dear me, what an interest it must be!" She sighed, and stared with unseeing eyes at a scarlet pimpernel which had seized a little root-hold for itself in a crevice at the foot of the steps. She remembered, dully, that she must go down to the barn and see about putting up the stanchions for her Jersey heifer, a pretty creature who was now a mother, and so must have a stall, and put her deerlike head between the stanchions, and forget her careless life in meadows and upland pastures.

Miss Susan had been greatly interested in Clover's pedigree, and her "coming in," and the butter quality of the milk; but somehow, this morning it all seemed dull and flat. To look after a cow's comfort, or decide on the necessity of tan bark for the strawberry bed, or point out the need of a tin patch on the corner of the corn-bin, — all the imperative interests of her quiet life looked suddenly dreary and useless.

It is a pity, for the mere human sympathy of it, that the heads of households, deeply concerned with joy and sorrow and themselves, do not oftener remember this pain which comes to the unmarried woman, — the consciousness of unimportance. Almost every unmarried woman experiences it at one time or another in her life, whether she is the necessary maiden aunt, whose usefulness can scarcely be exaggerated, but who feels the lack of the personal element in the appreciation of her labors, or whether she is that melancholy creature who solitarily eats and drinks and sleeps, and prolongs a colorless existence, ignorant forever of either joy or sorrow.

"Nobody cares," Susan Carr thought, with wistful but matter of fact intelligence. Yet she must go on building stanchions and stopping mouseholes, over, and over, and over again. Then the fresh color deepened a little in her face: if it had been possible for her to return his regard, Joseph Lavendar would have "cared." She sighed, and tapped her heavy boot upon the step, and rested her chin in her strong hand. She almost wished it had been pos-

sible! And that made her think again of her duty
to Joseph Lavendar. Yes, Lyssie would probably
miss the choir-practicing, if this young Carey meant
to come down often to spend Saturday and Sunday
in Old Chester; then it came to her as quite an inspiration that perhaps Mrs. Pendleton would come
and sing in the choir. "Not that she *can* sing,"
Miss Susan reflected, "but she'll be there, and I'll
always walk home with her. Oh dear, I ought to
have been more neighborly, and then I should n't
feel as though I were making a convenience of her
in asking her to come." Susan Carr got up carefully, so that her skirts should not brush the pimpernel. "I'll go in and ask her now," she said.

But while she waited in the little widow's trim
parlor, Miss Susan began to wish she had chosen
some other method of protecting Mr. Lavendar.
She looked about her, and became conscious of the
brown of her ungloved hands, and the limp lines of
her woolen gown, which had shrunk in many rains,
and faded to a yellow-gray along the edges of the
plaits; she felt large and clumsy, and touched timidly a bit of delicate fancywork on the table, and
wondered why she did not care to do things like
that.

Mrs. Pendleton's parlor was a pretty, ladylike
room; there were canary-bird cages hanging in the
windows, and there was an open piano, and an embroidery frame. And when the little lady came in,
with her delicate, hasty step, and her sleek brown h‥r
nearly hidden under a small square of lace, and her

neat black silk apron over a white dress made mournful by occasional black dots, she seemed to match the
femininity of the room ; she had all the comforting,
caressing, feminine ways which were so impossible to
Susan Carr, but which must have made life very
agreeable for the late Mr. Pendleton. She ran to
get Miss Susan a footstool, and then pulled a shade
down to shield the clear, strong eyes that were used
to the full glare of noon sunshine in open fields.

" How kind of you to come in, dear Miss Carr ! "
she said. " I was feeling very lonely this morning."

" Were you ? " said Miss Susan, in her loud voice,
which made Mrs. Pendleton wink. " Were you?
Why, so was I ! I think we ought to see more of
each other. Here we are, two lone women — "

Mrs. Pendleton sighed, and glanced at her husband's picture above the fireplace. " Exactly. Of
course I still feel rather a stranger here, though
every one is so kind. Roger's engagement to dear
Alicia seems to bring me nearer to you all, — although Frances Drayton and I were great friends
right off ; and Jane Dale, even if a little stern at
times, is always exceedingly kind to me."

Miss Carr never could suppress a quiver of surprise in her face when Mrs. Pendleton used thus
freely the first names of persons whom she would
never have dreamed of addressing so informally.

" I 'm sure Mrs. Dale and Mrs. Drayton have enjoyed your society," she said stiffly ; " and — "

But Mrs. Pendleton fluttered up from her chair.
" Dear, dear ! I did n't give you a fan ! " she cried,

and ran to fetch a little open-work ivory affair run
through with a pink ribbon, and clattering very
much when one tried to use it.

Miss Susan looked at it as though afraid that it
would break in her hands, and spread it carefully
open upon her brown linsey-woolsey lap.

"Yes," Mrs. Pendleton declared, "I'm truly
gratified by dear Roger's engagement. But do you
think dear Alicia is like her sister? Much as I admire and love Cecil Shore, I do hope dear Alicia is
not just like her?"

"Lyssie has n't Cecil's looks," said Miss Carr
gruffly, "but she has some of her sister's good points,
I am sure."

"Exactly. But I was thinking. I called on
Cecil yesterday, and her little Molly — dear me!
why, she never thought of obeying her mother. I
hope — it sounds a little indelicate, but still, such
things do happen, you know — I hope if Lyssie at
any time has — I mean if — if there *should* be a
family, I hope Lyssie will insist upon obedience. I
really felt it so much when I saw that little Molly
that I almost wanted to warn dear Alicia; but of
course it would not have been proper."

"It would have been premature, I think," Miss
Carr said. ("If I don't ask her now about the practicing, she will make me so cross I shan't do it at
all,") she thought; and said, abruptly, something
about Lyssie's being a good deal occupied just now,
and wondering whether Mrs. Pendleton would not
come and sing in the choir.

"I? But I don't sing very well." The color came into the little birdlike creature's face, and she sewed rapidly. Then, with a conscious look at Miss Susan, she added, "And I'm afraid it wouldn't do for me to come; I'm afraid I ought to keep away; considering the circumstances."

Susan Carr grew red and hot. Not do? Why wouldn't it do? Of course it would do! Her kind face was suddenly angry and alarmed. Was it possible that Mr. Joseph had confided his hopes to Mrs. Pendleton? But even if he had, it was most improper in her to make any such reference!

"Of course it will do for you to come," she declared loudly; "it will be much pleasanter for us all to have you, and we really need another voice."

"If I thought it wouldn't be harder for Mr. Lavendar?" Mrs. Pendleton pondered doubtfully.

Miss Susan stared at her. "I never met such an indelicate person!" she thought. She got up, and stood in a truculent attitude, her hand on her hip. "I assure you, Mrs. Pendleton, your presence will be a great addition; it will be a good deal pleasanter for Mr. Lavendar, and for me too." ("I don't know how much she knows," thought Miss Susan, "but that may enlighten her as to the real state of the case.")

"Do you really think so?" Mrs. Pendleton said slowly. "Well, then I'll come. Yes, I'll come."

XVI.

Your opinions are absolute to you because they are the opinions of your time and place. You have so thoroughly, so totally accepted them that you with greatest difficulty are able to believe that any man is a good man and a true man who believes that which you disbelieve, or disbelieves that which you hold true.

Phillips Brooks.

VIGILANCE being the price of success, Miss Susan Carr felt that, although she had thus far kept Mr. Lavendar silent, she must not relax her care; and for that reason she named an evening when he was not in town, for a little festivity in compliment to Mr. Roger Carey, when he should come down to Old Chester to have another glimpse of Lyssie. Mr. Carey was to spend four days in town, and go away on Tuesday; so Miss Susan sent out a number of neat little notes, requesting the pleasure of everybody's company at eight o'clock on Monday evening.

"It is quite marked not to have it on Saturday, when Joseph is in town; he will feel the slight, and it will show him there's no hope for him," she said to herself, with melancholy satisfaction. To consider and protect another person is one way of creating a tenderness for him. Miss Susan Carr's good intentions towards her unsuccessful suitor kept him constantly in her mind; and protected her, too, from that dismayed afterthought which follows an impulsive invitation, — an afterthought which even the most hospitable have been known to feel.

Her invitation had been given on the spur of the moment, when Lyssie had told her that Roger was coming.

"Well, we must have a little entertainment for him!" said good Miss Susan heartily, and oblivious, as such well-meaning persons are, to the bore it might be to Roger Carey to spend one of his precious evenings in company. "We must have a little party, Lyssie, my child. Ellen shall do some jellied tongues, and I'll make the cake myself. You will have to lend me some spoons, Lyssie, and I'll borrow Mrs. Dale's punch bowl."

Miss Carr beamed, and Lyssie kissed her and thanked her, all the pretty gratitude of youth speaking in her eyes.

"Yes, yes, I'm going," said Dr. Lavendar to Philip, on the afternoon preceding the social event. "I don't know why. I have my own home, and my books, and my pipe; so why I should go and chatter for a whole evening, and eat indigestible messes, I can't understand. Do you think Miss Susan would be offended if I went home at half past nine, Philip?"

"You must stay for the supper, must n't you?" Philip suggested. "You know, next to Lyssie and Carey, you are the star. Yes, I'm afraid you must n't leave until after ten."

“Well, well,” said Dr. Lavendar resignedly, “I suppose she meant well, — Susan means better than most people. She’s a fine woman, an intelligent woman, but really —”

“She does well, too,” Philip interposed. “She’s spent this whole day with poor little Eliza Todd. The baby was born this morning, and Miss Susan has been taking care of the mother and child as though she were a trained nurse.”

“In spite of anxieties about her ball?” said the old clergyman, smiling and frowning. “So the baby’s come? Is Job sober?”

“We don’t know. He beat Eliza yesterday, and this followed ; he promptly disappeared when he saw what he had done. That is what I came to see you about, sir. I think it’s time this matter was taken in hand.”

“Dear, dear! Why, this is very bad, — really, this is very bad. How is the poor thing doing, Philip? She’s in good hands if Susan Carr is looking after her. But it’s too bad!” Dr. Lavendar was greatly concerned ; he pushed his chair back from his lathe, and drummed on the table with worried finger tips. He had been cutting a green garnet when Philip entered, and his reluctance to put his work aside was evident ; but now all that was forgotten. “Too bad ; dear, dear!”

“What a poor, forlorn little thing she is,” said Philip ; “and I remember what a nice little body she seemed when they first came to Old Chester. That Todd is a perfect beast.”

"I never saw a beast who would n't be insulted at the comparison," Dr. Lavendar declared, chuckling to himself. "Well, women are strange creatures. Why did she ever marry him? Brown told me — Brown married 'em in Mercer — he told me he warned the silly thing; told her she was a foolish woman to marry a drinking man. But she would do it; would do it. Yes, in marriage, women have no common sense. Well, neither have men, for that matter," he ended, and sighed deeply.

He got up and hobbled stiffly across the room to a high-backed leather chair that stood by the hearth. It was cooler, on this glowing August day, near the dark cavern of the empty fireplace; it looked cooler, at least, for the soot on the chimney back caught cold, iridescent gleams from the pale light filtering down the chimney and falling on the dusty heap of ashes between the andirons. Dr. Lavendar drew a little leather tobacco pouch from the pocket of his faded dressing gown, and began to fill his pipe. "Sometimes this question of marriage seems quite puzzling," he said sadly.

"I've been struck by that myself," Philip confessed, with a curious smile, "but I must say it seems simple enough in this case. She ought to leave him." He had followed the old man, and stood leaning his elbow on the mantelpiece.

"What? Leave Job? Eliza leave her husband? Come, come, sir, we don't believe in such things in Old Chester."

Philip looked a little anxious; he wanted to gain

Dr. Lavendar's consent to a step he was meditating, — the breaking up of the Todds' wretched home, and the separation of the husband and wife. He knew — so great was the old clergyman's influence in his parish — that Eliza could hardly be persuaded to take such a step without his consent.

" See here, sir," said Dr. Lavendar, pulling hard upon his pipe, " you 've come back to the home of your youth, but don't put on airs ; don't bring any of your wicked, worldly ideas here to corrupt us."

" On the contrary," said Philip, with the affectionate impertinence of the young man who knows he is liked, " what I 'm afraid of is that you 'll corrupt me. In my wicked, worldly way, I had supposed we had some responsibilities to each other ; but I find Old Chester *particeps criminis* in an attempted murder, for you 've none of you interfered to keep Todd from attacking his wife."

" Interfered ? " cried the other indignantly. " Sir, I had a conversation with Todd only a week ago. I said to him, ' Todd ' — Young man, what are you grinning at ? "

" Grinning ? " Philip protested. " My dear Dr. Lavendar ! But look here, ought n't something to be done about it ? For the woman's safety, — to say nothing of other reasons, — for her personal safety, she ought to be taken away from Todd."

" And what, sir, will become of Todd ? " Dr. Lavendar demanded, twinkling up at Philip with his fierce little brown eyes. " When he is n't drunk,

his wife's an influence for good. And would you
have her leave him, to save her precious skin ?"

"There is something beside her skin to be considered ; the degradation — "

"She took him for better or worse," Dr. Lavendar broke in. " Well, she's got the worse. Let
her stick to her bargain and do her duty. The only
thing I wish is that she could be taught to hold her
tongue. She ought to be more intelligent, and not
talk to him when he's drunk. Well, well, poor
soul ! I may seem severe, but not at all ; I was
merely explaining. And this baby is the seventh ?
We must see that she has her coal this winter."

" But that's just the point," said Philip. " The
seventh ! and there may be seventeen. And you
and Miss Susan will go on supporting them. Now,
are n't you simply encouraging Todd in drunkenness
and idleness, when you two take care of his family
for him ? Why, as a mere matter of political economy it's bad."

" Political economy ! Upon my word, Philip, I
should n't have thought it of you, — to bring economics into a question of sentiment."

" Sentiment ! " said Philip Shore, with a gesture
of disgust. " There's no sentiment in a relation
like this ; it's simply debasing to the man and the
woman and the community."

" There's nothing debasing about it. They are
married. What are you talking about ? "

Philip hesitated, and then said gravely, " It seems
to me, sir, as shameful for a man and woman to live

within the law hating and despising each other, as these two poor things do, as to live outside the law with love. That 's why I say it 's debasing."

Dr. Lavendar looked at him, speechless with horror.

" One of these days," proceeded the young man thoughtfully, " perhaps we 'll be moral enough and civilized enough to have the state break up such marriages. The very idea of the seventeen possible children is shameful, and a menace to the state. For what sort of citizens are they likely to be, the children of such parents ? "

" The children are the Lord's affair," began Dr. Lavendar.

" The devil's, I should say. I tell you what it is, the human race will have to pay a high price some time for its philanthropy; you good people who are doing your level best to keep such poor little wretches alive, and advocating their being born, are trying to secure the survival of the unfittest ! "

" Well, upon my word ! " said Dr. Lavendar again, " is it murder you want? And you 're a fool, sir; you forget your Bible : ' Children are from the Lord; happy is the man that hath his quiver full of 'em; ' and as for breaking up marriages, ' Those whom God hath joined together let no man put asunder.' I never heard such sentiments in my life. You grieve me, Philip, I tell you; yes, you grieve me, sir."

Under all the anger of frowning brows and nodding head, there was genuine trouble in his face; it was the trouble which is as old as the relationship of father and son, — the resentment of being outgrown. We are constantly depressed, and, let us admit it, irritated, by the certainty of the younger generation that they have demolished our truths, truths which we evolved from our fathers' errors. But there is at least a satisfaction in realizing that this same confident and conceited generation will sometime experience the emotions which we now know, of being set upon the shelf!

Philip was distressed at the effect of his theories; he would have gone back to the danger to Eliza Todd of remaining with a husband who beat her, but Dr. Lavendar insisted upon an explanation. Yet he hardly had patience to listen while Philip tried to explain his position in regard to separation, and his belief that divorce was a concession necessary to the present stage of spiritual evolution, but deplorable as delaying the idealization of marriage. "But I do believe in separation," he ended earnestly, "and I think a higher morality will demand it."

"Higher fiddlesticks! You'd have people part as soon as they got tired of their bargain. How much sacredness would a bargain have if it could be dissolved for every whim? You are advocating free love, Philip! Do you realize that? You are advocating free love!"

"Well," said Philip, "if there's any choice between your ecclesiastical reason and my social reason for deciding upon the moment when a bad bargain should end, I must say I think the odds are with me. It's a matter of degree; you make another crime necessary before you will allow the criminality of a loveless marriage to end; I say, end it because it is a crime."

" Marriage a crime ? " Dr. Lavendar repeated, bewildered.

" A marriage without love is at variance with the interests of society," said Philip; " that seems to me a crime."

" But that is n't the fault of marriage; that 's because one or both of them are selfish fools. Let them try to love each other! But go on, go on," he commanded resignedly. " I should like to know just how lost to all moral sense you are."

But Philip was evidently anxious to change the subject; he said, restrainedly, something about the curious survival of Mosaic law in regard to marriage, while in other relations of life — parents and children, buyers and sellers — it did not prevail. " Some of those old laws have been the bulwarks of crime," he added; " think how they protected slavery, and burned witches, and did all sorts of unpleasant things."

But Dr. Lavendar fumed and fretted, and waved his pipe at him. " Well, never mind the Mosaic laws, — I 'm sure I 'm glad you are so well acquainted with your Bible, though there is another person of perverted views who can quote Scripture for his purpose, too, — but I want to ask you one question: Where does duty come in? Do you think we can get along without duty in this civilization you talk so much about? Young man, for eighteen hundred years the ultimatum of marriage has rested upon a divine word concerning it, and men and women have done their duty, and we 've gotten along pretty well, I think. Talk about your civilization and your economics! I tell you, Philip, you belong to this ungodly time of rooting up and casting out the things that were sacred to your fathers." He spoke in his angry way, frowning heavily, and shaking his lean, grimy forefinger at the young man. "And another thing I want to know is, what will you do with the children when you go about breaking up families? Don't you see any duties to the children and the home?"

Philip started as though something had stabbed him. "First of all, for the children's sake I 'd have such marriages broken up. The living together of a husband and wife divorced in everything but word is horrible for the children. Think of the partisanship! And when respect has ceased and love has ceased, what sort of a home does that make for the children? I 'm not talking of gross sins now; I mean the mere living together of a father and mother who don't love each other. Whether it 's their misfortune or their failure, or whatever you choose to call it —"

"Sin," said Dr. Lavendar.

"— they ought to part just because of the children, even if there were no desire for personal integrity."

"I never expected to hear you say you believed in

free love!" declared the other, too irritated to answer by any argument.

"I don't," Philip began. "I only said —"

"Oh, you used a lot of fine words," interrupted Dr. Lavendar, "but that's what it amounted to. Philip, the older we grow, the more we learn of what we call science, I tell you, the more we come back to God. And you'll find, when you get over being modern, that the old words, the simple words, 'Those whom God hath joined together, let no man put asunder,' — words that you, in your wisdom, have discarded, — hold the eternal truth for us. Yes, sir, this civilization you are so fond of talking about rests on marriage."

"Indeed it does!" cried Philip Shore, the personal reality breaking suddenly through his merely intellectual, argumentative statements. "My God! a man's salvation rests on it. Only, what do you call marriage?" He caught his breath, and stood silent, grinding his heel down on the hearth. "Why, Dr. Lavendar," he went on, in a low voice, "what God hath joined man *cannot* put asunder! Trouble can't sunder such a husband and wife, nor sin, nor misery, nor death itself, if God has joined them. But when the lust of the flesh, or the lust of the eye, or the pride of life joins a man and woman, is that marriage? If they are not sundered" — he stopped, and walked the length of the room, — "if they are not sundered," he said harshly, "if they have not the moral courage to part, it is degradation, it is defilement, it is —"

" It is duty," said Dr. Lavendar.

" This question of marriage and divorce," cried the young man passionately, " is the question of our day. We must meet it, we must answer it, — some of us. But we have no appeal except to eternal principles. This is n't a time to talk about Moses and the prophets ; we 've got to come to each man's own conscience. Yes, that is the only ultimate voice. But who has courage for it ? And if a man does n't have courage, look at the penalty : the continuance of a lie, for expediency or decency or mere comfort, shuts him out from all spiritual possibilities."

" Shuts him out from spiritual possibilities ? Shuts him out ? Man, it opens the door to him, if such continuance be his duty. Philip, my boy, no priest or prophet, no Bible or liturgy, no vision upon Patmos, ever exceeded the inspiration which comes to a man from the simple *doing of his duty !* "

Philip, lifting his head with sudden solemnity, as though he heard a summons in the words, said slowly, " I am sure of that."

XVII.

A party given by the smaller gentry of the interior is a kind of solemnity. It involves so much labor and anxiety . . . its spasmodic splendors are so violently contrasted with the homeliness of every-day family life. — O. W. HOLMES.

"Why, but Lyssie, it's our last evening; we don't want to spend it with a lot of gaping people."

"Oh, are n't you ashamed to say such a thing! Miss Susan is so kind to want us."

"Well, we don't want her — I mean we don't want to go to her old party. It would be a great deal kinder to leave us out," Roger grumbled; and tried to console himself by giving his little sweetheart a kiss; but she repulsed him with firmness.

"You'll crush my dress! keep away, — yes, at least a yard away. There! there's my hand. You may kiss that."

Roger kissed the hand humbly, but, with it in his grasp, took base advantage of her condescension, and caught her in his arms without the slightest consideration for her dress.

"*Oh!*" cried Lyssie, horrified, and then ran to look in the mirror with great concern; but finding herself quite unruffled, declared that it was time to start. "And please, Roger, be nice," she pleaded; "try to talk to people, and don't look bored. Nobody can be so very nice as you — when you want to."   From which it will be seen that Miss Alicia Drayton possessed a weapon used by most intelligent wives in most happy households.

Not even Mrs. Drayton's gentle resignation at being left alone had dimmed Lyssie's young joyousness. As for Roger, he had not noticed her resignation; he had only said, good naturedly, "I have no doubt you 're glad to be rid of us, Mrs. Drayton." But when she was alone, Mrs. Drayton squeezed out a few tears, and sighed, and prayed a little, and enjoyed the sense of being deserted by her child; when suddenly a pang of reality dried her eyes, and made her sit up straight, while her lip trembled in earnest. The thought had come to her of the time when Lyssie would marry Roger, and go away to be happy in a home of her own; and she, Lyssie's mother, who had done everything in the world for her, she would be left alone — alone!

"A girl never thinks of anybody but herself," she thought, with angry apprehension; then she really and truly cried, and when Esther came in to make her comfortable for the night she waved her away impatiently. "No; I must begin to learn to take care of myself. I must get used to being uncomfortable. Go away!" she gurgled.

But Esther went calmly about her various duties in the invalid's room, only saying now and then, "There, now, Mrs. Drayton, I would n't."

"I 'll never live to bear it," Mrs. Drayton sobbed. "Lyssie will have *that* to think of, — that she just killed her mother. But I don't suppose it will make the slightest difference to her; she 'll be happy."

"Turn your head a little, m'm, so I can brush the other side," said Esther.

And Mrs. Drayton turned her head, still weeping, and saying, "Yes, I had far, far better die, — you're pulling, Esther! — and let her be happy. Ah, Esther Brown, you don't know what it is to have your child prefer some one else, a stranger, to you!"

"No, m'm," Esther agreed calmly; an assurance scarcely necessary from the sedate spinster who had served Mrs. Drayton since Alicia's birth.

"It's a little bitter to think that she's enjoying herself," said the invalid, "while I — "

Yes, Alicia was enjoying herself. For the first time in her young life she was important, and of course that is a great experience; but added to that was the new and exquisite joy of proprietorship. To follow Roger with her happy eyes, as he talked with this or that old friend; to watch him "being nice" to Miss Susan's guests; to listen, radiant and assenting, to the pleasant things which people said to her of him; and to feel that he was *hers*, that he belonged to her, was engaged to her, — ah, it was very wonderful, very uplifting. "He's being appreciated!" she said to herself triumphantly.

So far as guests went, Miss Susan's party was a great success. The library, and the two parlors on the other side of the hall, long, cheerless rooms, rarely used, and smelling of linen furniture covers, were comfortably filled. Mercer was represented, and even Ashurst; for Colonel and Mrs. Drayton, of that sleepy town, had come, in spite of the length

of the journey, to make the occasion yet more distinguished. Of course all Old Chester was present.
Mr. and Mrs. Dove were there, each uncomfortable
for the sake of the other, and Mr. Tommy so plainly
unhappy, so unconventionally unhappy, that twice
his wife found him standing in front of the clock in
the hall, gazing wistfully at the stretch between ten
and eleven which must be gotten through before they
could go home.

Dr. Lavendar had arrived full of fierce good
nature and unfailing kindliness. Cecil had come;
very late, to be sure, which made Lyssie anxious for
appearance sake. Mrs. Shore was superb in a
gown the color of that green moss that lies deep in
wet woods, — moss on which the sunshine, sifting
down through the leafy darkness of lacing boughs,
strikes faint glints and spangles of light. About her
throat was some yellow lace, caught together on her
breast by a great square topaz in an old-fashioned
setting of pale gold. She did her part nobly. She
talked to Mr. Tommy Dove with genuine kindness,
and gave the little gentleman, who responded " Yes,
ma'am," and " No, ma'am," to her remarks, the only
happy moment he knew that evening. She was elabo-
rately civil to Mrs. Dale; the more so, perhaps, as
that excellent woman's disappointment in discovering
nothing of which she could disapprove in the younger
woman's manner was quite obvious to Mrs. Shore.
She stopped and spoke to Dr. Lavendar; a little
nervously, oddly enough, for the old man always
made her uncomfortable. He did so now, by his in-

tent, half-pitiful look, rather than by his words, which did not impress her, being merely, " Well, Cecilla, I hope you are a good wife? Your husband has views about marriage which are no credit to his wife." She was glad to leave him, even though it was to go and sit down by her aunt Maria Drayton. ("I touched my highest level then," she told Roger Carey afterwards, with entire seriousness.) Colonel Drayton, who never shirked the duty of letting people speak to him, gave his niece his hand, and then left her, while he proceeded to make a tour of Miss Susan's rooms.

"You must not mind your uncle's leaving us. He always tries to speak to every one ; he is so considerate," murmured Mrs. Drayton.

" He is," Cecil responded gratefully ; " so nice to have him go and speak to people."

" Ah well, your uncle never hesitates at any duty," said the other, with that closing of the lips and nodding of the head which means, " I wish as much might be said for *you!* "

Cecil was humbly silent.

" I heard in Mercer that Joseph Lavendar was very attentive to some Mrs. Pendleton," Mrs. Drayton digressed. " Who is she?"

" I beg your pardon ? "

" Which is Mrs. Pendleton? Oh, that little body? Very nice looking, I 'm sure. I hope Mr. Lavendar will be happy. She must be introduced to the Colonel ; it will please her. Cecil, my dear, how is your husband?"

Cecil's pause to remember was filled by Mrs. Drayton's expression of opinion about Roger Carey, which turned her niece restless, and made her say that reminded her that she must go and speak to Mrs. Pendleton, if her aunt Maria would excuse her?

"It 's the Colonel's example, you see," she said indolently; and Mrs. Drayton told her husband, afterwards, that she really believed there was good somewhere in poor Cecil. "I always felt that that child's privilege in living in your house would some-time express itself in her life, my dear," said Mrs. Drayton adoringly.

Mrs. Pendleton was plainly nervous at Mrs. Shore's attentions, but, with a view to being interesting, she did her best to say pleasant things; and as it was a peculiarity of this amiable woman that she could never say pleasant things to one person without saying unpleasant things of some other person, her conversation was generally interesting. How pretty Molly was, — how much prettier than any of the Old Chester children! How charming Mrs. Shore's dress looked; what a pity that dear Susan Carr had not a handsome dress! She hoped Mrs. Shore would not mind if she told her how beautifully she walked. "So gracefully, dear Mrs. Shore. I wish our dear Lyssie had your walk. I hope you are not offended at my speaking out? I never flatter, but I am very impulsive, and speak right from my heart; I shall outgrow it, no doubt." Cecil's involuntary smile and instant gravity made the somewhat mature widow uncomfortable, so she made haste, nervously, to speak of other things. She wondered when dear Dr. Lavendar was going to print his book? He had been so long about it! For her part, she thought it was not well to be too long in writing a book; there was danger in polishing it too much; did not Mrs. Shore think so?

" It is apt to make it shorter," said Cecil.

" Exactly! " Mrs. Pendleton agreed eagerly; " that's just it." And then she said, modestly, that she would like to present Mrs. Shore with a copy of her poems. " There 's nothing in them that a child may not read," said Mrs. Pendleton. " Ah, I 'm not like the authors of to-day, Mrs. Shore. I would never write anything that could not be put into the hands of the youngest child."

" Adults must appreciate that," Cecil told her, so cordially that Mrs. Pendleton was encouraged to patter on about her " works " for the next ten minutes. She confessed that she was about to print another book, which she had named — " so much depends upon the name," she explained — which she had named Thoughts.

" But whose? " said Mrs. Shore simply.

" Oh, I shall not sign my name," Mrs. Pendleton answered, not catching, perhaps, the significance of the question; " I shan't even put 'Amanda P.,' though that would insure the book attention from all the readers of the poems. I shall just say, Thoughts: by a Lady. Don't you think that is a nice, ladylike title ? "

"I never heard anything more ladylike," Cecil assured her warmly; and Mrs. Pendleton told several persons, afterwards, that poor dear Cecil had a good heart, she was sure.

As for Cecil, she felt her endurance at an end. She excused herself on the ground of wishing to speak to some one, and, unfastening one of the long French windows which opened upon the piazza, stepped out into the August night.

"Dear me," she said, "I beg your pardon!"

Alicia and Roger, standing by the balustrade, laughed: Lyssie, with pretty consciousness; Roger, with the embarrassment that is angry at being embarrassed.

"Why, Lys, Lys!" Cecil remonstrated, smiling and coming out into the shadows where the lovers stood, "is this the way you entertain Miss Susan's company? Mr. Carey, you won't endear yourself by carrying Lyssie off."

"I ought to go in," Alicia said penitently; and then, with shy authority, "Roger, you must n't — I mean, Ceci, don't say 'Mr. Carey.' Roger, it is n't 'Mrs. Shore;' it 's 'Cecil.'"

"Oh, Mrs. Shore thinks me too quarrelsome for such friendliness," Roger returned, frowning.

Cecil simply ignored the suggestion; she said something about the heat and being bored to death. Poor little Alicia looked blankly at them. "Why won't they?" she thought. "Why don't they like each other more?" Lyssie was stumbling very early in her life of love upon that rock of offense:

"Why do they not love each other, when I love them and they love me?" But in love two things which are equal to a third are not necessarily equal to each other, and two hands which, from opposite sides, give themselves to one friend fail sometimes to enter into a friendly clasp on their own account. Too often, with vehement futility, the middleman insists that these two hands must and shall clasp each other, and his endeavor results only in pain to all three.

"Roger," the young girl said, too straightforward to know how to keep the disappointment from her voice, and making still another exasperating effort, "I must go in, but you need n't; stay out here with — It's cooler here. Ceci, entertain him, won't you?"

"It is Mr. Carey who entertains me," Cecil answered, and Roger felt hot. He said to himself that he would much rather go in with Alicia, but of course he must not leave Mrs. Shore alone — confound it!

"Shan't I get you a wrap?" he said stiffly.

"No, thank you."

She sat down on the balustrade, leaning her head back against one of the big wooden columns that supported the porch roof.

"Did you ever know anything so stupid?"

Roger frowned, and appeared not to understand.

Cecil laughed a little under her breath. "You do it very well, Mr. Carey."

"Do what very well? I'm enjoying myself, if

that's what you mean. Miss Carr's kindness in planning pleasure for Lyssie of course makes it pleasant for me."

" Do you think, in contrast to my remark, that your flagrant goodness is quite polite?" she said, and turned her face away and seemed to forget him.

What was the evil thing about her that made him ashamed of his simple and obvious love-making?— for he was tingling with the embarrassment of having been, as it were, discovered. He was angry with her in a brutal way that made him feel that impulse of the very fingers to punish her.

" You don't seem to credit anybody with simple human feeling in such things," he told her, wincing at his own tone. " You may not appreciate Miss Carr's kindness, but I do."

Cecil turned and looked at him with interest. " You speak of virtue as though it were a discovery you had made," she said, in her slow voice; " but, do you know, I too, in my humble way, have thought that Miss Susan meant to give pleasure? Only that does not prevent me from finding the occasion stupid."

If she had not been sitting there before him, the lines of her gracious figure seen faintly in the half-light, and her white throat melting into the lace that filled the bosom of her dress to her waist, his anger might have lasted; but he could not be angry as he looked at her, and he could not take his eyes away from her. His admiration began to speak in his voice,— in the warmer tone, the softer words; but he made his fault-finding raillery instead of rudeness. He teased her, and contradicted her, and laughed at her. When she defended herself, he answered with a man's good-humored contempt of a woman's opinion, which, while it made her confused and petulant and half irritated, gave her also that strange pleasure, which only strong women know, of coming, as it were, to heel.

In the midst of it Philip came along the porch, and Cecil called to him to know what time it was.

"Isn't it almost time to go home? Oh, Philip, what bomb have you been exploding at the rectory? Dr. Lavendar assailed me because of your views about marriage. Really, it does seem hard that I should be held responsible for your opinions."

"It's nearly ten. You won't go before supper, of course?"

"Ten! I thought it was two. Oh, must we stay for supper? Mr. Carey, you'll have to," she ended maliciously, "for Lys won't want to leave until the last moment. How you will appreciate Old Chester's idea of a salad!"

This time Roger Carey had no protest for the violated hospitality. "I'll try what influence can do. Perhaps we can get away right after supper."

"It is just ready, I believe," Philip said, and would have left them, but Cecil stopped him.

"What is this thing which has agitated Dr. Lavendar? Do tell us. Your ideas are always so amusing."

"If I amuse you, I have not lived in vain. Carey, will you bring Mrs. Shore in?"

"No, no! You must tell us first, Philip. Come! here is Mr. Carey; he's in a most receptive state of mind on the subject of matrimony. Are you going to reform marriage or abolish it?"

"There is room for reform," he said; then, as though impatient at his own evasion, he added, "I was talking about that man Todd and his wife. I told Dr. Lavendar I thought they ought to be separated."

Cecil looked at him in genuine astonishment. "Why, really, Philip, I did n't suppose — why, but that's quite sensible!" She was so much in earnest that she had an instant's surprise at Roger's involuntary laugh. "Why, but it *is* sensible," she insisted. "I should have supposed you would say just the other thing, Philip. Of course Dr. Lavendar was dreadfully shocked?"

"Yes, he did n't approve of me," Philip answered, pulling a red carnation down into his button-hole.

"I can fancy Dr. Lavendar's dismay," Cecil said lightly. "I have what might be called a respectful dislike for Dr. Lavendar, but I'm sorry for the poor old gentleman's distress. It was too bad in you, Philip."

"Upon my word, the Shore family needs a missionary," Roger Carey declared. "Do you remember the night you told me you thought the little Todd woman ought to leave her husband, Mrs.

Shore?   I did n't know that Philip shared your perverted views."

Philip looked at his wife quickly. " You think so, too ? "

" Why, certainly I do.   I 'm sorry to shock you, Mr. Carey, but I believe the world would be much better off if divorce were easier.   In fact, I think, it 's a pity people have to wait until they actually come to blows before they can separate."

" There are blows and blows," Roger said, in that tone which meant, " You are charming, but you are not to be taken seriously."   " Some people's fists would be luxury compared to other people's tongues."

" Ah well," Cecil commented, " the great thing is to be able to be articulate in one's woes.   We are too polite, even when we use our tongues.   The husbands and wives who throw dishes at each other are the really happy people.   They are articulate; they have all the relief of expression."

" Might n't you call it action ? " Roger suggested.

" You and Lyssie will never throw dishes at each other," Cecil went on gayly, " and you 'll suffer ever so much more on account of your repression.   Philip (I never saw anybody so anxious for his supper !), don't you think it 's a pity that people have to come to blows before they can separate ? "

" Yes, I think it 's a pity," Philip said dryly.

But a certain reality in his voice made Roger suddenly interested.   " Why, Shore, do you think divorce should be easier ? "

"Yes; I think it would conduce to a higher morality."

"Well, I suppose I'm rather an extremist, but I don't believe in divorce at all."

"Ah, but you've never been married," Mrs. Shore reminded him drolly.

He had turned his shoulder toward her, and did not notice her remark, even to snub her; he was launched into discussion, and he cared more for discussion than for a pretty woman. "Mind you, I think separation is desirable occasionally, but never divorce. I mean, of course, divorce *a vinculo matrimonii*, and the right to marry again."

"Oh, divorce is concession to human nature, I admit," said Philip; "deplorable, but necessary."

"Never!" Roger declared, with the joyous dogmatism of the man whose argument has no personal bias. "It's hard on the innocent, sometimes; if the law frees a woman from a wretch, it's a pity that she can't marry some good fellow and be happy; but the individual has got to be subservient to the race. Divorce seems to me like suicide, not inherently or specifically wrong, but socially vicious; both lower just a little the moral tone of society. Besides, our progress is in direct proportion to our idea of the sacredness of marriage; and even the innocent mustn't tamper with that ideal sacredness. They've got to suffer, — that's all. It's a pity, but they've got to suffer."

Philip shook his head. "The idealism of the individual is what has made progress, and that may imply a theory of marriage which necessitates divorce."

" Ah, but," cried Roger, " that's just where you make your mistake: *divorce can't be considered from the individual's standpoint.* It 's a social question, a race question. If no man lives to himself or dies to himself, still less does he marry to himself; and besides, abstract idealism must always be subjugated to the needs of living."

" But, my dear fellow, it is the individual conscience which forever revises and corrects standards; society is made up of ' Me's.' "

" ' Me ' is a mighty selfish critter, when it comes to this question of divorce," Roger said quickly. " Lord ! how I have seen ' Me ' show the cloven foot when he was talking about his wrongs. Why, Shore, I believe that half the time, when the charge is cruelty, or drunkenness, or — or unfaithfulness, it 's just the expression of the resentment of personal humiliation and mortification. It 's vanity, that 's what it is ! Sometimes the children are made the excuse; but I tell you, it 's Self, every time; you can see that when ' Me ' goes and gets married again. No, sir; legal separation would answer every purpose."

" It might; but we are not ready for it. Human nature is n't ready for it."

" Human nature has had a great deal too much of it, as it is ! " Roger asserted emphatically. " Even separation comes too easy here."

"I don't agree with you, I don't agree with you," Philip said restlessly.

" Why, but Shore," the other persisted, "just see where your theory leads you. See what a poor, cheap sort of thing it makes of marriage, — a thing dependent on mood."

" It is dependent on love," said Philip Shore.

" But is n't duty to be considered? Is n't there to be any effort to hold love?" Roger protested.

Philip and Cecil both began to speak, and each stopped for the other, both with a certain astonishment in their faces that they thought alike.

" Love has nothing to do with effort," said Philip.

" It is absurd to talk about the duty of loving," Cecil declared ; and then there was the look at each other, and Cecil laughed. " Love is as unmoral as art ; you can't talk about the duty of loving."

" Love may have nothing to do with morality," Philip broke in, " but it has everything to do with spirituality. When love has ceased, marriage has ceased, and separation should be permitted."

" It would certainly be more agreeable," Cecil said. " But do you think a man and woman, even in our class, should part if they are tired of each other ? "

Roger Carey made some flippant remark about " theories." He was exceedingly uncomfortable without quite knowing why.

Philip's face, in the dim light on the porch, looked drawn and pale. " I don't know what you mean by a husband and wife being ' tired of each other.' "

"Excellent Philip! I mean bored to death. Were you never bored? Being bored takes the place of having dishes thrown at you in that state of life where it has pleased God to call us. Well, do you think such people ought to part? Heavens! society would tremble to its base; it would be a sort of puss-in-the-corner, would n't it? Everybody would run in every direction. Is that what you think, Philip, really?"

"I think a man and woman have no moral right to remain together when they no longer love each other."

"Well, I believe I agree with you," Cecil said thoughtfully, — "if only for the interest which it would impart to one's immediate circle." Then she took Roger's arm, while he, conscious and uncomfortable, declared, in a tone artificial even to his own ears, that they were both wrong.

"Absolutely wrong! Come in and have something to eat. Come down to earth, Shore, and teach your wife better sociology. By Jove, though, would n't the lawyers thrive if your views became general!"

XVIII.

"WHEN you get home, Cecil, I'd like to speak to you, if you'll be so good. I won't detain you very long."

Philip said this as he helped his wife into the carriage, at the close of Miss Carr's festivity.

"Very well," she said crossly. Her tolerance of his scrupulous politeness failed her for a moment. In that talk upon the porch, she had had, under her careless gayety of argument, a sudden passionate realization of the dreariness of her life. How tired she was of Philip, but how impossible — for she never dreamed of applying the theories she advanced for Eliza Todd to herself — how impossible was any escape from such dreariness! She had a bleak vision of the years before her: the years of hearing him talk to Molly; the years of seeing his face every day at the opposite end of the table; the years of dull household questions, — shall this horse be bought? shall that servant be discharged? — long, level, horrible years! She had a swift, angry remembrance of his "ways," — those harmless, unconscious habits of the body which go so far toward making the individual, and which love finds half touching and wholly dear. She recalled his way of cutting open the pages of his stupid quarterlies and reviews; of absently twisting his mustache while he read; of pressing his lips together as though to taste his wine while putting down his wineglass: all the little mannerisms of the Human suddenly filled her with disgust. Oh, how tired she was of him! Yes, plates as missiles would be far more bearable than this expanse of arid virtue, this monotonous faultlessness. His very courtesy at the carriage door gave her a feeling of irritation.

"Get in!" she said impatiently.

But he shook his head. "I'm going to walk. I'll be at home almost as soon as you are. Will you wait for me in the library, please?"

Then he shut the door, and turned on his heel into the darkness. An hour before, the difficulty of telling a woman (for Philip, before he was an idealist, was a gentleman) what he thought of their relation — or, to put it crudely, the difficulty of telling his wife that he did not wish to live with her any longer — had appeared to him almost insurmountable. But as he listened to her there on the porch, a sudden determination came to him. Perhaps it was because her carelessness and superficiality seemed absolutely unendurable; or perhaps it was because she chanced to say, "I agree with you." Of course he knew that her agreement with his proposition went no deeper than the effect, and never touched the cause. It indicated no conviction of hers, but it made it easier for him to express a conviction of his own. He went home through the darkness, too ab-

sorbed to notice the soft, fine rain that had begun to
fall. He carried his stick behind him, gripping it
with both hands; his head was bent, and his lips
were hardened into a stern line; his whole body
stooped forward, as though his will and haste outran
his hurried stride.

"*Will she consent to a separation?*"
Over and over he asked himself the question.
Not that he expected to put his fate to the touch
that night; he only meant to test this flimsy and obviously selfish opinion of hers. Would it be strong
enough to break down the bars of convention, and
give him freedom? He had never a moment's hope
that it would have in it the strength of any spiritual
desire for freedom for herself. He had long since
ceased to hope anything like that for her. No; his
only thought was that he might use her unworthy
impulse as a means of escape for his own soul.

When Philip Shore opened the door of his library,
he found his wife awaiting him. Her face had
cleared in that drive home, — it had been so comfortable among the cushions of her carriage; and
after all, life cannot be absolutely dreary when one
has plenty of cushions! She had sent upstairs for a
box of candy when she came in, and then she went
into the library, and sank down upon a lounge, half
reclining, half sitting, her strong white fingers clasped
behind her head, and her half-shut eyes full of lazy
good nature. Yes, things might be worse; and besides, everybody else was in the same trap. It was
the old miserable but mighty consolation of unhappy

souls : every one else is involved in the same calamity ;
so bear it, make the best of it, — in fact, be as comfortable as you can.

" And things are pretty comfortable," she said to
herself. " Oh, what a soup that was at dinner !
Jane must never leave me if she can make such soups.
She reconciles me to my lot." Then she heard the
door open, and knew that Philip had entered.
" Well ? " she said, without turning her head.

Philip pushed up a chair, and sat down ; he looked
at her in silence. Cecil opened her eyes, and took a
piece of candy.

" It 's about John, I suppose ? Is n't it a nuisance
to have him leave ? Don't give him a character ; it 's
the only way we can retaliate. Have you any one
else in mind ? "

" I have spoken to him ; he will stay," Philip said
briefly, and then stopped, and looked down at the
floor a moment, and drew in his lips. " I want to
speak to you of what you said to-night."

" Of what I said ? " Cecil frowned, and tried to
remember. " Why, what did I say ? Oh, you mean
about divorce ? Oh, Philip, now don't be argumentative at this hour ! "

She rubbed her foot softly against the lounge, and
one slipper dropped with a clatter to the floor ; then
she yawned, and stretched herself lazily, and un-
fastened the square topaz upon her bosom, loosening
the yellow lace a little, so that she might feel the
cool air upon her throat. Her *abandon,* her comfort,
her look of enjoying her body, strangely disgusted

him. He wanted to say to her, "Sit up; remember you are not alone!" He pushed his chair back, and frowned, with lowered eyes.

"Your — dress?" he said, with a gesture.

"No, I never take cold," she answered. "Yes, Philip, I supposed for once we agreed; but don't, for Heaven's sake, try to prove anything to me now." She laughed a little, and rubbed her eyes. "I'm nearly dead with sleep," she declared.

"We do agree," he returned quickly. "Only, it seems to me more than a pity that a man and woman must wait until they come to blows, before they can separate. It seems to me a sin."

"Oh well, that's as you look at it," said Cecil, with a yawn. "When one says it's unpleasant, one says the whole thing. If that is all you wanted to tell me, Philip, I'm going to bed. Oh, Philip, you have so much Soul! is n't it fatiguing?"

"Have you any?" he said, half to himself; "sometimes it seems as though your soul had never been born!"

"Perhaps not; perhaps not. But who knows? It may be twins. Just think how superior I'll be then to you. Don't be jealous, Philip; make a pincushion for the poor little Soul, with 'Welcome little stranger' on it, won't you? Oh, dear, I wish there was anything very good to eat in this house, — anything interesting, like mushrooms and aspic, perhaps. I think I'll wake Jane and tell her to find something for me; I'll take bread and cheese, if there's nothing else."

She sat up, and moved her foot in its thin silk stocking about upon the floor to find her slipper; then a sparkle of laughter flew into her eyes. "Put it on for me, Philip," she commanded, and thrust out a charming foot; and as he, his very fingers shrinking, touched the warm, lithe ankle and put the slipper on, she gave him a little poke with the green satin toe. "You goose!" she said drolly; but there was contempt as well as amusement in her voice.

He understood it, but he replied, quietly enough, "There is something more than unpleasantness in a marriage where the husband and wife don't love each other:" and then he gave her a look that made the color sweep into her face. But she was too sleepy to lose her temper.

"If you knew how perfectly ridiculous that sounds! Love! What do you mean by love? Exchanging locks of hair and vows of eternal constancy?"

"Hardly."

"Well," she answered slowly, "I don't believe in love, — except in maternal love. The other kind is nothing but selfishness."

"It need not be."

"But it is — while it lasts," she said, sighing; and rose, and stood silent a moment, looking down at the floor; then she said abruptly, "You wanted to say something, Philip? I don't know how we got off on this subject; it's disagreeable enough! What was it?"

"It was of this I wanted to speak," he answered, rising also; then he took a turn about the room, his hands in his pockets, and came back to her. "It has been in my mind a very long time."

"What has been in your mind? Marriage or love?"

"Marriage without love."

"At least that is more respectable than love without marriage," she said lazily. "Well, what about it?"

"I doubt if it is more respectable."

"Good heavens, Philip," she remonstrated, with good-natured amusement, "what on earth have you got hold of now? Is it some plan for abolishing marriage? You love to reform things, don't you? But do undertake something a little more reputable. Now I must go to bed; I can't keep my eyes open a minute longer. Do you want some money, to print pamphlets about reforming marriage, or do you want to start a fund for free divorce, for *mariés incompris*, so to speak? Take it, take it, — only let me go to bed!" She turned away, her hand on the door-knob. "Good-night," she said.

But he stopped her. "We've begun to speak of this, let us go on. I might as well say now — I ought to have said it long ago — that this is a very real and terrible question to me."

"Oh, Philip, must you be ecstatic? Consider the hour."

"For God's sake, drop your flippancy!" he said, with such sudden passion that she looked at him apprehensively. Was he going to have an attack of soul on the question of marriage? " I think the time has come when we must talk this out. You and I have failed as husband and wife. Of course we both know that perfectly well. Where the greater blame lies does n't matter now. The fact is the important thing."

" Failed ? " Cecil repeated, with that surprise which is uncertain whether or not to be anger, — " failed ? Do you mean we don't love each other ? Why, Philip, you are letting truthfulness get the better of politeness. Well, I don't know; you may not love me, but I — I don't mind you, Philip." Then it occurred to her that he wanted her love; was this what he had been leading up to ? She felt the color come into her face; she was very much amused, but she was interested. His next words enlightened her.

" You and I can't talk of love. Forgiveness is all I can ask you for. But there 's the fact, — we 've failed; the question is whether our failure involves any duty."

She was standing with her hands behind her, leaning back against the table; the light from the lamp beside her gilded the long line of her moss-green gown from her shoulder to her heel; the topaz caught it, and gleamed suddenly, like a watchful eye. Her face was full of delicate color, and her neck and bosom were as white as down; about her forehead, warm still from the cushions of the sofa, her hair broke into shining rings. She caught a shadowy glimpse of herself in the mirror between the windows, and she thought, with whimsical contempt, that Philip would have been just as indifferent to the beauty imaged there had it belonged to some other woman instead of to his wife.

"Well," she said scornfully, "you are perfectly absurd about some things, Philip. So long as you seem to be saying disagreeable things, I might as well tell you that you are perfectly absurd. We get along as well as most people. I don't know what you mean by a duty that may be involved. The only duty I know anything about is to have good manners, even though you bore me to death. And you do, you know, Philip, — I'm sorry to seem rude, but you have introduced truth, — you do bore me very much, sometimes. What do you want me to do? Try and take up love's young dream? Why can't you reconcile yourself to the fact that every marriage is a failure, in the sense you mean?"

"Other people's marriages are not our affair," he answered harshly; "and it isn't true, anyhow. But because we are miserable we need not blaspheme."

There was something in his voice that made her turn and face him. For a moment there was silence; then she said, in a very low voice, "Are you — are you — making this question of divorce *personal?*"

There was a breathless instant before he answered her.

"How can it be anything but personal, when you and I talk of the immorality of a marriage without love?"

Cecil made no reply.

"You said, — I don't know whether you were in earnest, — but you said that you thought that when a husband and wife did not love each other they ought to part."

Cecil, her head bent upon her breast, watched him closely, but did not speak.

"I, also, think they ought to part; because a marriage without love is legalized baseness; or else it is a lie."

Cecil, looking up at him, said distinctly, "Who is the woman, Philip?"

He looked at her, with a broken word of disgust, and turned away.

A flame leaped in Cecil's eyes; she stood upright, and struck the table violently with her clenched hand. "You come to me," she cried, her voice tingling with passion, "to *me*, to prate about the sanctity of marriage and the duty of separation! You want to be free, for reasons of your own, — illegal baseness, perhaps? But no! You? You have n't blood enough in your veins for that. I know you! Good heavens, you are not a man! But there is some reason under this fine talk, some ulterior motive. What is it?"

"You know better," he said, between his teeth.

She laughed loudly. "I know there 's no woman, because you have n't it in you! But when you come here and whimper about morality, I know there 's some cold-blooded reason behind it all. I 'm not a fool, Philip Shore. You put off our marriage on the ground of duty, — you wanted to go to Paris to study. You gave up your art because of duty, — you wanted to dabble, in your dilettante way, in politics. Now you come and talk of the duty of divorce! *What do you want?*"

It was terrible to see flash out through the refinement of tradition and training this loud vulgarity of soul.

" Well, answer, answer! Can't you? Of course we don't love each other; how could I love you? But I don't see what you want. You are perfectly free; you can go to Paris and study again, if you want to!"

Philip looked at her, and looked away for very shame of what he saw; under his breath he said, with sudden passionate pity, " Oh, you poor soul!" For an instant the tears stood in his eyes. " But I can't talk to her," he thought desperately. Yet when she said again, furiously, something of this separation which had existed in fact for three years, he tried to tell her, curtly, with averted eyes, that such a condition was a lie.

" We pretend to be married," he said, " but we are separated; we both know it, but no one else knows it."

" And you want it known?" she cried, — " you want to take the world into your confidence?" She was so amazed that she forgot her anger.

"We are living a lie — " he began ; but she interrupted him.

"Be explicit, be explicit," she said sternly; "don't rhapsodize. You offer me an insult. At least state it plainly."

"I think we ought to separate, openly."

"Do you mean be divorced ? "

"I don't think any legal steps are necessary. I mean separate. Stop profaning a sacrament."

He seemed to her so absolutely preposterous that her anger broke into a laugh.

"Sit down ; there's no use standing here as though we were on the stage. You use fine words, Philip ; I don't, though I know the *patois*. I prefer the stupid truth : we're tired of each other. But there is one thing you overlook : we are so unfortunate as to have been born in a class where a prejudice exists against publicity. We don't talk of our diseases or our infelicities ; yet we have our doctors, and though we don't 'separate,' we 'travel,' — like my dear papa."

It was a curious scene : these two, the woman in her lace and jewels, the man with the red carnation in his buttonhole, with every suggestion about them of the reserves, and dignities, and conventions of living, standing there face to face, speaking passionately the primitive realities of life! Cecil sat down opposite her husband at the library table ; a shaded lamp burned between them ; except for its soft glow, the room, with its book-covered walls, was full of shadowy dusk. One window was open, a black ob-

long of rainy night, and through it the smell of wet
leaves wandered in from the garden, and sometimes
a faint, cool breath of air, although there was no
wind; there was no sound, either, except for Philip's
voice and Cecil's playing with a paper cutter, —
lifting it and letting it drop between her fingers, and
then lifting it and dropping it again. She was perfectly calm; she rested her chin in one hand, and
watched him closely; only, when he came to speak
of Molly, her eyes blazed. He told her that the existence of the child made their duty greater in this
matter. And then he said that, under circumstances
such as theirs, neither father nor mother could claim
the right to the child, and therefore, if they should
decide to separate, the only thing to do was to divide
Molly's time; they should each have her for half
the year.

When he said this, his wife flung her head back
and laughed silently. He saw it; he sat there
speaking from the depths of his soul, speaking with
terrible restraint, speaking as a man speaks for his
life; he saw the laugh, and knew what it meant.
The hopelessness of the situation took him by the
throat. What was the use? He had no words; he
and she spoke a different language.

Cecil tapped her lip with her paper cutter
thoughtfully. "I can take Molly abroad to school,
I suppose, though she's rather young for that."
She did not even notice his concession; then she
looked over at him, and laughed angrily. "You
hypocrite! you have n't told me the truth yet."

He looked at her with a kind of terror. "My God! she *can't* understand!" he said, almost in a whisper.

"Oh, you need n't doubt my intelligence. I merely want to know the object of all this. What is at the root of this passion for duty? You know, Philip, I have seen it in you before. I tell you that I am willing to travel, — so drop that; now tell me the meaning of it all."

"Cecil," he said, with great gentleness, "you know that I have never lied to you, and —"

"Never!" she agreed dryly; "you would have been so much more attractive if you had."

" — so believe me, even if you can't understand me: your proposal of a secret separation has no bearing on the purpose in my mind."

"It is, however, the only ground on which I will consent to your suggestion," Cecil answered calmly. "I am quite willing to travel. In fact, if it were not impolite, I should say that I would be glad to travel. Oh, and about Molly. Of course that is perfectly absurd. I should n't think of giving her up, — I should n't think of such a thing!"

The blood rushed into Philip's face. "What! do you think I will allow you to have her?"

The threat in his eyes made her wince, as though he were going to strike her.

"I am responsible for Molly's soul!" he said; and then into the moment of tingling silence between them came the sudden banging of the front door, and Roger Carey's step in the hall.

" Hello, Eric, old man !   Don't knock me down," they heard him say. " Shore ! Philip ! what are you burning the midnight oil for ? "   He whistled, and shoved the library door open, and came in and saw them, the husband and wife : Philip, ghastly pale ; Cecil, crimson and panting, her lips parted for some furious word.   But in a flash the vision was gone.   He heard, in his embarrassed dismay, his hostess murmuring something about Lyssie and the rain, and the voice of his host declaring that Eric ought to have been locked up in the barn. For his own part, he was able to observe, sleepily, that it was funny how late twelve seemed in the country ; and then he said good-night with careful unconcern, and went out and left them, saying under his breath, " Good Lord ! "

They heard his door close ; they heard the clock in the hall begin to strike twelve.   Cecil suddenly drew the lace together across her throat ; her breath caught in a sob ; she leaned both hands upon the table and bent over toward her husband ; the light shone up upon her trembling lip, upon the fierce tears in her eyes, upon the anger and terror in her face.

" Yes," she said in a whisper, " we 'll separate.   I agree, I agree ! "

XIX.

Ah, love, but a day,
   And the world has changed!
The sun 's away,
   And the bird 's estranged;
The wind has dropped,
   And the sky 's deranged:
Summer has stopped.

BROWNING.

ROGER was to go away the next day, but he did not have to start until late in the afternoon, so he and Lyssie had planned to take a long walk in the morning. They were to go over to the hills on the other side of the river. There was a road there that Lyssie knew, — a road where the grass grew tall between the wheel ruts, and the wayside bushes pressed close upon the passer-by, and the trees dropped pleasant shadows all along the grassy track; a road where two might walk very close together, and know that no eye more curious than a squirrel's would be apt to pry upon them; the very road for a long talk, the very place for endless variations upon three noble words, " *I love you!* "

The thought of having Lyssie all to himself for a whole, still, sunshiny morning enchanted Roger Carey, and he was, not unnaturally, annoyed to have her come downstairs and say that her mother was so fatigued by the party that she had a bad headache.

“And of course,” Alicia ended, “I must sit with her; so I can’t go out to walk. I’m so sorry.”

“Why, but Lyssie!” said Roger blankly. “Why, this is our last chance for a month. Your mother fatigued by the party? How can she be fatigued by the party? She did n’t go; it ’s just a headache, and—”

“Yes, that ’s all; my going excited her, you know.”

“Can’t Esther take care of her? You seem to forget that I ’m going away this afternoon!”

“Esther? Esther can’t take my place. Or perhaps you think anybody can take my place, sir!”

To contradict this gave Roger some pleasure; and when Lyssie, with glowing face, slipped out of his arms, he supposed he had gained his point. But she shook her head, and sighed. “Oh, Roger, don’t encourage me to be selfish. I ’d like to go; that shows you how selfish I am. Selfishness is my be- setting sin,” she informed him sadly; “you ought to help me to be good.”

“You selfish?” Roger cried. “You are an an- gel!”

“I? I am not good at all—if you only knew! Why, Roger, I can’t imagine what you ever saw in me to love.”

“Bless your little heart! It was your goodness that made me love you. For me, I ’m like a crow beside you.”

Thus and thus the regal humility of love! What a pity it is that so often, when marriage has given two perfect beings to each other, admiration should be exchanged for criticism.

"You know, Lyssie" (confession is delightful when one's sweetheart is the priest, and her absolving, unbelieving, happy eyes look up and smile denial of the fault confessed), "I don't pretend to any great goodness, and I have a nasty temper; but there is one good thing about me: — I am reasonable. I don't insist on having my own way, unless, as a pure matter of reason, I know I'm right."

"Of course," Alicia agreed eagerly. "But then you always are right, Roger."

Roger whistled. "Lys, the king can do no wrong. But is it prudent to let him know you think so?"

"Yes!" said the girl proudly. "I'm not afraid to tell you all I think of you. I think nothing but what is true. And I see all your faults. No one is more critical of you than I."

"Well, you shall tell me all about them," Roger assured her. "We'll talk of my faults all the morning; it will take all the morning. Now go and get your hat; it will be too hot soon to climb the hill."

"But Roger — mother?" Alicia's smile vanished.

Roger looked annoyed. "Well, I'm sure she wouldn't want you to stay at home on her account?"

"I know she wouldn't; but it's my duty, don't you see?"

"No. I think you have some duty to me; though that doesn't seem to strike you."

"Oh, Roger!" said poor little Lyssie, her eyes full of reproach. "Mother is ill, and you know that is very different from just a mere walk."

"Well, of course, just a mere walk with me," he began crossly. "You don't care about it as I do, that's plain enough."

"Roger!"

"Then come. Don't be foolish, Lyssie." He was beginning to lose his interest; insistence, after a certain point, does lose its interest.

"Please don't urge me!"

He drew back stiffly. "Oh, certainly not. I suppose I may come in after dinner and say good-by?"

She looked at him, and her lip shook.

"Oh, *please!*" she said despairingly.

But Roger turned on his heel, with a concise though unuttered epithet in his own mind, coupled with the name of Mrs. Drayton.

"All right; I've nothing more to say. I think you are wrong; but never mind. I'll come in this afternoon and say good-by before the stage starts. I suppose you can leave your mother long enough for that? There! I'm a brute, Lyssie, I'm ashamed of myself; but you are all wrong, darling."

Then, still irritated in spite of being ashamed of himself, he left her, and Lyssie, after she had swallowed some tears, went up and spent the morning in the darkened bedroom, where the air was heavy with the sickly scent of cologne, and where she listened to feeble sobbings of reproach that she had stayed downstairs so long. In the afternoon it all came right, of course. Roger was repentant and Lyssie forgiving, but somehow the parting was less perfect than it should have been. A bewildered dismay still lingered in Alicia's eyes, and Roger was dully unhappy, with a self-reproach which took no definite form; he only knew it had nothing to do with his unreasonable temper in the morning.

Now, the stings of conscience are bad enough, as everybody knows, when they are definite; but when the still, small voice only mutters, when the stings are wandering pains which refuse to localize themselves and be treated, remorse is a little more unbearable by the addition of bewilderment.

Roger's self-reproach was connected with his manner of spending the morning after he left Alicia. Yet he could not say why he was dissatisfied with himself. When he tried to analyze his conduct, he found nothing definite; only a vague uneasiness, an intangible disapproval. Smarting at Lyssie's slight, — for so he chose to consider it, — he had gone back to the Shores', meaning to make his host entertain him. Philip had not appeared at breakfast, which Roger had taken early, so that he might be at Alicia's door by nine; and now he was shut up in his library, — "very much engaged," John said.

Roger wondered, moodily, if he had not better have taken the morning stage.

"I 've stayed one day too long in this place," he reflected. He wished Mrs. Shore would come downstairs; he wanted to talk to her of Lyssie's foolish self-sacrifice; not that he meant to complain of Alicia, but it would be a relief to say how, for Mrs. Drayton's own sake, he wished Lyssie were wiser in her devotion to her mother. It is strange how rarely we recognize in ourselves the meaning of this impulse to find fault with those we love to a third person. We call it sincerity, sometimes, — sometimes, duty: we are mightily serious in our task of justifying to ourselves our disloyalty.

Mrs. Shore did not appear, however. The day seemed to Roger to stretch interminably before him. He had really nothing to do but think how badly he had been treated; he even said savagely, "Very likely I 've been a fool to think she cares for me at all. I don't know why she should, of course." This with that angry humility which is so amusing to the persons who do not feel it.

A little later, for want of something better to do, he went out into the garden, and walked down to the stone seat by the pool. It was very still here. There was a sleepy blur of sunshine on the meadow opposite, where the grass was scorched into fading yellow and bronze by the August droughts; here and there, a patch of intense, vivid, almost wet green held its own under the shadow of an apple-tree or along the edge of the water. There was the drone of bees in a little border of sweet alyssum, whose faint, clean perfume came to him in hot, wandering breaths; the shimmering haze on the water was laced by the noiseless zigzag of dragonflies; sometimes a yellow leaf floated slowly down through the still air, to make a silent anchorage on the silent water. The warmth and the play of shadows from the faintly moving leaves above him soothed him, so that, in spite of his injured feelings, Roger would no doubt have taken a nap, if Eric, with Molly pulling at his collar, had not walked majestically down the path, and, catching sight of his friend, poked a cold nose under his relaxed hand; at which Roger was instantly awake and good natured. "You rascal," he said affectionately, taking the great, anxious, friendly face in his two hands, "you scoundrel, how dare you wake me up?"

"He would do it," Molly explained. "I was coming to fish for crayfish, an' he came. He lets me hang 'em on his ears by their pincers. He does n't mind."

"Do you suppose the crayfish mind?" Roger asked. But that did not interest Molly. Instead of discussing the feelings of the crayfish, she climbed up on the seat beside him.

"Tell me a story."

"Don't know any," said Roger, beginning to get sleepy again.

"Everybody 's so unobliging," Molly assured him : "mamma 's awfully cross, and father won't let me talk at all. It is n't very pleasant for me," she ended sadly.

"Well, perhaps you 'd better go and make it pleasant for the crayfish," Roger suggested, yawning. Then he looked at his watch, and discovered that it was only ten minutes past eleven. "Con-

found it!" he said. "Molly, where is your father?
In the library still?"

"I don't know. Maybe he is. Father was out
of doors all last night, walking and walking around
in the rain. Rosa told me so. John told her. And
I told mamma, and she said —"

"Never mind!" Roger broke in hastily.

And Molly, with great cheerfulness, changed the
subject. "I 'll show you something, Mr. Carey, —
something I 've got in a box in my pocket. Want
to see it?"

"Oh, very much," said poor Roger; but did n't
Molly think she 'd like to catch some crayfish? And
then, with an eye to the interrupted nap, he made
several suggestions for her diversion: Rosa? The
nursery and her paper dolls? "That would be delightful," he said, with insidious enthusiasm. "Just
think! playing with those nice dolls in the nursery.
Dear me! how pleasant that would be."

"It 's pleasanter with you," Molly informed him,
hugging him with much affection; and Roger sighed,
and said, "Well," and submitted to many caresses,
and showed his watch and Lyssie's picture, and
yawned a good deal.

"What 's in the mysterious box?" he asked.

And Molly, her little face very serious and eager,
took a small ring-box from her pocket and shook it
close against his ear. "Guess!"

"A rocking-chair?" said Roger.

"Why, there could n't be a rocking-chair in this
little box, Mr. Carey. Guess again."

" Can't imagine. Show us."

Molly, twinkling with excitement and the pleasure of giving pleasure, opened the box a very little way. " Look! it 's my tooth. Rosa pulled it yesterday."

" Great Cæsar's ghost! "

" I thought I 'd keep it for the Resurrection," Molly explained shyly.

" Oh, you 'll have nice false teeth by that time, Molly," Roger told her gravely.

" Well, but God will know where this is, if I keep it in my pocket," the child said simply, and grew red and resentful when Roger laughed long and loud. He was so wide awake now that he suggested they should hunt somebody up.

" Come and see if your mother is downstairs yet. Have you told her about the Resurrection? "

Molly replied coldly, " No; father knows." But her little anger burned out in a moment, and she was eager and confidential again. " Let 's go up to the porch. I guess mamma 's on the porch by this time. Mamma said maybe she 'd take me to Europe in a ship ; but father is n't coming. Father is going to stay at home."

" By Jove! " Roger thought, with real concern, " has their squabble gone as far as that? " He found himself thinking what Cecil must be in a passion ; and his eyes brightened a little and his jaw set.

When he and Molly reached the house, and found Mrs. Shore on the porch, he was full of interest in her. It is very subtle, but it is very real, that interest which a man feels in a woman who is quarreling with her husband. Perhaps it is because, when a woman marries, she shuts the door of her possibilities; but when she quarrels with her husband, she opens it a little, and archly peers out again into men's faces, if only for a moment.

Cecil hardly looked at Roger when he came up the steps, Molly dragging at his hand, and Eric close to his heels. She was sitting in a big reclining-chair which was full of yellow cushions; the old bamboo, smooth as golden lacquer, yielded to every movement, and was as absolutely comfortable as even Cecil could desire. Generally, when she sat thus on the porch, with, very likely, some deeply fragrant flowers at her elbow, she had an air of absolute, delicious comfort, the luxurious satisfaction one sees in an animal basking in the sunshine. But to-day she was unconscious of her comfort, apparently; a dull anger was smouldering in her eyes, and there was a heavy look about them as of fierce, unshed tears. Now, in a weak woman a man finds the hint of tears repulsive; but in a strong woman they rouse only a consciousness of his own strength, or a leaping impulse of tenderness. Her sullenness bites into his thought like some teasing, stimulating, exquisite pain. He would like at once to comfort and to hurt her.

Roger, sitting down beside her, had no longer any inclination to resent Alicia's slight. In Cecil's presence it seemed too small, too silly. He half smiled at himself for having felt it. Alicia, with her droll little obstinacy, was only a child, after all, so ignorant, so foolish, and so sweet! He felt that he loved her very much, and might therefore say to Mrs. Shore this and that of her sister's fantastic idea of duty.

Yes, yes, it was a great pity that Mrs. Drayton should have had a headache that morning!

Cecil made but little response. Roger, disappointed, but desiring sympathy, found himself inviting it by a hint of his conviction that " *votre belle mère* " — this with a hesitating look at Molly — was very — he supposed it was the result of illness, but she was not what one might call unselfish?

" Scarcely," said Mrs. Shore.

Roger felt, resentfully, that he had been encouraged to express an unworthy sentiment, and now his instigator stepped from under, as it were, and declined responsibility. " At least, you have given me that impression," he added.

" The woman tempted you? " Cecil commented.

" It's a way she has had from the beginning," Roger declared more good naturedly, and added frankly, " It was shabby in me to say that; the fact is, I suppose, I am out of temper because I lost my walk."

Cecil showed no interest in his penitence. She looked sullenly straight in front of her; she answered shortly, " yes " or " no," when he went on talking; she seemed to shrink a little as though she were half afraid of him when he brought his chair to her side. But after a while, quite suddenly, and with a curious fierceness, she turned, and began to talk with a recklessness which Roger had never before seen in her; it was as though she had slipped some leash which had been holding her back. She said she was sorry he was going away; that Lyssie had been very foolish not to walk with him; that Mrs. Drayton was really " impossible." In fact, she condoled with him so warmly upon his prospective mother-in-law that he grew uncomfortable.

" Mrs. Drayton has a talent for tears," she said, " and Lyssie believes in them. Is n't it funny? "

" Well, weakness is a great bully without knowing it," Roger defended Alicia's mother, " and she 's in wretched health, you know."

Molly, lounging on Roger's knee, announced that mamma said that grandmamma was as well — oh, as anybody, if she just would n't pretend to be sick. At which Cecil laughed, but Roger said abruptly, " You ought n't to let that child know how you feel! " and Cecil, sobering, winced at his tone.

" I suppose I ought n't," she acknowledged. " Molly, never say anything about grandmamma that mamma has said. Will you remember? I 'm very fond of her."

" You 're making fun."

" You naughty little girl! " cried Cecil, much amused. " Of course I love grandmamma, and so must you; remember you 've only one grandmother, so you must make the most of her, and love her very much."

" Oh, she's only a step," said Molly, with contempt. " Step-grandmothers don't count."

" What shall I do with her?" said Cecil, in despair.

" Your sin has found you out!" Roger commented significantly.

But his reproof annoyed her, and she dropped the subject of Mrs. Drayton.

" Isn't it funny how they understand the things we don't say?" she said. " Really, we ought to converse in another language after children are five years old."

" Wouldn't it be just as well to let the Young Person have a reforming effect upon our conversation?"

" It would be a little dull."

" Perhaps so," he admitted; and added that then, probably, slander and impropriety would become extinct.

" That *would* be dull!" Cecil said.

Roger looked at her thoughtfully. " Why do you say things like that? You don't mean them. And — "

" Well?"

" Well, I think they are rather silly," he explained cheerfully. " Would you mind if I lighted a cigar, Mrs. Shore?"

Again, as a dozen times during these last six weeks, his indifference touched her like some fine and stinging lash. She colored, and defended herself gayly, but with an undertone of eagerness. She

was full of that spirited docility which is so flattering
to a man; she wanted to know his opinion on a
dozen topics, and yet she had her own opinions, and
held them with a charming and feminine insistence,
which, however, being always based upon intelligence,
put her companion on his mettle. He grew keen and
interested. He overlooked his grievances. He did
not have to forgive Lyssie : he forgot her. Perhaps
the spiritual as well as the material world has its
spring and autumn, its summer and winter, its seasons of alert life, its time when virtue hibernates.
It would seem so when one watches the hardening of
a sensitive honor, the wavering lassitude of a hith-
erto robust conscience.

But to the vigorous soul the approach of such
torpidity is attended with more or less discomfort.
Roger, thinking this talk over afterwards, was
vaguely uncomfortable; he could not put his finger
on any one thing that he wished he had not done,
unless indeed it were his first impatient speech about
Mrs. Drayton. But he had apologized for that, and
defended her; he had overcome, yes, even forgotten,
his resentment at Alicia. To be sure, he had seen
with a fierce appreciation the whiteness of Cecil
Shore's throat, the color of her lip : he would have
been a fool, or blind, not to have seen them ; and they
certainly had not prevented him from giving her a
piece of his mind, once or twice, in good, hard words.
She had looked tired and unhappy, and he had been
sorry ; it would have been brutal not to be sorry.
Lyssie would have been the first to wish him to be

sympathetic. . No, he had not a thing with which to reproach himself; yet he felt dull and irritable; he was inclined to blame everybody about him, which is a state of mind characteristic of an uneasy conscience. He looked back, in his thoughts, to the disappointment of the morning, and wished that Alicia had just a little less of that feminine obstinacy in the matter of duty which is so aggravating to the masculine mind, — unless indeed the feminine idea of duty and the masculine idea of comfort chance to be synonymous. He said to himself that he hoped she was not going to be like her mother. Now this is a most significant wish in an engaged man, and one which, if he is wise, will turn him to examining the quality of his love.

When he went, later in the day, to say good-by to Lyssie, Roger was very penitent for his crossness of the morning, and confessed it humbly enough; for even the reasonableness of his position did not excuse crossness, he said.

But his penitence did not lighten his conscience of an uncommitted fault.

XX.

OLD CHESTER liked Roger Carey and approved of
him; although, indeed, one involved the other, for
Old Chester never did anything so ill judged as to
like where it could not approve. But even though
Roger had won regard, his departure had not been
entirely a regret.   A love affair is a pretty thing to
watch, but there are other matters in the world;
Miss Susan Carr said she should be glad when
Lyssie could put her mind on her choir-practicing
again; Dr. Lavendar felt that one or two families in
the upper village needed visiting; and as for Mrs.
Drayton — but Mrs. Drayton's opinion can easily be
taken for granted. She did, however, confide to her
step-daughter that she had been very much upset by
the engagement.

"I have been shaken by it; much shaken," she
said. "Of course, I have not had, have not expected, my usual comforts; but then I 've been glad
to contribute my discomfort to Lyssie's happiness.
It is a little bitter to think that a poor, miserable,
useless invalid like me has nothing to give except
discomfort."

"At least, your contribution has been unstinted,"

Cecil said sweetly; but her face was dull, and she turned away from her step-mother, feeling for once no desire to torment her.

It was the morning after Roger had gone. Cecil was very restless; she came down to see Lyssie for the mere occupation of moving about.

"Oh, how glad I am to get rid of him!" she thought once or twice. To have company at such a crisis as had come into her life might well seem intolerable. It was no wonder that she drew a deep breath and said, "Thank Heaven, he's gone!" and braced herself for the struggle which was at hand. Yet she was restless. "One is always restless when one's company goes," she explained to herself. Perhaps it was because with the departure of her guest departed also those commonplaces which pad the sharpnesses of life to us all. The necessary smile, the formal gayety, the mere requisites of eating and drinking, cover decently many things, among the rest that naked and primal passion which underlies existence; a passion which, smouldering long, had sprung into flame in that talk between the husband and wife, — the passion of self-preservation, with its terror and bitterness and horrible intensity. Cecil may have missed the comfort of the commonplace, or she may have missed the man, with his daily revolt of impetuous indifference, followed by the flattery of his daily subjugation. But she did not stop to analyze her state of mind; in fact, in those next few terrible days — days of discussion, of incrimination, of violent disagreement about Molly on the part of the husband and wife — she forgot everything except the lust of strife. Yet she had felt the vague and restless discomfort of missing a man whom she had known but a little while; a man who was her sister's lover.

There was, however, nothing apparent in the relations of Mr. and Mrs. Shore which could start a ripple of excitement in Old Chester. They met once a day at the dinner table, with Molly sitting chattering between them; themselves quite silent to each other. This gave no particular ground for comment; the maids only said, " She 's got the sulks again," and Philip's man remarked that he was " a fool not to settle her."

Of course, alone, they did talk, these two. Neither spared any truth to the other. It is only when they are husband and wife that two human souls can achieve absolute cruelty.

But until they were able to agree upon something, it was obviously best to keep up appearances; and so they saw each other at dinner every night, and listened to Molly, and talked to her, and despised each other. For, oddly enough, now that Philip had put his desire into words, his feeling for his wife dropped to a lower plane. He recognized this, but said to himself that it was because of what she revealed of herself in these terrible interviews; the subtlety of his meeting her upon the lower ground of self-interest escaped him.

Each was fighting for the possession of the child. Philip stood by his first opinion, that Molly should spend half of the year with each of them ; Cecil violently refused to listen to such a proposition : and there the matter stood, while the long, still August days faded into the yellow haze of September.

Meantime, the excitement about Lyssie having subsided, life in Old Chester slipped back into its ordinary channels of sleepy self-satisfaction.   Even at the rectory the tension had relaxed a little.   Mr. Joseph was still uncertain about Mr. Pendleton's will ; to be sure, he might have found out, but the idea of going to the probate court to make the necessary examination offended him.   Dr. Lavendar, aware that at least the momentous question had not been asked, was very conciliatory, and full of conversation about Miss Susan Carr.   Mr. Joseph accepted the friendliness, and, when he came home on Saturdays, walked in the garden at sunset and looked at the hollyhocks, just as usual ; but his kind heart knew its own bitterness.   Yet with the bitterness was a strange, new happiness, for with opposition his mild regard for Mrs. Pendleton had begun to glow and deepen ; and faintly, like the thrill of spring in November sunshine, the ardors of youth and love began to stir in his blood.   He thought of his weekly visit to Old Chester with a perceptible heart-beat ; and when he walked home with her from the choir-practicing, there was a haze before his eyes that hid the wrinkles about Mrs. Pendleton's temples, the sharp lines around her tight little mouth, the shrewdness of her light eyes ; he saw again the plump girl, silly and silent, who, twenty years before,

blushing and giggling, slid into an engagement and
out of it without a quicker heart-beat or falling tear.

"Old Chester," said Mr. Joseph, upon one of
these occasions, as they paced along together in the
pleasant September dusk, "is very fortunate to have
such an addition to its social circle this winter as
you will be, ma'am. We are somewhat narrow, I
fear, and need widening."

"Exactly!" Mrs. Pendleton agreed.

"I assure you, I feel it a privilege to return to
Old Chester from the less agreeable, if more worldly
life of Mercer," Mr. Lavendar continued.

"But I suppose the stage journey tries you a
good deal as you grow older?" Mrs. Pendleton said
sympathetically.

Mr. Joseph looked dashed, though only for a
moment. "I am older," he said, "in one way, but
not, my dear — Mrs. Pendleton — in every way.
My heart, as the poet says, is ever young, ever
young; and I think he adds, fresh. Of that, however, I am not certain."

But Mrs. Pendleton preferred to talk about
Mercer rather than about Mr. Lavendar's heart.
"I suppose (not that I am inquisitive; I have no
curiosity, but I'm so impulsive that I speak just
what comes into my mind), — I suppose your income
must be quite large, for you to live in Mercer?"

Her interest in him touched him very much.
"No, ma'am, no; not large, but sufficient; and we
expect it to be greatly augmented when my brother's
book is published."

Mr. Lavendar's heart was beating tumultuously; a declaration trembled upon his lips, but the curb of honor held it back. He must know about that will first. With admirable self-restraint he tried to talk of less personal things, — the choir, the weather, the difference of the seasons now and in his youth; and that led Mrs. Pendleton to remark that she and Susy Carr were soon coming to Mercer to do some autumn shopping. " Wednesday a week we are coming," she said ; and Mr. Joseph asked eagerly if he might have the honor of waiting upon them in town, and escorting them to the shops. Mrs. Pendleton consented, with a neat smile, and he left her, determined to learn at once whether he were "free" to address her. " For I may have a chance in Mercer," he thought, palpitating.

This visit to Mercer had been arranged nearly a month before, when Susan Carr, in one of those moments of rash good nature common to us all, had promised to " shop " with Mrs. Pendleton. When the day of fulfillment came, Miss Susan was as miserable as we all are when our amiable weaknesses come home to roost. The night before the fatal Wednesday she looked hopefully at a threatening sky ; but the morning was full of placid sunshine, and she sighed, and said to herself, " Well, Susan Carr, it 's your own fault ! " which comforted her as much as such statements usually do. She thought of all the things to be done upon the farm ; all the things she might do about the house ; nay, even the books she would read, the letters she would write, if

only she could stay at home. For there is perhaps
no moment when we so much appreciate our homes
as the moment of departure from them upon some
rashly accepted invitation.

Miss Susan put on a short, stout skirt, for she
could not endure the thought of any clothing of hers
touching those nasty streets ; and her oldest bonnet,
because the stage ride was dusty ; and her water-
proof cloak, for fear it might rain. Then she took
down from the top shelf in the spare-room wardrobe
a large bag with " Susy " worked on one side in
brown and yellow worsteds : this was to be filled with
the commissions with which she had taken kindly
pains to burden herself. " Can I do any shopping
for you in Mercer ? " she had asked everybody ; and
the result was that when she climbed into the coach
with Mrs. Pendleton, she was naming over on her
fingers a dozen errands for other people.

" Lilac ribbons for Fanny Drayton's wrapper ;
patterns of red flannel for the Sewing Society ; six
silk handkerchiefs for Jane Temple's Mr. Dove — I
think I must write the others down," said Miss
Susan, " or else I'll forget 'em."

" Exactly," Mrs. Pendleton agreed.

Mrs. Pendleton looked very pretty : her bonnet
had fine hemstitched lawn strings like a clergyman's
bands ; her hair came down in sleek waves upon her
pink cheeks ; her round, fresh face was rounder and
fresher for the spreading black veil that seemed to
take up a great deal of room ; a stiff fold even
touched Miss Susan's cheek now and then, or fell

forward in a wiry shade across the little window of
the coach. Mrs. Pendleton took very good care of
her crape ; she had been heard to say that she had
never let a tear fall on that veil, for fear of spotting
it ; she said that spotted crape was pure carelessness,
and a disrespect to the dead. She plaited the hem
gently between her fingers as she answered Miss
Susan : —

" Yes, it 's a very good plan to write things down ;
I always do, and especially to-day. I 've so many
things to think of." She sighed as she spoke ;
" I 'm going to lighten."

" Lighten ? "

" Exactly ; — my grief. And there is so much
to see to, for everything must be consistent. You
must n't have a black-bordered handkerchief when
you take off your veil ; and it 's the same with
gloves, — they must be stitched with white. I think,
in such a matter, one should always be consistent."

Miss Susan said she supposed so.

" Oh, dear me, yes ; and I 've had so much experience in it ! I was in lilacs for my dear mother
when my dear father died, and of course I went at
once into crape ; and I 'd hardly gotten into half
again when aunt Betty went, and that set me back
with jets, — no crape. I was married when I 'd
just begun to wear black and white, and had put my
note paper into a narrow edge, — just for an aunt,
you know, — and then my dear, dear husband ! "

Miss Carr looked sympathetic.

" Of course," Mrs. Pendleton ended, drying her

eyes on a handkerchief still in grief, " then I was in black all through; I did n't wear a white collar for three months; even my petticoats were black lawn, I do assure you."

Miss Susan murmured something appropriate, and sighed. Susan Carr had lived too long not to know that grief, that most precious possession, subsides; not to know that there is a pathetic instant when the mourner recognizes that life still holds some interest for him; that the world is still beautiful, though but a year ago — nay, a month ago — he had thought it but the blackness of darkness! It is an instant of terror, of remorse, and of fearful joy. Susan Carr knew this; and she looked at the widow with that pity for the little creature's littleness which only large and tender souls can feel, — for this strange moment had come very soon to Mrs. Pendleton.

It was a pleasant September day: there was a scent of wood smoke in the still air; in the fields along the turnpike road the corn had been cut, and stood upon the yellowing stubble in great tufted shocks which rustled if a rabbit went springing past, or a faint wind stirred the dry, sword-like leaves; the brook, which kept in friendly fashion close to the road, had dwindled in its shallow bed, and left bare the flat, worn stones which a month before had been covered with the dash and foam of hurrying water; the woods were yellowing a little, and a soft haze hung all across the smiling valley.

The stage jogged along in a cloud of dust, or

rumbled under covered bridges, where, from between
the dry, creaking planks, lines of dust sifted down
upon the sunny water below, and from the openings
in the roofs streaks of powdery sunshine fell like
bars across the gloom, making the horses swerve a
little to avoid them. As they pulled up the hills,
Jonas pounded with the butt end of his whip on the
wide tire, to keep time to a monotonous, jolting
song : —

> " So there, now, Sally,
>   I kiss ye once again ;
> So there, now, Sally,
>   Don't kiss no other men ! ' "

Mrs. Pendleton chattered steadily, and Miss Susan
thought of her last ride in the coach with her impatient and ardent lover. At least, she thought of it
until she fell asleep. Occasionally her head nodded forward ; but Mrs. Pendleton's remarks rarely
needed more elaborate answers.

Did Miss Susan know if Dr. Lavendar were dependent upon his salary, or did he have an indepen-
dent income ? How old was he ? How much did
she suppose Joseph Lavendar was worth ?

" I 'm sure I don't know ! " said Miss Susan
sleepily.

After that Mrs. Pendleton was silent, and sighed
once or twice ; then, with an effort to change the
subject, she began to talk about her works.

" I mean to give a copy of the Thoughts to Philip
Shore's little girl."

Miss Susan opened her eyes at the sound of
Philip's name.

"Oh, is it a child's book?"

"No; oh, dear me, no; it is for grown persons; but there are lessons in it for all. Though it is very delicate, — nothing which a child might not read;" and to show the character of Thoughts Mrs. Pendleton took the trouble to recite a poem about a little girl who went to the spring with

"A long-lipped pitcher of lovely shape."

The moral, she told Miss Susan, was detached, to impress it upon the mind, thus : —

MORAL.
"So if you chance to make a sad mistake
On any lovely summer morn,
And pretty dish or long-lipped pitcher break,
Be sure, my dear, and tell mamma 't is done."

"You see, a book like that will be good for that poor little Shore child," Mrs. Pendleton ended, waving her veil back. "She is sadly neglected."

"Neglected? Molly?" said Miss Susan hotly. "She has the best father in the world, and — and her mother is very fond of her; and —"

"Exactly," Mrs. Pendleton broke in, nodding her head; "but it 's hard on a child to be brought up by a father and mother who are not united."

"Oh, indeed, I think you must allow that I know them best," Susan Carr said stiffly. "Mr. and Mrs. Shore are both very reserved people, but — but they are devoted to Molly," she ended lamely. She felt as though she wanted to shake Mrs. Pendleton. "It serves me right for promising to go to Mercer with her!" she thought, and looked at the floor so forbiddingly that conversation flagged. She would not look up until they entered Mercer; and when she did, as the stage stopped, it was to see Joseph Lavendar, his face beaming with a friendly smile that turned the corners of his blue eyes into a network of wrinkles.

"My dear Miss Susan, pray take my hand!" he begged, pulling open the stage door, and letting the hinged steps drop with a clatter. His happiness was apparent in his very voice.

Susan Carr had not a word to say. She got out, and watched him offer Mrs. Pendleton the same courtesy; she felt rigid, and when she tried to smile she had that consciousness of the stiffness of the muscles about her lips that most of us know in those moments when we try to assume enjoyment when we have it not. She flashed a stern and suspicious glance at the little widow cowering by her side, who whispered, "Oh, I hope it was all right? I knew it would give the poor man pleasure; though nothing can come of it, I'm afraid."

"Of course nothing can come of it," Miss Susan replied, so loudly that Mrs. Pendleton shrank, and said, "Sh-h-h!" "But it makes no difference to me. I'm going to make a call. You can go to the shops with Mr. Lavendar."

"Oh, won't that be too marked?" remonstrated Mrs. Pendleton, under her breath. "And consider my errand, too! Oh, that is quite marked."

"I wished it to be marked," said Susan Carr dryly. "I'll leave Mrs. Pendleton to you, Joseph," she said with deliberate malice, turning to the nervous and happy escort. "Take her to White's and Eaton's; they are the best shops. We can meet at the hotel for dinner. We'd better have dinner at half past two, I think."

And then she tramped off, with the heavy, swinging step that comes only from having walked between the furrows of new-ploughed fields.

"Of course she told him I was coming!" she said to herself, angry at Mrs. Pendleton's meddling and Joseph's persistence; but with her anger was a certain pride in being so ardently sought.

When she had made her call, she tried to find some interest and pleasure in her shopping; but her heart was hot at the memory of Mrs. Pendleton's perfidy, and heavy with the thought of Joseph Lavendar's disappointment. Nor did she feel more cheerful when, across the street, she caught sight of the two culprits talking so earnestly that they did not see her. Indeed, she even experienced that unreasonable resentment which comes to the best of women when they see a rejected lover consoling himself.

Yet that did not prevent her, when they met at dinner at the hotel, from putting Mrs. Pendleton between herself and Joseph; and when, later, grudgingly enough, she went with them to make some further purchases, from using Mrs. Pendleton as a protector, and placing her in the middle as they walked down the street.

But her conscience reproached her for her severity

to them both, and when the stage started she tried to apologize to Mrs. Pendleton for her neglect. " I 'm afraid I seemed a little ungracious, but I really had to go and see some people; and I knew Mr. Lavendar would be as good a guide as I."

Mrs. Pendleton shook her head hopelessly. " Oh, I never supposed you were not going to be with me, or I should n't have let him meet me," she said.

But Miss Carr would not pursue the subject; she did not want to talk about Mr. Joseph. She said she must put down her accounts. Yet even while she was adding up her columns of figures, and counting out everybody's change, she was wretched at the thought of her unkindness to her too devoted lover. Indeed, when she got home, and sat down to her solitary supper table, and heard Ellen scolding her for looking tired, she was almost ready to cry, to think how she had hurt his feelings.

She did not follow Ellen's report of the day's happenings very closely : Miss Lyssie Drayton had gone to the upper village on an errand; Ellen believed that the child would work herself to death over those shiftless people in the upper village. Mrs. Dove had had a whole hind quarter of lamb cooked for Mr. Tommy's dinner; Ellen did n't see how ever cold meat was used up in that house, they had so many joints. " We don't cook no whole hind quarters," Ellen said ; " but *we* believe willful waste is woeful want." Mr. Philip went away on the afternoon stage ; did Miss Susan know he was going? And then Ellen coughed a little, and said there was

a tablecloth in last week's wash that needed darning.
" He ain't looking real good, Miss Susan ? "

Miss Carr came out of her remorse with a start.
" Oh, I think he 's pretty well," she said.

" Well, Mr. Philip was never what you 'd call
pious," Ellen commented, shaking her head, " so I 'm
sure I 'd like to see him comfortable in *this* world ;
but Mrs. Shore's Rosa was in to-day, and — well, I
don't know ! — she says *they had words* last night.
Poor Mr. Philip ! Well, he 's gone ; and Rosa says
that he won't be in no hurry to come back. Dear
me, I don't know how it will end."

Miss Susan's heart was in her throat, yet she
waited for Ellen to finish before telling her, sharply,
that she did not know what she was talking about,
and that Mr. Philip was very well ; and why should
n't he go away on business ? Miss Carr had thought
that Ellen had more sense ; she thought she was
crazy ! and she might go and get some hot tea.
" This is cold as a stone," said Miss Susan ; " and
you are very foolish, Ellen."

" So people are beginning to see it ! " she said to
herself, with a groan, as Ellen disappeared with the
teapot. But Miss Carr did not realize that this was
not the " beginning " of the seeing which she de-
plored. If she had only known it, Ellen had " seen
it " long before she had ; and so had Esther and
Betsey, and half a dozen other Esthers and Betseys.
It was only the little thrill of excitement caused by
Mr. Shore's abrupt departure which made their
knowledge come to the surface.

We rarely realize how astoundingly complete is our servants' knowledge of us and our friends. Our weaknesses belong to them, our errors and our misfortunes; we are to them what the theatre and the latest novel, nay, what other people's scandals, are to us.

And though poor Susan Carr shrank from believing it, it was just about this time that all Old Chester, through the lowly medium of the Shores' servants, began to know how bad, how very bad things were up in the big house on the hill.

XXI.

THERE had, indeed, as Miss Susan's Ellen hinted, been "words" between Mr. and Mrs. Shore; and the result had been that Philip had taken the stage the next afternoon and gone to town.

"When are you going away?" Cecil had said to her husband, suddenly, at dinner, after John had left the room. "Or shall we leave you here? I am going abroad next month with Molly, and I want to close the house."

"Mamma, is Eric going?" Molly clamored.

"Polly, run upstairs and bring me a box of cigars that is on the table in my room," Philip said, his face pale, his fingers tightening upon the stem of his wineglass. When she had gone, he said between his teeth, without looking at his wife, "I will answer you when we are alone."

Cecil cut a peach, smiling. "I'm not sure that it is proper for us to be alone. Do you think Mrs. Drayton would chaperon me, if I asked her? Oh; arrange, of course, about the money you will want; you must n't deprive your art student of his income."

"This is not decent, before the child!" he said passionately.

"Father," Molly called from the first landing, running her hand back and forth across the balusters to make believe that she was playing on a harp, "there is n't any box of cigars here. Father, may I take some cologne out of your green bottle?"

"Yes.   Look in my dressing-room for the cigars," Philip called back.

Cecil put her peach down; she leaned forward, her eyes narrowing like a tiger's. "Very well, then, you understand: *I take Molly with me.* Listen! If you try to 'divide her time,' I 'll carry it through every court in the land, and I 'll tell — everything! I don't care! I 'm going to leave America, so I don't mind the scandal. Besides, people will think you are mad; 'not a fit guardian,' you know."

"Father," Molly said cheerfully, coming downstairs one foot at a time, with the box of cigars in her arms, "I put some cologne on your cigars to make them smell sweet."

It was like a keen edge laid against some tense chord. Philip's face, set with anger, suddenly quivered with a laugh; then his eyes blurred. But Cecil rose, with a passionate exclamation.

Molly, leaning against her father, was pulling out the cologne-soaked cigars with all the pride of the benefactor.

"Just smell 'em! Oh, father, may Eric go on the ship?"

"Do you want Eric to go, darling?" Cecil asked. "Then come here to mamma, and she 'll tell you all about it."

And Molly joyously deserted her father, and ran to hang on her mother's hand and chatter about her dog.

Later, when the child had gone to bed, Philip came into the parlor, where his wife was reading. " I am going to town to-morrow — " he began.

" To see your lawyer ? " Cecil interrupted sardonically.

" Yes. I want you to give me your word of honor not to go away in my absence."

Cecil laughed. " Oh, Philip, how melodramatic ! "

" Give me your word."

" I had n't thought of abducting her," she assured him; " that sort of thing is n't my style. I much prefer you to find out from your lawyer how absurd you are to suppose that you have any claim." And then she took up " Monsieur, Madame, et Bébé," and he went away.

" How silly in him to make all this fuss ! " she thought, looking absently over the top of the book; " but I suppose I must consult somebody."

And later in the evening, half reluctantly, half eagerly, she wrote to Mr. Roger Carey, saying that she wished to see him on a matter of business. As she sealed the letter, she remembered, with some annoyance, that she did not know his address. She could find out from Lyssie; and yet, oddly enough, she did not want to ask Lyssie. So the letter stood on her writing-desk for a day or two; stood there, in fact, after Philip had consulted his lawyer, and had learned that, as he had supposed, if the question of the disposition of Molly were pressed to a legal decision, she would undoubtedly be given to her mother.

"The court does not recognize your subtilties, Shore," his lawyer told him, and looked as though he would like to add his own opinion on the subject. But his client's face did not encourage him.

Philip Shore did not go back at once to Old Chester. He must, he told himself, be alone to meet the question of giving up Molly to her mother or giving up his convictions. Nor did he communicate with his wife; and, her letter to Roger still unsent, Cecil was ignorant of the legal probabilities. She was not exactly anxious about them, but she was irritated at the delay. If there were going to be any complication, she wanted to know it. Roger Carey could tell her; and yet some strange instinct made her still delay to ask Lyssie for his address; perhaps an unconscious application of the Mosaic command that at least one shall not seethe a kid in its mother's milk.

She explained this reluctance to herself by saying that Lyssie would wonder why she was writing to him. "And there's no use in telling her until the last moment," she thought, softening. "Poor Lys! she'll be so distressed." The grief of it all to Lyssie was in her mind, as, in the small jewel of a room which she used as a morning-room, she sat, after dinner, idly looking at a pile of unanswered letters on her writing-desk. A little fire was burning on the hearth, repeating itself in faint gleams on the dark furniture, in the sconces high up between the windows, and in the long mirror that, divided by gilded pilasters, hung lengthwise above the mantel.

To Lyssie, pushing the door open, and coming smiling into the room, it had never looked more peaceful: the flickering fire; Eric on the white rug before the hearth, his great nose between his paws; Molly asleep on a sofa in a dusky corner; and Cecil sitting at her desk, writing, — perhaps to Philip. Lyssie, poor child, hoped it was to Philip; she had been greatly troubled of late by Cecil's manner to her husband.

" Am I interrupting you, Ceci ? " she said gayly. " Mother seemed so bright this evening that I thought I 'd run up for a little while. Esther escorted me."

" No, kitty; it 's very nice to have you," Cecil said, in a preoccupied way, getting up from her desk, and letting Lyssie kiss her before sinking down into a chair before the fire. " Oh, shut the door, will you, dear ? There is a draught on Molly."

" I thought Molly went to bed at eight ? " Lyssie commented, as she closed the door.

" She did n't want to, to-night."

" But she 'd be so much more comfortable in bed than lying here with her clothes on," Alicia urged ; for Molly's face was flushed and troubled, and she moved uneasily in her sleep.

" I like her near me," Cecil said calmly.

Lyssie opened her lips to protest, but apparently thought better of it, and began to talk of other things. She told Cecil that Eliza Todd's baby had died that afternoon. " I never saw death before," she said, her voice a little awed, " but it was n't dreadful. The poor little thing was so sick and so tired, and it just stopped breathing, — that was all. I was holding it on my lap, and I did n't know until poor Eliza said, ' Oh, she 's gone ' ! "

" It 's really the best thing that could have happened, though," Cecil answered. " Poor little Eliza ! I suppose she cries just as much as though she had not six other empty stomachs to think about. When is it to be buried ? Do you think she would be pleased if I sent her some flowers ? "

Alicia looked at her lovingly. " How sweet in you to think of it ! Yes, indeed she would. The funeral is to be to-morrow." And then they were silent a little while, until Lyssie asked her sister if she had been out. " It 's been a perfect day. You lazy thing, I believe you 've just poked over the fire all day ! "

" I 've read a very bad French novel," Cecil assured her ; " that is exercise enough. I feel it my duty to keep up my French when I 'm in the country."

" I suppose a bad book is better exercise than a good one ? " Lyssie retorted. " I don't see any use in reading bad books, Ceci."

" That 's because you 've never done it, my dear."

" Well," Alicia returned, hesitating, " Roger said once that he thought — "

" Now, Lyssie, for Heaven's sake, don't be the

kind of woman who is forever quoting what ‘ he ’ says!   Your own opinions are good enough.”

“ They are not so good as Roger’s, and I don’t know anybody else’s that are, either! ”

“ Oh well,” Cecil declared, “ you must n’t talk so much about him !   If you are forever talking of his superhuman virtues, you ’ll make people hate him. I hate him now, a little.”

“ Then you are a very narrow-minded person,” Lyssie said placidly, sitting down on the rug in front of the fire, and dragging Eric’s head over into her lap. “ Wake up, old fellow ! ” she commanded, squeezing his black nose with her two pretty hands. Eric flopped his tail heavily, and opened one eye, and then dozed again. “ To prevent your hating Roger, I ’ll change the subject.   When does Philip come home ? ”

“ I don’t know,” Cecil answered ; and then added, yawning, “ and I ’m sure I don’t care.”

Lyssie’s face sobered.   She was so happy herself — for she had Roger — that the pity of it all made the tears spring to her eyes.   She came and knelt down at Cecil’s side, putting her arms around her sister’s waist and kissing her shoulder softly.

“ Ceci darling, you know you ought n’t to say those things.   Even if they were true, they ought not to be said.”

Cecil, clasping her hands behind her head, and smiling with a dubious droop of the corner of her mouth, looked down at the sensitive, quivering face before her.

"Lys dear, Philip and I are going to separate. So, naturally, I don't concern myself as to his movements."

"Separate?" Lyssie repeated vaguely; "separate? Why — why, what do you mean?"

"To separate means to live apart, ordinarily."

"Live apart — I don't understand," Alicia said faintly. "Cecil, what do you mean? · Cecil, you don't mean — ?" She grew white to her lips.

"Why, Lys, you surely have n't thought us such a united pair?" Cecil said, surprised. Alicia's speechless pallor troubled her; she put her arm about the girl's waist. "Come, now, you must n't be so upset. I did n't mean to tell you just yet, but there is really no reason why you should n't know; only you must n't be so upset about it. And don't speak of it, please." She paused, and patted Alicia's head. "Why, you poor little thing!"

"Oh, Cecil, it is n't true? You are not telling me the truth?"

"My dear," Cecil answered impatiently, "of course it 's true; it is n't a subject on which I would romance. Now, please don't cry, Lys; it always makes me cross to have people cry."

Alicia lifted her face, and caught at Cecil's wrists with trembling hands, leaning heavily against her. "You can't be in earnest? It 's wicked! Leave Philip? It 's wicked. *Cecil!*"

Cecil frowned. "If you are going to be so silly, I 'm sorry I told you. But I thought perhaps you could help me about Molly. Philip has an idea that he wants her part of the time, — a sort of King Solomon arrangement, you know, and just about as healthy for Molly. Of course I shan't allow it. But he will probably make a dreadful fuss. I thought you might advise him to have more sense; but you just sit there and cry! I tell you, I'll be much happier when it's all settled. I'm going to take Molly abroad, and I'll be very happy."

"Cecil," said Alicia faintly, "do you mean that you and Philip are going to be — ?"

"Divorced?" Cecil ended dryly. "No, that's horrid and public. Besides, we neither of us want to marry anybody el —"

"Don't!" Alicia put her hands over her ears. "You mustn't speak, you mustn't think — such things! Oh, I —" She stopped; she had no protests, no arguments, nothing but horror.

"We don't want to marry again," Cecil went on calmly, — "at least, I'm sure I don't; I've had enough of it! But I simply cannot endure Philip any longer. And I suppose that is exactly the way he feels about me. Which really, Lys, — I don't want to be egotistical, but really, that is very odd in Philip. So we are going to separate. I shall go abroad with Molly. Oh, don't sit there and weep, Lyssie!"

Cecil got up angrily, pushing past Alicia's crouching figure, and going over to Molly, who, cramped by her clothing and the straight lines of the sofa, was looking very uncomfortable.

Cecil Shore knelt down beside the child, the

anger in her eyes melting into the passion, not of motherhood, but of the mother, — the dam. Her voice trembled with caresses: "Sweet! Sweet! Sweet! Open your little eyes, my own, open your eyes!" She pushed her arm under the pillow and drew Molly toward her, gathering her two small hot hands in one of hers, pressing them against her lips, her throat, her bosom, in a fierce caress. "Molly, kiss mamma! kiss mamma!" Molly stirred, and sighed, and burrowed her head in her mother's breast. Cecil, panting, and with passionate, inarticulate murmurs, devoured the little neck with kisses; she strained the soft body against her, so that Molly struggled and gasped, and then said, with the heavy tongue of slumber, "Don't!" and pushed out her arms, fretting to be asleep again.

"I'm *so* discomfortable," she said.

Alicia looked at her sister, then turned away her eyes; why, she could not have said. It was not because this outburst of maternal love was sacred; on the contrary, it was not even human; it frightened her, it almost shocked her.

"Mamma, you squeeze me so tight," Molly complained.

"Cecil!" Alicia burst out sharply, "don't!"

Cecil, rocking back and forth, looked over her shoulder and smiled, with a tightening of her lips. "Well, do you think I would give her up?" Then, as if fatigued, with a smiling sigh, her arms relaxed; and Molly, with a catch at her mother's dress to save herself, slipped to the floor, and stood on her unsteady little legs, blinking with bewildered, sleepy eyes at her mother and aunt. Then she turned as though to climb on the sofa again, but Cecil restrained her gently. " No, darling; you must go to bed now, kitty. I 'll call Rosa."

Molly whimpered, and broke into a fretful wail.

" Don't, precious; mamma does n't like little girls who cry! " and, half impatiently, she pushed the child toward the door. " Take her, Rosa! Molly, if you don't stop, I 'll punish you."

She put her fingers in her ears, and came back to her chair before the fire. " Does n't a shriek like that go through you? Now, Lys, I want to say just one thing about — what we were speaking of. There is no use making yourself miserable over it. I shall be much more comfortable. I have our beloved father's example, you know, and —"

"You must n't say those things to me! " Alicia interrupted, with indignant grief. " It reflects upon my mother as well as papa, and I won't hear it."

" Well, then I have n't his example, if that pleases you better. It is original sin. But what I wanted to say is, don't say anything about it, please, until I 've made my final arrangements. It may be a week or two yet," she ended, frowning.

Lyssie did not answer; she was too heartsick for any more words. Cecil began to walk restlessly about the room; once she stopped as though about to speak, but checked herself, and went over to her desk, and seemed to arrange some letters ; then, suddenly, as though the words had broken free from her will, she said, standing with her back to Alicia, "Oh — where is your Mr. Carey, Lys? What is his address? I 've got to write to him on business."

For once Roger's name woke no happy consciousness in Alicia Drayton's face; she gave the address, and then, with quivering lip, kissed her sister, stammering, brokenly, something of duty, of Molly, of Philip's goodness. "Oh, Cecil, say you won't leave him!"

But Cecil drew back impatiently. "Ach! your face is all wet," she said, rubbing her cheek.

"Good-night, Cecil," Lyssie said, in a low voice, and went away.

XXII.

As she walked home through the darkness, the sense of her own helplessness in this dreadful matter fell upon Alicia Drayton like some tangible despair. Her most agonized efforts beat against her sister's flippancy like wind against some crystal barrier.

"Oh, if Cecil would only listen to me!" she said to herself. "But she won't; she never has." Alicia did not cry; she was too terrified for tears.

When she reached home, she was so absorbed that she did not notice the traces of tears upon her mother's cheek, although Mrs. Drayton's elaborate concealment of them might well have called her attention to them. She went silently about her task of arranging things for the night: she rolled Mrs. Drayton's thin hair into a thicket of curl-papers, and put the shade before the night-lamp, and said, gently, "yes" or "no" to this or that sighing question; then she kissed her mother good-night, and turned to go away. But a smothered sound arrested her, and she came back.

"What is it, dear? Did you call me?"

"Oh no, no; it does n't matter; it 's nothing. Go to bed. Don't mind me," and Mrs. Drayton sobbed

But Alicia's grave patience did not relax into any girlish burst of tenderness.

"What 's the matter, mother darling? Your head does n't ache, does it?"

"You are so absorbed now, Lyssie, in your own happiness, of course I don't expect you to think about me. I 've been crying here alone all the evening, while you 've been enjoying yourself at Cecil's. Not that it matters; I 'm glad to have you enjoy yourself."

"I know you are, dear," Lyssie said simply. "But I 'm so sorry anything troubles you. Won't you tell me what it is?" She knelt down by the bedside, and, lifting Mrs. Drayton's hand to her lips, kissed the finger tips once or twice gently. "What troubles you, mother dear? Were you lonely?"

It was the first time in her life that Alicia had felt that sense of effort in showing affection which is such pain to a tender heart.

"I 'm always lonely," Mrs. Drayton reminded her severely.

"I know," Alicia said sympathetically. "But maybe papa will be home soon. I really think, from his last letter, that he is stronger, and perhaps he will soon be able to come back."

Mrs. Drayton caught her breath, and sat up in bed excitedly. "I don't know why you say so! I don't think so at all!" she cried shrilly. "What makes you say such things?"

"Why, I only thought perhaps he might," Lyssie began to explain, wearily; "that was all."

"Then why do you startle me so?" demanded Mrs. Drayton, sinking back on her pillows, and panting, the tears of anger and relief glittering suddenly in her eyes. "You speak of his coming home, and then you — you just disappoint me! As if I did n't suffer enough from his absence, without having my nerves shattered in this way!"

"I 'm sorry, dear; I did n't mean to."

"And I 'm sure I 'm unhappy enough without your making me more so. I 'm very unhappy; I 'm a great sinner."

At this Alicia at once resigned herself to an hour's battle with hysteria; she knew too well the various phases through which her mother must pass in struggling with a sense of sin, before finding comfort "in the bosom of her Heavenly Father."

She was never impatient with or suspicious of these struggles; she was only tender, with a tenderness which kept her reverent even of those peculiar phrases with which Mrs. Drayton was apt to clothe her religious emotions. We sometimes grow impatient of such phrases unless we have love like little Lyssie's; yet, after all, there is not one of them but once was body to a living thought. A human heart must have beat its way through a terrible or uplifting experience in those words, a soul found them the portal to eternal things. Long since the life has gone out of the phrase, though its dead body still goes about among the churches, and thrusts itself into formal prayers, and comes at last to be what one might call spiritual slang upon the lips of persons like Mrs. Drayton. Yet for its beginnings of truth, let us be reverent of it, as Lyssie was.

"I've lost my sense of intimacy with God," said Mrs. Drayton.

"Do you feel sick, mother?" Alicia asked anxiously.

"Sick!" said Mrs. Drayton, with a reproachful look. "Do you think a sense of sin is a matter of digestion? No; I'm not any more sick than I always am. I've done wrong; and my Heavenly Father is showing me that He is offended with me."

"I don't believe you have done anything very bad, dear," Alicia comforted her; "but — you know, mother, if you are sorry, why — it's all right."

Lyssie had never been able to speak her mother's religious language; she could not talk of God's forgiveness; she could only say it would be "all right."

"Not at all!" Mrs. Drayton retorted. "You don't understand, Lyssie, what a high ideal I have. When one has walked with God daily, and then does something which makes Him hide the light of his countenance, why, it's — it's trying," said Mrs. Drayton, weeping. "And I *have* sinned; I acknowledge that. And now I suffer from the withdrawal of his favor."

Alicia murmured some appropriate word; she wondered how soon she might, without offense, suggest a sleeping-powder. The knowledge of Cecil's intention hung over her as such an appalling reality that it was an effort to speak or think of anything else. Mrs. Drayton still wept. She said she must get up, and kneel and pray again. "He will be displeased with me unless I kneel down," she sighed.

Alicia combated this gently. "You'd take cold, dear; please don't. And — God understands."

"Well, I shall just tell Him you wouldn't let me! I tell Him everything, you know. Oh, what it is to be intimate with God! and I am, generally. I saw a hymn somewhere, and the last line of each verse was, 'My God and I;' — I can't remember the rest. But that's just the way it is with me, usually. He knows all my thoughts, and I ask Him for everything I want; I wish you'd do that, Lyssie. I just say, 'Now, Lord, I leave it in your hands; I want it, and you really must attend to it.' And He always does. I said that when I wanted the parlor sofa covered, and you remember how you found the covering in the garret? Yet, kind as He is, I've — I've displeased Him!"

Alicia consoled and comforted; but all the while she was searching, passionately, for some help for Cecil and Philip. She did not hear the meaning in Mrs. Drayton's moans and sighs of repentance, until, suddenly, the sin which kept the poor lady from an intimacy with God was put in half a dozen clear words. It was not that she had been impatient with Esther last Tuesday; it was not that she had left Lyssie's dear papa's letter unanswered for three days (and there was not a single word in it to lead anybody to think he was coming home, — Lyssie would please remember that); it was not even that she had seemed to criticise Dr. Lavendar to Susy Carr.

Alicia knew all these sins well. It was something which, as the whimpering woman told it, made a look come into Lyssie's face that turned her mother sober, and brought a note of reality into her voice.

"You said you wouldn't get married while I was very ill, Lyssie. You promised, — do you remember?"

"Yes, I remember," Lyssie answered patiently. "But Roger wouldn't want me to. You needn't have asked me to promise, mother."

But Mrs. Drayton could not hear so delicate a reproach. "Well," she faltered, her heart beating hard with excitement and interest, "well, I — oh, of course I know it was a dreadful sin, but I was *so* unhappy. I had made up my mind, before I asked you, that if you wouldn't promise, I should — commit suicide."

Alicia was silent.

"Take my own life," Mrs. Drayton explained tremulously. "I had Esther get me a little bottle of laudanum from Mr. Tommy's. I said it was for a toothache. Well, so it was. You remember I had a toothache? But I didn't use it all, and so I meant, if you wouldn't promise, to — Oh, I suppose it was a great sin?"

Alicia put her hand across her eyes. "Oh, mother!" she said faintly.

It was really too bad that poor little Lyssie did not know how meaningless is this vain and silly threat from the lips of an hysterical woman. Yet perhaps, if she had known, she could have found no wise answer. To receive such statements with the laugh they justly provoke is seldom beneficial; to take them seriously is an outrage upon truth; to point out their selfishness and silliness results, generally, in an outcry against the hardness of the listener. Alicia Drayton, covering her face with her hands, only said, half whispering, " Oh, mother, mother ! if you loved me, you could n't think such thoughts."

" Why, it 's just because I love you ! " cried Mrs. Drayton, growing shrill and frightened. " I don't see how I can live when you get married and go away. I thought I 'd much better die ; and so, if the Lord did n't think it wise to remove me, I thought I 'd just do it myself. I thought — "

And thus and thus she babbled on ; Alicia listening silently. It was a long time before things were peaceful enough for the tired girl to creep away to her room. She forgot to light her candle; she sat down in the dark, her hands folded listlessly in her lap ; once her breath caught in a long sigh. After a while she took Roger's last letter out of her pocket and held it tightly, as though it were the strong clasp of his hand, full of comfort and assurance. She could not understand all this misery, and pain, and puzzle; but — Roger loved her ! She held on to that, while she felt the shock and surge of human passion all about her sweet young life ; while she saw Hate hidden by a shallow wash of flippancy, like a scum of foam and froth over treacherous sands ; and Selfishness lying like a dreadful rock below the currents of daily living, ready to make shipwreck of the hopes and happiness of young souls like hers. It was as though the bad world suddenly lifted the veil from its face and laughed.

Alicia Drayton hid her eyes, and kissed her lover's letter, and had no prayer but his name repeated over and over.

At last, when the night was far gone, she got up and lit her candle, and wrote to him. It was only a cry that something dreadful had happened, something dreadful for Cecil. She would not tell him what, but would he not come? Now! He could help things, she thought, if there were any help. "But oh, come, — come and help Cecil. She will tell you all about it, and I know you will help her!"

XXIII.

THE post that brought to Roger Carey Lyssie's terrified and confused appeal brought also a brief communication from Mrs. Shore. She was anxious to consult Mr. Carey on business; could he run down to Old Chester for a day or two ? She would be greatly indebted to him if he could spare the time to come.

As it happened, Roger really could not spare the time very well, and a stern sense of duty might have made him write to Lyssie, with anxious regret, that he could not possibly leave his office at what chanced to be an important moment; but he was able to silence his conscience for stealing a day off with Alicia by the business terms in which Mrs. Shore's summons was couched. " I 've got to go," he assured himself. " Business is business ; but I 'll stay over Sunday, and maybe Lyssie will be willing not to go to church this once; — and then she 'll tell me what troubles her," he thought, a little amused, but tender. Roger had forgotten his vague self-reproach for something he had not done on the day that he had last seen Lyssie and her sister, and he was aware now of nothing but eagerness to see his sweetheart again. " I 'll take the Friday afternoon stage," he told himself, with great satisfaction.

It happened that Mr. Joseph Lavendar took the same stage, and he, with instant hospitality, insisted that Mr. Carey, instead of putting up at the village tavern, should come to the rectory. "My brother will be delighted to see you," he said, " delighted ! "

Roger, alarmed at the prospect of the rectory, and morning and evening worship, and no food to speak of, protested that the tavern was very comfortable ; that he was in town on business, and would be much occupied ; that he could not think of bothering Dr. Lavendar : in fact, he offered all those excuses with which we try to evade undesired hospitality, and which never save us.

Mr. Lavendar pooh-poohed them all. " My brother 'll be delighted," he insisted, beaming.

And Roger, with a sigh for the freedom of the tavern, declared that, in that case, he should be delighted, too ; and so it was settled.

Mr. Lavendar was honestly glad to see the young man, because he was a young man, and in love, and on his way to Old Chester, — three things calculated to arouse a kindly sentiment in the mind of Joseph Lavendar ; but he suddenly remembered that Mr. Carey was also a cousin of Mrs. Pendleton's, and he was at once conscious of a distinctly warmer feeling for him. As they sat side by side on the box-seat, he scanned Roger furtively over the rims of his spectacles, and seemed to find the inspection satisfactory. He liked the young man's gray clothes ; he liked his straw hat ; he liked his clean-shaven face, his strong mouth, his keen eye. "He has a look of Amanda," Mr. Joseph thought sentimentally, indifferent to the claims of blood on the part of the late Mr. Pendleton.

They did not talk very much. Roger, until the long, slow jog in the sunshine made him sleepy, was wondering what on earth Mrs. Shore could want of him; and the other had his own affairs to think of.

Mr. Joseph sighed once or twice, and looked at his companion as though about to speak. Yet they were more than half way to Old Chester before, in the most casual way in the world, though with a flurried note in his voice which Roger might have noticed had he been less sleepy, Mr. Lavendar began to say something of his young friend's interesting relative Mrs. Pendleton. He spoke of her writings, her garden, her pleasing and most feminine manners, and then he ventured the criticism that she must be somewhat lonely, being (comparatively) a stranger in Old Chester.

Roger yawned, and said, Well, yes, he supposed so.

Then there was a little silence, after which the older man observed, hurriedly, that the afternoon was charming, and he wondered that so agreeable a lady had not married again.

"Yes," said Roger, glancing off across the russet fields.

"It surprises me a little," Mr. Lavendar remarked, and paused to cough gently behind his hand, " that she has not made another choice; though perhaps it is a little soon to think of it, and I am certain that your relative would observe every propriety. However, I have no doubt that she will make another choice at some future time?"

"Very likely," Roger agreed absently. He had waked up enough to say to himself again, "But why does she send for *me?* Where's Woodhouse? He looks after their affairs. I wonder if Shore advised it?" He did not notice how instantly the furtive anxiety had cleared from Mr. Lavendar's face, nor how he drew a full breath, and smiled, and began to talk to the stage-driver with a certain excited gayety.

When Mr. Carey climbed down at Alicia's door, and said he should not come to the rectory until late, for he thought Mrs. Drayton would give him some supper, Mr. Lavendar hardly protested. His mind was too full of the conclusion he had drawn from the young man's assent to his statement that Mrs. Pendleton would no doubt make another choice.

"That settles the question of the will," he thought, his heart beating hard. For the rest of the evening he thought of nothing else, even while the preface to the chapters which were to be written upon The Relation of Precious Stones to the Science and Practice of Medicine was being read aloud to him, and while he told his brother all the Mercer news.

After supper, as usual, the brothers played dominoes, with Danny snuggled into Dr. Lavendar's chair; the old clergyman was constantly addressing the little grizzled dog with fierce epithets, and threatening that he would give him away to the first person who would take him. "You are•a scoundrel, sir!" his master assured him, edging forward in his chair to make more room for him.

"Go on, Joey, it's your draw. You're slow, boy!"

Mr. Joseph drew. "Ah, brother Jim," he said, continuing to draw, "I spoke—I should say, young Carey spoke, of my friend Mrs. Pendleton. You recall your fear that she was hampered, as you might say, by the will of the late Mr. Pendleton?"

Dr. Lavendar, about to mark his gains with a broken match upon an old cribbage-board, looked up, his jaw dropping.

"Young Carey said," Mr. Joseph went on (still drawing), "he said that—but I won't trouble you with what he said; only, brother Jim, I wished you to know that there are strong probabilities that the —impediment which you mentioned does not exist."

"But nine hundred and ninety-nine other impediments do!" cried Dr. Lavendar, choking.

"I am not aware of them," said Mr. Joseph, with dignity; but he breathed hard, and drew three more dominoes very rapidly.

"Have you asked her yet?" the elder brother demanded. ("Hold on! How many are you going to draw?")

Mr. Lavendar checked himself and apologized; beginning, with a shaking hand, to arrange a fence of dominoes like a Druid circle about the altar of a double-six. "I have n't asked her yet; but now I mean to. I don't think we need pursue this subject; it is painful for us both."

"The result will be painful for you, sir!" Dr. Lavendar answered loudly. "But if Ephraim is joined to his idols, I suppose one must let him alone; only I should like to say one thing, and then we 'll drop the subject: Are you prepared to live on your wife, sir?"

"I have my profession," returned poor Mr. Joseph, matching a five, and turning off the snaky line to the left; but he quivered under the thrust.

"Well," said Dr. Lavendar, throwing himself back in his chair so suddenly that Danny squeaked, and scrambled out from under his arm, "in my young days, a young man would n't have had the face to go to a rich woman and say, 'I can earn my coach-fare, ma'am, and a dollar or two beside, but I 'll be obliged to you if you will marry me.' But never mind, never mind. Things have changed since then."

"James!"

"Well, he *would n't*," Dr. Lavendar said tremulously. Then he opened and shut his lips several times before he succeeded in adding, "I did n't mean that, Joey. You make me seem irritable sometimes; but not at all; I am merely impatient. Of course you earn more than your coach-fare. But I don't like her, Joey; that 's the fact. She threw you over once; she 'd do it again."

"You 've no right to say that, brother Jim," Mr.

Joseph said; then, the gibe about his money still rankling, he went on with some spirit: "And beside, it is n't as though I were a fortune-hunter; not at all. I have something beside my profession. There 's the income we shall have from the book."

Dr. Lavendar was silent. He got up, and went over to the mantelshelf and filled his pipe, forgetting to light it; then he came shuffling back. "It 's your draw," he said, and stroked Danny's ears violently. "I — I, of course, expect a good income from my book. But you 've no right to reckon on that. It belongs to me."

Mr. Joseph did not speak. Dr. Lavendar played excitedly; the tears stood in his eyes. "Don't you want a light, Jim?" his brother said, and got up and brought a live coal in the tongs; and then they played in silence.

Joseph Lavendar could hardly see. If he did not match his dominoes, his brother let it pass. "You 've no right to reckon on that:" Mr. Joseph said it over and over. He forgot Mrs. Pendleton. Such a threat had no bearing upon his purpose, but it broke his heart. Jim's book — Jim's income — he had "no right to reckon" on them! He played on blindly; he felt as though he hated Mrs. Pendleton; but he matched a doublet and turned and twisted the long line across the slippery top of the table, and made no protest.

It was a dreadful evening to these two brothers: they wished Roger Carey would come in; they could not meet each other's eyes as they sat there alone, and it would be something to have the young man to talk to and to look at. But he did not come; and by and by, at half past nine to the minute, they went out together to look, as usual, at the thermometer, and to mark the temperature upon a sheltered clapboard at one end of the porch, where a line of such marks showed the age of the habit. Then they had prayers; after which, still as usual, they together conducted Danny to his bed in the barn, and blew out the lights. They put a candle and a match upon the hall-table for Mr. Carey, and left the door on the latch. Then they said good-night, and each shut himself up in his room.

Both of them were awake when, the night half over, Roger Carey entered, and, with careful stealth, climbed the stairs to his bedroom.

XXIV.

" 'T is very possible," replied I, " when a man is thinking more of
a woman than of good advice." — *Sentimental Journey.*

WHEN Alicia's first delight at seeing her lover had
worn off, her face settled into anxious lines.   But
she was incapable of putting into words, even to him,
the " dreadful thing," the " shameful thing," as she
thought it, which had happened to her sister ; all
that she told him, the color coming up into her face,
and even her slender neck flushing, was that something troubled Cecil and Philip.   " I 'm sure you
can help them," she said.

Roger did not press her for any explanation.

" Very well, dear, I 'll do my best," he told her
gently, and saw the painful color ebb, and her clear
eyes meet his again.   He was very gentle with her,
as one is with a child whose modesty is a beautiful
ignorance ; but it removed him very far away from
her.   In his own mind he smiled a little.   " They 've
quarreled, I suppose," he thought, " and Lyssie, bless
her little heart ! wants me to reconcile them.   But I
can't do anything.   The fellow who tries to mediate
between husband and wife is a fool.   But why in the
world did *she* send for me ?   It can't be this
squabble ? "

And when, directly after supper, he left Lyssie,
with the promise of an early return, and went up to

Mrs. Shore's, he was still in the dark as to why he had been summoned to Old Chester.

No, Mr. Shore was not at home, he was told. Mrs. Shore was in, yes; the servant would find out whether she would see Mr. Carey. Roger, waiting, received a leaping welcome from Eric, and responded as warmly. "You old scamp!" he said, lovingly, as the dog showed that beautiful and joyous affection which the human creature is as unworthy to receive as he is incapable of experiencing in himself. But all the while he was listening intently for a step upon the stairs, and he was aware that he was breathing quickly. Then the maid came to say, Would Mr. Carey please go up to Mrs. Shore's sitting-room?

She did not rise to meet him, but she smiled, and held out her hand without speaking. That reception of smiling silence is strangely flattering. Roger felt it so now.

"You see I come at once," he said.

"You are very good," she answered cordially; and then said something of the bore of a stage ride, and asked him if he had had dinner, and would he not have a glass of wine?

"No, thank you," Roger said. The situation itself was suddenly like wine to him. Behind her, high on the wall, a cluster of candles burned in an old sconce, and a shower of soft light fell on her bronze hair wrapped in two noble braids about her head. At her suggestion, he threw a fresh log upon the fire, and, with a leaping rush of sparks, the small flames curled about it as tremulously as the fingers of a

player about the neck of his mandolin; the light
shone on her face, and glimmered in a square topaz
that caught the lace together at her throat, and
spread itself in a sheen upon her lap. — Roger Carey
could not hold his eyes away from her!

Cecil talked, in her slow voice, — a voice that had
color in it, — of this or that : told him Molly was in
despair to have to go to bed without seeing him;
laughed a little at the invitation from the rectory;
said Eric had pined for him. Eric, outside, heard
his name, and rapped on the door with his tail.
Roger answered recklessly and gayly. He had no
longer any curiosity to know why she had sent for
him; he was here, and he could look at her, and
that was enough. He said to himself that he had
never seen a more splendid creature. She was not
Mrs. Philip Shore to him; still less was she Lyssie's
sister: she was a " splendid creature."

" Yes," Cecil continued, " it is very good in you
to come so promptly." She was drumming her fingers carelessly on the arms of her chair, and looking
into the fire; " I have some business matters I want
to put into your hands, Mr. Carey. Mr. Shore and
I are going to separate."

The blood flew to Roger Carey's face. " *What?* "

" Yes. Oh, I don't mean that I am going to need
your professional services. Did you have a vision
of the divorce court? No; we are most amicable,
Mr. Shore and I. We are a perfect Darby and
Joan in the way in which we agree about this. We
are going to live apart; that 's all. What I wanted

to ask you was only a question about Molly. And
I want you to take care of my money, too, if you
will ? ”

Her words were like a dash of water in his face;
he dropped abruptly from that haze of impersonal
appreciation of the “ splendid creature ” to keen interest and very honest dismay. His friend’s wife
was going to leave him !

“ Oh, Mrs. Shore,” he cried, “ this is very dreadful ! It is — why, it is incredible ! Surely you
don’t mean — it ’s only a passing impulse ; you can’t
mean — ”

“ Yes,” Cecil answered quietly, “ I do mean it,
Mr. Carey. I need not bother you with my reasons, but I do mean it.”

“ But I don’t understand ! You ’ve had some
difference, I suppose ; and now you think — Oh,
Mrs. Shore, it ’s impossible ! You must let me see
Philip and tell him you think better of it. You
must let me — do something.”

“ You are very kind,” Cecil said, with an annoyed look, “ but it ’s all settled ; thank you very
much. I merely wished to ask you one or two questions.”

“ I ’ll answer any questions I can, but first please
let me say how distressed and shocked I am at what
you tell me. Of course, if — if Philip has offended
you in any way — ”

“ Oh, not at all. We have nothing against one
another, — except each the existence of the other.
Oh yes ; the daily aggravation of Philip’s good ex-

ample has been very trying. My dear Mr. Carey, we are bored; that is all."

Roger was too dumfounded at the folly of it for words; his face grew rigid with consternation.

"I thought you believed in separation?" Cecil said. "Did n't you, say the Todds ought to separate? Or, no; it was Mr. Shore who said that; I had forgotten. But you certainly told me you believed in separation?"

"Under some circumstances I do. The Todds ought n't to live together, perhaps; but such a separation ought to be made *by the State, for the State;* — not by themselves for any selfish reasons. But how ridiculous to speak of such a thing! You and Philip are educated and responsible people, who propose to do this — this terrible thing, for apparently no reason or motive whatever!"

"Oh, we have very exalted reasons," Cecil answered with a slight smile. "Mr. Shore knows that I no longer adore him; Love's young dream is over, so to speak; so on high moral grounds we think it right to part." Her color deepened as she spoke, and there was an instant's silence between them.

Then Roger said, constrainedly, something about false ideas of morality. "It 's all very well to hide the fact under fine sentiments; but I tell you what it is, it is a case of the Emperor in Hans Andersen's story, who said he was so finely dressed: — do you remember what the child cried out? I don't care how exalted your reasons and Philip's are, the real naked fact is selfishness! But I refuse to think it possible that you will do such a thing. It's only an impulse, as I said. Will you not authorize me to go to see Philip and tell him that you think better of it?"

"You would like to arrange a reconciliation, would n't you?" she said drolly. "Do you want Molly to fall ill, and then join our hands over her cradle? Or shall one of us die, and uncomfortably remorseful love ensue? No, Mr. Carey; the dramatic does n't happen. Molly is very robust, thank Heaven, and neither Mr. Shore nor I mean to commit suicide to give freedom to the other — "

Roger interrupted her, frowning. "This is too grave a matter for flippancy. Let me discuss it with you seriously."

But even while he discussed it the old excitement crept over him, this time with a shadowy terror in it; his earnestness held a singular note of fright. He did not want Cecil Shore to be free! Every argument of conventionality, of duty to Molly, of ecclesiastical force, was hot upon his lips. She could not, he declared, find a word of complaint against Philip; Philip was the best fellow in the world. He sternly bade her realize her husband's worth. He was convinced, he said, that the fault was hers, if Philip, for this preposterous reason which she had given, wished to leave her. "You are a selfish woman," he said, — he was bending forward, one hand behind him, gripping the arm of his chair, the other outstretched, almost touching hers in his excitement, yet never unconscious enough to really touch hers, — "you are a selfish woman, and you are flippant, which is worse. Even now you are flippant. Here is a matter of awful seriousness, and you regard it — or you pretend to regard it — lightly, and from a simply selfish point of view."

Roger was battling for his friend with all his heart, but he looked all the while — he could not take his eyes away from her — at this beautiful woman, who, despite the matter of which they were speaking, was again only a beautiful woman to him.

But defense of her husband was an insult to Cecil. She flung out at him that she only wished to consult him about Molly, — unless, of course, being Mr. Shore's friend, he did not wish to advise her? In which case she would consult some one else.

"I am here to advise you, whether you want it or not," he returned; "now just listen to me, please." He stood up in front of her, one hand in his pocket, the other emphasizing his curt words. "There shall be no question about Molly; you and Shore will both do your duty, and keep a home for her."

His indignation, his apparent feeling that her views and reasons were beneath argument, his evident and rude belief that if she would only behave herself like an intelligent woman Philip would "be willing" to give up this mad and wicked plan, made Cecil furious. She was not for a moment impressed by the value of anything he said. It is not impossible that this was because of its insincerity. He was arguing as he believed, but not because he believed it.   He was arguing from absolute, dismayed selfishness.

" As for Molly," he said, " I can't help telling you frankly that I consider you the last person in the world to take charge of her ; you spoil her, you amuse yourself with her, you neglect her, just as it happens to suit you."

" Mr. Carey, you force me to remind you that I have not asked your opinion about my conduct. I —"

" Well, I 'm sorry to appear to thrust my opinion upon you, but it 's certainly just as well you should know what people will think and say if you carry out this preposterous idea.   Upon my word, Mrs. Shore, it is amazing to me that a man of Philip's integrity, and a woman of — well, of as much horse sense, in the long run, as you have, can seriously consider such a thing !   I shall tell Philip that he 'll sacrifice Molly if he carries out an abstract idealism (of course that 's what it is in him), because she will be left without his influence.   It 's the only influence for good the child has," he ended, looking at her sternly.

She defended herself as well as she could, but his words beat her like whips.   In spite of her anger and her pride, she cowered ; tears, even, rose in her eyes.   " You are very unjust — you are very unjust," she murmured.

" On the contrary, I am only just ; I tell you the truth.   As for your having Molly, — yes, I suppose she would be given to you, if you did anything so wicked as to push this matter to a question of law. Unfortunately, the court would not take cognizance of the fact that you are an unfit woman to be intrusted with her. But there must n't be such a question ; you must go back to your husband, — and you must remember you 're his wife. This matter of flinging off an obligation because it is n't agreeable is vicious and pernicious, I don't care what the ideals are! Ideality can be responsible for damnable crimes." He spoke with that brutal indifference as to his choice of words that a man reserves for men, and for the woman who loves him. It did not strike either of them at the time, but he did not excuse his indignant excitement on the ground of his approaching connection with the family.

He stood looking down at her, his chin set, his eyes narrowing in a certain aggressive masculinity that made all the woman in her shrink. "You ought to be ashamed of yourself!" he said.

She rose ; his words and the jarring anger of his voice were as tangible as a grip upon her wrists, pulling her to her feet before him. "Don't say such things; don't talk to me that way. It 's done. I can't help it. It 's done. I wish you would help me instead of talking that way."

He said, breathlessly, that he *was* helping her when he told her she must not leave her husband ; for Molly's sake, for — for — "My God! Philip Shore 's a fool!" he burst out. But instantly, as though a quick rein tightened upon him, he again stammered something of duty. " Promise me to do your duty ! "

" I 'll think over what you 've said," she answered faintly. She felt as though he had compelled the words; she was afraid of him. Her breath came in a sob, and she swayed a little as though about to fall.

" You are faint!" he said quickly. Her arms fell along his own stretched out to support her; he felt her warm, swaying weight upon his breast; their eyes met in one full, pulsating look, — met with a clash of exultant shame; and dropped, cowering.

Cecil drew back violently, flinging her hands behind her as though she had touched fire. Neither spoke. Roger Carey trembled to his soul.

" I — I beg your pardon; I thought you were faint —"

A spark from the fire leaped suddenly out across the hearth and fell on the white rug at their feet.

" How that wood does snap ! " he said, breathless.

" Yes — yes; it 's a nuisance to have it snap so. Oh, are you — must you go ? "

" I think so. Yes. I will see you to-morrow. Good-night."

" Good-night."

XXV.

SHAKESPEARE.

"No, it was so late when I left Mrs. Shore's, I thought I 'd better not come in."

"Oh, Roger, could you make things straight? Oh, is n't it dreadful that she should have thought of such a thing? I felt sure you 'd show her how wrong it was."

" Well, I said everything I could think of. Yes, I produced some effect. I had a note from her this morning, and — "

" Oh," interrupted Lyssie, " won't you please begin at the beginning? Tell me everything! I 'm so worried. What did you say to her? How did you begin? Tell me every word."

But there was singularly little to tell.

" She promises to reconsider it," he said. "There 's her letter; she sent it down this morning; read it, if you want to. She just says she will reconsider it. Lys, after I left — Mrs. Shore's, I took a walk. That 's another thing that made me late. The fact was, I wanted to think."

" About this, I suppose ? "

" About you."

The color came into Lyssie's face, and she smiled, in spite of the grief of the world. "You might have found a better subject!"

They were in the parlor; Lyssie near the window, for the room was dark with a steady sweep of rain against the glass, and she was busy with a bit of sewing. Outside there was a glimpse of a frosted garden standing forlornly in the mist; there was a yellow litter of fallen leaves under the chestnuts, and in the sodden border a single blot of scarlet, where a late geranium burned bravely in spite of its pallid, hanging leaves. Once or twice a drop splashed down the chimney and sputtered on the hearth; but the fire flamed cheerily, with a low murmur of sap, and Eric lay comfortably in front of it, steaming a little, and twinkling up at Roger from under anxious, deprecatory brows.

"He met me in the village, and he would come," Roger explained, and touched the dog's big nose with his foot. "Come, wake up, old man!"

Eric lifted one eyebrow, and flopped his tail, but he had no intention of moving.

"What a beastly day it is!" said Roger; he was wondering whether he looked as stupid as he felt.

"Yes," Lyssie assented, glancing up from her sewing. "Just see this yellow leaf the rain has beaten against the window! It's too bad about our walk, but perhaps it will clear by this afternoon."

"I don't believe it will," Roger said gloomily; and then he came and sat down by Lyssie's little work-table, and took her scissors and began to snip off bits of thread; when reproved for such untidy ways, he built the spools into pyramids, and then drummed on the table to make them totter and fall. He had nothing to say of Cecil and Philip, except that "it was all perfectly absurd," and just a passing impulse. "It will come out all right," he told her impatiently.

"Oh, Roger, are you *sure?*" Lyssie entreated, ready to cry with the relief of it. She wished he would be a little more explicit, but she would not tease him with questions; perhaps he felt that such a matter ought not to be spoken of.

Roger knocked all the spools down at a blow, and rose, and stirred Eric up, rolling him over with his foot, and worrying him with grumbling affection. "It's beastly, this rain," he announced again; which made Alicia put down her work and say with decision, "We will go out to walk. You don't mind the rain, do you? I don't. And it will be pleasanter than staying in the house."

Roger brightened up at once, but protested faintly: "You might get damp; your mother will think I am insane. Of course you must n't go out in the rain. We can talk here just as well. I want to tell you what it was that I thought about you last night."

If this suggestion of a confidence by the fireside was any temptation to Alicia, she did not betray it. "Damp? What does that matter! I'd love a walk in the rain;" and she silenced him by running away to get her cloak.

Left alone, Roger stood looking moodily out of the window; the fact was, he had decided, after a night's sleep, that when he had left Mrs. Shore, the night before, he had taken himself too seriously.

There was certainly no doubt about it, — he had taken himself seriously. He had gone down through Cecil Shore's silent house, out into the amber dusk of the moonlit autumnal night, half drunk with excitement. All the man, for one glowing moment, had spoken in his eyes; all the woman had answered in hers; then had come the speechless outcry of fear and triumph, the ringing silence — those words of the habit of conventionality neither of them had heard. When he had shut the door behind him, he stood for a moment on the porch, staring into the night and breathing heavily. The stone steps were wet with mist; there was a scent of dead leaves and damp earth. Some one closed a window in the house, and he caught his breath with a start, as though he were awakening. Mechanically he walked across the terrace, and down along the flagged path to the pool. There was a light gauze of mist over the water, and the fallen leaves under the two old poplars were heavy with moisture. At the sound of his step along the path, the frogs stopped suddenly their bell-like clangor, and there was a splash somewhere under the mist, and then silence. Roger sat down on the stone bench, and passed his hand over his eyes.

"Good Lord ! suppose I had kissed her ? "

His danger made him shiver. A breath of colder

air came straying across the pool, and touched his hands, clasped listlessly between his knees. Yes: she had leaned against his breast; he had felt the satin warmth of her arm along his wrist. Again the blood leaped in his temples, he felt hot pulses in his fingers; he drew in his lips, and his eyelids drooped into a smile that drove the soul out of his face. Ah, that swaying weight in his arms!

He exulted, even while he cowered at the danger he had been in; but he lifted his wrist to his lips and kissed it savagely, and cursed himself, with a laugh, for a fool.

"Well, I did n't. But damn Philip Shore!"

Then the shame of it grew upon him, and that inescapable fright which comes with the recognition of a possibility. His self-knowledge struck him insolently in the face. "But I did n't do it!" he insisted sullenly. He almost forgot Cecil, as he thus came to himself and saw his possibilities before him; his friend's wife had only opened the door to facts. He could forget the doorkeeper, face to face with the drunken crew whom she had admitted. In his dismay, he had no concern for any dismay that she might feel. A little later, to protect her in his thoughts, he decided that she was unaware of that hot impulse of his, and that he had read no consent in her eyes; but just at that moment, in the mist under the poplars, he did not think of her at all.

But how keenly aware Cecil had been of it all! When Roger Carey closed the door, and the flames of the candles swerved and bent, and then burned in a pointed gleam, she had stood quite still for a moment. She looked down at the charred bit of wood on the rug, and even pushed it away with her foot, and stooped, as if to see whether the white fur were burned. Then she walked the length of the room with violent haste, and stood, panting.

"Suppose he had kissed me? What could I have done? Why did n't he? He's not a fool."

She came back to the fire, and leaned her arms along the mantelpiece, resting her forehead on them. She felt herself smile and blush; and she shut her eyes and closed her teeth upon her lip. She stood there a long time, — longer than Roger Carey sat on the bench under the poplars. And when at last a log smouldered through, and fell apart with a soft crash of sparks, the light shone upon a face that was full of a strange terror.

She went over to her writing-desk, and hunted among the litter of notes and papers, and found some telegraph blanks. She addressed one to her husband, but she sat at her desk a long time, making idle marks upon her blotting paper, before she wrote: "Pray come back to Old Chester at once. Important."

Cecil, too, had had a glimpse of her possibilities; all her instincts and traditions revolted in alarm. She fled to cover; she summoned her husband. "Lyssie — Lyssie — Lyssie!" she said to herself, her face hot with shame. "Oh, he is *good!*" she thought. She had decided swiftly that Philip should give up his foolery, and she her freedom, be-

cause Roger Carey was " good." She did not reason about it, but she wanted to meet him on his own
level.

It was curious that, as he fell, he lifted her. Yet,
absorbed in the selfishness of remorse, — and nothing may be more selfish than remorse, — Roger,
sitting there on the stone bench, had not a thought
for Cecil Shore except perhaps of dull dislike.

.   .   .   .

But all that amazement and shame had been last
night. By daylight things looked different; so different that, standing there at the window, in Lyssie's
parlor, grumbling at the rain, he assured himself
that he had not been guilty of the slightest impropriety; all the world might know that, seeing Mrs.
Shore about to faint, he had supported her — and
that he had come within an ace of kissing her! So
long as he did n't do it, what an ass he had been to
feel himself dishonorable. Good Lord, if a man is
to agonize because he has had the impulse to kiss a
pretty woman, he had best go into a monastery at
once! He was morosely amused at himself. He
had been too intense; and the reaction was an irritated conviction that he was a fool. It was this irritation which made it an effort to speak on a certain subject to Lyssie: he had made up his mind to
ask her to be married at once; and then, as he put
it to himself, " clear out, and let the Shores settle
their own messes." He had not, in this connection,
the slightest impulse to confess to Alicia his experience of the night before. Confession would be as

absurd as his remorse had been; he never thought of it; if he had, it would have been to say that "Lyssie would not understand," — in which he would probably have been correct. No, he was not going to confess; he was only going to catch at her tender hand to save himself from his possibilities. He did mean, however, to say that he was not good enough to tie her little shoes; and having told so much truth as that, he would feel, like the rest of his sex, that he was square with his conscience. That such statements only enhance his virtue in his beloved's eyes never troubles a man.

Roger Carey, to protect himself, was going to beg Lyssie to name the day. Now, when a man wants to urge a speedy marriage on the girl he loves, he may well hold her hand in his, and perhaps kiss the finger tips, softly, and slip an arm around her waist to bring her shy face close to his, that he may hear her whisper, "Yes — yes; if you wish it!"

But any action seemed an effort to Roger; he was dull, he acknowledged listlessly; it would be easier to tramp along in the rain and hold an umbrella over Lyssie's head, and be perhaps just a little matter of fact. He was glad to start out; the fresh air would brighten him up, he thought.

The street was quite deserted. Dr. Lavendar's old hooded gig, sagging on its C springs, went slowly past them, leaving wheel-ruts full of running yellow water; the shaggy fetlocks of the little old blind horse came up from each step with a pull, and went squashing down again into the mud.

“Well, well,” said Dr. Lavendar over the rubber apron, “are n’t you young folks allowed to stay indoors to-day? Mr. Carey, you ’re welcome to my study, if Lyssie won’t give you her parlor. What weather! What weather!”

“Is n’t it funny,” said Alicia, as the gig bobbed along ahead of them, “ that old people don’t seem to see the pleasure of walking in the rain? ”

“It depends on whether they are walking with their girls,” Roger explained.

“No, it’s pleasant anyhow!” Roger’s girl declared. Her young face was wet with mist, and glowing with the color of a peach blossom ; her eyes were shining under the dark brim of her hat.

“ Lyssie, do you know what I was thinking about, — I mean when I took that walk, last night? I told you I was going to tell you what I was thinking about.”

Lyssie’s face sobered. “ Cecil ? ”

“ No! Why should I think of — of Mrs. Shore ? Oh, you mean — oh, about that? That ’ll come out all right,” he said, frowning. “ I was thinking of you, Lyssie. Look here: this thing of seeing you for a day, and then going off for a month, is preposterous. I can’t stand it. Let ’s put a stop to it. What do you say? This is the 28th of October ; can’t it be on the 1st of December ? That ’s Wednesday. I looked it up on the calendar.”

“ Can’t what be ? ” cried Lyssie. “ Why, you don’t mean — Roger, you are *crazy !* ”

“ I never was more sane. Lyssie, listen ! Don’t laugh. And please say ‘ yes.’ ”

“ What are you talking about ? ” she said. “ I never heard of anything so absurd ; you might as well ask me to fly ! ” And then she sobered a little. “ It ’s simply impossible, you know. In a month ? If you had said a year, I should have laughed.”

“ I should have laughed if I had said a year. Be serious, Lys. Lots of people are married when they have n’t been engaged as long as we have. There ’s no reason to wait. It ’s just waste of time. Let ’s begin to be happy. I know of a house, and I can have it all in order by the 1st of December.”

“ In the first place, you could n’t. It takes ever so much longer to put a house in order — Oh dear ! ” she interrupted herself, “ would n’t it be lovely ? ” All the domesticity of the sweet woman stirred in her, just as some women’s eyes lighten when they look at the picture of a baby. “ Yes, it takes a long time to put a house in order ; but that is n’t the question. I could n’t, possibly, Roger.”

“ Could n’t what ? ”

“ Be — married,” she said, looking up at him with clear, sweet eyes, but with the pretty color deepening suddenly in her face. “ Oh, I could n’t for ever so long.”

Roger looked at her blankly, standing still, and holding the umbrella over his own head.

“ What do you mean ? Can’t be married for a long time ? Dear, consider ! ”

He was very gentle. Her shyness seemed so exquisite. He had no idea of her reason. It was not until they began to climb the hill on the further side of Old Chester that he realized that she was unwilling to leave her mother.

" I 'm young," she said ; " I can wait."

" Well, but what about *me?* " he asked, in the simplicity of his astonishment.

Then Alicia looked at him with pathetic anxiety in her eyes that her ideal should not fail her. " Would n't it be just thinking of ourselves, if we — got married now ? "

" I 'm sure I don't know who else ought to be thought of ! And look here : you may have a right to sacrifice your own life, but do you think you have a right to sacrifice mine ? And that 's what you will do, you little saint ! Lyssie darling, if the 1st of December is too soon, really and seriously, why of course I 'll not urge. I 'll put it off a month, or even two months."

Alicia was silent with dismay. They had stopped on the top of the hill, and turned to look down into the valley, lying in a gray mist. The low sumacs that fringed the road were still burning their small red torches, but they had dropped a carpet of crimson leaves upon the path. Eric, very muddy, and panting, flung himself down to rest ; no doubt he thought of the fire and the rug, and decided that his two young friends were fools.

All Roger's listlessness had gone ; Alicia's resistance made her more charming than he had ever seen her. As they walked back, he began again, so confidently that her little sad interruption, "It's impossible, Roger," was like the steel to his flint. But it brought love as well as anger into his voice.

"I believe you'd like to put it off a year!" he declared.

"A year?" returned Alicia, sighing. "There's no use thinking of a year; perhaps in two, in three — "

"In three years!"

"Oh, Roger, don't! Somebody will hear. Roger, listen. Why isn't it happiness enough to go on a little while as we are? You know I love you."

"I hope you do," he answered meanly.

"You know it. And I don't see why that isn't enough, — just to know I love you."

"Well, it isn't," Roger said, half mollified by her voice and words; and he proclaimed a dozen reasons to the contrary; in his earnestness, he almost touched the true reason: "I need you, Lyssie."

"But mother needs me, and — "

"She'll need you forever, if you're going to let that come into it," he interrupted angrily, again forgetting to hold the umbrella over her head, and gesticulating with it to emphasize his words. "Besides, I need you as no mere mother can."

Alicia was silent.

Roger talked on until they reached home; then he paused long enough to take off her rubbers and scold her for being damp.

"Eric's feet must be wiped before he can come

into the house," said Lyssie absently, and went to get a cloth.

Roger, looking cross and worried, wiped the great paws; and Lyssie, watching him, laughed nervously at the dog's serious expression, and his sudden affection in trying to lick his friend's cheek; but Roger never smiled. Then they went into the parlor, and Roger put a log on the fire, and Alicia took up the bellows and sent a puff of flame and smoke crackling up the chimney, and the discussion went on as though there had been no interruption.

"You say your mother needs you. Dear, I need you. Your husband needs you, Lyssie."

The sudden color throbbed in her face, but she did not answer. Roger could not see how she was trembling, for she held the bellows hard to keep her fingers steady.

"And see the effect of your unreasonableness," he went on: "you make me — well, annoyed at your mother. Of course it is n't fair to be annoyed at her because of your — your obstinacy (that's the only word)! but I can't help it."

Alicia looked at him hopelessly. "I don't seem able to put it right, or else you would n't feel so. Oh, I think it would kill her if I got married now."

"Kill her!" said Roger, and paused, for it would scarcely do to express his belief that there was no such luck to be expected. "Kill her! Why, in the first place, she has all the wonderful vitality of the invalid; it would n't kill her at all. She 'd be awfully interested ; and it's the best thing in the world for hypochon — I mean for people sick as she is, to be interested. It makes them forget themselves. And then she'd enjoy coming to visit us sometimes, and —"

"Visit us ?" Lyssie broke in blankly.

"Why," said Roger, as blankly, "you did n't think she'd *live* with us ? " And then they looked at each other.

"If you wish it, of course," Roger hastened to say ; but in his own mind he added, "Good Lord!"

"I had thought so — when the time came," Lyssie faltered.

"Dear, with all due regard for your mother, — and you know I'm very fond of her, — but as a matter of common sense, I do think it is a mistake for people to have their mothers-in-law live with them. I mean any mother-in-law, even a nice one — I'm not making this personal to Mrs. Drayton. Lyssie, please don't think I mean to be unkind!" he ended, in a burst. "I'm very fond of her, you know."

Lyssie drew in her breath, and looked away from him.

"I'd say it of my own mother, if she were alive," he protested, "and *she* was an angel. But she never would have wanted to live with us ; she had too much sense," he floundered on.

"I don't want to thrust my mother on any one," said Alicia. "I had thought she would have a home with us ; but — never mind."

Roger was silent for a moment; then he told her, as courteously as though he were not engaged to her, "Your wish settles it, my darling. And of course your mother is always welcome in my house. But if she is to come to us, you must see that there's no reason why we should n't be married at once."

"There's every reason, Roger. For one thing, she'll have to get used to the idea of leaving her own home. It would be dreadful for her. I have n't even dared to propose it to her yet. But I will. I promise you I will. And perhaps in two years, or a little more —"

Roger tramped back and forth across the room. Eric sprang up joyfully and capered to the door; but nobody noticed him, and he subsided under the piano.

"Lyssie," the young man demanded, standing before her, with his hands in his pockets, "have you made any promise to your mother about this thing?"

"I said something once. But that has nothing to do with it. It is n't because of my promise. It's because I must n't."

"Well, may I ask how long you are going to prefer your mother to me?"

"Oh, Roger!"

"You need n't say 'Oh, Roger!' That's what it amounts to; but Lyssie, don't, *don't* push me off this way! There's so much uncertainty; and — I do need you. Don't push me off!" His voice trembled.

Lyssie, her fingers quite cold, her voice breaking, came up to him, and put her hands on his shoulders.

"I'll have to tell you. I didn't mean to, but I'll have to tell you. Then you'll understand." And with her face flaming with shame and pain, she told him of Mrs. Drayton's threat of suicide.

Roger Carey listened, — grimly, at first; then he swore under his breath; then he laughed, with the exuberance of gleeful relief and contempt.

"You poor blessed child! don't you know what that's worth? Just that!" and he snapped his fingers. "Kill herself? She'll outlive us both; they always do!" He would have kissed her, though he was still irritated: but she was rigid, and drew away from him stiffly.

"You mustn't say such things. You have no right to say such things. You are cruel!"

Her anger lasted only long enough to kindle his; he was already out of patience. He said something bitter about "selfishness," and "that sort of love," and "having been mistaken, no doubt, in her feeling for him." He did not mean what he said, but, unfortunately, the effect of such statements is not in proportion to their sincerity.

Alicia's face whitened and whitened. These two young persons, with the little work-table between them, and Eric's head poking itself under Alicia's nervous hand and upsetting Roger's tottering columns of spools, looked into each other's eyes, and used words like swords, while each declared the other wrong.

"Then I am to understand that you dismiss me?" said Roger Carey.

"You shall not put it upon me!" Lyssie cried piteously. "It is n't my fault. You are perfectly selfish about it. I am doing what is right. Of course our engagement is broken, but it is n't *my* fault!"

"Of course not; there 's no fault about it. You simply choose between your mother and me. I don't blame you; I 'd be the last person in the world to blame you. I always told you I was n't worthy of you, and I suppose now you 've discovered it for yourself."

Lyssie was silent.

"Well, good-by. I — oh well, there 's no use talking! Good-by."

Roger swung himself out of the door and out of the house without another look. He had never been so much in love with her before.

Eric jumped up with a great bound; the work-table rocked, and all the spools went rolling about on the floor; then he whined, and scratched, and looked at Alicia, and whined again.

She, with poor trembling hands, and with the breath catching in her young throat, opened the front door, and the dog, impatient for his friend, rushed past her, and went bounding with splendid leaps out into the rain.

XXVI.

ROSSETTI.

LITTLE Lyssie could not, just at first, tell even her mother of her broken engagement. There had to be hours of staggering on alone, dumbly, under her grief. She went about her daily duties on Sunday and Monday, dry-eyed and calm. She had taken off her ring, looking at it silently a long time before she put it away. She was too unconscious of self, and unfamiliar with the conventions of life, to think of sending it back to Roger. Her mother did not notice its absence from the slim, girlish hand; Mrs. Drayton had too many cares of her own to notice such things; she "was failing rapidly," she told every one who came to see her. "But perhaps it is just as well, for now Lyssie is happy, I am no longer needed," she sighed ; and added that Alicia's present selfish absorption in her own happiness was doubtless the Lord's way of driving her, Mrs. Drayton, closer to Him for companionship ; which, to the curious mind, opened up interesting questions as to the propriety of the Lord's methods.

But if Mrs. Drayton was no longer needed, she had still some needs. When Alicia began to creep out of her daze of pain, and feel tears starting in her eyes and a sob swelling in her throat, and recognize that she must have the relief of speaking, Mrs. Drayton " needed " her so much that it was not easy to fly to Cecil to tell her troubles, as it was her impulse to do.

"I think I'll go and see Cecil, mother dear," she said, "and Esther will bring your dinner up. I may not be at home for dinner."

" Esther ? " returned Mrs. Drayton, opening her eyes. " Oh, Lyssie, you know how I dislike to have Esther come into the room when my nerves are so racked ! "

But Alicia, for once, thought of herself. She felt that she must be with Cecil; she must put her head on her sister's breast, and cry, and cry, and cry. She could not come back so early as dinner-time.

" Oh, mother darling," she entreated, " if you would n't mind just this once ! Oh, I *must* see Cecil," she said, in a sort of wail, and then steadied herself, her breath catching. " I'll fix your tray, dear, all nicely, and then you won't mind letting Esther bring it in ? "

Mrs. Drayton closed her eyes. " Oh, go, of course. Don't mind me. But I don't want Esther to bring in the tray. I'll wait, and have my dinner when you come home. I suppose you 'll be home by tea-time? Oh, Lyssie, when I am gone, I hope you won't remember things like this! Remorse is very painful. But I have such a sensitive conscience; perhaps you won't suffer as I should."

" I don't mean to be neglectful, mother, but —"

"Oh well, I shan't allow you to stay at home now. I only spoke of your selfishness from the highest motives, — because it was my duty, not because I wanted to keep you at home. My motives are always the highest and the best. For myself, I don't mind waiting for my dinner until it 's convenient for you. I have little enough appetite, anyhow."

Of course Lyssie brought up the tray.

In the afternoon, as she went up the hill, she thought, almost for the first time in these two days, of Cecil's own troubles; and yet Cecil's troubles only made her think of Roger's promptitude in helping them. Compared to a broken engagement, how foolish and unreal seemed the senseless quarrels between husband and wife! Beside, it was all right now; Roger had said so — *Roger!* and the long-withheld tears rose burning to her eyes. She felt as though she could hardly wait to reach Cecil, and as she went swiftly into the house, and upstairs, she had only a word for Molly who was playing with her dolls in the hall.

She found Cecil's room empty of everything but confusion. Two great trunks, half packed, took up much space; the small pictures and photographs,

the pleasant litter of books and little dainty furnishings, stood forlornly about on tables or chairs, waiting to be packed; the curtains had been taken
down, and a streak of pale sunshine fell across the
carpet and into the fireplace, laying a moving finger
on the busy fire, whitening the flame, and glittering
on the brass andirons.

"Oh, she's going away!" thought Lyssie hopelessly. Then she went into the hall, and called her
sister in a listless voice. Cecil answered from the
floor above, and a moment later came downstairs.
She kissed Lyssie, and shut the door, and threw herself down on the lounge.

"I'm tired to death!" she said crossly. "I had
a headache last night, and endured the torments of
the very bad, and could n't sleep; and now to-day
I've had to see about closing the house. Should n't
you think, with four able-bodied women, this house
could be closed without supervision? Where have
you been, Lys? I have n't been able to hunt you
up, I've had so much to do."

"You are going away?"

"Yes. I telegraphed Philip to come back. I've
thought it over, and I've decided that — I won't
leave him. But we must get back to town."

"I'm so glad everything is smooth," Lyssie said
absently. "Cecil, I want to tell you something."
She sat down on the floor beside Cecil's couch,
twisting her fingers in the soft white rug, and seeing the pallid flames in the sunny fireplace flicker
in two great tears that trembled behind her eye-

lids. " Roger and I have broken our engagement, Ceci."

Cecil sat upright, and opened her lips for a reply; but she was speechless. There was alarm, but amusement too, in her face. Was it possible that Roger Carey had been so absurd as to tell — But there was nothing to tell!

" *Lys!* Why, what do you mean? What did he say to you? Now, Lyssie, don't be absurd! Break your engagement? He has n't done anything that — "

" Of course he has n't done anything; it is n't his fault. He wanted to be married right off, — next month. And I could n't. You know I could n't, Cecil. How could I leave mother? And he did n't want to wait; and so — and so — " And at last came the relief of a fit of crying, with her face on Cecil's knees, her arms about her waist.

" Did he — did he want to be married right away? " Cecil said slowly above Lyssie's bowed head. Was it possible that it had been so much to him as *that?* Oh, it was well she had sent for her husband! She was frightened, exulting, renouncing, all at once. But mechanically she stroked Lyssie's head, and murmured vaguely, " It will all come right. I shall make it come right." Oh, she was glad she had sent for Philip!

" If I could only just die! " Lyssie said.

Cecil listened with angry remorse; she put her arms about Alicia impetuously, and her voice broke with tenderness. " There, darling, don't cry. Lyssie, it breaks my heart to have you cry." It came to her with a great impulse of affection that she would bring Roger Carey back to his duty. "Now, dear, stop crying," she said heartily. "No man is worth so many tears. I'll see him in town, and I can patch it up; with no injury to your pride, of course."

"Pride? Oh, Ceci, I have n't any pride! Why, I'd go and kneel down before him if I had been wrong, or if I could make him feel differently; only, it's the principle, don't you see? We could never be happy, if he could n't feel as I do about mother."

"Lyssie, that is absurd; of course he could n't feel as you do about Mrs. Drayton."

"But he said — oh, I can't tell you how he spoke of her. He does n't love her; I know he does n't."

"But good gracious, child, why should he? He does n't know Mrs. Drayton. Do you expect him to divine all her admirable qualities?"

"Oh, but Ceci, he could n't ever have loved me, if he feels that way about her."

Cecil's impatience at this did Lyssie good. Not that she thought her lover would come back to her, but it made her feel that she, too, had been to blame, a little; that it was not all his fault.

She sat there, leaning against Cecil, talking out her aching heart, while the room darkened, and the fire glowed and brightened. She was less miserable, she thought, now that she had told her sister, yet she realized, heavily, that though she might be comforted, she had nothing to hope for. She knew, poor child, that beneath all these superficial explanations which she was making, the real difficulty of the situation lay in the fact that she and Roger could part; not that they had parted. Cecil said very little. Her color deepened once, suddenly, and she smiled; then she set her teeth hard upon her lip, and drew in her breath, and looked down upon Lyssie's bowed head.

"Lys dear, I 'm sure he will come back; and you must forgive him."

"You don't understand. You don't see how bad it is. His coming back would n't make any difference in the question of mother."

"The 'question of mother' will settle itself," Cecil declared, and paused, listening. "That is the stage!" she said, in a low voice. She put her hands up to her eyes a moment. "Philip has come, Lys."

"Oh, I 'll go!" Alicia said quickly.

Cecil made no effort to detain her. She was impatient to be through with what she had to say to her husband.

Philip, however, was in no haste to see his wife; he was hungry and thirsty for his child.

Molly was in the nursery, and when he opened the door she flew toward him with a shriek of delight.

"Oh, Molly, let me fasten your dress," Rosa expostulated.

Philip took the child in his arms passionately. "I 'll finish dressing her. Say to Mrs. Shore that I have come. I 'll bring Molly down to dinner."

He sat down, and Molly, standing between his

knees, demanded eagerly, "Father, what did you bring me for a present?"

"Why, you don't say you wanted a present!" Philip remonstrated with great show of dismay. At which Molly joyously flung herself upon him and hunted for his pockets.

"I wish you 'd have your pockets hung on the outside," she informed him, rumaging through his coat.

"You can't have presents until you are dressed," her father said, trying to button her frock down her little back. But his hands were trembling. "How does this thing go, Polly?"

"You put the holes over the buttons," Molly instructed him. "Hurry, father! I want my present. Oh, father, that feels queer; it pulls. I don't think Rosa fastens it that way."

"It looks queer," Philip admitted anxiously. "Have n't you got anything easier to put on than this?" And between them they took off the somewhat elaborate frock, and Molly frisked about before the fire, in her petticoat. Philip got her on his knee, and cuddled her inside his coat to keep her warm, and told her a marvelous tale of gnomes and fairies. He rested his cheek upon her soft, straight hair, and felt her little warm body against his heart, and gathered her swinging foot into his hand. Once his voice shook so that Molly noticed it.

"Father, why did you laugh?" she said reproachfully, for it chanced to be at an affecting point in the tale.

"I did n't laugh," Philip told her, truthfully enough. "Now let's find an easy dress to put on, and then look for presents!"

The toilet accomplished, the presents were discovered to have been left on a chair outside the nursery-door. Molly, quivering with excitement and happiness, tore off the wrappers, and uttered a succession of shrieks as each new joy revealed itself, — a tin steamboat, a picture-book, a little bow and arrow. At last, fairly tired out with pleasure, she gathered her treasures in the skirt of her dress, with a long, happy sigh.

"I'm going to put 'em in my trunk. Do you think I can shoot my bow and arrow on the ship?"

Philip's exclamation made her look up; but he said nothing of the ship. He told her that he had an idea there was a small box in his waistcoat pocket; did she care to look? Her eager eyes showed how much she cared. The box found and opened, a little ring revealed itself, — a tiny thread of gold clasping a small dark garnet shaped like a heart. Philip's hand was unsteady as he slipped it on her finger, but his words were gay enough, and he gave her a kiss, and perched her on his shoulder in the way in which he always ended their frolics.

But his face was ghastly when they reached the dining-room.

Cecil met her husband with an affectation of carelessness. He was very good to have come so promptly, she said. She found a good deal of fault with the dinner; she spoke sharply to Molly once or twice;

she told John, in a low voice, that his silver was disgracefully dull, and the man blushed to his ears; she looked at her husband across the table, sometimes, with a cold dislike in her eyes, very different from the old good-natured contempt.

"I wish you 'd come into the library, Philip, when you 've finished your cigar," she said, when dinner was over.

He rose at once. "No, Polly; run upstairs to Rosa, darling," he told Molly, who demurred, but obeyed.

Philip could scarcely wait to close the library-door before he burst out: "I shall not consent to Molly's going to Europe! Neither you nor I have the right to take her where the other can't see her."

"Will you please wait until Europe has been mentioned?" Cecil said. She was standing by the fire, her hand resting on the mantelpiece, and one foot upon the brass fender. "I don't mean to take Molly abroad. I don't mean to go myself."

"I — I beg your pardon," Philip stammered.

"No," she went on, without turning her head, "no; I am not going anywhere — except to town, as soon as I can possibly get there. These idiots of ours apparently want weeks to pack up in! But I think I can get off on Friday."

"Why did n't you send for me sooner? I could have hurried things. I suppose you 've sent word to town, and the house will be in order for you?"

"Oh yes; I telegraphed when — when I decided. You did n't share your legal information with me,

Philip," she said, over her shoulder, and laughed ; then she turned round and faced him, her eyes full of hate. " I suppose you were afraid I would take advantage of you? You see I have had some legal information. I know that Molly belongs to me."

" So far as any legal question goes," he answered coldly, " we both knew the probabilities when I went away. There seemed to be no reason why I should communicate with you until you had decided what you wished to do at present. As for Molly " — he paused ; " you know my wishes. Her time must be divided between us."

" If I agree ! " she reminded him, with strident malice in her tone. " I may not agree, you know. But grant, for the sake of argument, that I do : do you think, devoted father, that my influence over her is good? Oh, pray don't hesitate, on any grounds of politeness, from expressing your opinion, — I know what it is ; I ask, only because I want to understand why you are willing to resign her to the tender mercies of the wicked for six months in every year."

" I have no choice," said Philip Shore grimly.

" Oh yes, you had a choice," she assured him. " You could have given up being so good, could n't you, and stayed with her? But I did n't mean to discuss it. I only asked out of curiosity. It does n't really matter. The fact is, this is all nonsense, Philip. I sent for you just to tell you that it is nonsense."

" What is nonsense ? "

" Oh, this plan of ours. Come, now, you ought

to be flattered! I can't tear myself away from you.
I 've decided not to leave you."

It seemed to Philip Shore as though the ground
moved suddenly under his feet. He grew white, and
did not speak.

Cecil looked at him. "See here, Philip," she said
kindly. "I quite understand that this takes you by
surprise; but things need n't be changed, really.
You can go abroad, if you want to, for a while.
Only, I 've decided not to do anything public." She
sat down wearily, and reached over for the paper
cutter, playing with it restlessly, as she had done on
that other night when she had consented to Philip's
proposition. She bent the broad tortoise-shell blade
back and forth against the palm of her hand, and
then held it up between her eyes and the lamp, and
yawned slightly. "This winter I shall go out a
great deal. You can put Molly to bed every night,
if you want to, in intervals of 'learning to be an
artist,' as Mrs. Drayton says."

She was so perfectly matter of course that Philip's
astounded questions died upon his lips. He said
quietly, "What are your reasons for changing your
mind?"

"Reasons? Oh, as Molly says about step-grandmothers, 'they don't count.' I don't want to talk
about reasons. It is convenient; that 's enough.
I 'm willing to go back. I 'm willing to let things be
as they were. That 's all. But don't, for Heaven's
sake, talk about it!"

She was feverishly anxious to get through and be

alone, and have the chance to think. She had not dared to face the fact that Roger Carey was free until she had made herself a prisoner again. But now, having taken up her chains, she wanted to think the whole thing out; to realize what his desire for a speedy marriage meant; to give free rein to that fierce satisfaction of conquest, which in such a woman has an almost masculine intensity, but which, it must be admitted, is not confined to such women. The Very Good can experience it — if the opportunity is afforded them.

" We've got to talk about it. You seem to forget that the principle underlying this idea of separation transcends any mere personal convenience."

" Ah, but Philip, you forget; I have no principles! I tell you I can't tear myself away from you. Is n't that enough ? "

" What are your reasons ? "

" They are my own, at least," she said contemptuously, and rose. " I don't think we need talk any more. I simply am not willing to carry out an arrangement which would have been (there is no use choosing words) a very great relief to me " — She stopped, and then turned upon him with a sudden furious look. " See here ! Did it ever occur to you that I — that I am human ? that I am flesh and blood ? Did it ever occur to you that all these years may have made me hate you ? that — that perhaps if — Oh, my *God !* why did I marry you !" She stood facing him, panting, her teeth set in a passion that turned her white.

Philip's eyes narrowed. " We never were — married," he said, with deliberate and deadly meaning.

" Oh, don't be such a fool! You don't know what I was talking about. I feel like saying, 'Get thee to a nunnery,' whenever I look at you!"

" And still you propose to remain with me?"

" I propose not to make a fool of myself. The amount of it is, Philip, that you and I have been acting as though we were the only people in the world to be considered ; well, I 've come to my senses, — that 's all. I have n't any reasons to proclaim or to discuss. I merely tell you I 'm willing to let things be as they were."

" But I am not."

She flung up her head as though he had struck her. " You ! "

" It is n't as though there were any possibility of your loving me, of — "

Cecil broke in with furious candor. " Love you ? *I ?*"

Then Philip Shore spoke his mind. He told her first, very clearly, their position in the eye of the law in regard to Molly ; then he went over the arguments which were burned into his conscience for the ending of a false relation, — a relation only less base, he said, than those other loveless marriages where the wife is her husband's mistress. " For that 's what it amounts to," he ended, beside himself with his sincere and brutal panic for personal safety. The protest which he and she would make by separating was for the honor of marriage. He was convinced, he declared, that this preservation of their individual integrity would in the end, by its effect upon her character, more than compensate Molly for any pain and embarrassment which would come to her.

Cecil did not speak.

"You do not tell me your reasons, but these are mine. I give them to you because I cannot do otherwise in view of what you have said. Nevertheless, if, after hearing them, you insist that we must go on living as we have been living, I must submit."

"Live with you?" she said, in a low, vibrating voice. "I would not live in the same world with you if I could help it!"

They stood facing one another in this dreadful duel of souls; stabbing each other with naked words; and one of them, at least, struggling spiritually with the same ferocious selfishness with which, ages ago, his ancestors of caves and forests struggled physically. Then it was as though he suddenly threw down his sword.

"Oh, can't we put self out of it?" Philip said hoarsely. "Can't it be because it is right?" A wave of agitation moved in his face. "Oh, Cecil, this is the end. If you will — "

But she threw herself forward, flinging out her arm, and striking him full on the mouth with the back of her hand.

"*It is the beginning!*"

.   .   .   .

Alas for the smoking flax, the bruised reed!

XXVII.

BYRON.

IT was not until nearly a fortnight later that Old Chester woke to its privileges in the way of gossip: two great and exciting events to discuss, — a broken engagement and a divorce. A week before, the village had found food for conversation in Eliza Todd's affairs; for Job had " burst out " again, as Miss Susan expressed it. The infelicities of the poor Todds were very interesting to Old Chester, but of course these other two affairs were much more interesting. There are people, no doubt, who do not consider the breaking of a girl's engagement a very important matter; but that only goes to show that they never lived in Old Chester; and there may be some to whom marital quarrels are commonplace; but such a point of view merely reflects upon their own characters.

Alicia's disappointment stirred the whole village; in fact, only such a matter as Philip and Cecil's separation could take precedence of it. As a topic of conversation, the Todds were almost forgotten.

Each of the great sensations had been characteristically announced.

Mrs. Shore had mentioned to Mrs. Drayton, in answer to some trivial question as to Philip's plans, that she did not know anything about Philip's plans. "We have separated, Mrs. Drayton; so, naturally, I don't trouble myself with Philip's affairs. I have enough to do to attend to my own," she said.

An hour later, through the medium of Mrs. Pendleton, Cecil's shocked and distressed step-mother had informed Old Chester of what she called her "affliction." "Of course you won't speak of it; I only tell you, to unburden my mind," she declared, with tears. "I assure you I've always loved Cecil as though she were my own child. Why, my dear, when she was little, people did not even know which was my own child, Cecil or Lyssie! I think that shows how I have treated her," said Mrs. Drayton, much affected; "and it is a little bitter to have her behave so now, in spite of the way I brought her up."

The news of Alicia's broken engagement was given to the world with all decent accessories of feeling and reserve, but still characteristically; for Mrs. Drayton confided it to four persons, with the caution to each that it was not to be spoken of.

"There's no use talking about such a sad thing," she told Susan Carr, shaking her head.

Miss Susan, however, had no wish to speak of it; sorry as she was for Lyssie, the greater matter was heavy upon her heart. Philip, after the dreadful scene with his wife, had come to her, ghastly white, with a smear of blood where Cecil's rings had cut his lip, and had asked her to take him in for the night.

"Cecil and I are going to live apart," he told her briefly.

Susan Carr loved him so truly that she asked not a single question. "Come up to your room, my darling," she said; and brought him a glass of wine, and kissed him, and left him. The next day she heard it all. Philip was very quiet and direct as he talked to her; but once, as he spoke of Molly, he got up and paced the floor, and she could see that his hands were clenched upon each other until the knuckles were white. He told her of the long estrangement in thought and motive and principle. He said that gradual irritation had culminated in absolute dislike, with its inevitable differences and quarreling, — a state of things revolting to both Cecil and himself, and horrible for Molly. And then he explained, gently, that under such circumstances he believed marriage to be morally annulled.

"Are you going to be divorced, Philip?" Miss Susan asked, in a frightened voice.

"Real divorce takes place without a decree," he answered.

There was something in his face that terrified and silenced her; yet his arguments did not convince her. For a moment it seemed to Susan Carr that his own righteousness was more to him than his child's welfare, and infinitely more than Cecil's welfare. But she would not allow herself to think that.

What that talk was to Philip, agonized to a point where physical endurance wavered, she, dear soul, could never know. He went away from her with the courage which comes to a man who, in the midst of stress and storm, has laid his head upon his mother's breast. That Miss Susan did not understand him, that she did not approve of him, was nothing : she loved him.

In spite of Mrs. Drayton's cautious confidences, by the Thursday that the Sewing Society met, everybody looked pitifully or critically at Lyssie, as chanced to be their disposition ; and sighed or shook their heads, and said, "Isn't it dreadful about Cecil? Oh, it 's a great grief to us all !"

But Old Chester went to the Sewing Society with an eagerness which the preparation of the wardrobe of a missionary's wife had never aroused. It was Mrs. Drayton's turn to receive the society, and there was a little anxiety among the ladies to know if Alicia would be present ; they hoped not, and they explained their hope by saying that it would be awkward for the child to see them. "Though of course nobody will speak of Mr. Carey," said one lady to another as they walked up the street together, "but I do want to ask Frances about poor Cecil, and it would be scarcely proper to speak on such a subject before Alicia."

"'Poor Cecil'?" repeated old Mrs. Dale. "*Wicked* Cecil, I say !"

She glared at her gentler companion, but had no time to say anything more, for they had reached Mrs. Drayton's door, and Lyssie, a little pale, a little older, stood smiling in the hall, ready to help them take off their wraps before they went into the parlor, where Mrs. Drayton, in her wheeled chair, was waiting to receive them.

Mrs. Drayton was full of subdued excitement, but her manner had a marked hesitation. One moment she showed grief and dismay for Cecil, and a " proper pride " that Lyssie had broken her engagement; the next, rabid curiosity concerning her step-daughter, and heartbroken acceptance of Alicia's disappointment. The fact was, it was all so new, so hurried, that she had not yet chosen her rôle, and skipped from one state of mind to the other, in a way bewildering even to herself.

Mrs. Drayton's chair was close to the hearth, and she wore a white shoulder-shawl, for the day was chilly. She looked very pretty and frail. She had on a plum-colored silk with some gray fur around the throat and wrists, and she wore a cap with blond tabs resting on her shoulders; a miniature of Mr. Drayton hung by a slender gold chain around her neck, and she was apt to lift it and look at it as she conversed, which sometimes made her manner a little absent; but she always came back with a start, and apologized with a faint sigh. She sighed a good deal that afternoon, and looked at the picture very often.

" Oh, this is all very sad! " she said to Mrs.

Dove; "it makes me feel my loneliness doubly. If it were not selfish, I should long to have my dear husband come back to help me bear it all; and he would know what to do about Cecil. She came and confided in me at once, and I did all I could, — all any mother could. But Mr. Drayton would know what to say to Philip."

"But what does Philip say?" cried Mrs. Wright, a plump, anxious-looking matron. "If it is not an improper question, Fanny, what does Philip say?"

The fact was that, so far, Philip had said nothing to his mother-in-law, so Mrs. Drayton was only truthful when she replied, a little stiffly, "Ah, I think I cannot tell you that. He does not want to say anything severe about Cecil, but — poor, dear Cecil!"

Mrs. Drayton might perhaps have been more explicit, but at that moment Alicia came in to ask some question about tea, and said, under her breath, "Oh, mother, *don't* talk about Cecil!"

Mrs. Drayton frowned, and motioned her away. "Lyssie is a most sensitive child," she told Mrs. Pendleton, — "so different from poor Cecil, who is just like her own mother; she can't bear to have me talk about this sad affair. But it is very foolish in her, for, in my position, I can understand and defend Cecil better than anybody else. It has been a great blow to me, in my weak state; still, I do defend her, for of course she did not stop to think how it would upset me."

"How unselfish you are!" murmured Mrs. Pendleton.

“Ah no, no; I fall short of my ideal! I had a high ideal of a step-mother’s duties, and I never quite reached it. I think one ought to have one’s ideal just out of reach, don’t you? Still, some one once said to Susy Carr, — you remember, don’t you, Susy? — some one said, ‘Which — ’ ” But Mrs. Drayton was talking to empty air, for Mrs. Pendleton was listening to Mrs. Dove’s gentle assurance in her other ear that Cecil had fine qualities, “ very fine; and so has Philip. I sometimes think it is only because they can’t understand each other.”

“ Well,” Mrs. Pendleton answered, hesitating, and looking down at her sewing, “ perhaps there ’s more in this than appears? Perhaps Mr. Shore has some motive that — that it would not be quite delicate to speak of. There may be some other woman ?”

But Mrs. Dove’s horrified look and little gesture of drawing away made Mrs. Pendleton hasten to retrace her steps; for Mrs. Pendleton always kept pace with her companion’s thoughts.

“ Not that I think so. Of course I know that there is nothing like that in this case. But that is what people will say, I am afraid,” she said, with such regretful simplicity, that Mrs. Dove felt vaguely ashamed, as though the insinuation had sprung from her own mind.

Mrs. Pendleton looked very meek and mild and sympathetic as she sat there in the Sewing Society that afternoon; always ready to listen to the two sides of every story, and showing such sympathy with each that she endeared herself to both.

And there were distinctly two sides to this story of Philip and Cecil. Everybody said that Philip was an exemplary young man; everybody knew that Cecil had been Old Chester's black sheep: so, on the one hand, it was no wonder poor Philip wanted to leave her; but, on the other hand, marriage was marriage, and Philip had made his bed, and ought to lie in it.

Lyssie, coming in sometimes, and finding the buzz of conversation drop at her innocent footsteps, and hearing it rise eagerly as she left the room, knew, with heartbroken helplessness, that all the dear old ladies were " talking about Cecil." " Why do they want to *talk* about it ? " the child thought, being a child, and not knowing the vulture delight of scandal latent, one often thinks, in the kindest soul.

" Frances, you had better tell us all about it," commanded Mrs. Dale, looking at her hostess over her glasses. " Alicia is out of the room, and of course we are interested to hear; though I must say I am mortified that such a thing should happen in Old Chester."

There was a murmur of assent, and a sighing comment or two. " It 's all so sad." " It is n't just curiosity that makes us ask about it, — we are so attached to poor Philip."

" Curiosity ? Of course it 's curiosity ! " said Mrs. Dale. " I am curious to know how these two misguided people defend themselves. Has James Lavendar reasoned with them, do you know, Frances ? "

"He went to see Cecil at once," Mrs. Drayton began; "but she sent word she was 'not at home,' and she was sitting upstairs reading a novel the whole time!"

"I don't think she meant to be untruthful," Jane Dove protested, in her timid voice; "it is quite customary — "

"Not in Old Chester!" interrupted Mrs. Dale; "Go on, Frances."

Mrs. Drayton looked at the miniature of Mr. Drayton and pressed it to her lips; then, with a start, seemed to remember that she was not alone. "I am so saddened, you know, by all this, I quite forget where I am, sometimes. I can only think of my dear husband, and pray that it may come right in the end. Well, as I understand it, they've been very unhappy ever since Molly was born. Maybe Philip wanted a boy. I can't think of anything else, though Cecil's temper may be the real reason!" Mrs. Drayton's voice trembled and her face flushed, as she said that. "I never knew any one so ill-tempered as Cecil, though I 'm sure I tried to bring her up well."

"Yes, but she did n't come to you until she was seven," Mrs. Pendleton murmured, "and the early years are the impressionable ones, I am told."

Mrs. Drayton protested politely, but with a simper. "Maria Drayton did her best, I 've no doubt, but I fear Cecil was born with a bad disposition. She has quarreled constantly with Philip. Oh dear, the idea of a husband and wife quarreling is so shocking to me! I’m sure she never saw it in her own home.”

Only Susan Carr smiled at that, thinking of William Drayton’s intelligent absences.

“I am sure,” continued Mrs. Drayton, growing shrill and wiping her eyes, “if Cecil has talked to Philip as she has to me, I can excuse him. But I believe that what has made the present trouble is that she wants to live abroad, and Philip does n’t want to; which I think is so strange in Philip, for he could learn to be an artist again. But they had a dreadful quarrel about it, and then they decided to part. That ’s the whole story. And I never knew anything so distressing! I suppose Cecil gets her terrible temper from her own mother; I ’m sure it does n’t come from me.”

“I don’t know how it could, unless by example,” Susan Carr thought; but was discreetly silent.

“Well, it is perfectly incomprehensible,” said Mrs. Dale solemnly. “A girl brought up in Old Chester! If Philip had any bad habits, I could understand that she might have the impulse to leave him.”

“I don’t know that he has any bad habits—” Mrs. Drayton began.

“You know he has n’t!” said Susan Carr, indignantly.

“—but Cecil said to me, once, that he had ‘didactic hysteria,’ and you know she never liked sick people. I had always thought he had very good health, but perhaps this has come on lately.

She has no patience with it, I suppose — which is something I can't understand in her! I should think any wife would be grateful for the chance to wait on a sick husband. My poor dear William! how happy I should be to attend his sick-bed."

The ladies of the Sewing Society looked at each other, but only Susan Carr smiled broadly. Then Mrs. Wright said with some haste, as though to hide embarrassment, "But what's going to become of Molly? Which one of them will have Molly?"

"Oh, Cecil, I suppose. Poor Molly!" Mrs. Drayton answered mournfully.

"Well, I don't see how Philip can make up his mind to part with her," said Mrs. Wright. "I always thought he was so fond of her."

Then Susan Carr broke through the silence which she had set upon her lips that whole afternoon: "Philip wants to divide Molly's time between himself and Cecil. She won't consent to that, and she's going to keep the child; but Philip is to see her as often as he wants to."

"Well," said Mrs. Pendleton mildly, "Mrs. Dove and I were just saying, we wondered whether it would not be best that the real reason for this most regrettable affair should be known? One fancies — anything! Why, I have no doubt that there are people who would say — I quite hesitate to repeat such a thing," and she glanced at Mrs. Dove — "who would say, 'Who is the woman in the case?'"

"Why, Jane Temple!" cried Miss Carr angrily. "I wouldn't have believed that of you!"

"But I did n't mean — I did n't say — " protested poor Mrs. Dove. But the conversation swept past her before she could explain or deny.

Miss Susan, her face flushed and agitated, declared that, rather than have such things said, she would say what she knew of the matter: Philip and Cecil did not love each other any longer. That was the whole story. They had long ago parted in everything but word. "It 's nothing worse than just not loving each other."

"Not love each other? "

"You mean they quarrel? "

"I never heard anything so absurd! "

"So wicked, I say! " old Mrs. Dale proclaimed.

"Let them try to love each other," Mrs. Wright said emphatically; " and, dear me, what have they got to complain of? Philip is n't a religious man, I 'm afraid, but he 's always very polite. And Cecil is the best housekeeper I know. Do you remember how she taught her cook to broil grouse, and then put that jelly and stuff all around it? Cecil makes him very comfortable. Gracious! I could keep my husband good natured from one year's end to another, if I could have a table like Cecil's."

"I fear Cecil is one of those persons to whom St. Paul refers in the third chapter of Philippians, who make a god of their belly," said Mrs. Dale, in a deep voice, fixing her eyes upon Mrs. Wright, whose face immediately grew very red.

Susan Carr, listening, felt helplessly that all those things which Philip had said to her of honor and

purity could not be repeated here. They would not
be understood. " When people don't love each
other," she began, " it does seem not nice for them
to go on living together —" But severe voices interrupted her.

" Susan Carr, when you 've lived as long as I
have, you 'll know that *duty* is a form of love," Mrs.
Dale rebuked her.

" Well, I think that a nice, feminine, ladylike
person always does love her husband," Mrs. Pendleton observed, with great gentility ; and added to Mrs.
Drayton, in a low voice, that sometimes dear Susan
Carr was almost indelicate.

Miss Susan sighed, and accepted the various
reproofs meekly enough. No doubt the ladies were
right, she said ; only sometimes, just for a moment,
it did seem wrong to insist that two people who
quarreled like — like cats and dogs should go on
living together. But still, of course, the ladies were
right. And certainly Philip and Cecil were wrong.
She had told Philip so.

" Well, what is Philip going to live on ? — that 's
what I 'd like to know," some one said ; and then
the Sewing Society looked at Miss Susan.

" I don't know what he 'll do. But he 'll find
something. I 'm not afraid for Philip," she answered proudly.

" Well, I suppose Cecil will give him something
for managing her money for her ? " some one suggested. But Miss Susan shook her head.

" Cecil is going to ask " — she dropped her voice,

and glanced toward the door — "to ask Mr. Carey to do that. Oh dear, I do hope and pray the young man will try to reconcile them."

"Oh, then very likely he'll come down to Old Chester to see Cecil about it!" said the Sewing Society; and the possibility of a reconciliation between Alicia and her lover instantly struck these kindly women, and for a little while the greater and more interesting subject dropped. But Lyssie, coming along the hall with some plates and napkins, stopped, trembling, at that mention of Roger's return.

" Though it 's nothing to me," she thought, very pallid and breathless.

Tea, and Alicia, put an end to all interesting conversation. The ladies rolled up their work neatly, and chattered about the missionary's wife, and looked with quick, sidelong glances at Lyssie, as she stepped, smiling, about, handing the cake, or the little tray that held the decanter and glasses.

" She looks pale," they said aside to one another, and dipped up their chocolate custard from tall glasses, and broke off crumbling bits from their slices of cake. Only Mrs. Dove showed the pity in her heart : she took Lyssie's hand, as the girl passed her, and patted it without speaking. But tears came to the child's eyes.

Susan Carr, as she went home, hoped nervously that she had not been indiscreet in what she had told the Sewing Society. " I could not have those things said about Philip," she thought. Her mind was full of Philip; and yet, that night, as she sat by the round centre-table in her parlor, sometimes reading, but oftener thinking of this dreadful affair, her newspaper slipped once into her lap, and she looked absently over the top of her glasses, and smiled a little, and sighed.

"I wonder if Joseph *will* try again?" Her face grew as conscious as a girl's. "Of course I must n't let him; but if he does —"

XXVIII.

There are occasions when a man dares not look into his own eyes for fear of what he may see there.

In spite of Alicia's assurance, Roger Carey's return to Old Chester could not but be something to her. It meant the instant thought on waking, " Will he be here to-day ? " and the last ache of pain at night fading into a dream that he had come. It meant staying indoors lest he might have arrived, and she should have the pain of meeting him in the street; it meant long, aimless walks for the chance of seeing him, and the start at every tall figure in the distance. To be sure, she might have ended the uncertainty by asking Cecil when he was coming. But she could not ask any one. She could not speak his name.

Over and over, in her mind, she enacted possible meetings; especially that scene so dear to youth, of her own deathbed, and a beautiful and satisfying reconciliation. If she should be going to die, — and it seemed to Lyssie that she should not live long, — why then she would tell them to send for Roger. And he would come, — oh yes, she was sure he would come when he should hear that she was going to die; and he would be so unhappy, — her eyes always filled and her lip quivered at the thought of his repentance and grief; but she would comfort him;

she would tell him it was n't his fault, it was just
fate !

Sometimes she thought that instead of summoning
him to her deathbed she would leave a letter for
him, "explaining" everything; and she even went
so far as to write, "Dear Roger, I want you to
know that I don't blame you — " But she stopped
there, for the date of her letter must not be too far
in advance of her demise, and no mortal disease had
as yet declared itself.

She knew no better, poor child, than to read over
and over the letters she had received from Roger
Carey during their short engagement, and she suffered accordingly. For very exquisite pain, there is
nothing which may be more highly commended than
the reading of old love-letters after love has died.
It is like touching something dead; the pain is
mixed with a curious disgust, as though the scent of
corruption entered into the very soul. Alicia read,
and remembered, and suffered. She went through
those weary alternations of excusing and condemn-
ing herself; those wearier moments of realizing
that the whole difficulty lay in something far deeper
than circumstances which might be either excused
or condemned, — the radical and hopeless difficulty of a conscientious difference in the point of
view.

Those were dark days for Lyssie Drayton; but
she made no public moan of sickness or of neglected
work. In her simple way, she was glad of the silent
friendship of pity which she knew was all about her;

and she cried a little sometimes at the disapproval
which went hand in hand with pity, — for the disapproval of her elders was grief to Lyssie. She knew
that Mrs. Pendleton thought her a jilt, and Dr.
Lavendar was disappointed in her, and even kind
Miss Susan was surprised and sorry. But she made
no explanation or excuse for the broken engagement.
Why give any one cause to blame her mother?
Why give her mother the pain which comes to one
who accepts the sacrifice, even the necessary sacrifice,
of another's life?

Mrs. Drayton, after the first delight of hearing
that she was to have her child "forever," had grown
a little impatient with Lyssie's quiet; later a half-
sullen indifference fell upon her, until the flat and
tasteless moment when she recognized that Alicia
had robbed her of a grievance; then she was frankly
cross.

Alicia for once did not try to understand her mother's moods. It was hard for her to try to understand or to be interested in anything. Even her
dismay and grief for her sister came with a sense of
effort.

Cecil gave her no information beyond the fact
that she and Philip, on thinking it over, had decided
that it was best to part.

Cecil was cruel to her little sister in those autumn
days: she seemed uneasy in Alicia's presence; she
snubbed her violently; she said things about Mrs.
Drayton that brought the angry color into the girl's
cheek. Perhaps that was why Lyssie never asked

her when Roger was coming to Old Chester. And
Cecil did not volunteer the information.

But she had referred Philip's lawyer to Roger
Carey, who would, she said, take charge of her affairs. "Why not?" she asked herself angrily.
"He is free, and I am free — or I shall be; and
there's no reason why he should n't look after things
for me." Yet it was some days after this decision
that she wrote to him; and meantime Roger Carey's
first intimation of the temptation before him had
come in legal form : —

DEAR SIR, — I have been consulted by Mr.
Philip Shore in relation to certain family matters,
and I am advised by Mrs. Shore, whom I have seen
in this same connection, that you will represent her
interests. Kindly let me know when it will be convenient for you to meet me.

Very truly yours,
GIFFORD WOODHOUSE.

Roger was sitting gloomily before a cluttered
desk; his feet were supported by the yielding edge
of his waste-basket, a pipe warmed the hollow of his
left hand, while with his right he was making aimless marks and dashes on his blotting-paper. He
had been thinking of Lyssie. He had thought
much of Lyssie in these weeks that had passed since
the engagement had been broken. He went over
and over in his mind her unreasonableness, her foolishness, her unkindness. He did not think much of

his own. He sucked away at his pipe, and looked at the red glow brightening and fading in the brier-wood bowl, and assured himself that it was far better that the engagement was broken. "Confound an unreasonable woman!" said Roger Carey; he could stand anything but unreasonableness, he told himself angrily.

He had never been so much in love with Lyssie before; but he did not know it. All he knew was, that he recognized, in a half-sneaking way, that he had not been very much in love with her when he had proposed to her.

He nestled the hot bowl of his pipe down into the palm of his hand, and set his teeth, and said that unreasonableness was the only thing he had no patience with. And then he thought how much he should like to talk the matter over with Mrs. Shore. She was a reasonable woman. She would see how preposterous Lyssie's conduct had been, and how fair was his demand. "I offered to wait six months," he justified himself. Mrs. Shore would appreciate all that; though she would not see the fear which had lurked behind his entreaties to Alicia. In that fear, he admitted, *he* had been unreasonable.

"Yes, I'd like to talk it over with her," he thought, an absent look softening his eyes.

Now, Roger Carey was not that objectionable sort of man who, when he is in any difficulty, must needs run crying to some woman's knee for sympathy; so, when he felt the impulse to tell Cecil his woes, he might well have mistrusted it. But Roger was not given to analyzing his impulses.

Sitting here in his office, in the darkening November afternoon, with love for Lyssie tugging at his heart, with his pulse quickening at the remembered look and touch of another woman, he put his hand out listlessly for a letter a messenger brought into his office.

When he had read it, he got up breathlessly and walked the length of the room; and came back, and stood by his desk, and read it again. "Shore's a fool!" he said, and struck the letter across his hand sharply; his face was alert and vivid.

He stood there a moment, and then flung his office-door open. "Here, you! Johnny! come and light the gas; why don't you attend to your business?"

Yet when his boy came in, stumbling with haste, Roger Carey did no more than pull down the cover of his desk with a bang, and fling himself out of the door. He would go and take a walk, he said to himself.

In his mind two thoughts were struggling for control: an intellectual appreciation of Philip Shore's purpose; and, beating the appreciation down, a rude and brutal wonder, a fierce joy, an exulting contempt. "He's a damned fool!" he said again.

In aimless, irritated haste, he walked on, under a low and melancholy sky, far out into the country. His mind was in a tumult, but the situation, so far as the Shóres were concerned, seemed perfectly pa-tent to him. He had, of course, no idea of that last quarrel. He took it for granted that Cecil's promise to him to "reconsider" had not amounted to anything, and that she was going to carry out the plan of separation; probably she had refused to give up any part of Molly's time, and the result was that Philip was going to bring the matter to a legal issue. "But he hasn't any case; he hasn't a leg to stand on! What's Woodhouse thinking of to let him push it?" he thought, frowning. He was not surprised that Mrs. Shore wished him to represent her; and he said to himself, with entire sincerity, that he had no doubt Philip wished it, also. "It's better that it should be a friend of Shore's as well as hers," he declared, and struck out with his stick at a dead mullein-stalk standing by the roadside. His mind leaped ahead to all sorts of possibilities. When it was settled, where would she go? What would she do! Live abroad, probably, after the fashion of the *déclassée* American woman. "She has a gorgeous sort of nature," he reflected. How curious it would be to lose sight of her! In these few months she had impressed her individuality profoundly upon him, — "in a perfectly impersonal way," he reminded himself.

"This whole row is as unreal as the theatre, but it's mighty interesting to the observer," he thought. He overlooked the fact that one who observes the play from the wings, awaiting his own cue to rush upon the stage, feels a different interest from one who sits before the footlights.

He tramped home in the mud and darkness, still too absorbed to know that he was a great fool to have walked six miles in a rainy fog. Now, a man who does not, upon viewing his boots after such an excursion, call himself a fool is decidedly not in the " impersonal " stage.

The next day came Cecil Shore's letter; a brief and somewhat ill-tempered summons that he should come and advise her about the necessary steps in the divorce suit which she proposed to bring.

" Divorce ! " said Roger Carey contemptuously. " She does n't know what she 's talking about; she can't get a divorce in any decent way ; and I would n't let her, if she could."

But so it came that he went down to Old Chester.

He went to receive instructions from his client ; he went to advise her to the best of his ability; he went because the devil, masquerading as professional duty, beckoned him from the white page of the lawyer's letter. And before he went he looked up the Dakota divorce laws.

And here was a strange thing: under all his anger which refused to recognize it, he loved Alicia Drayton. But this phase of his experience was as remote from that love as is the hunger with which an artist falls upon his bread and cheese remote from his passion before his canvas. One does not contradict the other.

That journey to Old Chester was a crisis in Roger's life. He went as far as Mercer in company with a friend, and had no time to think about himself, in their talk of the political situation and the recent election. Not that Roger cared the snap of his finger about the election. " They might have elected the devil, if they 'd wanted to ; I should n't have cared!" he swore softly under his breath, driven to the verge of madness by his companion's earnestness. But conversation upon the high theme of the moral purpose in government served to shut out connected thought on other purposes not moral. And when, at last, he climbed up on the box-seat of the coach at Mercer, it was with the profound relief of a man who can get his mental breath, who can think and reason and decide.

Yet, in spite of such an opportunity, Roger seemed to find nothing particular to think about : the off leader had an ugly way of throwing his head ; the whiffletree was obviously cracked ; how strange it would seem to be in Old Chester merely on business. Then the driver got on the box and gathered up his reins, and there was the tug and pull, the sagging pitch forward, and a rush of memories to Roger Carey's mind that hurt him like lashes. He wanted, with the mere impatience of pain, to forget them, — to forget that first journey across these rolling Pennsylvania hills, brown now, and swept by a bitter wind. He could not endure the remembrance of his arrival, six months ago, in Old Chester : the stately house, with its garden and orchards up on the hillside ; Philip opening the stage-door ; a young girl, with serious, pleasant eyes, standing, smiling, on the steps, leaf shadows from the great

locust-trees moving across her. face and hair. The
difference between that journey and this was intolerable.

He made spasmodic efforts at conversation with
the driver. He observed that Jonas ought to cure
the leader of throwing his head back that way. ·
" I 'd put a martingale on him," he said ; and added
that he thought the off mare was spavined.

" She cast her shoe first, and went lame," Jonas
jolted out.

" And she 's been lame ever since, I suppose ? "
Roger said absently, bending forward to watch the
twist and give of the mare's leg. He was reflecting
upon the truth, which is inspiring or depressing as
one looks at it, that, after passing through a great experience, a man cannot remain what he was ; he must
either be better or worse. " Yes," he was saying to
himself doggedly, " better or worse. Well, I 'm
worse; and," he added meanly, after the oldest
fashion of his sex, " it 's Lyssie's fault ! "

It seemed as though always his thoughts came
back to Lyssie. He was angry at her because it gave
him such pain to think of her. Nor would he allow
himself to think of Mrs. Shore save as the commonplace, business reason for his taking this journey.
He never once looked behind the professional need
there was for him to come ; he never uncovered the
shame lurking under his well-turned phrases : " I 'm
glad to be of any assistance, but it 's beastly to have
to come to Old Chester." " I wish she had sent for
somebody else. Still, it would have been unfriendly

to Philip as well as to her to have refused to come."

Then he began to speculate upon the divorce laws of Dakota; but started, to see beneath the veil he stretched between his inner and outer self a glimpse of the real and shameful meaning of his thoughts. After that, for some time he talked resolutely to Jonas.

Yet as the stage turned from the road, and went down to ford the creek so that the horses might drink, Roger found this suggestion of divorce again leering up at him from under the flimsy pretense of being an impersonal comment: "She could bring suit for desertion." He looked over the wheel at the shallow, racing little stream, and heard the pebbles grate against the tire. The horses, steaming a little, drank, and shook their necks in their heavy collars. There was the clash and rattle of buckles and trace-chains. Roger listlessly followed with his eyes the course of the brook which, from far up across the fields, came chattering down to the ford, whirling itself into foam around a big stone that broke its path before it slipped under the bridge and was off into the woods.

"Yes, she can go out to Dakota; it can easily be arranged."

It came dully to his mind, — the instinct, perhaps, of the gentleman, an instinct which at such moments seems artificial, or at least acquired, — it came to his mind that such a proceeding was not for Cecil's honor. But a fierce selfishness leaped up and choked this refinement of civilization, and left her in his thought merely the woman ; himself merely the man.

Then again, angrily, he insisted that he was considering only the legal possibilities ; that it was nothing to him one way or the other.

When at last, in the early November dusk, the stage drew up at the tavern, he was fatigued in body and soul by this wrestling with a vague, elusive, nay, a denied temptation. / If he had been willing to face it for what it was, if he had summoned the devil out from behind his phrases, he could have fought him like a man, and found a certain vigor in the conflict. But he waited, as, strangely enough, most of us wait, allowing the temptation to gain its full strength before meeting it with deliberate and desperate resistance.

Even as he walked up the hill to Cecil's house, that night, he kept on lying to himself. He was only " doing his duty " in coming. Suppose he had had that moment of emotion in Mrs. Shore's presence? He must come when she summoned him. He " had n't any choice." Indeed, so low had he fallen, in the swift descent of this one day, that he could say, " I 've lost Lyssie, but the least I can do is to be helpful to her sister in this unfortunate affair."

There he touched his lowest level. No actual sin could compare with such degradation of the mind.

XXIX.

Fal. Of what quality was your love then ?
Ford. Like a fair house built on another man's ground.

SHAKESPEARE.

AFTERWARDS, alone in his room in the tavern, while midnight whitened into dawn, the supreme words scorched themselves into Roger Carey's mind; it was as though a flaming finger wrote them upon his bare soul. They crashed and clamored in his ears; he could hear nothing else because of them. He found himself repeating them over and over as he walked back and forth, back and forth, across the bare and meagre bedroom of the tavern.

Years afterwards, Roger could see every detail of that room, yet at the time he did not know that he was aware of anything in it. He was absorbed in seeing again Cecil Shore's face, in feeling her hair against his lips, in listening in horror to those words his own lips spoke; but all the while he was following the pattern on the thin red and black carpet, study-ing the landscape upon the green paper window-shades, counting his footsteps from the door to the fireplace, the last step ending on a sunken brick in the hearth. He looked at a bunch of pallid wax flowers under a glass shade on the mantelpiece ; he saw the blue wool mat under the lamp on the corner of the bureau; he examined two faded and yellowing photographs in black walnut frames hanging near the ceiling. He stood before one of these for a long time, staring up at the dull face and the big hands hanging limply between the knees,— staring at them, but seeing only a room half lighted by the glow of a fire and by the gleam of candles high on the walls; seeing a bowl of violets that spread a delicate perfume through the warm air; seeing the glitter of a silver dagger between the uncut pages of a book; and seeing himself, leaning forward, holding her hand between his own, pressing it to his lips, once, twice, fiercely; then, still holding it in a grip that, but for its own returning strenuous clasp, would have made the rings cut into the white flesh, leaning nearer, nearer; kneeling —

He began to pace the floor once more. Each time that he stepped upon a certain board the bureau shook, and then the lamp flared. Eight steps from the sunken brick to the door, sagging a little in its old frame; eight steps back again. Had anybody ever lifted that brick? he wondered. He stopped once and thrust a bit of wood under the castorless corner of the bureau, adjusting the clumsy piece of furniture with careful precision, and looking to see that it was straight.

"*But I love you! Good God, I love you! Do you hear me? I love you!*"

"*Yes.*"

"*Do you care, you cruel woman,— is it anything to you?*"

"*Yes.*"

Then silence; the small flicker of the fire on the hearth, the little puffing burst of flame; but silence — silence.

"*May I kiss your face? May I kiss your lips?*"

"*Kiss me.*"

Then what? He could not seem to remember. Had he pushed her aside? Had he run for his soul?

Here he was, pacing up and down, up and down: eight steps from the door to the sunken brick; eight steps back again. The latch of the door was brass, with the thumb-piece worn thin, and with little black specks in it; it clattered faintly under the jar of his steps; a screw-eye and a hook answered for a bolt: not much protection should the landlord of fiction wish to break in and murder the sleeping traveler, and then bury his plunder under the sunken brick. The fire on the hearth brightened suddenly, as a stick, smouldering under a film of white ashes, broke in two, and a shower of sparks flew up into the thick soot.

Yes; he had pushed her away from him, brutally, breathlessly.

"*When you are free. When you are free. Not till then.*"

That he should have said that, that he could have said it, that he had been able to repulse her, yielding, soft-breathed, glowing, filled him with astonishment that had in it something of awe. What had thrust his arm out, turned his head away, defended him from himself? It was not his own will, not his own desire. No; the habit of integrity had driven him into mechanical virtue; had pushed him, raging against it, from her presence; had dragged him here, at midnight, and set him pacing back and forth, up and down; all his body summoning him to her side, all his decent past holding him in this room. Roger Carey, caught by the fetter of the habit of honor, was saying to himself that he had been a fool to leave her. What difference would it have made to have caught her in his arms for a mad instant, and kissed her face, her throat, her mouth, before the carrying out of the plan bound up in that single utterance, " When you are free," — a plan founded upon the convenient, soul-destroying variance of the divorce laws in the different States? What difference would it have made? Truly none, in the soul and spirit of things. Nevertheless, the letter which killeth had for the moment saved him. He beat against it; he set his teeth in shame at his schoolboy scruples; but he still paced back and forth, up and down. He wondered how early the next morning he could go back to her, and put into tender words, words that might fit an honest love, the outrageous proposition that, when the sham righteousness of obeying the law should have invested her with a sham respectability, he and she should marry.

A mouse nibbled in the wall, but stopped at the creak of the loose board under his foot.

"*But I love you! Good God, I love you! Do you hear me? I love you!*"

"*Yes.*"

"*Do you care, you cruel woman, — is it any-thing to you ?*"

"*Yes.*"

She had leaned her head against his arm; the warm, white hollow of her throat was under his eyes, under his lips —

Yet here he was, counting his steps, studying the landscape on the green window-shades!

"Fool! fool! fool!" he said to himself. He thought he knew how this scruple looked to her; the idea of her contemptuous amusement made him loathe himself; how she must have laughed when, after his theatrical protest, he had gone! It made him hate her, — a hate which stamped his love for what it was. But Roger Carey did not stop to think of that.

All of a sudden, the room, with its tawdry furnishings, its faint light, seemed insupportable to him. He must get out of doors; he must move about; he must walk. He lifted the little clattering latch, and went stealthily down the narrow staircase. He felt the oppression of sleep all about him, and the brush against his face of the lifeless air, with its wandering scents of the closed house. In the office there was still a faint glow from the open door of the stove, and he could see upon the walls flaring notices of horse-fairs and mowing-machines; a cat moved in the seat of one of the chairs that were standing about the square of zinc under the stove; she yawned, and sharpened her claws on the brittle splints, and watched him suspiciously as he opened the door and stepped out into the darkness. It was good to draw a full, cold breath, and let the silence of the strong world dull for a moment the clamor of those terrible words.

He walked aimlessly out into the road, and turned to go up the street, but stopped sharply. No, not that way, not that way ; not past — Lyssie's house. He would go down the river-road to the bridge. He heard his steps ringing on the frosty ground ; and then he felt a cool touch upon his cheek, and looked up to see that there were small, wandering flakes of snow in the air.

" The winter is pretty tough in Dakota," he thought ; "she must get in the ninety days' residence early in the autumn." It was lucky that he was a lawyer ; he knew how to arrange things. No one need be consulted ; they could manage their own business ; he knew just how to plan the easy iniquity of compliance with law. He smiled to himself at the bad humor of the situation, and he observed, with curious, impersonal interest, how, since he had spoken those words to his friend's wife, his mind refused any longer to be hoodwinked by words ; he was seeing straight and thinking clear ; being a lawyer, he knew just how to cover Lust with the decent cloak of Law.

" She 's got to prove a year's desertion. Well, that 's easy enough. Fortunately, those three months in Dakota are included in the year. Still, at best it will be next November before — "

It was very dark down on the bridge, but far up behind the hills there was the faint lightening of dawn.

Yes; she should be divorced, and they would marry. He remembered that he had said that he did not believe in divorce; what a fool he had been! Why, without it crime must inevitably exist; for human nature was human nature. He even used, for the sake of illustration, that old, fallacious, pitiful argument that divorce must be permitted to prevent sin, even to put an end to sin if it has begun, — as though the legalization of an immoral relation made it moral! This young man, who had felt the stern passion for his profession that a priest may feel for his, was ready to urge that Law, majestic and relentless, the expression of the human creature's best, should degrade herself by pandering to vice, by abetting crime, by making lust legal. The time had been when all this had been clear enough to his eyes; but how different it looked now! He said to himself that divorce was necessary to the moral life of the community. His old argument that the one must suffer for the many was forgotten — because he was the one.

He had not come to this opinion without a struggle; he had held to his belief as a man holds to some last chance of life, only dropping it at the lick of flame across his hands. The fire of selfishness seared Roger Carey's very soul; he flung over his belief, and fell. Yet he remembered that before those dreadful words were said he had told her what he thought of divorce; had pleaded with her as a man may plead for his own life, — for he knew what her freedom would mean to him. Later, when this was of no avail, he had told her that, if she insisted upon carrying out this deplorable plan, at least Molly should be spared.

"You are no fit woman to bring up a child; she ought to be with her father," he said. Then, as it were, he made her prove the truth of his assertion by those answers to his mad words.

But instead of thinking again of those words he listened to the river, and suddenly, cringing at the memory, he heard others, spoken one summer night, with the splash of oars and the brush of lily-pads against a little rocking skiff.

The river and the bridge grew intolerable. He went back into the village and up the street, his breath catching in an oath that was almost a sob. He could not bear such memories. He drove his mind back to that firelit, perfumed room; he felt once more her panting breath upon his cheek; he saw the mad surrender in her eyes!

"*But I love you! Good God —*"

"Why, I must — I must see her again," he said vehemently, as though answering some silent Forbidder in his soul. How many hours must pass before he could go back to her! He wished he could blot out the day and find it night; the thought of taking up that midnight scene, with the stern, cold daylight staring in her face and his, gave him a shock that turned him sick. Such a scene needed darkness rather than light. " But I *will* see her! " he said, with the panic of the man who finds himself helpless in the grasp of an unsought repentance.

It was very still; the frozen furrows of the road were beginning to fill with feathery white; the cold, pale dawn spread itself behind the hills; there was hoar frost on the leafless twigs of the hedge that lay, in the darkness, like a band of furry black along the edge of Mrs. Drayton's whitening lawn. Far off, from some distant farm, came a weak crow; and then a dog barked.

In that hour Satan desired to have him. And he desired Satan.

He did not know why he should have come to stand thus under Alicia Drayton's window. How dark and cold the house looked! She must be asleep now. Oh, if he could speak to her, if he could see her! It was not the desire of the lover; it was the human need of help.

" Lyssie! " he called out sharply, and started, and stepped back into the shadows. " What am I thinking of! " he said, and held his breath lest she might have heard him. There was no sound except the faint rustle of the flakes in the dead leaves of the oak above his head.

Scorched and blackened as he was by the fires of these last hours, he knew she would not shrink from him; she would not shrink from any soul in trouble. She might not understand, — that made no difference; she would take care of him.

He stood there a long time.

.   .   .   .

When he went away, he did not know whether he loved Alicia or not ; he did not think of that. He only knew that he would not see that other woman again.

XXX.

There is the nice and critical moment of declaration to be got over. — STEVENSON.

WHEN Roger Carey awoke the next morning, he did not, for a moment, understand the void of dismay in his mind.

Then it all cleared, and his intolerable self-knowledge surged back upon him. Like some insulting hand, his shame struck him again and again in the face, while, with set teeth biting through a cigar which he had forgotten to light, he moved about the room, getting his things together for his departure.

For of course he was going away. There was nothing else for him to do, — nothing except to write the letter which must be sent up the hill. The brutality of such a course made him shiver; but what else could he do?

He looked at his watch to see how much time he had before the stage went, and discovered with dismay that it had gone. Under his breath he cursed his luck. To lose the stage meant that he could not leave Old Chester until afternoon, unless, by good fortune, he could hire a vehicle, and a driver willing to face the heavy rain which had begun to fall since dawn.

Here he was, in this primitive little tavern, pulled every moment by soft, invisible cords, in the midst of surroundings which stabbed him at every glance, with the steady rain shutting out the river and the hills, but revealing the dreary street, the drearier barnyard; how could he endure it until four o'clock? Suppose he should see Lyssie? She did not mind the rain, he remembered.

" I 'll walk before I stay here till four!" he said to himself; and then he drew a small, painted pine table up to the window, and sat down, a sheet of the tavern note-paper and a bottle of watery ink before him.

He must write that letter even before he sought for means to escape from Old Chester.

He thrust his hands down into his pockets, and stretched his feet out under the table, and stared at a blue wool mat on the bureau. Then he lifted his pen, looked at it critically, and put it down with a fling.

" My God!" he said.

It was hideously ludicrous; the incongruousness of the words she had heard him speak the night before, with those which he was about to write on this thin bluish sheet ruled in pink lines, with a picture in the upper left-hand corner of a bird sitting on a fence-rail.

He put his hands in his pockets again, and looked out at two dripping hens which had sought shelter under an empty cart. The rain fell with an increasing pour. The spout from the eaves above his window gurgled and chuckled, and there was a gush of water into the pebbly gutter below. " And of course I have n't an umbrella," he thought absently. "Curse this rain!" He took up the pen and stabbed it into the ink-bottle; then he looked out of the window again. He felt a sullen envy of a hostler, who, his hands in his pockets, stood chewing a straw at the stable-door; suddenly the man buttoned up his jacket, bent his head against the rain, and went running across the yard to the house, to sit for the rest of the idle morning, with steaming clothes, by the kitchen-fire. If that red-faced, good-humored fellow caught one of the plump maid-servants about the waist and gave her a smacking kiss, once in a while, it was as natural as eating and just as unmoral. "What a row we make about nothing!" Roger thought, looking with savage resentment at the blank sheet of paper.

A dog, with a dripping coat, trotted across the overflowing wheel ruts of the road. A sulky came jogging down the street, and drew up before the tavern-door.

The recollection of the last rainy day when he had seen Dr. Lavendar's sulky pierced Roger Carey's heart; he got up impetuously, nearly overturning the table, and flung himself away from the window. So it happened that he did not see the old clergyman emerge from under the streaming rubber apron, or hear him say, "What, upstairs? I'll just come in, then, for a minute."

But that stab of memory, that vision of the fresh and wholesome past, — the rainy day, the old clergy-man and his little blind horse, and — and Lyssie, —

made the sheet of thin paper, and the words of
renunciation which he was arranging in his mind,
seem melodramatic and disgusting. After all, he
had been a fool; that was the amount of it. "There's
no use palavering!" he told himself. He pulled
out one of his cards, and wrote on it, with that fierce
haste which fears to be overtaken by a change of
mind, "I must not see you again. Forgive me if
you can. But I will never see you again."

He loathed himself; he said between his teeth
that he was a brute and a coward; but he slipped
the card into an envelope and sealed it, pounding it
with his fist until the little table shook. He did not
hear Dr. Lavendar's step upon the stairs, and leaped
back, as though detected in some shameful deed,
when, under a thundering rap, the door flew open
with such suddenness that the old clergyman pitched
forward into the room.

"Dear me!" said Dr. Lavendar, "I thought
that door was shut! Well, sir, this is first rate."
His face beamed with pleasure. "Van Horn told
me you were up here, and I thought he'd lost his
wits. But I never heard better news. Come, now!
the boy's writing a sonnet to her eyebrow. Well,
that's right, that's right. Young things will have
their quarrels, being young. But they make up,
when they're good for anything. They kiss and
are friends, as the children say. Well, sir, have
you kissed?"

"It's very good in you to hunt me up," Roger
stammered. "I'm just packing, just leaving. I—"

"What!" interrupted Dr. Lavendar, sobering. "You don't mean that little Lyssie would n't?" He unbuttoned his great-coat, on which the mist stood in fine drops, and sat down on one of the lean, unsteady chairs. "She's a most superior young woman, sir!"

Roger murmured an assent. He looked desperately about the room for means of escape.

"Most superior; and therefore, if she would n't kiss, it's because you did n't go about it in the right way. Now, I tell you, young man, it don't do to be proud. Tell her you were a fool! Of course you were?"

"Oh yes; yes."

"And ask her to forgive you, like a man, sir!"

"You're very good, I'm sure," Roger said hurriedly, "but I came down here on business. I have not seen — Miss Drayton. Mrs. Philip Shore wished some advice; legal advice." His voice shrank, and fell; but Dr Lavendar did not notice it.

"Oh, is that all? Not but what I'm glad for you to try and bring those two mad people to their senses; but I hoped — I would n't have spoken if I had n't supposed you had come down on — another matter."

"Do you think I can hire anybody to drive me over to Mercer in this storm, Dr. Lavendar?" Roger said, shutting his portmanteau with a snap, his back to his guest.

"Oh, don't hurry," commanded the other. "Now you're here, stay over till the afternoon. Perhaps

you can make it worth your while!" he insisted
with vast significance, his eyes twinkling very much,
and feeling himself to be exceedingly subtle.

"I'm obliged to be back in town to-morrow,
thank you," Roger answered stiffly.

Dr. Lavendar sighed. "Well; tell me about
Philip, then. Could you persuade Cecil to go back
to him?"

"I hope she will," answered Roger Carey; behind
his shut teeth he was swearing softly. "I'm afraid
I'll have to leave you now, sir. I've got to go
down and see Van Horn, and get him to hunt up
some sort of conveyance for me."

Dr. Lavendar was silent. He got up from his
chair and tramped over to the window, and stood
staring out at the steady downpour; then he turned
around. "Look here, my boy. *Don't.*"

"Don't what?"

"Go away without seeing her."

"My dear Dr. Lavendar, it's perfectly impossible.
You don't understand. It was all my fault."

"Why, then go and tell her it was your fault!"
The old sentimentalist came and put his hand on the
young man's shoulder. "My dear boy, you are
young. I'm an old fellow, but I was young once,
too. And I was a fool—just like you. We fell
out, and I could n't make up my mind to eat humble
pie. Well, she married somebody else. And every
tear that girl shed —and she shed enough of 'em!
—was my fault. Don't you see? It was just
because my wicked pride kept me from telling her

I 'd been a fool. Now don't you do that, Carey ; don't you do it, boy ! ''

" Good Lord ! " Roger burst out, and then begged pardon. " You are very kind, sir, but I must not intrude upon Miss Drayton."

" Well," said the old man, and sighed. " I suppose you know your own business. I won't say anything more. I hope I have n't offended you ? But you 're wrong, you 're wrong."

" Yes, I 'm wrong."

Dr. Lavendar looked as though he would like to make one more plea ; but he closed his lips, and silently followed Roger downstairs. He heard him arrange for a carriage, and watched him give a note to the landlord, with instructions to have it sent at once to Mrs. Shore. " These lawyers have no feelings," he thought indignantly, for Roger stood staring at the note, even after it was in Van Horn's hands, as though he could think of nothing else. " Absorbed in his everlasting legal quibbles, and that poor child crying her eyes out ! Well, I don't know ; I believe she 's well rid of him ! "

He said good-by to Roger rather coldly. " Joey is not showing intelligence in his choice," he thought, as he climbed into his gig, " but I 'd rather have him have some heart than be as intelligent as this young man."

Dr. Lavendar was distinctly gentler to his brother, when, in all the rain, Mr. Joseph arrived by the morning stage. At dinner he told him of his talk with that cold-blooded young jackanapes, Carey, and he declared that Lyssie Drayton was well rid of him.

" Most superior girl ; really intelligent," he said.

Mr. Joseph nodded, and agreed ; but there was a look of absent melancholy in his mild face. Joseph Lavendar had had a blow : he had learned, beyond any shadow of doubt, the particulars of the late Mr. Pendleton's will.

The information had come to him casually, but it was not the less deadly. Coming down from Mercer, a passenger on the coach announced himself as the man of business of a lady who resided in the charming village of Old Chester, — a Mrs. Pendleton. Did his fellow-traveler chance to know her? He had to get her signature to some papers, he said, and he had come to Old Chester for that purpose. Then, with a generosity ill befitting a man of business, he gossiped most entertainingly about his employer. Mr. Lavendar, thirsting for one particular bit of information, tried, faintly, to stop him, but held his breath at the reference to " Pendleton " and his will. " If she marries, she loses every cent. But I guess she won't marry. That kind of thing works both ways : it keeps the widow from marrying a poor man, and it keeps a rich man from marrying the widow ; " and the man of business laughed very much.

Mr. Joseph felt sore and bewildered. He thought that it would be generous to tell James this melancholy news ; James would be so relieved to hear it. But he could not, just yet. He must think it over a

little longer. He thought about it all that afternoon.
It was in his mind when he climbed listlessly into
the organ-loft for the choir-practicing.

He felt that blank which comes to a man deprived
of an interest, — a blank which may easily be mistaken for grief, so it was a relief to him that Mrs. Pendleton was not present. "She's afraid of the rain,
I suppose," said Susan Carr, with a curl of her lip.
It seemed to Mr. Lavendar that Susan Carr's voice,
of late so unsympathetic, was kinder; so he could
not help being kinder himself, and resolving to
overlook that officiousness which had so annoyed
him. He told her, while they picked out the
voluntary, several bits of news, and he asked her
advice about a new chant with all his old simple
friendliness.

Miss Susan answered politely, but somewhat at
random; in fact, they were both preoccupied. "I'll
have to tell Jim; and he will be glad; glad of my
unhappiness," Mr. Lavendar was saying to himself,
sadly; and Susan Carr, her cheeks hot, was thinking that Mr. Joseph would walk home with her, as
Mrs. Pendleton was not there. "I ought to have arranged something so that he shouldn't have such an
opportunity," Susan Carr said to herself, severely,
her eyes shining with content.

The practicing had never seemed so long. When
it was over, Lyssie hurried out into the rain, and Mr.
Tommy ran after her, to beg to hold his umbrella
over her head; but Miss Susan found several things
to detain her.

She picked up two Prayer-Books from the floor, and said that it was a bad day.

She wished that she knew how to say to Joseph that she was sorry she had been disagreeable; then, if he *should* press it again — At that a sudden fear touched her like a cold finger: suppose he should not press it? Suppose her systematic snubbing had discouraged him so that he was not able to recognize her contrition? Susan Carr drew in her breath and set her white teeth on her lip, and said to herself that she was not a silly girl, but a middle-aged woman; she and Joseph had known each other all their lives, and if he did not understand, if he should be afraid to speak, why, then, she must just say — something friendly!

" I wish it was n't raining so hard," she announced in a fluttered voice, listening to the persistent sweep of the rain on the roof.

Mr. Joseph agreed absently. The trouble in his face brought a remorseful mist into Susan Carr's eyes. Oh, how unhappy she had made him! Well, it should stop now; yes, if she had to say plump out, " Joseph, I was a fool. I did n't know my own mind. But I do now. And — and — "

She beat the two Prayer-Books together, and said, tremulously, that they were shamefully dusty. " I think your touch grows finer every year, Mr. Joseph," she continued, with much agitation for so simple a remark.

" You 're very good to say so, ma'am," he answered, with a melancholy air, shaking some loose sheets of music evenly together on his brown broad-cloth knees.

"I don't know what St. John's would do without you. I've often been afraid you would have an offer from some great city church." She bent down to put on her overshoes, and her voice was muffled and breathless.

Mr. Lavendar shook his head. "You're very good. I don't know; sometimes I've thought it might be well to stay away for a while."

"Oh no!" she burst out, stamping down into her rubbers, her face scarlet; "no, indeed, Mr. Joseph."

Mr. Joseph did not insist; he sighed, and peered over the rail of the loft down into the church.

"How early it gets dark now! It seems to me that when I was a boy it did n't get dark so early in the afternoon in November." Then he opened the loft-door politely, and Miss Susan started down the narrow circular flight of stairs. Her breath came fast; she stopped abruptly by the narrow window, where, through the mat of ivy stems, the gray light struggled in.

"We'd better shut this," she said, pulling at the cord of the little swinging sash. It was quite dark here on the stairs, and Joseph was behind her.

"Mr. Joseph, I've been wanting to say to you — I've been wanting to tell you — that I've thought over — what you tried to tell me. Oh — you know?" she ended faintly, tying down the window-cord in a series of bewildering knots.

She could say no more. The tears were in her

eyes from the effort of her words. Joseph Lavendar
was quick to feel the frankness of her repentance for
her hardness.

"You are most kind, Miss Susan," he said, looking down at the top of her bonnet from his height of
three stairs above her, "most kind; but I had n't
any right to trouble you in the first place."

"Oh yes, yes, you had! and I did appreciate it.
I felt it was a great honor; only, I had never
thought of such a thing, and — and it did n't seem
right."

"I quite understand, ma'am," he said, the wrinkles deepening on his high forehead. He felt no
bitterness, even though Susan Carr put into words
his own scruple. Her sincere friendliness was too
apparent for offense. "No, it was n't right; and
you were kind to try to hold me back. And I realize myself that I 'm a poor man. I 've only my
small earnings. I had no right to ask —"

She turned around quickly and looked up at him;
even in the dusk he could see that her straightforward eyes were full of tears, and there was a deeper
color on her cheeks. She made a quick gesture.
"Oh, how could you think such a thing? I never
thought about money! It was — Donald. And I
did n't know my own mind. But I do — now."
Then, with great energy, she tied another knot in
the window-cord, and went on down the little dark
winding stairs.

Joseph Lavendar, with his mouth open, looked
after her. He grew pale, and then red. He said

something under his breath, violently, and turned, with two skipping steps, as though to flee for shelter back to the organ-loft.   Then he stood, palpitating.

"Miss Susan!" he called faintly, and went stumbling after her. "Miss Susan, I'm afraid you — I'm afraid there's some misunderstanding; you are so kind — I'm afraid —"

"No," she said boldly, smiling, but with her eyes full of tears, "no; it's only that I know my own mind now.   I didn't let you speak because I thought I couldn't return it.   But now I know my own mind.   And so — I've told you.   It isn't as if we were young things.   We are such matter of fact, middle-aged people, not two young things — I thought I could tell you?"

Joseph Lavendar gasped; he rubbed his hands together, and opened and closed his lips.

All Susan Carr's strength and force had melted into shyness.   "I hope you didn't think I was forward," she murmured.

Mr. Lavendar swallowed once; then his face grew very gentle and noble. "Take my arm, my dear Susan," he said. "I hope I may be worthy of the honor you have done me."

XXXI.

Lest she should fail and perish utterly,
God, before whom ever lie bare
The abysmal deeps of Personality,
Plagued her with sore despair.

TENNYSON.

ALL that day the rain fell steadily. Roger Carey, his face bent against the wind, driving in an open wagon across the hills, was following in his mind, with deadly humiliation, his letter to his friend's wife. In imagination, he saw John receiving it at the door; carrying it upstairs on his tray; fingering it, perhaps, with the supercilious curiosity of his kind, but handing it to his mistress with his usual immobility. Probably she would be in that very room where — Roger's hands tightened upon the reins, and his teeth set.

Well, she would take it; open it, perhaps with that silver dagger on her desk; read it! He reached forward for the whip, and struck the horse viciously. " This confounded beast never goes out of a walk," he told the boy on the seat beside him.

Yes; she would read it; he tried to remember what he had said : —

" *I must not see you again. Forgive me if you can. But I will never* — " Was it " will never " or " must never," in that last sentence? Why had he not made some excuse? " Unexpectedly summoned to town — will write — " Anything, rather than that confession of fright, and shame, and remorse. For the moment, all his self-loathing was concentrated on his *gaucherie :—*

"*I must not see you again. Forgive —*"
"Good Lord!" groaned the young man; and the boy beside him said, "Sur?"

"I could walk faster than this brute!" his fare told him, angrily.

But the note did not reach its destination quite as early as it should have done. Van Horn said it was a shame to send a "human critter" out in such a rain just for a letter; he would wait till he saw some one driving up that way. He waited until nearly noon; then John came down to the post office for the morning mail, and stopped at the tavern for a chat, and there was Van Horn's opportunity. Mr. Carey's dollar for immediate delivery went toward paying for the extra oil which that young man had burned. " Fer I give you my word," said Van Horn in confidence to John, " that young feller burned the lamp all night; it was burning there this morning when my wife went in to red up after him."

So it happened that when Cecil Shore read Roger's card twelve hours had passed since, with that terror-stricken look, he had left her; twelve hours of reality. When she heard the door bang behind him, it was like some frightful awakening; she stood, gasping, staring about the empty room; then sank down, cowering, and hiding her face. She shut her eyes, quivering and crouching, as though she still felt the

storm of his presence. He loved her! And he had
gone — at such a moment! Her heart rose in passionate exultation at his strength. But he loved her.
" When I am free! When I am free!" she repeated
in a whisper.

She got up, and walked hurriedly up and down,
her breath broken, the tears wet upon her face.

" I love him!" she said to herself, and covered
her face with her hands. Then, standing still, swaying back and forth, she burst suddenly into dreadful
crying.

" *I love him*," she said again.

As she spoke, her eyes fell on some little scraps
of paper which he had torn with nervous fingers as
he talked to her ; and she stooped over and brushed
them into her hand and kissed them, — once, twice.
Then she stood still, trembling for a moment, before,
with violent haste, she went to the window and flung
it open. As she leaned out, the cold air struck on
her neck and face, and the spasm in her throat
stopped ; it had seemed as if she could not breathe.
Touched, for the first time in her life, by the great
Human Experience, her whole body answered to the
summons of the soul.

But she had no consciousness of morality, she
had no thought of self ; she had forgotten that she
was Philip's wife ; or that Roger had been Alicia's
lover.

A great experience transcends morality, because it
bursts the shell of personality ; and in the empty
moment which follows it identity seems lost, swept

out on the surge of those eternal currents we call Life.   At such a moment a soul knows all things but itself ; it apprehends the knowledge of beasts, it feels the thrill of the stars shining ; it understands the color of crimson in the sun ; it is acquainted with grief ; maternity belongs to it, and death.   It is a moment of terror and magnificence ; it is the moment of Moses on Sinai ; but whether it be for good or evil, only that discarded personality can say.

When Cecil drew back and shut the window, her face had curiously changed.   Living was stamped upon it.   Eagerness, fear, desire, all those emotions from which her satisfied life had shut her out, began to dawn and deepen in it.   She paced up and down, her lips tightening upon each other ; but her eyes softening, and glowing, and dimming.   She had decided swiftly not to see him in the morning ; she, too, would be strong.   No ; they must both wait ; "and he must have nothing to do with the case," she thought ; " we must not speak, we must not look, until I am free.   He said, 'when you are free.' Oh, how few men could have turned back when he did ! "   An adoring tenderness shone in her eyes ; she smiled, her lip quivering, as she stood looking over at the spot where he had repulsed her.

She watched the dawn come cold over the hills ; the candles in the sconces sputtered and guttered, and went out, and the lamps burned with a sickly light.   She walked softly about her room : " He stood there.   He looked at that picture.   He touched this book."   But over and over and over she came back, exulting, to that moment of renunciation when he had left her, — when it seemed as though he dragged her heart out of her body.

And so the morning broke, gray with sweeping rain; the wind rumbled sometimes in the chimney, and a chill crept into the room, for the fire had burned out.

"He will be here soon," she thought, a deep color burning in her face, and her breath quickening. She would hear his voice asking for her; hear him being sent away. Well, thank Heaven, he would understand; he would even care more for her because she would not see him; because she would meet him on his own level! For, with this first appreciation of anything but herself, such mere decency of life seemed high to this poor soul.

She had had her coffee, and put on a charming gown of some soft silk; her face was full of delicate color. Though she did not mean to see him, she felt the impulse to be beautiful just because he would come and stand in the doorway downstairs, even though it was only to be told that he must go away.

And so she waited.

The day darkened as the morning passed; the rain shut her in upon the passionate centre of herself.

But it was curious that he did not come.

Somehow or other, the morning wore on. Molly clamored at the door, and came in to play with her paper dolls on the rug before the fire. The cook wanted instructions for dinner; Cecil gave them carefully, speculating a little as to whether a certain white soup could be made with this sort of stock or that; she stopped once, abruptly, as she was speaking, and listened. Then she said dully, "Yes, try it, Jane; but don't put in too much wine;" and listened again.

By noon she had begun to pace up and down, up and down. She sent Molly away, telling her sharply that she was a perfect nuisance with her dolls. She stood with her hands behind her at the window, her mouth rigid, her eyes troubled and wandering.

Very likely he had gone back to town at once. How like him! how superb in him! But he ought to have sent a line. For, though he might have known she would not see him, it would only have been civil to come — under the circumstances.

At noon his note came. She grew white as she read it, and sat down, trembling. Then she dashed it from her, and flew to the door, bolting it and clinging to the door-knob, her teeth grinding down upon her lip, her eyes furious.

"So: it was an insult."

The color surged into her face, and left it white again. She raged back and forth across her room, breathing hard.

"How dared he!" Her hands gripped and twisted upon each other as though they would tear the life from the throat of the man who had kissed them, and kissed them.

He had *dared* — and then gone!

"The insult, the insult, the insult!"

She was suffocated by hate. Standing with clenched hands, she ground her heel into the floor. "I wish it were his face!" she whispered, quivering all over. The card was lying where she had thrown it on the rug before the fire. "I despise him!" she said, and stooped to pick it up, crumpling it furiously in her hand.

Then, suddenly, she carried it to her lips, and burst into tears.

"Oh, why do I love him, when I hate him so?"

.   .   .   .

It was late in the afternoon that, very curiously, she went and looked in the glass. She sat before her dressing-table for a long time, leaning forward, staring into the mirror with miserable, hopeless eyes. It was as though her soul looked out of the windows of its prison. Yet it was only now that she had recognized that it was a prison, this ruthless body of hers that dragged her into all its dreadful delights; this body, with its love of sloth, its sensual droop of the lip, its cruel indifference to anything but itself.

"No; I shall never be good," she said aloud. "I'll get over this in a week, and I shall see how amusing it is."

The consciousness of this ultimateness of the environment of the body is very horrible. (Some time in our lives every man and woman of us, putting out our hands toward the stars, touch on either side our prison walls the immutable limitations of temperament.) "I can never be good," she said hopelessly, watching her heavy, tear-stained face in the mirror; "and perhaps I should n't like it if I were. No, I 'll get over this, and then I 'll want to *kill* him. I know."

But she was wrong: Cecil Shore's was not one of those fluid souls which slip, quicksilver-like, between the fingers of circumstances, returning always to the unimpressionable sphere of self. This experience was moulding her as molten steel is moulded. She would never think of it with amusement; she would always be a better woman, no matter how bad she might become, because of this one shuddering glimpse of righteousness.

She held the crumpled card in her hand, and looked at it now and then. "*I must not see you again. Forgive me if you can. I will never see you again.*"

"He does n't care," she said to herself; "it was n't love. What must he think of me?" Her face scorched under the slow tears; she could not bear the shame of it; and yet — and yet — "I love him !"

"I 'm not good enough for him," she thought piteously. "I was wicked. He belonged to Lyssie. I was wicked!" She groaned as she spoke. The soul is not born without agony; this beginning of the moral consciousness knew the throes of birth.

He had told her that she was not good enough to take care of her own child. Well, he was right. She saw herself in Europe, living the lazy, easy, suffocating life that she loved. He was right; such a life would be dreadful for Molly; it meant meanness, selfishness, unrestrained impulses, sloth; it meant all that intellectual enjoyment of materialism which is a sensuality of the mind. But it could not be helped, unless — unless she gave Molly up?

"If I have her, she will be as bad as I am," she thought dully. She wished passionately that she were dead, so that Molly would be safe.

"Oh, she ought not to be with me," she said, with a wail. "I'm no woman to be trusted with a child; he said so. He was right. He knows what my life is."

Molly ought not to know such a life; Molly ought to be good.

"Not like me! Not like me!" she said, dropping her head down on her arms crossed upon the dressing-table.

. . . .

It was nearly a week later that she wrote to him : —

I am going abroad for such an indefinitely long time that it will perhaps be better to put my affairs in the hands of some lawyer on the other side, instead of troubling you with them. You were right about Molly. I think it wiser to leave her with her father, though I should like her to be under my sister's influence to some extent; may I ask you to try to arrange this for me? It would be rather a bore to have her in Europe, and she will do very well with her father. I hope he will give an occasional thought to her soul, in intervals of saving his own. Will you tell him so from me ? I will never see him again. Nor you. I shall be in Rome for the season, and later in London. You must look me up, if you come over.

Sincerely,	C. S.

XXXII.

"SHORE, are you at liberty? I want to see you."

Philip put down his pen, and stretched out his hand. "Why, hello, Carey! Look out, don't tumble over that waste-basket. It's so dark in here, I did n't know you for a minute."

The afternoon dusk was rising like a tide in the small office, and the pale sunshine was climbing the wall to escape it; climbing the wall, creeping across the papers on Philip Shore's desk, breaking into rippling shadows on the ceiling, as a flag on an opposite building blew taut and strong, or swerved and clung to its mast, and then whipped out again in the high wind.

"You are just the man I wanted to see," Philip said. "I did n't know you were in town."

"I 'm not. At least, I only came this moment. I was in Old Chester last week; and I 've come now to see you."

"Ah," said Philip. "Well?" His caller, it appeared, was his wife's legal adviser, rather than his old friend or Lyssie's lover, — he had not heard of the broken engagement; so with some formality he offered Roger a chair, and braced himself for a conflict of words about the situation. He had expected a fierce and friendly remonstrance, such as this which he thought he saw in Roger's eyes, before Carey should assume his professional character, and betake himself to the attorney in whose hands Philip had placed his affairs; or rather, to whom he had stated his position and his wishes about Molly. For Philip, having given up the management of his wife's money, had in fact no "affairs" of his own. Indeed, when Roger entered, he had been engaged in adding up columns of figures, and subtracting the smallest possible living expenses from the sum total of his probable assets, and he was aware of that curious mixture of poignant anxiety and absurd humor which can be felt only by the man who, never having known the necessity of work, finds suddenly that if he does not work, neither may he eat.

"I can't even be a bricklayer. I 've had no experience," he thought, morosely amused. He had meant to consult Roger Carey, for the fact that Cecil had put her business matters in his hands had no bearing, in Philip's mind, upon their friendship. But in the younger man's set face, as he stood beside his desk, Philip instantly read the impossibility of this.

"Well?" he said, curtly, again.

"I 've come to see you on — Mrs. Shore's behalf."

"So I supposed. I knew that she had asked you to look after her affairs. I 'm very glad of it, Carey."

Roger sat down, bending his stick across his

knees in a fierce, unconscious grip; his face was pale, and had in it a suggestion of struggle, — a struggle which had burned something out of it, and left it strangely refined, but almost haggard.

Philip said, impulsively, "Are you under the weather, old man?"

Roger did not even notice the question; his hands tightened upon his stick until the knuckles whitened.

"I'm not here in any professional way—"

"My dear fellow, that is the reason that I appreciate the professional part of it," Philip began warmly. "I know what your friendship is, and—"

"Yes. Well, never mind that; I've come to ask you to go back to her."

"What!"

"I want you to go back to your wife."

"Did she send you here with that message?" said Philip.

"She send me! Don't you know her better than that? No, I'm here on my own account. This plan of yours is so incredible to me that I can't believe it! You cannot be aware of what you are doing."

Philip sighed, and seemed to draw himself together. "We don't agree on this subject of divorce and separation, so what is the use of discussing it? Although I appreciate your motive in wishing to discuss it."

"You do, do you?"

A thread of anger in his voice made Philip look at him, but Roger went on calmly: —

"No; of course there is no use in discussing your theories. I don't believe in divorce. I think I told you that some time ago. I — I still don't believe in it."

"So far as I am concerned, there should be no question of divorce in this matter," Philip said.

"I know; you want to separate. And I believe you put it on the ground of morality!"

"Absolutely," the other answered, with a surprised look. "Why, Carey, look here; put the personal equation out of this for a moment. What makes marriage? A priest's gibberish, or a legal decree, or the tyranny of public opinion, which holds a man and woman together who are separated in every thought and impulse and belief? They are husband and wife by a Law that transcends all these things; or else — they are not husband and wife!"

"If you don't mind, I 'd rather not go into that kind of thing," Roger said. "The duties of a citizen I can understand; but when you come to 'higher laws,' I 'm all off. Common law 's good enough for me. But what I 'm here for is not to discuss the abstract; it is to ask you to go back to your wife."

"Apparently you are not speaking for Mrs. Shore," Philip answered, frowning; "and as we don't agree as to the principle, what 's the use of talking about it?"

Roger was silent for a moment; then he said quietly, "I have a message for you, Philip, from — your wife. She is going abroad (unless I can persuade you to prevent it), and she has decided to leave Molly with you."

Philip Shore half rose. " Leave Molly ? " he repeated, in a dazed way.

" Yes."

" I don't understand. She told Woodhouse — I thought she meant to bring suit, and get possession of the child? Carey, what do you mean ? "

" What I say. If this theory of yours is carried out, and she goes away, she proposes to leave Molly with you. She told me to say " — his eyes narrowed with angry satisfaction as he spoke, — " she told me to say she hoped you would give an occasional thought to Molly's soul in intervals of saving your own. She has also made certain arrangements as to money matters in relation to Molly. But I don't want to go into that now. I hope it may never be necessary to go into it. I hope you will go back to her."

Philip's face was sunk in his hands ; he was silent for several moments. Then, in a low voice, " What are Mrs. Shore's reasons for this decision ? "

" Do you think," answered the other, " that you have any right to ask Mrs. Shore's reasons ? "

Philip got up and went over to the fireplace ; he leaned his forehead upon his arm along the mantelpiece, and looked down at a little fire that was shrinking and creeping back into the narrow grate. Roger watched him silently.

" No ; I 've no right to ask her reasons."

" I suppose," said the younger man, in a hard

voice, "that you are perfectly willing to let your wife make this sacrifice?"

Philip turned upon him savagely. " Is this a time to say whether it is agreeable to me to accept a sacrifice? I 've got to think of Molly! You know she ought not to be with her mother."

" So you 'll accept the sacrifice?" Roger insisted, with contempt that was like a blow.

" I accept my child!" said Philip Shore hoarsely. " You can't understand this thing, Carey, —"

" You 're right.   I can't."

" — but the humiliation to me of letting Cecil give up is not to be considered. Good God, do you suppose, if it were just *myself*, that I would let her do it?"

" I can't say, I 'm sure.   You 're letting her do a good deal."

" I don't know what you mean."

" You are letting her take advantage of a theory which you consider essential to your personal integrity, whether it is for her welfare or not."

" It is for her welfare."

" Is that why you are doing it? I wonder if it has ever occurred to you that salvation can cost too dear!"

" I don't understand you," Philip answered impatiently.

" I mean that the pursuit of righteousness for personal ends is just a yielding to a spiritual appetite; and it may be as demoralizing and debauching as — as the yielding to a physical appetite!"

Roger Carey's stick broke suddenly across his knee; his hands trembled.

"Race regeneration begins with the individual," Philip began.

But Roger broke in with a sort of groan: "Who is going to be regenerated, in this case, — beside yourself? That part of the race included in your immediate family? Your — your wife, for instance?"

Again in the darkening room a note in his voice made Philip stare at him.

"Let's look at the value of this sort of regeneration: suppose every man who got tired of his bargain — "

"Carey, you go too far!"

" — every man who thought the preservation of his own precious integrity depended on it, should throw over his wife — "

"What the devil is the matter with you?"

"I want to make an illustration," Roger said between his teeth. "Suppose he left his wife, feeling that the honor of marriage and the salvation of his own soul depended on it, — you see, I am granting absolute integrity of purpose."

The blood came up into Philip Shore's face as if at the touch of a whip-lash.

"Of course," Roger went on, "it is conceivable that, the woman being left, some other man might be attracted; and — but I need n't go into all that. You see what possibilities it opens up?"

"Yes," Philip agreed; "and why not?"

“Why not?” Roger stammered, recoiling. “Why, because public morals are to be considered!”

“Public morals will not suffer by private virtue,” Philip said contemptuously. “I maintain that a loveless marriage is n’t a marriage. The question of absolute divorce is n’t a question of re-marriage, but of marrying at all. The first relationship is n’t marriage, it is legalized prostitution; but we are not ready, yet, to make the results of such a mistake permanent, so the right to marry righteously and decently is necessary. It 's a concession to human nature, I grant, but it 's perfectly reasonable and proper, even though one may repudiate it for one's self.”

Roger said something under his breath, looking at Cecil Shore's husband with a sort of terror.

“Of course,” Philip went on, “I realize the possible abuses of freer divorce, but I do not believe such abuses are inherent in divorce. And beside, other people’s weakness or wickedness does not affect individual duty.”

“There 's no duty that makes other people either weak or wicked,” Roger burst out. “ ‘If meat cause my brother to offend, then will I eat no meat.’ ”

“My brother’s offending is his own business. Beside, meat-eating is not a necessity. Purity, honor, decency even, are necessities.”

“Shore,” the other answered, his voice trembling, “hell might be a necessity, if you went there to keep somebody else out; it's the old idea, to lose one's life for somebody else's sake is to find it. If it was expedient for one man to die for the people, it is conceivable that it may be expedient to be damned for the people. I can't talk religion, but that's the way it seems to me. You've got to consider society, not your own soul, in this matter of divorce."

He was profoundly agitated. He got up and walked over to the window, and stood looking through the glass grimed with the smoke from innumerable chimneys below; far off, beyond the crowding, huddling roofs covered with streaked and dirty snow, he could see a yellow line of sunset; his anger and his shame fighting for words left him silent. He came back and sat down again by Philip's desk.

"Shore, I'll take your motives for granted. I will believe that you believe in them; but go back, go back!"

Philip was silent for a moment; he watched Roger closely; then he said quietly, "There's no use prolonging this. You don't understand the situation. Mrs. Shore wishes to leave me."

Then the rein broke. "You know the proposition was yours. For God's sake, don't be a Jesuit; it's bad enough to be a saint! And you are willing to accept your freedom at any cost to her? You'd go over dead bodies or dead souls to save yourself! Damn you, you're not worth saving!"

"You're mad, or else you're drunk. There's the door."

"You'll listen to what I have to say first. The Lord knows I'm not anxious to talk to you, but you've got to listen, — and I've got to speak! What about your wife, if you leave her? and what about the fellow you dig a pit for when you send her out into the world?"

"Your words are an offense. You will speak with respect of Mrs. Shore in my presence or I'll put you out of it!"

The two men were standing. Philip was trembling with rage. Roger's hand was clenched on the edge of the desk; there was a solemn frown in his face which made it almost beautiful, and strangely devoid of self. The sunset, loitering and lifting on the wall, had been swallowed by the rising tide of gray, and the room was quite dark.

"You've got to hear, Philip," Roger said. Then, lifted far above self-consciousness, using, as it were, his own sin as an instrument of salvation, he leaned forward and touched him on the shoulder.

"*I love her.*"

There was no answer.

"Well, what's the matter? 'Why not?' as you said yourself. I love her. How do you like that? I held her in my arms. I held your wife in my arms. I — Keep back, keep back! You've no right to resent one word I've said! You throw her over, I take her —"

Philip's hands leaped at his throat. There was

no resistance.   Flung neck and crop like a dog out into the narrow entry, Roger Carey leaned, breathless and ghastly, against the whitewashed wall.   His face was full of exultation ; it was as though some mighty hand of justice and insolence and insult had wiped shame out of it.

XXXIII.

THE grimy sunshine, lifting and lifting in Philip Shore's office in the city, resting on crowded roofs, gilding with sudden pallid glory the edge of a chimney, or striking a red shine on smoky windows, was lying in an ebbing tide of placid light on the white hills around Old Chester. It crept across Cecil Shore's leafless garden, and up the west front of the house, touching the closed shutters, and peering for a fading instant into the open doorway of the hall, where everything was confusion and haste.

"The stage and baggage-wagon will be here at five," said Mrs. Shore, fastening her long glove as she came slowly downstairs. "Just see that everything is put on, John; then tell Jonas to drive down to the rectory for me. Come, Polly, come along with mamma."

"Will Eric come with John? Can't he come to say good-by to Dr. Lavendar, too? Shall we say good-by to aunt Lyssie and grandmamma over again?" Molly chattered, as they went down the steps.

"Come, hurry," Cecil said crossly. "What did you bring that dog for? He'll fight Danny." She looked down at the child running to keep up with her, and drew in her breath in a sob. Molly was full of questions: Where was father? What made the moon so thin? Had the sun bitten a piece out of it? Should they see father to-morrow in town?

"Do you want to see your father?" Cecil asked, her voice strained and harsh.

"I don't mind," Molly answered cheerfully. "I'd like to see Mr. Carey. He loves Eric."

"Is that why you like Mr. Carey?"

Molly shook her head, and took two little skipping steps. "I don't like him *very* much. He laughed at my tooth. I like father better. Don't you like father better? Mamma, when shall we go on the ship?"

They had come to the iron gates at the bottom of the garden, and Cecil lifted the great rusted latch; but when they closed behind her with a clang, she stopped, shivering, and looked back at the garden, leaning her forehead against the bars.

"I'd better say good-by to her here," she said; and called the child, who had run on a little distance ahead. Yet when, with laggard obedience, Molly came, her mother only said, with a curious breathlessness, "Take mamma's hand. Don't run ahead that way. (No, I can't yet; I can't yet!") she told herself.

As they walked down the lane in the gray twilight, she kept putting off those last words; she talked constantly, but so entirely at random that once Molly said, in a puzzled way, " But, mamma, you told me ' yes,' and now you tell me ' no.' I don't know *what* to do ! "

" Molly, you will be a good girl ? " Cecil said feverishly, as though insisting upon something to herself. " You must be good. That's the main thing. Promise mamma you 'll be good ? "

Her voice frightened the child, whose face puckered into a sort of whimper. " I 'm not a naughty girl ! "

" Oh, I know, darling, I know ! But promise mamma you 'll try and be good. (I 'll wait until I get to the rectory,") she thought, gripping the child's hand until Molly cried out, and pulled it away from her.

They came along the narrow path to the sunken door of the rectory. The shades were not down, and they had a glimpse of Dr. Lavendar sitting in his shabby dressing-gown by the hearth. The little dusky room was full of lurching firelight, brightening and fading, and brightening again. This was his free hour, and he was sitting by himself, his pipe between his lips, thinking of many things. With one hand he rubbed Danny's gray head, and the other was fumbling in the pocket of his dressing-gown with some uncut topazes. Once he pulled out a handful of them, and held them close to his eyes, gloating over them with the greatest satisfaction ; then he thrust them deep down into his pocket again. He was trying to decide a matter of taste :

was it better to preach on the New Jerusalem descending out of heaven like a bride adorned for her husband, her walls of chalcedony, jacinth, amethyst, and jasper, the Sunday before Joey and Susan were married, or the Sunday after?

"That match," he was saying to himself, "was about as good a thing as I ever accomplished in my life!"

As they drew near the house, Cecil stopped and looked in at the tranquil scene. "I'll wait till I have spoken to Dr. Lavendar," she thought, shivering. "Molly," she said hoarsely, "give me a kiss before we go in." The street was deserted and nearly dark; no one saw her crush the child against her breast, kissing her until Molly, out of breath, laughed and struggled, and tried to wriggle out of her arms.

("I'll say it the last thing; the last thing.) Oh, Molly, you will be good? That is all I want. Promise me you will be good! Come, we must go in."

Then she pushed the door open and went down the little narrow hall to the library.

She came in, wrapped in her great crimson cloak, and smiling, in the firelit dusk; yet for an instant, until she spoke, the old clergyman felt the grip of actual terror upon his heart.

"I came to say good-by, Dr. Lavendar —" She stopped and caught her breath. "The stage is to come here for me. I felt that I must have the blessing of the Church before I left the home of my childhood for good."

"Left for good?" he stammered, but she interrupted him.

"It may be for bad. But it's leaving, anyhow. May I sit down? Polly, don't drag at mamma's cloak. Dr. Lavendar, I want you to do something for me."

"Sit down, Cecilla, sit down," he said, waving his pipe at her. "I am glad to see you: I've something to say to you. I've been four times to your door, Cecilla, but was not admitted."

"Oh, not really?" she said absently, her eyes fastened upon Molly.

"The person who opened the door," proceeded the old man, "said you were not at home. *But I heard your voice, Cecilla!*"

"Really?" Cecil answered, vaguely; and then suddenly laughed, as if at first she had not heard him.

"I fear he is an untruthful person; but that was not why I wished to speak to you, though I do feel that you are responsible for the morals of your servants —"

"My dear Dr. Lavendar, my own morals are more than I can attend to properly," she said, smiling, "and I have only five minutes; the stage will be here, and I must speak to you."

"Send the child away, for I must speak to you," he began, sternly; but Cecil shook her head.

"Oh no, please don't. In fact, you can't, before Molly," she reminded him maliciously. "Beside, it's no use; everything is settled. But I've come

(I'm so glad *you* are at home) to ask you to give Philip a message from me."

"Mamma, are we going to see father to-morrow?" Molly asked fretfully.

"You will, kitty, in a day or two. There! don't you want to go and play with Danny? Dr. Lavendar, I am going away. I am going to sail for Europe on Saturday."

His bushy eyebrows twitched with angry anxiety; "I can't believe that you will do any such wicked thing. I went to implore you not to, those four times that I called. My child, you can't do such a thing! I have written to Philip — I think you are both beside yourselves," he ended incoherently.

Cecil sighed impatiently. "Dr. Lavendar — " But he interrupted her.

"Lyssie, poor child, is heart-broken about it; she sat here yesterday and cried until she could n't see!"

Cecil started, frowning. "If I've given Lyssie any grief, the sooner I get away the better. Yes, she 'll be happier when I 'm gone. That 's one reason I 'm going. Oh, please don't talk to me; there 's no use. Listen to what I want to say: I 'm going away, and I 'm going to enjoy life. I want that distinctly understood. I 'm going to enjoy life. Only, I 've thought it all over, and I won't take Molly. She would be — she would be in the way. But I want you to tell Philip Shore one thing: say, 'Cecil says, *You saved yourself, so you could not save any one else.*' Possibly he will understand. Yes, I think he will understand. ‘You saved yourself, so you could not save any one else.’ Will you remember? You might add that, having saved his life, he may lose it; but no; he’ll find that out for himself, perhaps.” She rose and pulled the crimson cloak about her, shivering a little.

“I know what you mean,” he said tremulously, “but Cecilla, my dear child, just let me make one plea; not for yourself, not even for the child. Listen to me, my dear. There is nothing in the world so awful as the knowledge that you have injured a soul. If you go away, Philip will understand that. Yes, you will grow harder to reach, Cecilla, and it will be his fault. He will have injured your soul; there is no anguish so dreadful as such a realization! *Can’t you spare him?* Aren’t you generous enough to spare him?”

It was a high appeal.

She turned and looked at him, and laughed, drawing in her breath between her shut teeth.

“I hope the thought of it may take him down to hell. I should be willing to go there, if it would make him suffer!”

As she spoke there was a trampling at the gate, and the rattle of harness-chains, and the scraping of a wheel against the gatepost. “Here’s the stage,” she said lightly, her face white to the lips. “I’ve arranged that Molly is to go to Lyssie, until her father comes for her. Come, Polly, you are to stay all night with aunt Lyssie; shall you like that?”

“And Eric, too?” clamored Molly.

"I told Lyssie I would send her over by Rosa at half past five; I didn't want to make my adieus under Mrs. Drayton's windows. Good-by, Dr. Lavendar." She held out her hand carelessly, as she went into the hall; the front door was open, and the stage loomed up in the dusk, with its lamps glimmering through the evening fog.

" Molly! Come here!" Cecil said sharply.

Dr. Lavendar had followed them into the hall; Rosa was standing in the doorway; the stage-driver was leaning down from his seat, tapping the wheel with his whip; John had come up the path to ask some question. Cecil looked about her like a hunted creature.

"Jonas is in a hurry, ma'am," John ventured.

"I'm coming, I'm coming," Cecil said breathlessly. "Have you got everything, John? Is Rosa here? Rosa, take Molly right over to Miss Lyssie's—"

"Mamma!" Molly began, half frightened.

Cecil looked at her, and then suddenly knelt down in front of her. "Kiss me! *Kiss* me!" she whispered, and hid her face in the child's bosom; then she rose, brushing past the little girl as though she did not see her.

"I'll miss the train at Mercer if I don't hurry. Dr. Lavendar, congratulate Mr. Joseph for me. At least his choice has not been impulsive; they have known each other all their lives, haven't they?"

Then, smiling out of the coach, she kissed her hand to Molly. " There, kitty, don't cry; you are going over to grandmamma's to stay all night." She pulled the stage-door in with a bang. "Tell them to start," she said hoarsely. "Why don't they start? Oh, hurry, hurry! Good heavens, are they never going to start?"

XXXIV.

When April-time was melting into May. — Earthly Paradise.

IN April, in southern Pennsylvania, there comes one day when the brown fields dim suddenly with green, as though a warm breath passed over them. The full, white clouds hang low, but part now and then, and bursts of sunshine move swiftly over the meadows and up the hillsides ; the little runs brim and bubble in their narrow beds, and the larger streams whirl against the big stones in their paths, and hurry on, streaked with foam and chattering loudly. In the orchards threads of water gush out from under tussocks of winter-bleached grass, or spurt up under a footstep, and when those sunbursts travel swiftly over the countryside, all the fields are agleam with these innumerable springs. The air has been warmed through and through by the sunshine behind the clouds, yet it has a cool edge that comes from its touch upon patches of melting snow up in the northern hollows of the hills. The buds have hardly begun to open, but it seems as if there were a faint green smoke in the woods ; and the stems of the willows are reddening as though some mysterious wine were rising in them.

Such a day is full of peace and promise ; one feels a springing joy that reason does not explain. No doubt the grief of the world is just the same ; the grave is still new in the churchyard, perhaps; faiths have been broken; the soul has earned its own inviolable soltitude; nay, the sordid anxieties of life and living are all unchanged;—yet on such an April day of sunshine moving over brown fields, of brimming brooks, of greening hillsides, the heart rises, the feet dance, and a song comes bubbling to the lips.

Alicia Drayton felt this unreasoning joy as she walked slowly up the long hill on her way back from the upper village. Far down the road, behind her, the stage came tugging along. She had meant to hail it at the cross-roads, and spare herself a half hour's walk; but she had not waited for it, and had walked on absently, yet with this April joyousness nestling warmly at her heart. Once she stopped to look back at the stage crawling up the long slope, and saw a great stretch of sunshine flood all the valley, and move swiftly up the hill. The fields looked greener for its touch, Lyssie thought. She drew a long breath and trudged on, saying to herself that it was pleasant to be alive.

This was a new feeling to little Lyssie. It had been a hard winter for her.

First there had been the bewildering grief about Philip and Cecil; then the interest and beauty of life had seemed to go out on the day that Roger Carey slammed the door behind him and went off into the rain; and, while that pain was still new, the filial instinct had been killed in her: Alicia Drayton had learned to know her mother.

With such knowing had come the tenderest love and pity; but the reverence of the child for the parent, that noble reverence which makes life deep and beautiful, was dead.

This grief had come to the girl in mid-winter. A letter had arrived from Mr. Drayton announcing his immediate and final return to Old Chester; and there was a dreadful scene when his wife, in the miserable fright of a selfish woman, had had no decent reserves before Lyssie. The dignity and sacredness of marriage were insulted before the child's eyes: her mother had cried and screamed with disappointment and passion; she had revealed her hatred of her husband, and her fear of his interference with her comfort. Afterwards, there was the simpering smile to her little public; her upraised eyes; her "heartfelt gratitude for her heavenly Father's goodness in thus blessing her by her dear William's restoration to health." It turned Alicia sick. The instinct of the child for the mother agonized and died; and with it went the divine and beautiful believing of youth. But she went on loving. Other knowledge had come to Lyssie in connection with this same experience: Mr. William Drayton had come back looking very broken; his health was just the same, he said curtly; he had returned because he had lost a — a friend by death, so he did not care to live abroad any longer.

"At least it must be a comfort to feel that he is at rest in heaven," Mrs. Drayton said. "Who was he, dear William?"

“ You would n’t be any wiser if I mentioned the name,” he said slowly ; “ and I don’t care to talk about it, please.”

Perhaps the look in his face suddenly instructed Alicia Drayton as to what that friendship was. She grew deadly pale, shamed to her very soul. The somewhat conventional affection with which she had welcomed him went out in swift indignation. For a long time it was an effort to speak to him ; she shrank from his touch, and his commonplace questions and comments were answered almost curtly. But that did not last : she knew her mother. So in spite of shame, pity began to take the place of anger. At first she was sorry for him, then, after a while, came a sort of friendliness. That she could make excuses for him was a sad commentary on the child’s loss of youth. She thought about him now, as she walked up the hill in the scudding sunshine, and noticed, with a pang of joy, a bluebird balancing on a rail, and the sharp greenness of the grass in the sheltered triangle of the zigzag fence. “ If only he had come sooner,” she said to herself, “ I need n’t have said three years ; and it would all be different now, perhaps.”

Mr. Drayton had been told of the broken engagement, and had called Lyssie to him one day, and said quietly, “ Tell me why it was, child.” She had told him, simply enough. He had listened, and nodded, and looked at the end of his cigar, and told her to bring him another light. That was all ; but he had pulled her ears at tea-time, and called her his little monkey; and it was after that that this silent friendship grew up. There were no explanations; they were sorry for each other, and understood; and one forgave.

"But if he had been here, it would have been different," she thought, and stopped to look back at the stage; she did not reproach her father, even in her mind.

Alicia had had a swift hope that his return would mean some way out of the distress and grief and shame that had come to Philip and Cecil. But such hope had quickly died. Mr. Drayton showed no inclination to interfere. He listened to the story, drowsing through Mrs. Drayton's excited and pious embellishments of it, and then he took his cigar from between his lips and knocked off the ashes.

"They know their own business," he said, in his slow, dull voice. "I'm glad there was no scandal. I'm glad everything was done decently and in order;" there was a flicker of humor in his half-shut eyes at Mrs. Drayton's disappointment at his indifference. "And on the whole, I think they were very sensible; it's better to be open and aboveboard."

"I do not know what you mean, dear William," said Mrs. Drayton.

Her husband smoked on stolidly. "No, I don't suppose you do."

"But," sighed Lyssie to herself, beginning to go down the hill into the village, "it was too late, anyhow; nothing could have been done; Cecil would never have gone back to Philip."

She was quite right. The tragedy of human selfishness destroys the fabric of life beyond repair. Yet Lyssie had tried to repair it. When Philip, with passionate haste, came down to Old Chester, only to be confronted by the dark silence of the empty house, — Alicia had done her best.

"Oh, Philip, did you mean to come back? Philip, Philip, hurry! go after her; you may catch her before she sails! Oh, perhaps she will forgive you!"

He was very gentle with her, but he silenced her.

He had come to accept Molly from her mother's hands; to let gratitude overcome his humiliation; to defer to Cecil in every possible way, — but that was all. The citadel of his spirituality, where Self had intrenched herself, was absolutely fast.

"If Philip and Cecil would not listen to — Roger, there was no use for me to talk," she thought, as she stopped a moment on the bridge, and looked down into the water. And then the stage drew up behind her, and some one got down, and came and stood beside her.

"Lyssie, will you please — speak to me?"

And she turned and saw him; older, graver, his face quivering, his eyes imploring her.

.   .   .   .

There was not much explanation. To talk over a quarrel, with its inevitable accompaniment of self-justification, is too much like handling cobwebs to be very successful. Roger said "Forgive me" and Lyssie said "Forgive me," and that was about all there was to it. Of course Roger had to shake hands with Mr. Drayton, and be forgiven by Mrs. Drayton, and dine with the family, and feel exceedingly like a whipped puppy; which, after all, was perfectly right and just.

Late in the afternoon, they went out to walk; and somehow Roger fell silent, and Lyssie did all the talking. She said, softly, " Cecil will be glad. I will write and tell her."

Roger stared down the road.

" Do you hear from Mrs. Shore often ? "

" Not as often as I should like to," she answered sadly; " she is so busy; she is very gay. But oh, Roger, she is n't happy; though she does n't seem to miss Molly much, she hardly speaks of her. Only, I know she is n't really contented; and I am so happy! — it does n't seem fair. Did you see her before she went away ? "

Roger shook his head.

" Well, then, you don't know how dreadful things were. I heard afterwards that you came down, just before the end of it all, to try to reconcile them. It must have seemed strange to be here, and not see me. Did you think of me, Roger ? "

He pulled a budded maple-twig, and twisted it between his fingers.

" Yes. I — thought of you."

" What did you think ? "

" I 'll tell you — another time."

" Philip came down for Molly," Lyssie went on, telling her little story, " and I said everything I

could. But it was n't any use. He was dear and
sweet, as he always is, but he would n't discuss it.
He said Cecil wanted Molly to be with me sometimes, and he wanted to arrange about that. But
he would n't talk about Cecil. Molly is to be here
this summer, and Philip will come when he can.
I suppose he has told you all about it ? "

"No."

Alicia looked troubled. "Have you felt as if he
was n't friendly, because — because our engagement
was broken ? I know it never made any difference
in his feeling for you. Let me tell you what he
said that day he came for Molly. Just as he was
going away, he came back and took my hands, and
he said — oh, Roger, he said, 'Lyssie, if he comes
back, forgive him. He is a good man.' He meant
you, Roger. (Of course, Philip did n't understand,
or he would n't have said 'forgive.'")

The twig snapped between the young man's fingers, and he looked away from her.

"What did you say ?" she asked him softly.

"Nothing; nothing. Do you forgive me, Lyssie ? "

Her look told him.

"Oh, I don't deserve it," he said brokenly. It
was growing cold as the twilight fell upon the river-
road; they stood quite silently, with a little sadness
in their joy which they had never known when they
had loved each other less.

"You ought n't to be standing here," he told her
suddenly, "but I 've got to say something ; I 've

got something to confess, Lyssie." They were standing under a little dogwood-tree, its shelving branches white with blossoms; it was very still in the soft spring dusk. Roger looked up and down the deserted road; then he said, " Will you kiss me just once, first? Perhaps you won't forgive me when I 've told you."

There was something in his voice that sent the color out of her face. " There is nothing you could tell me that is not forgiven already ; so — don't tell me."

"Yes, I must tell you," he said ; but turned away from her, and stood staring into the dusk for a little while. " Lyssie, I do love you. I 've loved you more every minute since we — "

" Yes, I understand," she murmured, " since we — " But neither of them spoke the cruel word.

" I 've loved you all the time. But once — you will never understand! but I 've got to tell you ; once I thought I loved — your sister."

She started and shivered, her hands tightening on each other ; but she did not speak.

" It was that Friday night I came down. I — "

But she stopped him, tenderly, though truly with no understanding of what he meant ; with only love — love — love. She took both his hands and pressed them against her bosom in ineffable tenderness.

" Oh, Lyssie, do you forgive me ? "

" There is no talk of forgiveness between us."

And then he said passionately, " *I love you!* " and dared not kiss her, even.

Afterwards they talked of other things, and Roger, square with his conscience, was able to forget that he had had cause to be forgiven, but Alicia was a little absent; until she said, suddenly, tremulously, "I just want to ask you' one thing, and then we 'll not think of it again : I want to know if — if *she* cared ? "

There was no pause between her question and Roger's instant and generous lie ; but her lover was quiet for a while afterwards.　It was a pity that she had asked him ; but a woman in love rarely knows the value of ignorance.

After a while, as they walked home, Roger began, timidly, to say that he would wait as long — as long as she wished.　But she interrupted him.

"There is n't any need to — wait — very long."

www.ingramcontent.com/pod-product-compliance
Lightning Source LLC
Chambersburg PA
CBHW020859130726
47900CB00014B/1145